Previous books by Bill Sheehan

MARAGOLD IN FOURTH

MARAGOLD IN FIFTH

MARAGOLD IN SIXTH

ROMAN WOLFE'S ADIRONDACK ORDEAL

ROMAN WOLF 2
CLASSROOM TERROR

Bill Sheehan

iUniverse, Inc.
New York   Bloomington

iUniverse books may be ordered through booksellers or by contacting:

iUniverse
1663 Liberty Drive
Bloomington, IN 47403
www.iuniverse.com
1-800-Authors (1-800-288-4677)

Because of the dynamic nature of the Internet, any Web addresses or links contained in this book may have changed since publication and may no longer be valid. The views expressed in this work are solely those of the author and do not necessarily reflect the views of the publisher, and the publisher hereby disclaims any responsibility for them.

ISBN: 978-1-4502-6167-8 (sc)
ISBN: 978-1-4502-6168-5 (ebook)

Printed in the United States of America

iUniverse rev. date: 09/29/10

An old Cherokee is teaching his grandson about life: "A fight is going on inside of me," he said to the boy. "It is a terrible fight and it is between two wolves. One is evil; he is full of anger, envy, guilt, resentment, lies, sorrow, regret, greed, arrogance, self-pity, superiority, false pride, and ego. The other is good; he is joy, peace, love, hope, serenity, humility, kindness, benevolence, empathy, generosity, truth, and compassion. This same fight is going on inside you and inside of every other person, too."

The grandson thought about it, then asked, " Grandfather, which wolf will win?"

Grandfather replied, "The one you feed."

American Indian Proverb

"Wolf is the Grand Teacher. Wolf is the sage, who after many winters upon the sacred path, and seeking the ways of wisdom, returns to share new knowledge with the tribe. Wolf is both the radical and the traditional in the same breath. When the wolf walks by you – you will remember."

Robert Ghost Wolf

Wolf Man

The wolf appeared in his dream,
To his surprise he did not scream.
He thought for sure it was the end,
But he glared back, did not bend,
Wolf's eyes red with bloody madness,
Instead Wolf said it was his sadness.
Blood stained Wolf's fur so white,
Crimson on white gave quite a fright,
Until Wolf spoke, "Have no fear."
The man approached, got very near.
Then Wolf growled into his ear.
Wolf's request was clear, but queer.
"A man like you is hard to find.
May I live in your courageous mind?"
The man accepted Wolf as a peer.
There Wolf lies dormant, year after year,
Until great danger appears too near.
A ferocious growl that man will hear.
Then man is wolf and the wolf is man,
As Wolf Man, they staunchly stand.

Liam Anthony

Dedication

To Sandy, my wonderful wife and to Mara, my precious daughter.
I am incredibly lucky to have their love.

To Mark French, my nephew and all-around great guy.
To Tony French, my nephew and good friend.
To Mike French, my nephew and the funny man in the family.
To Lori Bullock, my niece and, also, my lovely Princess.

To Todd Bonnewell, my hard-working son-in-law.
To Gus Kovalik, a great friend and fellow "shootist."

Prologue

Dear Diary,

What do you say to someone who asks you how many people you've killed?

What if that person with the curious mind is your ten year old daughter?

What if your daughter has seen you kill viciously, but in self-defense?

Do you ignore her or lie to her when you've always tried to be honest with her?

Is answering with a lie better than the truth? I thought it was, but, luckily, I didn't have to lie. I kept my response short, bland, generalized. I simply told Grace that I had killed, in self-defense, when I was in the Vietnam War and let it go at that,— no details, no heroic stories, no showing of medals and no bragging. I wasn't proud of what I did in Vietnam, though other, higher ranking, military people were.

Was all the killing worth it? Not to me. Not to the dead, nor to the amputees, nor to the physically and mentally wounded, not to the PTSD (post-traumatic stress disorder) victims, nor was it worth the civil strife in America.

I told Grace that, in my opinion, Vietnam wasn't worth saving from the communists; not at the cost of over fifty-eight thousand American lives.

The world is littered liberally with unjust opinions— perhaps mine is one of them— and lies, even in the bible-thumpers. Truth and justice are often lost in the shuffle and complexity of everyday life, while lies, much too often, become tools of everyday life. It's nice to think the best of people, but being realistically honest is more important to me. So accepting lies, fantasies and/or myths, that encourage self-deception, and demand a rigid, unquestioning mind-set, without proof, is a life I can't live. There definitely are atheists in foxholes; they fight just as hard and die just as easily as anyone else. The good may die young, but the honest die bravely without religious lies burning their tongues.

I cannot believe that an ancient storybook (like the Bible), in which religious mythology is interpreted differently all over the world, should be the standard for guiding one's modern life. Logically, it's like asking millions of people to still believe that the universe operates as it is said to have operated in a book that was written two thousand years ago, and to believe this voluntarily, unquestioningly, without regard to two thousand years of technical and scientific progress. It requires a mentality that's capable of vast, self-imposed ignorance, a mind-set with the ability to deny the immense strides in progress and knowledge that science has made during two millennium and to revere the myriad religious fallacies and myths that have been exposed during those two thousand years of knowledge and progress.

So religion, all religions with a supernatural God, to me, are exactly as Richard Dawkins has stated: "Religion is about turning untested belief into unshakeable truth through the power of institutions and the passage of time."

Billions of people believe in a personal God (Christians, Jews, Muslims, etc.). But I think that the existence of a God described by Christians, Jews and Muslims is a world-wide lie; perhaps not a deliberate lie, not even a white lie, but simply a grandiose lie that people both like and need to believe. It's an example of a lie that people desperately want to believe, despite its irrationalism, despite its lack of proof, despite its nonsense.

Ironically and technically, we are all atheists whether we want to accept it or not, because most modern people do not believe in the ancient Gods of Rome or Greece or the Gods of any other early civilizations. We are all atheists when it comes to those Gods. But, to their credit, atheists simply believe in *one less God* and that God is the God of the Christians, Jews and Muslims. So what gives these religions, that bathe themselves in myth and false pride, the right to decide how modern, knowledgeable people live their lives? Is it coercion? Fear? Intimidation? Heritage?

Popular religions are an immense tangle of falsehoods, exaggerations, impossibilities, contradictions, inconceivable fantasies, absurdities, irrational thoughts, out-right lies, revisions, errors of consistency, ineffable thoughts and concepts and, in many cases, just plain nonsense. Religion loves the Aristotelian tradition of articulating opinions, fantasies and myths without requiring any objective support. That's the only way they can survive.

I wonder, how many religions there are in the world? Over one-hundred, maybe? And they all differ in numerous and significant ways, yet each considers itself to be the true advocate of God. That fact itself has the thunderous ring of human ignorance, confusion, error, desperation and centuries of deceitful manipulation, with the end result being millions of lives using guidelines of mythical, ritualized dogma entrenched solidly in most of the world's societies and cultures.

So, I ask myself, what is truth? Perhaps truths and lies are simply evolutionary. Perhaps knowing when to lie and when to be truthful is a characteristic of the human genome, something in the DNA sequence that assists humans to survive; survival of the fittest. Lying convincingly could save someone's life or the lives of others, whereas telling the truth may get someone killed and vice-versa. Perhaps when it came to evolutionary survival, belief in falsehoods was advantageous. Perhaps so advantageous that religious falsehoods were needed, liked, kept and obeyed without question. Then belief was easy; whatever mom and dad believe is what all their children believe, ad infinitum.

But truth, lies and religious myths don't bother me as much as the fact that I'm uneasy with the knowledge that I can so easily and skillfully kill and that I've done it too many times. For me, it's a disturbing feeling, unrelated to religion, that makes me question my own humanity, even when justified by war or self-defense. But that's probably as it should be or killing would be much more prevalent.

When I've killed, I've taken away all of a person's sunny days, all his hopes and dreams. I take away all he has and all that he could have had. I take the most precious thing life has to offer, life itself, and I annihilate it for all eternity. How could I not think about that? How could I not feel guilty about that?

I only know a few things for certain— though I cannot prove them beyond all doubt. One of those things is that God, all Gods, are myths. Perhaps useful myths, but still myths, and another thing I know is that the truth will, many times, not set you free, but rather, it will imprison you physically and/or emotionally. Evil watches us, sometimes invades us and even commands us, especially those of us with major character weaknesses and whose portals are invitingly open to Evil's invasion. We can each look into ourselves and find that darkness, though few people have that kind of courage. Evil has always been there; it's a primordial, innate, human characteristic.

I also know that evil is immortal, but not omnipotent. It can't be wounded or killed. It occupies the shell or the husk of a person. It claws, rips, dissolves and destroys the brain's sanity and the brain's ability to use logic and reason as guidelines for a happy life.

It has been well documented, by physiologists and psychiatrists, that most happy people have important, similar character traits, but that most unhappy people are unhappy in their own unique ways of forming feelings of discontent. But killing a person whose husk evil occupies does not kill the evil. Evil simply finds another shell to occupy and to eventually destroy. And evil has thousands of brothers, sisters, cousins and friends that perform the same function in their struggle against the forces of good.

I think that Evil is a traveler, like a breeze blowing an ill-fog. It surrounds you, entering your pores and orifices. You can't help but breathe it into your lungs where it enters the bloodstream and travels to all regions of the inner husk that it will temporarily inhabit and eventually annihilate. Evil can overpower a person, but it can also be defeated. It can be refused access to the brain, but only by the strong, the determined, the persistent, the indomitable, those persons who are willing to repel it in their own way.

So, dear diary, here lies my last dark thought for this entry. I think, since adulthood, I've had a death wish. I've always thought that I'd die young. I think that may be why I didn't fight the military's mistake in drafting me when drafting guys with families wasn't usually done during wartime. I have always sensed an uncomfortable darkness within me; the fingers of death reaching out for me; a black, cold and quiet tomb waiting for me to take permanent residence; a place where guilt, shame, tragedy and savagery don't exist; a place where the absence of light is normal and not evil; a place without pain, without disturbing thoughts, without stress or responsibility, and without heroes or cowards; a place where the weary, like me, can finally rest, peacefully.

These are some of my secrets, dear diary. Keep my secrets safe.

Diary entry by Roman Wolfe

1

★★★★

"To himself everyone is immortal; he may know that he is going to die, but he can never know that he is dead."

**Samuel Butler **

THE NIGHTTIME AIR LIT up with bright, enemy tracer-fire; taut ropes of green lights cutting through the air like laser beams zipping past our bodies, lighting the moist, hot jungle as we dove to the ground and returned fire.

Then our own staccato-like, red tracer-fire filled the air, but not before we heard the anguished, desperate sound of our dying men, wounded and screaming in agony through clenched teeth, feeling their lives dripping or pouring away as their blood pooled, then soaked onto the jungle floor.

In the morning, if they survived, the sight and smell of the blood would be as appealing as being a horse racing sulky driver behind a horse with full-blown diarrhea.

Each man in the platoon desperately sought refuge behind anything they could find. Some men, in a state of panic and terror tried to bury themselves by digging into the dirt like burrowing animals.

One soldier was digging a small hole and placing his head in it, as if he thought that doing an ostrich routine would save the rest of his body from being seen and shot at. In any other context, that action would have been hilarious. But it was a time of fear, terror, panic, a life-and-death situation. Absurd, nonsense things like that happen when you're terrorized and feel death's squeezing grip around your heart and its hellish breath in your nose.

Roman's body reacted to the terror; the sweat flowed freely, tunnel vision occurred, a numbness cloaked him, while, at the same time, adrenaline saturated his blood. His muscles soaked it up as his body prepared for the inevitable "fight or flight" reaction. But he knew that panic was the worst thing to do. Panic means the loss of control, loss of power, both mentally and physically. It means almost certain death because it often causes a person to freeze, to stand dazed and helpless as if paralyzed inside a cloud of chaos.

Roman's M-16 rifle was bucking at his shoulder. He fired bursts of three bullets at a time so he could shoot a running man, by aiming ahead of him, whereas single shots usually hit behind a running man.

The enemy could hardly be seen, and even if Roman could see them clearly, they appeared as nebulous, dark shadows flitting back and forth in the background like fleeting, black wraiths.

Roman's Colt 1911, .45 pistol was in a shoulder holster, under his left arm. Outside his uniform, his Marine combat knife was strapped, upside down, and attached to the left shoulder of his uniform— where the breast pocket would normally be— for easy, quick access. His throwing knife lay in its sheath, under his uniform, inside his back collar, aligned with his upper spine and extending down the back of his neck. These three items were mostly useless in a firefight; the Colt was used for close targets, the combat knife was used for up-close and personal, hand-to-hand combat or when he was night stalking and silently killing with it, and the throwing knife was the most useless of all in the jungle, because there were too many dense trees, bushes and vines to deflect the blade from its target. However, it made a useful fork and knife combination if the real utensils got lost.

Sweat was pouring off his forehead, into his eyes, stinging and making him blink, blurring his vision, frustrating him. His moist hands slipped easily on the plastic-like, fiberglass rifle stock. He tightened his grip, then swore silently as he gritted his teeth.

It was difficult to see. The jungle foliage made the jungle floor look as thick and black as India ink so that the standing men could not see their shoes.

Roman knelt, minimizing the size of his body. He reloaded the M-16 and suddenly Christmas came to his mind. It was an absurd thought, especially now. He wondered why his mind would do that, then noticed the red and green tracer-fire, the colors of Christmas, so maybe— "Damn! pay attention," he screamed at himself as a green laser beam passed just to the right of him. He could feel its lethal breeze on his cheek. He moved away quickly; someone must have me in their sights, he thought. He needed to change locations. Roman was well aware that at night, with tracer fire, he could be located easily by simply following the laser-like beams right back to the rifle that shot it.

Shit! Dammit! Where's Billy? he thought, then said, "How the fuck could I forget about Billy?" Roman surged left to get out of the rifle fire that was zipping past his right shoulder like crazed bees. He accidentally smashed into Billy, who fell farther to the left.

Roman had told Billy to stay close to him, that he'd try to keep him safe. Billy was the new guy.

"Billy?" Roman whispered.

Billy didn't respond, nor was he firing his rifle.

Must have frozen in panic and terror, Roman guessed.

Green tracers were shooting off to his left. Roman knew that the VC saw him lunge left and were trying to catch him running, so they shot ahead of where they thought he would be, hoping he'd run into their bullets. But Roman had fallen to the ground with Billy.

Roman's mouth felt as if he'd licked sand. He didn't have enough moisture to even swallow his own fear. He was concerned for Billy, which took precedence over his dry mouth.

Roman forced himself to focus. Damnation! That was damn lucky for Billy and me, he thought. The tracer-fire stopped just ahead of Roman; the bullets hitting a tree with rapid thump, thump, thumping sounds. He saw the liquid-like shadows of flying bark with each thump.

Roman hugged the ground. He saw Billy doing the same. "Good. Stay down," Roman said to Billy.

Roman still hadn't heard Billy shooting, but was less worried now because they were both prone, a position that made them a very difficult target, due to the thick brush, broad-leaf plants, vines, and tree trunks.

Roman knew that Billy was terrorized, probably in a static state of panic. It happens a lot, he thought. Guys freeze, becoming perfect, immobile targets, like statues, then die riddled with enough bullets to make them a human sieve.

Billy was still a teenager; only eighteen, with peach fuzz for a beard. Roman was trying to get him safely through the initial fear, panic, and terror of his first firefight— quite a bit different than shooting paper targets at the Marine boot camp on Parris Island.

Billy was a short, thin, shy, farm boy who always showed nervousness. One way he showed it was by talking almost non-stop, as if his life depended on it. He talked rapidly and continuously as if there was no such thing as a period at the end of sentences. You could hardly detect even the pause of a comma in most of his sentences. If he had been Wyatt Earp, in a gun fight, he'd be shooting from the lip. Luckily, he had to pause to breathe. But he was a good kid, just too young and innocent to be here, thousands of miles from home and trying to stay alive with too few combat skills. Probably got drafted. He should have joined the Air Force, Roman thought.

Roman again whispered to Billy. No answer. Roman kept his head down as he crawled ahead using his elbows until he bumped his head into Billy's boots. Roman's initial thought was that Billy was performing the ostrich routine until he realized that the toes of Billy's boots were pointing skyward. A fleeting, but ominous feeling stabbed his heart like a thick needle, then flew away on bat wings. Roman shook, then pushed Billy's boots. Roman whispered impatiently for Billy to get moving, but Billy only slightly moved one leg.

With tracer-fire all around him, Roman got pissed-off and dragged himself up to Billy's shoulder. Through grinding teeth he whispered, "Goddamnit Billy! We've got to get out of here. Too dangerous. Stay down, but get your ass moving! Crawl behind that large tree." Roman pointed straight ahead, about ten feet. When Billy didn't respond, Roman's anger choked him as it became a lump that lodged in his throat. Roman slapped Billy, hoping to snap him out of his immobilizing panic and terror.

Billy's head turned slightly to look at Roman, who was so close to him that their noses almost touched. Roman saw the dreamy gaze in Billy's eyes. Shit, Roman thought, Billy must have dove forward and hit his head on a rock or tree root. He must have been knocked out for awhile and that's why he didn't answer or respond.

Billy smiled weakly as a thick stream of chewing tobacco juice slowly traveled between his lips and ran down his cheek.

But, then a rocketing icicle cold fear shot up Roman's spine. Icy tentacles gripped Roman's heart, making it skip a beat. Oh, fuck no, Roman thought. No. Please, no, Roman thought. Oh, shit. Billy doesn't chew tobacco. Then, as suddenly as a broken shoelace, Roman's head fell into the tightening claws of a monster migraine. "What the fuck's happening?" he uttered to himself, amidst the cacophony of rifle fire and screams.

Roman knelt close to Billy and placed his hand on Billy's chest to check his breathing. His chest was wet, felt slick like oil. When Roman removed his hand and peered at it, it too looked as if it had chewing tobacco juice on it. His head pounded as if it were an anvil being hit with sledge hammers. He stared at his wet hand. Not oil. Not tobacco juice. Blood. Blood that looked black as tar in the jungle darkness. His hand was slick with Billy's warm blood. Roman froze, as everything became quiet. He didn't hear the screaming, the rifle fire, nor did he see anything, but Billy. "Damn me to Hell!" he screamed, but he couldn't hear himself say it.

Billy blinked sluggishly as Roman stared down at him with horror and sympathy. Billy was dying— three bullets in his chest and abdomen. Roman realized what had happened; it was one of the most devastating events in his life. He'd promised to protect this kid, this teenager, and he had failed miserably. A monsoon of guilt poured over him.

Billy coughed. A mist of unseen blood sprayed Roman's face as more thick blood poured down Billy's cheek, onto his neck. Blood pooled in the hollow of his neck. Then the tragic epiphany hit him like a brick to his head. The thump, thump, thumping sounds that he'd heard were not bullets hitting a tree. They had hit Billy. And the flying bits of bark that he thought he saw? They were really blood spray thickly out of the wounds.

Then Billy's words, like daggers, stabbed Roman in the heart. Those few words hurt more than bullets would have, especially because, when Roman had time to think about it, Billy's words were true. Billy struggled to talk, then said, "You push . . . pushed me . . . int . . . into . . . th . . . the . . . bull . . . ets."

Roman's jaw dropped in horror as Billy's eyes were losing their spark of life. Billy's final words strangled Roman. Billy gurgled, "Yuh . . . kilt . . . me," Billy weakly grabbed Roman's arm.

Tears flash-flooded Roman's eyes. They streamed down his dirt-crusted cheeks. He gasped, wheezed, choked on his own saliva. He struggled not to vomit, then hyperventilated while completely unaware of his surroundings. He grabbed Billy, leaned over and put his lips to Billy's ear. "I'm so sorry. It was an accident. I'm sorry Billy. So sorry." But his words fell on dead ears. He sat up and held Billy's head in his lap, not caring about the danger. "Shoot me, you fuckin' bastards! Put me out of my misery!" he screamed into the blackness of his mind and into the blackness of the jungle.

Roman became bloated with rage. He stood up and screamed maniacally at the VC, their bullets whizzing all around him. He screamed again, "Fuck you, you gook bastards!"

Instantly he pushed himself off the ground and charged the nearest enemy movement. But before he could get to full speed, Hawk Eye tackled him, forced him down. Roman fought viciously, animal-like, as rage filled him with energy and strength. Roman and Hawk Eye were vaguely aware of puffs of dirt spraying upward all around them as they struggled, as miniature, lead jets looked for a soft runway of flesh to land on.

Hawk Eye quickly realized that he couldn't hold onto Roman any longer. Hawk Eye screamed at Roman to stop and when Roman fought him even harder, Hawk Eye crashed the butt of his .45 against Roman's skull.

Numbness. Relief. Blackness and tranquility relaxed Roman's body within the safety of unconsciousness. Then, under covering fire, Hawk Eye dragged Roman behind a vine infested tree trunk.

Upon waking, Roman's first thought was, I accidentally killed Billy. Then, the platoon ran into an enemy kill zone and here I am alive, not a single scratch, except the lump on my head. Roman's stomach churned with self-disgust.

Nighttime in the jungle was like a bug infested cemetery. Only an occasional animal noise pierced the inky darkness.

The next morning the enemy was gone, just vanished silently. Roman took care of Billy's body, not allowing anyone, not even Hawk Eye, to assist him with the body bag. Roman carried Billy a quarter of a mile, to the nearest clearing, where he placed Billy into the helicopter, with all the other dead bodies and the seriously wounded.

Thereafter, Roman wouldn't allow anyone to get close to him, except Hawk Eye.

*　*　*　*　*　*　*

The war has been over for a years, but Roman often awakens fearful, sweaty, cold, confused and always angry. He had awakened this morning just that way. It was that terrible dream again. His face and hands were slick with sweat. Each time he had that dream, the sweat felt like, even smelled like, Billy's blood. The nightmare was always so clear, as if it were actually happening all over again. He'd tried so hard to cast the nightmare out of his mind, but it was an unfailing boomerang.

He got out of bed gently, feeling the bottom sheet sticking to his back, wet with sweat. He straightened his twisted boxer shorts, then moved quietly so he wouldn't awaken Sam. In the bathroom, he sat on the toilet— more to think than to pee— elbows on knees, fingers covering his eyes, crying silently. His body shuddered, quaked with guilt. The guilt hung precariously over his head, heavy, pointed and sharp; the Sword of Damocles. Roman whispered curses at the nightmare, cursed himself and pleaded for Billy to forgive him, which was his frequent act of contrition after each of those nightmares.

But this was not Roman's only nightmare. There were other nightmares that would not let him forget the terrors of war; all the horrible things men are willing to do to each other for a chunk of land or power or anger or ideology or just plain, ruthless stupidity.

Roman lived with his nightmares, dealt with them the best he could simply because he now knew that he wouldn't be able to forget them. They were like the sucking, poisonous tentacles of an octopus, a different nightmare occasionally grasping him, squeezing him until the guilt poured out of him like water from a hose, draining his energy and filling him with remorse, then enveloping him in emotional depression.

Roman continued to think about Billy and all that Billy might have been, all that he might have done. The good things he could have done; the family he could have raised; the friendships he would have made. Roman knew that Billy was neither brave nor a coward. He was just Billy, a teenage boy in the wrong place, without adequate training.

Thinking of bravery and cowardice, Roman realized that bravery and cowardice both have the same root, which is fear. The only difference between heroes and cowards is simply whether or not a person can confront and conquer the fear. The brave conquer it and take preventative, life-saving action, while cowards panic and/or freeze and cannot act or act in a negative way. Roman knew that most of the guys thought Billy was a coward. Roman didn't. Billy needed help, training, guidance, but Roman couldn't give those to him fast enough. The irony of the hero and the coward, Roman thought, is that most people are both. We have in us the ability to be both— just like we are not all good or all bad. It's only the situation and circumstances of acting as a hero or a coward that differ in all of us. Like Mark Twain said, "Except a person be part coward, it is not a compliment to say he is brave." You have to conquer your own cowardice to act bravely.

Roman mused, Why do I worry about personal guilt, shame, pain and sorrow? Why do I occasionally think about suicide? The world is such a cruel place. "Of all the animals, man is the only one that is cruel. He is the only one that inflicts pain for the pleasure of doing it." (Mark Twain)

Thoughts of death slipped into Roman's mind like a snake into a mouse hole. Seems like most people think of death as something that must be delayed, fought, struggled against. You're considered a coward if you surrender to it, and definitely a coward if you cause your own death. On the contrary, Roman thought, a person has the absolute right to commit suicide. Roman remembered reading a quote by Arthur Schopenhauer that said something like this: "People tell us that suicide is the worst form of cowardice, that suicide is always wrong, despite the fact that it is extremely obvious that there's nothing in this world to which every person has an unquestionable ownership to his own life, to his own person, to his own body and, therefore, has the universal right to end it if he chooses to."

Roman continued to sit on the toilet, using it as a chair, and thought that Death itself was no big-deal. How he died mattered to him, but not nearly as much as fading away, being forgotten by those he loved so dearly. His mind drifted into darkness. He thought, *Facing my inevitable annihilation isn't nearly as bad as having loved-ones placing me into their mental attic to collect dust and cob webs, to wither and fade away as they think of me less and less each year. Then the once bright, clear, joyful memories fade into a misty cloud of vagueness, as if precious memories were sugar cubes dropped into a glass of water. It's bad enough to die and leave the ones you love, but much worse, you die a thousand more deaths as the pleasant memory of you dies within them, until all the memories of you are dead, buried in the dust of the unvisited attic, the closed and forgotten memory cemetery.* But remembering dead loved-ones can cause suffering and Roman didn't want that either. The dilemma was: Is suffering from the memories of dead loved-ones better or worse that not suffering by forgetting them? Roman also thought, *It's no consolation that the same thing will eventually happen to those who go on living.*

Roman quietly exited the bathroom and tip-toed to the living room where he sat, staring into the darkness, feeling depressed and angry and as empty and dry as a nun's vagina. He wondered if a *majority* of war veterans with actual life-and-death combat experience felt like he did: the bad dreams, the depression, the PTSD, the haunting guilt, as if his and their minds were like haunted houses with roving ghosts stirring up the dust of guilt in each room.

Serious depression was the worst condition for Roman. Luckily, PTSD plagued him less frequently now. Roman knew manifold ways of concealing depression. During his high school years he'd find a quiet, isolated corner of the cellar, or take a walk into the woods, or bury his face in a thick pillow and scream with rage and frustration, or he would perform one-hundred push-ups, sit-ups and knee-bends. Once he punched a hole through thick drywall, hitting a stud behind it. The edge of the stud splintered, resulting in abraded knuckles that didn't hurt, at first, because they were numb, but the one inch, needle-like sliver that penetrated half way through the skin around his index-finger knuckle was a pleasing distraction. The blood pooled, then ran along all his knuckles like a drunken, red worm. It was then that he discovered that exhaustion and pain were a panacea, a distracting, pleasing, satisfying, but temporary relief from depression. The high school bullies he readily fought had no idea how welcomed they had become to him. Some days, Roman had even sought them out . . . he needed to fight.

2

★★★★

"I found one day in school, a boy of medium size, ill-treating a smaller boy. I expostulated, but he replied: 'The bigs hit me, so I hit the babies; that's fair.' In these words he epitomized the history of the human race."

Bertrand Russell

THEY SAT IN THE prison cafeteria staring out of the grimy, spotted windows. Self-satisfied smiles etched into their faces as they viewed the hard and heavy April rain. They'd been waiting almost two months for this harsh, early morning downpour. It had to fall at the right time of the morning, but not on a weekend. It had been a long time coming, but today was finally their lucky day. Today they could escape this lousy prison, with its ubiquitous iron bars, myriad locks, manifold cameras, high electric fences topped with razor wire; its buried ground sensors; its cage-like cells, the depressing, chipped and stained walls and food that looked and smelled like vomit. Their cold, sinister eyes darted at one another, then sparkled with the joy of conspiracy.

Otto Fangzahn continued to smile at Charlie Miller as they sat at their over-crowded, cafeteria table. Otto ran his right hand over his flat-topped, crew-cut, feeling the vertical bristles of hair similar to the bristles on a hair brush. As he did it, his hand resembled a jet landing on the deck of an aircraft carrier.

The other inmates' eyes gave fleeting glances to the two of them. Many of the prisoners knew about the escape plan, but said nothing for fear of a protracted death. Fangzahn, the undisputed king of the prison weight lifters and vicious street-fighters was nobody to rat on, unless you were suicidal.

Otto Fangzahn. Everyone called him Fang because he insisted on being called that, but also because his right canine tooth was more horizontal than vertical; his upper lip often caught on the tooth, making a comical sight that everyone learned not to laugh at. Many other members of his family tree demonstrated the same tooth deformity, the result of hereditary influences.

Otto's surname was very appropriate, coming from the Proto-Germanic root "tunthskaz," an extended form of the linguistic root for "tooth." Otto came from German stock and was infamous for his sadistic viciousness. He would just as soon bite a chunk out of you or gouge an eye out if you crossed him. He liked to demonstrate a deadly, poisonous smile just before he bit off an ear or a nose, then spit it at his victim. He'd smile broadly, showing crimson teeth, lips and chin covered with blood, like fiendishly, scarlet lipstick. The blood also made the scar on his cheek appear prominent, the scar remaining white while the surrounding skin was bloody. When Fang smiled, his cheek stretched and the scar took on a bone-white color with reddish-pink edges. The scar looked as if was caused by a puncture, then a tear, resembling a keloid. It gave him an even more beastly grimace which he was quite proud of. He displayed the scar as a badge of courage and brutality, but, ironically, it disturbed him whenever anyone questioned him about it, even if it was Charlie.

One "supposedly" accidental killing in the weight room, combined with two prisoners with "accidentally" broken arms, were enough to insure the silence of anyone who was privy to information about the escape. Fang would personally rip the throat out of anyone who crossed him, and if he couldn't get to them, he'd order someone else to do the killing for him. Only extreme fools thought about crossing Fang. Not even solitary confinement could keep a person safe from Fang or from his loyal and sadistic, mindless minions.

Charlie turned toward Fang and whispered, "Yuh sure the get-away car'll be there? Yuh got someone a hundred percent reliable, right?"

"A course. Yuh think I'd forget? Don't be a moron. It's 'nough that my brother be one. An' speakin' a my brother; he's the one bringin' the car. An', no, he's not very reliable. But I made him a hundred percent reliable really fast with a phone call."

"Yeah? How'd yuh do it?"

"I tol' him that if he didn't help with what I need, then when I got outta prison, I'd kill 'im or maybe I'd have it done sooner by a friend on the outside. Then I tol' 'im that before I killed 'im, I'd cut his finger-tips off and make 'im eat all ten of 'em. Then I'd castrate him and shove his balls in his mouth and tape his mouth closed." Fang laughed quietly, not wanting to attract any attention. "He come aroun' ta my way a thinkin' real quick like."

Fang was the perfect example of a human gone terribly wrong; the perfect example of Darwin's Theory of evolution colliding with Murphy's Law. It was an evolution gone violently astray; seriously and unalterably warped so much that he personified evil. Fang was constantly a serious irritation to most other human beings, like a wool condom or wool tampon would to the ones wearing them.

"You'd do that ta yur own brother?"

"Fuckin'-A, man! Goddamn right I would. Anyway, he say it's all set up. He'll be waiting for us. Don't yuh worry."

Charlie smiled and said, "Great. Good ta know."

Fang smiled, showing brownish-yellow teeth, though he didn't smoke. He was excited by the sound of the drenching rain and the freedom it meant to him. He took Charlie's hand and placed it gently on his groin, rubbing it in sensual circles, under the cover of the table.

Charlie got the message. It was his job to satisfy Fang because Fang protected him from physical harm. But it was also a job that Charlie enjoyed. Charlie was very good at his job. He'd done this hundreds of times, in and out of prison. To Charlie, the word "succumb" was really two words.

What Charlie hadn't enjoyed, however, was when Fang gave him a painful prison tattoo on his butt cheeks. The left buttock tattoo said FANGS, and the right buttock tattoo said HOLE— Fang didn't know anything about possessive, proper nouns, so he didn't place an apostrophe between the G and the S.

Fang deliberately looked away from Charlie, following a preset sexual routine. He started talking to another inmate who sat across the table. After Charlie sneaked under the table, all the inmates on that side of the table slid closer together so the space that Charlie vacated didn't give a clue to the guards. Also, when this human barricade was formed, no one could see under the table, except at the extreme ends.

Charlie, now under the table, on his hands and knees, pulled Fang's zipper open. Fang seldom wore underwear because of his sudden sexual urges. He liked the feel of his penis rubbing against his jeans. He even liked the name given to wearing no underwear; "going commando." It gave him an even greater "macho" feeling, only this wasn't the power of swollen muscles, it was the power of his swollen penis, his sex weapon.

He thought that underwear got in the way of his sexual spontaneity, though he didn't use those exact words. Fang continued talking with the prisoner across the table from him. It was just idle chit-chat that would keep up appearances of normality.

Fang could hear and feel Charlie maneuvering under the table. Charlie was excited as his salivary glands gushed saliva into his mouth. At times, like this, Charlie had to spit excess saliva out of his mouth, his hyper-excitement making his mouth water copiously.

The sound of Charlie spitting onto the floor caught the attention of some inmates sitting at an adjacent table. Even though they knew that they shouldn't stare, they looked longingly anyway; the envy slowly spreading across their faces, like thick syrup across a pancake, as the crotch of their jeans started to bulge. Then they quickly looked away; adjusting the fronts of their jeans to relieve their discomfort.

Charlie carefully took Fang's erection out of his zipper. Charlie was always very careful with the zipper. He remembered the time when the zipper teeth got caught on Fang's flesh. He remembered even more the pain and bruises that Fang inflicted on him afterward. That's why Charlie placed two paper napkins over the zipper teeth of each open zipper half before he began stroking Fang with long, slim, velvet fingers.

Fang was pleased with how gentle Charlie was, with his smooth-fingered, even strokes. Charlie possessed soft hands; soft from the lack of hard work and further aided by his creamy, fragrant hand lotions.

Charlie thought that Fang's skin was like taut velvet as his fingers slipped up and down Fang's turgid penis. Charlie stopped temporarily, teasingly, to increase Fang's excitement and his own. Charlie spit again. He gently gripped Fang's near bursting and pulsating erection. When Charlie's delicate touch felt the mini-spasms of Fang's penis, he knew it was time to *succumb* to the pleasure of his job.

Swiftly Fang's moist, warm flesh came alive, like a baby boa-constrictor in Charlie's mouth. Charlie smiled triumphantly as Fang's body jerked with small, uncontrolled spasms. His eyes rolled upward, then closed. Fang opened his mouth wanting to scream with pleasure, but instead he clenched his teeth, imprisoning his orgasmic scream behind the walls of his teeth.

The muscles in Fang's neck tensed; his biceps bulged; his thighs hardened with strain, and his eyelids fluttered. He breathed rapidly and had trouble keeping eye contact with the inmate across the table, as a languid, semi-smile took command of his lips.

A couple of minutes later he was able to continue his conversation with the other inmate, though his speech was garbled by his restrained, spastic ecstasy and the post-orgasmic spasms that followed, like the aftershocks of an earthquake.

Charlie's face looked like a child's during a wonderful dream. Despite the obvious restriction to smiling, at this point. Charlie's smile drifted to his eyes which sparkled so brightly that you'd think he'd had an orgasm, too . . . and he had. While attending to Fang, Charlie would get a hard-on, too. That's why he always wore the end of a sock over his own penis, the sock pinned to his underwear so it stayed in place. While he was giving sexual pleasure to Fang, he was also giving himself sexual pleasure and when Fang climaxed, Charlie would swallow, which brought him to a peak of excitement that usually resulted with Charlie's own orgasm . . . into the sock. This preparation was devised so that his own orgasm wouldn't show by wetting the front of his jeans.

Charlie wiped up the spit from the floor with a paper towel. It was important not to leave any clues, even though the guards, except for new ones, knew exactly what was happening. They kept their eyes and mouths shut and didn't say anything because, when it was happening, there was no trouble of any kind. The prisoners behaved themselves so as not to interrupt Fang's pleasure. The fear of Fang in them was as strong as skunk musk.

Fang cherished Charlie because Charlie joyfully appeased his special sexual appetites. Being a pedophile, Fang liked having sexual encounters with little girls and little boys, girls in particular, but in prison he had to make do with the "fresh meat" that was available and Charlie was pretty good at arousing him, even if Charlie was normally too old for his special appetites. But Charlie did exactly what Fang wanted and needed, sexually. Charlie even made himself look younger by acting like a younger boy, talking like one, rubbing flesh-tone make-up over his closely shaven peach fuzz and keeping his head hair short. He also shaved off his pubic hairs as well as the hair on his legs, arms and underarms. A special trick that Charlie used to arouse Fang was to suck lollipops while makes slurping noises. That really pleased Fang's pederast desires.

*   *   *   *   *   *   *

Prison life frightened Charlie. He had noticed how many of the other inmates ogled him. Luckily, Fang had offered to protect him, and all Charlie had to do was give Fang exclusive sexual favors. Charlie often smiled privately, thinking that, actually, Fang was providing him with the sexual favors and not vice-versa, but the physical protection was an added bonus, though he was careful to keep that information to himself. It was a perfect symbiotic relationship for Fang and Charlie.

Fang pulled his now flaccid penis into his jeans, removed the napkins and zipped up his zipper, all of which was concealed by the table-top. He threw the paper towels on the ground for Charlie to pick up and place in his pocket.

Who needed bitchy women and crying girls? Fang thought, when I can have orgasms like this until I get out and find me some kid candy.

Fang hated women— a misogynist, with a capital "M"— and couldn't keep an erection with them, unless the sex act included humiliation and pain for them, which is exactly what he did to them if they angered him.

Charlie felt the same way. Most women angered him, just by being women. His anger towards women was intense and rooted in his hatred for his mother.

Charlie peeked at the guards. None were close to his table and, even if they were, they looked the other way when they suspected what was going on. Even the guards didn't want any trouble with Fang.

Charlie didn't want the experience to end so he pushed other thoughts out of his mind and thought about being under the table, on his hands and knees, in front of Fang's legs. He saw himself gently spread Fang's knees apart. The imagined, white shaft that he saw filled his eyes with delight and literally made him drool; the saliva dripping down his chin. He let it drip into his hand.

Fang's erection looked as if it could raise the table. Charlie saw the power in it and in the man. He loved Fang's power and felt as if he was sharing that power whenever he swallowed Fang's ejaculate.

He envisioned Fang's erection being pale and unblemished. Charlie's own erection grew quickly as he wrapped his moistened lips around the swollen head of Fang penis, feeling Fang's rapid pulse inside his mouth and grinning as best he could with his mouth so full of power.

Charlie knew that Fang leaned forward, putting his forearms on the table for support, prior to orgasm. Charlie could see it; a vivid vision. Charlie remembered sensing this and ejaculating into his sock, knowing that he could make this powerful and feared man weak with pleasure. He paid no attention to the sticky mess that his own orgasm made; the sock would absorb it. He was used to it. He liked the warm, sticky feeling. It was like an erotic glue that held him and Fang together.

Charlie pushed Fang farther into his mouth, working his moist lips and tongue around Fang's penis until he heard Fang grunt quietly and felt the final surging pulses. Then he licked faster as Fang's hot, creamy, seminal fluid filled the back of his mouth. He had to swallow in order to keep Fang's precious juices, his power, inside of him.

Charlie saw his own skinny frame easily slide out from under the table and sit next to a robustly, grinning Fang. They stared at each other almost lovingly, Otto squeezing Charlie's forearm affectionately.

Five minutes later, Charlie came back to reality when he felt Fang's elbow poke him.

Fang looked at his watch and stood. He whispered, "Come Charlie. Time ta go ta the unloading bay. Time fer some freedom." He sounded like a dutiful owner about to take his precious dog for a walk.

Charlie rose quickly, following Fang like a happy puppy might follow its master.

/--/.-/.-./.-/./.-/--/.--./.-./---/..-/-../---/..-./-.--/---/..-/

3

"Some men are alive simply because it is against the law to kill them."

Edward W. Howe

EVERY MONDAY THE SUPPLY truck arrived at approximately 9:00 A.M. Usually the inmates disliked having the duty of unloading the supply truck because it interfered with breakfast. But Fang had surprised everyone by volunteering his and Charlie's services to unload the truck and for two months they never missed it once. The guards expected them. Even the driver expected to see their familiar faces. The job had become routine.

The driver and his helper appreciated Fang's help, though they were wary and used extreme caution . . . at first. Fang, being five feet ten inches tall and two hundred forty pounds of bulging muscles—his neck was as muscled as a bull, his flexing biceps looked like two Rottweiler's fucking in a large sack, his thighs were as thick as the base of a mature oak tree, and his arms were like the largest branches of the oak— could lift and carry just about anything that would ever need to be taken off of or put onto the truck. He could pick things up with ease that would take three normal sized men. Once, the driver joked

that if he had a flat tire, he thought that Fang could lift the truck up
and the tire could be changed without a jack. He said it jokingly, but
there was an undercurrent to his voice that expressed sincerity.

Such thoughts of raw strength added to Fang's terrorizing reputation.
But there was more to it. Fang believed that when he scared someone,
he was controlling them. Fang prized control because control meant
power. Last year Fang had knocked a guy to the floor, then ordered
Charlie to bring him a spoon and butter knife. Fang threatened to cut
the guys nose off with the butter knife and scoop his eyeballs out with
the spoon unless the guy obeyed him. The guy was so terrified that
he peed his pants. Thereafter, the guy obeyed Fang's every order and
involuntarily trembled even at the sight of Fang. That's the power that
Fang savored: having a man held like a marionette, the strings in his
hands.

Usually there were heavy boxes full of canned foods and prison
clothing, ordinary supplies. Sometimes machinery needed to be
unloaded. Fang took care of the heavy boxes, his upper arms bulging as
stiff as a honeymoon hard-on. Charlie carried the lighter boxes.

Butch, the truck driver, already had the truck backed-up to the
unloading dock. Butch was average height, but stout and his plump
stomach made him look pregnant.

Butch was dressed in the company's casual, but heavy-duty work
clothes: a faded blue, long sleeve, industrial shirt with the company
logo COSTLESS, INC above the left breast pocket, heavy-duty work
pants— featuring stains and rips. His tan boots looked like Chinese-
made copies of Timberline, with steel-toes support. His Yankees
baseball cap was dark blue; the white NY stitching was grimy. He also
wore a sleeveless, waterproof, black vest.

Butch was nearly as heavy as Fang, but he carried too much of
that weight in fat. He had the quivering physique of a large water
balloon. Though his arms looked big, upon closer examination they
were mostly puffy flesh, like the soft, protruding stomach that hung
over his belt, hiding the buckle and top of his zipper. His baldness and
weathered skin made him look older than he actually was. His rotund
face was highlighted with sagging jowls. The effort it took him to walk
showed that his body struggled with the extra flab; his strides were
slow, lumbering and heavy-footed. His nickname was "Bull," but it

had nothing to do with that animal or with strength. With his flat face and his puffy, flabby jowls, his appearance was like that of an aging bulldog, thus the name "Bull."

Butch, like many people, thought that denying reality, fooling himself, would keep him happy. Butch subconsciously knew that "reality" has an evil cousin called "disillusionment." So Butch avoided disillusionment by living the fantasy of thinking of himself as being big and strong.

Jim was Butch's younger, slender assistant. If Butch resembled a bulldog, then Jim resembled a spry, young poodle, his steps being quick, short and bouncy. Wiry, curly black hair covered his head and arms. Out of the top of his shirt, under his Adam's Apple, protruded a patch of thick hair— his back was similarly carpeted.

Jim also had the company uniform on, but since he was relatively new, his clothes looked newer, cleaner, as if someone actually washed them regularly. Jim, however, wore a tan, sleeveless work vest. His tan work boots— hardly any scuffs or discoloration— were also an indication that he was a new guy.

Jim's ears were too large and out of proportion with his head. His nose, mouth and chin protruded, giving the impression of a dog's muzzle. The wiry hair and protruding muzzle reminded his co-workers of a poodle so, to his displeasure, they started calling him "Poo." To make matters worse, those same co-workers referred to Butch and Jim together as "Bull Poo."

Jim shoved open the vertical, segmented back doors of the truck. Butch and Jim both waited in their long rain coats and hoods, waited for the "lion" and his "cub."

Neither Butch nor Jim liked their jobs. They were lazy so they did as little as possible to make it to the next paycheck. That's why they were so pleased having Fang and Charlie unload the truck on Monday mornings.

Fang and Charlie were a few minutes late getting to the unloading dock due to a hurried phone call that Fang made just a few seconds prior to arriving at the dock. But they arrived with their usual smiles and seemingly cooperative attitudes. The lone guard relaxed any suspicions that he may have had about their slight lateness. The guard smiled and they all started working.

Butch and Jim shoved the boxes to the door of the truck, using a dolly for the heavy boxes. Fang and Charlie carried the boxes— Fang shunned the dolly. He viewed it as a sissy's toy— to the warehouse. The guard stood on the unloading-dock platform, in the pouring rain, and supervised; his mind mostly on getting out of the rain which was trickling down his back collar like cold, slithering snakes.

The steady, drenching April rain beat on the aluminum roof of the truck sounding like millions of small pebbles unceasingly plummeting from the clouds without a hint of stopping. Someone could easily get drenched in a few seconds of exposure. The rain was so heavy that it acted like a curtain, making the men strain their eyes just to see things that were close and making it impossible to see anything that was only a few feet away. The deluge made it seem as though the men had to peer through a waterfall to see even close objects. The downpour brought a chill with it, too, the kind of chill that went right to the bone marrow. But it didn't bother Fang, nor did the wetness of the rain itself, though Charlie was irritated about getting wet. Fang acted stoically, concerning the rain. He could walk outside in the dead of winter without a coat and wearing a short sleeve shirt and the coldness wouldn't bother him.

Forty minutes passed as the four men worked continuously. Normally Butch and Jim would have to take turns shoving boxes and crates to the back end of the truck, toward the doors, while the other person had to shove the dolly under it. They would switch jobs midway. Sometimes they both had to be in the truck to push a very large container to the back doors and sometimes it took both of them to get it onto the dolly. Usually they got tired quickly and had to take rest breaks. So, a job that took Fang and Charlie an hour to accomplish, took Butch and Jim a little over two hours to complete. That left Butch and Jim two hours of freedom that their boss didn't know about. They were free to spend it any way they wanted, usually at a fast-food place. That made Monday mornings feel wonderful to both of them.

Fang and Charlie brought the last load of boxes into the warehouse. But only Charlie returned, slapping his shoes down with every step and splashing water in all directions. He was fatigued and breathing heavily. He wiped the rain off his forehead and addressed the guard.

"Sir, Fang said that you'd better come in and check the contents of a box that just broke open by accident."

Charlie said it in a hushed tone so Butch and Jim wouldn't hear him. The guard was pleased, but didn't show it. Yes, indeed, he said to himself, I'll take any excuse to get out of this goddamn rain. The guard followed Charlie into the warehouse. He was unarmed, as prison guards usually are when they work directly with the inmates. Before his eyes could adjust to the darkness of the warehouse, Fang smashed the guard's face with his boulder-like fist, knocking the man unconscious before his body could crumble to the floor. The guard's jaw hung at an odd angle, broken. Blood dripped from his mouth and right ear. Fang dragged the unconscious guard behind some boxes to conceal him. Then, looking at Charlie through gimlet eyes and clenched teeth, he said, "I ken gag an' tie 'im, then yuh get them other two bastards in 'ere."

Charlie noticed the expansion of Fang's thick neck. The trapezoid muscles were like large tree roots attaching his neck to his shoulders. To Charlie, it looked freakish.

Charlie smiled, waited for Fang to gag and tie the guard, then walked out of the warehouse towards the truck. Violence done to other people, excited him, too. He could feel the tumescence in his groin. He reached down and pushed his erection to the side to decrease the bulge in his pants and to relieve his discomfort. When Charlie reached Butch and Jim he smiled warmly, saying, "Sorry guys. The guard wants yuh both to come back into the warehouse to see the strange stuff that came outta one of the boxes that fell and broke open. Might not be our stuff." Charlie continued grinning as if both men were his best friends. Charlie displayed his most disarming smile; almost angelic, though it's difficult to imagine an angel with a hard-on.

"What the fuck're yuh talking about," Butch said. "It's jus' cans of food and clothes in them boxes," he added in a voice the demonstrated his irritation

Charlie, the consummate actor, raised his eyebrows, pinched his lips together, then shrugged his shoulders, all movements reflecting ignorance and innocence. "Hey, don't shoot the messenger. Up ta you. Come or don't come," he said, then turned and slowly walked back toward the warehouse . . . waiting.

Butch paused for a second, looked at his wet boots and muttered, "Fuck." Then he looked at Charlie walking away and said, "Wait a second. Hell, let's go see," he said to Jim. Butch called to Charlie to wait. They walked quickly towards the warehouse door, catching up to Charlie, who stopped to wait for them; their boots' soles splashing water on each other's pants.

Inside the warehouse, about thirty feet away, stood Fang near what appeared to be a ripped open box. Butch walked straight toward Fang who was making arm motions that meant, "Come here." Jim was in back of Butch, as if he were Butch's shadow.

Charlie grabbed a piece of pipe that he had previously set by the door and walked up closely behind Jim, just as Butch stopped in front of Fang and looked downward. As Charlie smashed the pipe onto Jim's head, Fang thrust a pulverizing right fist into Butch's solar plexus, knocking the air out of his lungs and leaving him weak-kneed and gasping for air, his face grimacing in pain. Then Fang kneed Butch's bent-over head, breaking Butch's nose. Next, Fang landed a vicious blow to Butch's temple and within seconds of their arrival, Butch and Jim lay on the floor, unconscious, blood seeping from their wounds.

Charlie, though frail and pale, had a vicious mean streak that he usually kept well concealed. Fang didn't notice Charlie's eyes, nor the slit of his lips as Charlie stood over Jim with the pipe in his hand. Charlie looked deceptively like a devilish china doll, pale, stiff, fragile, yet cruel. There was unconcealed viciousness in his look and distortion of the skin around his eyes and mouth.

Sparks shot across Charlie's pupils like flaming meteors across the sky. Sadistic rage tugged his lips into a twisted smile, like a jagged edge broken off a fine piece of china. Charlie could feel his throbbing, turgid maleness. So excited was he, that he suddenly had the spasms of a standing orgasm. Violence thrilled him.

Fang and Charlie tied and gagged Butch and Jim quickly. A few minutes later Fang had Butch's clothes, raincoat and hat on, while Charlie had Jim's clothes, raincoat and hat on. The hats were pulled down low over their eyes as they walked out of the warehouse toward the truck.

To the tower guard it appeared as if Butch and Jim had completed another delivery and were headed for the truck to exit the prison.

Next, the tower guard checked the roof of the truck to make sure no one was hiding there, then said, "Roof is clear," into a walkie-talkie to the guards at the gate. One of the gate guards responded, "Roger that." The tower guard turned away and scanned other more remote areas of the prison yard. No one had ever escaped from the prison, though it was relatively new. He figured that if no one had ever escaped, then no one could escape.

A prison guard's job is repetitive, routine and dull. It created dull thoughts and minimal activity. Dull thoughts and minimal activity led to boredom and boredom led to carelessness, which, in turn, caused errors due to bored, slumbering complacency and drowsiness in the guards. The tower guard didn't notice that both exiting men had prison shoes on, not the ankle high, solid looking, steel toed boots of the delivery men. He also didn't question the fact that a guard that had entered the warehouse hadn't exited because it would be normal for that guard to be supervising Fang and Charlie inside the warehouse.

Fang and Charlie couldn't see the tower guard . From the outside, the bullet-proof windows looked like a series of giant, one-way mirrors which reflected the immediate environment. The windows were wet now, but they could still see reflections of trees with newly budding leaves, some sections of the fence topped with razor-wire, some buildings and the pewter gray, cloud-filled sky.

Fang and Charlie knew that the tower guard was watching them as they walked toward the truck, so they were very careful not to look up and show their faces. They continued to look slightly downward, with their hats pulled low over their eyes, and collars turned up as if to protect themselves from the driving rain. To the guard, it looked like a natural. Fang and Charlie had orally rehearsed this routine many times— during those times Charlie would often get distracted because he was joyfully addicted to practicing *orally*.

They climbed into the truck. Fang drove, just as Butch had been driving when the truck entered the prison yard. With their collars turned up, their raincoats and hats on, Fang and Charlie looked surprisingly like Butch and Jim. With luck, if the plan went correctly, they wouldn't have to ram the front gate. And if they got out undetected, they'd have plenty of time to travel two miles down the road to where the get-away car was waiting. Fang's hurried telephone call had gone to his brother,

Freddy, who was to bring the get-away car to a pre-arranged spot—
Freddy thanked God that he finally got the call, after waiting two
months for it. The car contained three Russian designed AK-47 semi-
automatic military rifles, like the Viet Cong and NVA had used during
the Vietnam War. There were also three .357 handguns, a couple of
knives and plenty of ammunition for the handguns and rifles, plus a
few extra goodies.

Fang drove the truck toward the gate. He looked straight ahead as
he slowly, but carefully, drove through a curtain of rain. He looked out
the windshield and his spirit lifted when he noticed that the windshield
wipers could barely keep up with the rain. He knew that the driving
rain would aid their escape more than any other single factor. The
heavy rainstorm was exactly what they'd been waiting for.

Fang spoke quickly, but clearly to Charlie. "The guard will come ta
yur winda. Keep calm, stay cool. Keep yur head bent down so's the hat
will cover most a yur face. Sit still. Don't fidget. If yur asked a question
just roll the winda down a crack an' mumble yur answer. Just answer
'yes' or 'no' if yuh can, an' don't panic. The windas are all fogged-up an'
wet, an' that will help hide yur face and muffle yur voice. Remember,
keep calm an' we ken make it outta here."

Charlie nodded his head up and down as the truck approached the
guard's booth at the front gate. Sweat rolled down his face and stung
his eyes. He felt a knot in his throat that he thought would surely
choke him if he tried to talk. He glanced at Fang, who sat calmly with
both hands on the steering wheel. Charlie noticed that Fang sat there
like a block of ice, stoic, strong and as frigid as a glacier. It appeared
that, as Fang grasped the steering wheel, it, too, was turning into a ring
of frosty ice.

Charlie calmed himself, went into acting mode and became the
suave deceiver that he needed to be. Plus, he thought, the sweat will
look like rain-drops. So no big deal.

Fang looked straight ahead as he slowly, carefully drove the truck
forward; the headlights making the rain look like tiny, beaded glass
pellets.

Fang looked out the windshield, then the side windows and smiled
when he noticed that the windows were all streaked, distorting the

view inside the truck. He was glad that he had been patient, waiting for this heavy rain. Fang stopped at the gate.

The two gate guards reluctantly came out of their booth, their heads lowered to shield their faces. One guard approached Charlie's side of the truck with a contraption that looked like a roller skate with a mirror. The mirror was tilted at a forty-five degree angle. Attached to the skate part, at one end, was a six feet aluminum handle, shaped like a broomstick handle. The other guard went to the back of the truck to inspect the inside.

Fang cracked his window, then signaled to Charlie to roll his window down a crack so he could hear if the guard said anything. Charlie could feel the stirrings of panic, but quickly crushed them and settled back into his actor's persona. Being a convincing actor had saved him during many awkward and sometimes dangerous situations.

Fang's instincts for opening the windows a crack were correct.

Charlie's guard said, "How yuh doing?" as he slipped his mirrored contraption under different parts of the truck's undercarriage.

The guard at the back of the truck peeked around the corner and yelled to Fang, over the roar of the engine and the pinging of the rain hitting the truck, "Piss poor weather. Could use some sunshine, right?" said the guard as he pushed the accordion door upward, then climbed into the back.

Fang turned his head toward the crack in the window, as he felt the truck bounce gently while the guard did his checking, which wouldn't take long since the truck was half empty now.

Fang knew that if he didn't answer or if his answer wasn't loud enough, the guard might actually come and open the truck door to talk with him. That would completely blow their chances of escaping. Fang wasn't worried about yelling his response, though. He raised his voice a little above the sound of the rain, saying, "Yes," while Charlie answered his guard with a simple, "Yeah." The sound of the rain and the roar of the engine covered-up the difference between the sound of their voices and the voices of Butch and Jim.

Fang's guard jumped off the back of the truck, but didn't try to start a friendly chat as he normally would have in order to break the boredom. He wanted to get indoors as quickly as he could, so he grabbed at the pull-down-rope to pull the vertically moving door all the way down. But the rope was wet and soggy which caused his hand to slip off the rope and hit a piece of metal. "Damn it!" he cursed, then grabbed for the rope again. This time he was successful. The back guard then walked around to Charlie's side of the truck. The guard with the mirrored contraption drifted toward the booth while the back guard slapped Charlie's door and said, "You're good to go. See you next Monday," to which Charlie briefly replied, "OK." Both Fang and Charlie rolled up their windows, then faced each other and smiled.

Fang whispered, "Yuh did good. We almost outta here."

The suspense was over and Charlie relaxed his facial muscles.

Charlie noticed that the side view mirror had been bumped, probably by the guard. Charlie could see his own face, though the rain distorted the image. He stared at himself and was disgusted when he thought of his mother who had said that he was an ugly kid and must have gotten it from his dad. Charlie stared at his face. It was pimply and showed pock marks; one of the things that his own mother taunted him about. His mother, instead of saying he was *adorable*, would tease him, saying that he was "*odor-able*," then she'd laugh at him. He would feel humiliated, then he would think of ways to kill her.

The guards ran for the comfort of the booth, then called the guard tower and the unseen tower guard pressed the button that electronically opened the front gate.Everything seemed routine, and boring, just as always, just the way it was supposed to be, the bored tower-guard thought. Boring meant there were no problems. Sometimes boring is very good, he thought.

Being a tower or gate guard wasn't the kind of job you took if you hated simplicity, inactivity, and boredom. It took a certain character to do most guards' jobs well and not become jaded, hostile, or afraid of the inmates. A person had to be lazy, but hide it convincingly; unmotivated, but only when alone or with someone that was trusted, and simple-minded, with no higher goals in mind and desiring no challenges to improve himself. He also had to be duplicitous, but good at these traits to prevent unsatisfactory, yearly reviews. No taxing physical or mental labor was expected— simply follow orders— and being, or getting fat did not count against him, since the jobs were mostly sedentary, so gaining weight was actually expected, though never mentioned.

Fang drove the truck through the gate opening while he and Charlie smiled broadly, like children on Christmas morning.

Fang turned on the defroster to clear the steamy windows. He grinned as he drove by the horizontally spiraling, razor wire which was attached to the top of the high fence that encircled the prison. And just before he went through the gate, he stopped to let a prison pickup truck go by. He burst out laughing when he saw the shotgun mounted inside the back window. It was one of the mobile guards who drove around the prison fencing twenty-four hours a day, just in case someone got past the motion sensors that were buried in the ground by the fence, or got by the razor wire that was connected to the fence. Fang laughed quietly knowing that he and Charlie were driving right out the gate, exactly where no one would have ever expected a prisoner to escape. All that fancy, complex, expensive, high-tech equipment to stop escapes and they were escaping right through the front gate, right under their noses.

At the end of the prison driveway, Fang drove onto the highway toward Rochester, New York. He turned to Charlie and said, "Don't worry, boy. I take good care a ya, like always. As soon's we get ta the car, we be safe an' free."

He took off his hat, grabbed Charlie's hat and threw them on the seat. Then, while Charlie reached over from the passenger side and steered with one hand, Fang took off his raincoat and rolled down the window. He took the steering wheel back from Charlie, sat back and enjoyed the cool air as it blew up his bare arms and onto his face. He growled with joy as Charlie also removed his raincoat and rolled down his window.

Both men sat back and relaxed. Neither of them minded the rain splattering their arms. They were free. Free to resume their lives. Free to find the children they needed to satisfy their pederast desires. Fang had pornography connections in the Rochester area and Charlie was anxious to learn who they were.

Charlie was thinking about his freedom. He was a person that lived day to day and was mostly oblivious to the future. As he thought, he felt the breeze on his cheek, then gazed out the window and smiled with great satisfaction. He was looking forward to a change in weather that would bring a wonderful day, a day of sunshine and warmth, with the sky looking like a cumulus field of cotton.

As he drove, Fang's thoughts drifted off to his trial, when he had been convicted of several counts of rape, sodomy, sexual abuse, and endangering the welfare of children. He smiled as he thought about the other charges that he'd been convicted of over the years: statutory rape, deviate sexual intercourse with a minor, promoting prostitution, corrupting the morals of minors, indecent assault, simple assault, and second and third degree counts of felony sodomy. Pretty impressive record, he proudly thought.

Then he laughed at the irony of his current conviction. He had murdered people for getting in his way. He had taken part in several robberies and car thefts and was a member of some nefarious gangs. He sometimes served as a money collector, an enforcer, for highly connected loan sharks. He would break fingers, ribs, legs and arms if the price was right. He helped in drug deals though he would never use drugs himself— he was concerned with the health of his body. And, yet, after all these criminal activities, he had only been convicted of child abuse crimes and sent to a medium security prison. Then self-doubt set in. He wondered if he had been foolish escaping from the Grove Correctional Facility. But then he decided that he had done the right thing. With his extensive criminal background and his activities within the prison walls, he'd never get a quick parole. They'd keep him waiting and waiting, maybe for years before they would parole him. He might have even been sent to Attica because he was such a mislabeled hard case. And a break from Attica would have been a whole lot tougher; perhaps impossible. He wanted his freedom, needed his freedom and what he wanted or needed, he took. That was his life's philosophy: You want something, you take it.

He felt the same way about kids: He wanted them, so he took them. It was easy to do that in any large city. He could find a porn broker or do it himself. Kids were all over the streets, many of them selling themselves, offering their sexual services. Fang would cruise the streets and pick up a young looking girl, sometimes a boy, promise them money, food, and a good time, then drive away. He wouldn't have to force them into anal or oral intercourse. They knew what their jobs were. They were street-wise at an early age. But after the anal intercourse, which purposely would not lead to orgasm, Fang sometimes had to use a little muscle to have them switch to oral sex. He liked to humiliate them; it heightened his sexual arousal, causing his pleasure to soar when he had to force them to complete the act which he also wouldn't allow to reach orgasm until he was good and ready. When he was ready, he would have them strip, continue the oral sex, and spank them with his huge hand. He would tell them that he wouldn't stop spanking until they made him have an orgasm, which they were forced to swallow. He further terrorized them by telling them he'd kill them if they bit him. The spanking was very painful for the kids, very pleasurable for Fang. By the time he had his orgasm the kids' buttocks were covered with red welts and blisters so that when Fang released them back on the streets they could barely walk. He paid them, of course. It was part of the pleasure of humiliating them. He wanted them to feel that they got what they deserved. He would smile as he watched them stiffly walk away on unsteady legs. Then he would look forward to the next day when he could pick up another one and do something different.

Fang's ego was gigantic and warped. He wondered, even wished that he could make the top ten in the FBI Pedophile Task Force. Then he could brag, use it like a trophy, wave it like a flag. His warped ego knew no bounds.

Fang continued his thoughts as Charlie's thoughts reverted to his days of "wilding." He was from the mean streets of New York City. It's one of the things that he and Fang had in common. Only he wasn't the loner that Fang was. Charlie had to depend on his gang. The gang protected each other; security in numbers. The gang had many skinny, wimpy looking kids in their early-to-late teens. They were quickly taught to be tough. They would roam the streets and wait for an opportunity to go wild. They had all sorts of weapons, since muscle wasn't their forte. The weapons were small and concealable. Barbed wire wrapped around a pair of thick welders' gloves was a unique weapon that could ruin a face, yet could easily be hidden inside an innocent looking backpack. Then there was a variation on the same theme, where the fists of thick welders' gloves was smeared with superglue, then pushed into a container of finely crushed glass which would stick securely to the glove's fist area. There were the usual assortment of knives, sharpened screw drivers, clubs (usually baseball bats), and chains (bicycle chains, usually, because they were light and easy to conceal; they gave a mean, scarring blow).

Charlie liked to carry a hunting knife because knives scared people. He had slashed quite a few unsuspecting citizens with his knife. As a matter of fact, he was caught robbing someone at knife-point and that's why he was in prison.

But he also liked to carry a four foot length of common rubber garden hose. It could be concealed easily under the back of his coat in cold weather or in a backpack in summer or simply hanging down the inside of one of his pants legs. But he liked the hose for more than gang fighting. It was a sadistic, but pleasing tool for him and the gang. The gang would capture someone, usually a young woman (but a girl or boy would do, if no one else was available), gag them in an alley, and strip their clothes off. All the members of the gang would then pull their zippers down and pull their dicks out into clear view of the victim. The victim was ordered to give each gang member a blowjob that culminated in an orgasm before they would be set free. Charlie liked the terrified look in the girls' and young women's eyes.

Usually the victim balked. That's when Charlie would beat them with the rubber hose. Charlie learned this trick a few years ago from an older gang member who was later stabbed to death in a gang fight. The hose beating would inflict great pain; actually, terrible pain that reached the point of agony. Eventually no one could really resist the pain and the gang all got their blowjobs sooner or later, each of them laughing and cheering and waiting their turn. Charlie enjoyed using the hose on females more than getting the blowjob. That's why, sometimes, he had orgasm before the blowjob. Either way, he had an orgasm. It was a game he couldn't lose. He loved it.

But the great thing, besides the delightful orgasms, was that a hose beating would usually leave no broken bones or skin cuts, so if the victim went to the cops, there would be little or no evidence of severe physical harm, so the cops would file the complaint and consider the person to be just another whining, crack-pot.

Charlie always came up with a goods, so the other gang members liked him. The gang members made him their leader even though he looked like a skinny adolescent. Charlie became especially popular when he thought of the idea of sticking thin finishing nails through the sides of rubber hoses, then using them in gang fights. Those hoses proved to be devastating weapons and propelled his gang to dominance over other gangs. Some of the gang super-glued finely crushed glass to the end of their hoses. The hoses could rip and slash their way through clothes and flesh and the victims couldn't get close enough to their attacker to retaliate in any effective way without, of course, getting ripped to shreds.

Fang slowed down after about two miles, pulled off onto a side road where there were tall trees and bushes that would hide the truck from view for a little while. The awaiting get-away car was parked on the opposite side of the road, facing the main highway. The get-away car was a black Pontiac and from the rumbling sound of its idling engine, it was a sure bet that whatever was under the hood was powerful and built for speed.

The young driver looked like someone from a school for retarded adults. It wasn't that he had classic Down's Syndrome features, but he did have a goofy look about him that was easily taken for stupidity. The driver's window was down as he sucked on a cigarette and released the smoke through his nose, while watching Fang and Charlie.

Charlie got into the back, while Fang slid into the front passenger seat. Fang shook hands with Freddy, then introduced Charlie to Freddy, telling Charlie that Freddy was his brother.

Fang looked in the back seat and saw that it was empty except for Charlie, then asked, "Yuh got the weapons, like I asked for, Freddy?"

"Yeah, Otto. In the trunk," came the quick response as Freddy flicked the cigarette out the window and into the wet weeds.

"Good. Now git us the hell outta 'ere, an' make it fast, liddle brother."

/../.-../---/...-/./.-.--/---/..-/.-../../.-../.-../-.--/

4

★★★★

"Intelligence without ambition is a bird without wings."

Salvador Dali

THE RADIANT, AZURE SKY, dotted with pure-white, cotton-puff clouds looked pristine. The sun shone brilliantly, but temperately. The warmth on his flesh was comforting, like a baby must feel in its mother's womb. There was a sense of moist, dreamy, floating comfort, as if he were lying on a cloud-like, heated waterbed.

He had the feeling that destiny and fate had formed a partnership that guided his life to a positive series of events. That is, until a dark figure rose from the horizon. It's blackness rivaling the ace of spades which, in Nam, was the *death card*— some guys placed it on the dead VC and NVA soldiers.

The horizon slowly blackened as the sun shied away behind a newly born, dark curtain of sinister-looking clouds, as if it knew that it was no match for the darkness that was approaching. Lightening flashed from the suddenly darkening, inky sky, looking more like daggers than lightening and the thunder sounded more like the raving, furious cries of Satan than the boom of a natural event. The luminous sun and its comforting warmth retreated farther behind his back as the furious storm approached on the flashing legs of lightening. The sound of thunder was the sinister screams of an evil being. Fear choked him. He could not swallow, nor could he look away. Uncertainty numbed and immobilized him. His legs became the stumps of dead trees; his arms became withered branches. He watched as the specter of a demon slowly approaching in the shape of a death's-head skull; its red eyes glowing. It opened its fanged mouth as it continued its threatening approach. The gaping, fanged maw, he realized, wanted to devour his goodness; masticate, crush, mush and swallow every diamond of goodness within him, then transform him into one of its myriad minions of cruelty. He braced himself for its onslaught as the wind whipped his face, stinging it with grit and debris, then pummeling it with stones. Stones, like bullets, punctured the skin of his forehead, cheeks, lips and chin, but almost purposely missed his eyes so he could see clearly his helplessness and his hopeless future. Serpentine strings of blood sprayed horizontally across his face, then into his flying hair. He summoned his inner strength and indomitable determination only to see it vaporize, sucked into the black maw of doom. He couldn't breathe; the air was being pummeled out of his lungs. Immobilized, breathless and in agony, he was suffocating as the skeletal specter robbed him of breath. His lungs burned. He knew that he was dying, could feel the emptiness of it as the blackness engulfed him. He struggled in vain like a landed fish gulping for air. His strength had vanished, drained from him by an overpowering force. He managed one final, desperate scream with his last breath, then popped up in bed like a jack-in-the-box. He panted, then breathed deeply and quickly to restore his energy and sense of life. The sweaty bed sheet stuck to his back. He rubbed his eyes and felt the slick, salty sweat on his face. The sweat was foul-smelling and snapped him out of his sleep induced haziness. He was now cognizant of the fact that he had had a nightmare, the same recurring nightmare that frequently visited him. He remained still, gulping air like a drowning person who's saved at the last second. He talked to himself: "A bad dream? A nightmare? A premonition? A sinister storm approaching?"

The bed shook gently, then he felt pressure on his forearm. Samantha's hand.

"Same nightmare, Roman?" Sam asked sleepily.

"No. Not the Nam one. A different one. I might as well get up. The alarm will ring soon, anyway," Roman Wolfe said, with a frustrating exhalation of breath.

"This Monday morning's already started out poorly," Roman whispered to himself, while approaching the bathroom to relieve his bladder. It was 5:12 A.M.

Roman did his normal, martial arts exercise routines in the basement workout room. When he finished, he shaved and showered, then dressed in dark blue pants, a light blue shirt with various muted colors in vertical lines, and shined black shoes. He ate breakfast with Sam and Grace. When Sam departed for her school— she's a teacher— Roman took Grace to the sitter's house to await the school bus. Then Roman, also a teacher, drove to his own school.

While driving to work, Roman thought of how pretty Sam had looked when she departed for school. Her make-up was perfect, hair styled nicely, fashionable, tan slacks and a silky blouse with muted orange, brown and tan patterns. Plus, she smelled flowery and had a happy smile. Roman thought that Sam stood out in a crowd, not just because she was five feet, nine inches tall. It was because she was like a beautiful and valuable painting, like Sandro Botticelli's painting of *The Birth of Venus*, while all the women surrounding her, comparatively, might as well be part of the painting's plain frame.

It was raining as if all the angels began pissing pure water at the same time. The large rain droplets smacked the windshield like hail, making Roman slightly anxious about his newly rebuilt and repainted, royal blue, 1968 Mustang. Quickly, he reached toward the dashboard to turn on the headlights and the windshield wipers.

All the way to school Roman was serenaded by the constant splash of water on the undercarriage of the Mustang and the tap-tapping sound of rain on the roof and windshield. The sound was like white-noise making him slightly drowsy.

The Mustang was hard to miss. It attracted much attention and questions. Roman was proud of his classic car. He liked the feel of manually shifting the gears. The Mustang hugged the wet road and handled beautifully. Iacocca could be really proud of himself for this car. It had blinding acceleration due to the 390 horse power, 427 cubic inch, over-head valve V8 engine. It was a speed demon. It was a beauty, a classic, and Roman's mechanical pride and joy. Roman turned into the nearly empty and shallowly flooded school parking lot.

Roman parked, got out of the car and put his brown briefcase over his head as he rushed for the back door of Kroy Central School. Another Monday morning, he thought. The weekend went too fast, as usual. He knew it would be a lot easier once he started working, so he quickly climbed the stairs to the second floor where his fourth grade classroom was located. He opened the hallway door and walked down the deserted hallway to his classroom— other than the maintenance workers, Roman was almost always first to arrive at school, before any other teachers.

Roman's long legs strode by rows of vertical lockers that stood like soldiers standing at attention. He grinned, looked up and down the hallway, making sure he was alone, then saluted the locker-soldiers. He laughed at himself. As he used his key to open the door, he wondered how many times he'd done this very same routine. He wasn't bored with the routine; rather he was thankful for it. It was thousands of times better than being in the jungles of Nam where the sight of blood was as prevalent as the green of lush foliage.

He entered the room, turned on the lights and walked to his desk, his heels clicking on the wooden floor. He set his briefcase on the table adjacent to his desk, then used a paper towel to wipe the rain off it. He took all the corrected papers out of his briefcase and put half of them on Alyson's desk and the same amount on Steven's desk so they could pass them out when they arrived. They both liked helping Roman do this chore.

The desks were all in nice, neat order: four rows, six desks per row, directly facing the blackboard. Each desk had an upside-down chair on top of it, the chair's legs pointed at the ceiling, like children's toy rockets. The tops of all the desks were cleaned off by the students the night before.

The floor was clean and the garbage cans were empty, thanks to the custodians. Everything was neat and clean, just the way Roman liked it; a place for everything and everything in its place. Even the counter-tops had been cleaned. Roman could smell the fresh pine scent of the cleaning liquid that had been used. Roman thought of the custodians and how important their jobs were, but, like teachers, they worked with little recognition and even lower salaries. Roman chuckled when he thought, Perhaps if we screwed up our jobs consistently, we could be promoted to Superintendent of the school or to the Board (Bored?) of Education, if the Peter Principal still works.

The rooms and hallway were quiet at this time of morning. Roman enjoyed that. He could get a lot of work done when no one else was around to distract him. He valued the peaceful, early morning hours.

He scanned his plan book to double-check what lessons he'd be doing that day. His lesson plans were usually completed a week ahead of time, so he knew exactly what he was doing each day of the week, although, sometimes, things had to be altered due to unforeseen circumstances.

He familiarized himself with all the lessons that he would be teaching and made sure he had all the equipment needed for those lessons. Then, when he was satisfied, he began thinking about what he would be doing the next day. He checked to make sure there were no snags in the lessons for each day of the week and when he was satisfied that there weren't any, he started correcting a pile of classroom work and homework that he hadn't brought home. There were always papers and tests to grade or correct. Being a teacher meant a never-ending pile of paper.

Roman liked to keep busy. It meant keeping the grasping tentacles of depression away from him. He thought about his bouts of depression, then connected it to his experiences in Vietnam. In Vietnam, the Viet Cong soldiers and the North Vietnam Army soldiers replaced the high school bullies as a temporary panacea for his depression. A blade through the throat or a garrote encircling a neck worked better than a Wellbutrin and Lexapro cocktail . . . in Nam. Roman wasn't bothered as much now-a-days by the PTSD that he'd had to contend with after his discharge, but the bouts of depression continued to haunt him.

After forty-five minutes of marking papers, he sat back in his chair to relieve his back pain. He always felt better after he checked all the students' work papers and his lesson plans. He smiled with satisfaction knowing that he was well organized for the day and the new week.

Soon he heard chatter in the hallway as other teachers arrived. The marble floors, that aided voice travel, made it easy to tell when someone was walking or talking in the hallway. The conversations and footsteps that Roman heard were quiet, almost like whispering, before the words reached his ears. That meant that no one was approaching his room. He smiled with satisfaction.

He glanced at the clock. Nearly 8:30 A.M., fifteen minutes before the students would start arriving. He left his room and proceeded down the stairs to the ground level. He used the faculty men's room, then entered the office to check his mailbox. There was nothing in it except the computerized attendance sheet. He was pleased that there was nothing else because the things that were usually in the mailbox often lead to more work or more meetings and on Monday mornings he especially didn't want to learn about unproductive meetings being scheduled.

He greeted the secretary with a pleasant "hello," then did the same when the principal appeared. He joked with the principal for a minute.

The overworked, but wonderfully efficient secretary was too busy to share in the jokes. Roman walked back down the hallway and greeted a few teachers as he passed them while returning to his classroom.

Roman noticed some lower grade students' classroom work hanging on the walls. The work was out for display, something that the students could be proud of and other teachers and students could enjoy reading or admiring. He wondered whose drawings and writings may, some day, be famous and valuable. He thought about so much potential, so tightly wrapped into such small bodies, with such curious minds. He wished them all the best of luck, then quickly ran up the stairs, two at a time.

Two fourth grade teachers were in the hallway; he greeted them. He entered his classroom, took his student attendance book out, put the computerized attendance sheet in it and waited for the children to arrive from their buses. It was 8:45 A.M.

As he waited at his desk, he thought of summer vacation and the fun that he, Sam and Grace— his daughter— had when they traveled to Freeport, in the Bahamas, during the second week in July. They stayed in the best hotel, the Princess Towers. It was mostly free, too, because Grace had won the trip in a New York State writing contest that she'd entered during the previous school year.

Then, in mid-August, he and Sam went to Keene Valley in the Adirondack Mountains of northeastern New York State. They'd stayed for three days at John's Brook Lodge and climbed Mount Marcy, the highest mountain in New York State (5,344 ft.). Grace had stayed with her maternal grandparents.

Now Roman thought about Sam. She was wonderful and he didn't deserve her, yet they were happy together, though it wasn't always smooth. They'd mixed their tears of happiness and pain with each other; the happy times diluting the painful times. And, in mixing their tears of happiness, they discovered that, in some ways, those mingling tears of happiness were more intimate than sexual love.

Roman heard the students entering the building. The hallway grew noisier and noisier, as was to be expected. When his students arrived at his room, he smiled at them, teased them a little and hoped he wouldn't disappoint them with his efforts to make learning fun. He always wanted to make learning fun. He wasn't always successful.

/../.-../---/...-/./-.--/---/../-/.../.-../.-..-/---/-././

5

★★★★

"The world is a dangerous place to live, not because of the people who are evil, but because of the people who don't do anything about it."

Albert Einstein

FANG'S BROTHER, FREDDY, DROVE the Trans-Am through the rain as if he'd only recently gotten a learner's permit. He tried to smile, to keep his head up, his chin thrust forward in a sign of arrogant confidence. But he wasn't confident at all. He'd stolen the car from the long term parking lot of the Rochester International Airport so that no one would miss it for a few days, then hid the car until needed. In the dark of night, he had to practice driving it so he wouldn't lose control during the get-away. He made sure that the car he stole was an automatic shift because he couldn't handle a manual stick shift. Even so, the car was too much for him. The car rumbled and bucked with power. He gripped the wheel tightly and fed the carburetor gas in spurts. He enjoyed the response of power. It made him feel powerful, but he was like a boy riding a stallion, not able to really control or steer the powerful horse. He had practiced enough to be able to drive the car at normal speeds and hoped that was all he'd have to use.

He looked at the rosary beads and crucifix hanging from the rear view mirror. He'd placed them there. He recited a silent prayer asking to be forgiven for stealing. He'd become a fanatic about religion while Fang was in prison. Previously he'd been indifferent towards religion. His life had been spartan, lonely and friendless, so joining a church group made him feel worthy of friendship and it assuaged his terrible loneliness and self hatred.

Fang saw the rosary beads swinging on the mirror and, with sarcasm dripping from his lips like syrup, he said, "What the fuck's that, liddle brother? Looks like candy on a string."

Freddy grinned nervously. "Rosary beads. I been saved from the torments of hell. I've been born-again while you was gone."

"One a them ridiculous born-again Christian things?" Fang responded with distaste.

"Not ridiculous. I go ta church real regular now and try ta do good things. I got some friends now."

"Shit. Yuh just as stupid, too. Yuh haven't yet figured out that religion's jus' like pro-wrastlin'. Every body know it's fake, but they pretend it's real or their fun goes outta it. Jus' like religion, pro-wrastlin' is showy, colorful; it's kind a addictin', too. Think of it like this, liddle brother: the alter area is the fightin' ring, the fighters be the priests, the fans are the con . . . congray . . ."

"Congregation?" Freddy corrected.

"Yeah. That's it. The fans are the congration. An' the fight rules is the ten comamets." Freddy didn't even attempt to assist Otto with the word *commandments*, but he did smile with contempt for Otto. "The wimen wrastlers is the nuns an' the ticket prices is the money given to the church. An' just like wrastlin' fans, my man, there be those jus' interested, some that be faithful and then there be the fanatics. Wake up, boy! Yuh bein' a sucker fer fairy tales."

Fang and Charlie burst out in another round of taunting laughter.

"I have faith. And yur wrong, so fuck you, bro, and you too, Asswipe."

"Yeah, well, if yur born-again bro, then show me yur two bellybuttons," Fang mocked Freddy. "Yeah, man, while in prison I become a born again atheist. Whaddaya think a that?" Then Fang and Charlie burst into louder mocking laughter.

Freddy thought, Otto hasn't changed at all. Still treats me like a retard, his personal gofer; his worthless slave. Bastard. I hate 'im. What the fuck'm I doin' here helping him? Dear Lord, my savior, forgive my swearing and hatred. Freddy glanced at Otto, thinking, Psalm 14:1 The fool says in his heart, there is no God.

"It's raining, bro. Why aren't the wipers on?" Fang snarled.

"Don't wanna take my hands off the steering wheel," Freddy said, lamely— actually he didn't know where the switch was and didn't want to look for fear of driving off the road.

"Pathetic," Fang whispered, then reach for the dashboard, flicked a switch and the windshield wipers activated.

Charlie started sniffing around the back seat, then sniffed over the back of Freddy's front seat, near Freddy's hair, and said, "Jesus Christ, man. Where da yuh buy yur after-shave? The Dollar Store? Shit, man. Smells like yuh got a bad case of the zackly."

"Yeah? And jus' what the hell's zackly?"

"Oh, it's terrible, man. It's when your mouth smells zackly like your butt hole." Charlie and Fang busted a gut laughing. Charlie laughed so hard that his stomach ached, then he farted.

The fart made them both laugh louder, then Fang screeched, "Charlie, I think maybe yuh bet on a dry fart an' lost that bet. Sounded juicy ta me."

Charlie, in the spirit of teasing Freddy added, "Hey Freddy. Of all the things yuh miss, I bet yuh miss yur mind the most, huh?"

Fang's and Charlie's contemptuous laughter increased so much that they both started crying. "Hey, guess who said that? It was Ozzy Osbourne, that dead-head, heavy-metal music, druggie." Now the laughter was so intense that tears were pouring down Charlie's and Otto's red faces.

"Screw you," Freddy said, then immediately became nervous. He thought, Yeah, Charlie, you'd be the one to know how someone's butt smelled, up close and personal. Pervert. Freddy's legs trembled and his sweaty hands slipped on the steering wheel. He would speed up, then slow down due to his nervous foot on the gas pedal. Then his foot had a spasm and he depressed the accelerator too hard.

Fang vice-gripped his brother's thigh, digging his fingers into the large muscle until Freddy got the message and slowed the car. "Don't need no goddamn cop chasin' us fer speedin', Freddy, so slow down ta legal, an' fer Christ's sake, stay on the road. Yuh weavin' an' some cop'll think yur drunk. It jus' like yuh ta steal a car yuh can't handle. I shoulda drove," Fang said, gruffly, making Freddy more nervous. Freddy used his left sleeve and swiped at the beaded sweat on his forehead.

"I thought a get-away car was supposed ta be fast," Freddy said.

"Just in movies an' TV. If yuh get chased. We do not wanna be chased, but yur drivin' this thing like yur drunk an' that attracts attention, yuh shit fer brains."

"OK, then, I can pull over an' let you drive," Freddy stated, meekly.

"An' that would attract even more attention. People look at stopped cars. If they see me, then hear a description a me on the radio or TV, then we been made. Yur still a damn fool, ain't ya? Goddamnit. Jus' keep drivin'."

Freddy stepped on the gas too much and went too fast, again. He corrected himself immediately, then remained silent, but feeling humiliated, especially when he heard Charlie smirking in the back seat. He could see Charlie smirking in the rear view mirror. Sucks on Otto's dick like a kid with a lollypop and he has the nerve ta laugh at me. Fuck 'im, Freddy thought.

Hard ta believe he's my brother, Fang thought about Freddy.

Fang tried to relax and pressed his back into the seat. He thought about how similarly his brother, Frederick, and Charlie were built. It would be easy to mistake the relationship of the three men. It looked more like Charlie and Freddy were the brothers. They had the same slender body build and the same taut-skinned faces, like leather stretched over a drum. Fang looked disapprovingly at Freddy and wondered if, perhaps, there was some mix-up at the hospital. Charlie had some brains, but Freddy often acted like he was a retard. Then Fang concentrated on Freddy's sloppy driving. Freddy was still slowing down, then over-compensating and speeding up too much. First too slow, then too fast. His sweaty hands slipped on the steering wheel causing a weaving effect. Fang's frustration heightened. Now is not the time for carelessness, he thought as if he was reprimanding himself. He turned and looked directly at Freddy.

"Listen up, okay?" Fang said in a pretentiously patient and soft-spoken voice. "The guard an' the delivery men we laid out will be found soon an' the delivery truck'll be found. We'll have cops all over us if we ain't extra careful. We probly don't have much of a lead, maybe ten or fifteen minutes; half-hour at most. Cops don't know what kinda car we in. That be an advantage fer us." Then his voice lost most of its patience. "But if yuh keep drivin' like a drunk, they gonna spot us an' pull us over fer a fuckin' ticket. Then we gotta shoot it out with 'em or try ta outrun 'em or both. So, bro, what I'm sayin' ta yuh is," Fang's voice turned into a low, deep-throated snarl, "keep the fuckin' speed ta the speed-limit. Ain't no use us gettin' stopped now when we almost have it made outta here." Fang's voice raised to a shout. "You understand!" Then even louder, full of rage, he started screaming, "I don't want no attention while we—" Abruptly, Fang's voice died in his throat as he lurched backward due to the force of the sudden acceleration of the car.

Freddy was so nervous, scared, trembling and humiliated that he leaned forward toward the steering wheel. Tears came to his eyes and, without feeling it, his foot jerked the gas pedal to the floor.

Charlie said, "What the fuck yuh doin', man?"

Just then a steak of blue and yellow passed them in the opposite lane, heading toward the prison. Then two more streaks just like it blazed by, roof lights flashing and sirens blaring.

Fang looked at Freddy with a combination of rage and disbelief. He wanted to strangle his slow-witted brother. His searing rage made him want to strangle Freddy. But he noticed the exaggerated fear in his brother's eyes; a fear that immobilized him, but made him tremble and spasm. Freddy was now driving like a robot. Fang looked over his shoulder, out the rear window, to watch the last New York State trooper car that had just passed them. The cop cars had all been travelling fast and heading straight for the prison. They must have quickly gotten word about the escape.

"Oh, fuck!" Fang screamed as he pounded the back of his seat. "The last cop car's turning around and comin' after are speedin' Trans-Am." Fang gave Freddy a mean, disgusted look, then shouted, "See what I mean, retard! Yuh got the cops chasin' us now."

"They're drivin to a prison escape," Freddy said. "They're not chasin' a speeding car when there's a prison break."

Fang slapped Freddy on the back of the head once, then twice. "Yuh ever think that a smart cop'll see a speedin' car goin' in the opposite direction as a prison break, an' maybe think they be connected? Prison break? Speeding car? Get it? Yur such a fuckin' retard. If yuh wasn't my bro, I'da kilt yuh long ago."

Uncharacteristically Freddy screamed, "I wish I was dead because I am your brother! So fuck you!"

Fang simply stared at Freddy, stunned. "Fuckin-a, man. Yuh do have some guts. 'Bout time yuh stopped bein' a pussy."

What Fang didn't realize is that it wasn't just the speeding car that made the cops suspicious. The cops had a description of all three of them. They knew that one of the escapees was body-builder large. It made Fang stand out in the car like a clown in a monastery.

Freddy slowed down, then glanced into the rear view mirror and started screaming and crying, "Jesus. Yur right. They made us! They made us! I'm sorry, Otto."

Freddy felt another hard slap to the back of his head as his head jerked forward hitting the steering wheel.

Charlie shouted, "No shit yuh goddamn, fuckin' asshole!"

Fang countered with, "Yuh goddamn fuckin' retard! Now's the time ta speed-up. Now we need speed. Go! Go!," Fang shouted. "Those cops wouldn't a made us if yuh knew how ta think an' drive like I tol' yuh. Yuh floored it an' got their attention. They put two an' two together when they saw this fuckin' speedin' Trans-Am an' they figure someone was nervous an' trying ta get away fast. Well, Mr. Asshole, it don't take much ta figure that this 'ere speedin' car of yurs is carryin' people in a hurry, an' maybe those people are escaped prisoners. Yuh bastard! We're fucked now, so step on it!"

Freddy glanced into the rear view mirror and saw that the troopers had completed their U-turn. Rain, like smoke, was wafting off the rear wheels.

"They on are ass now, idiot, so yuh might as well floor it! Let's get the fuck outta here!" Fang screamed. "Yuh shoulda brought a common, everyday lookin' car in the first place, not some fuckin' advertisement fer the Indy-500. Dammit, those fuckers woulda drove right by us if yuh hadn't panicked!" Then Fang lowered his voice, balled his hands into tight fists, shrugged his shoulders in anger and said to Charlie, "Meet my retard brother. The king of dumb-ass pricks."

"Otto, yuh know I don't like bein' called a retard," Freddy whimpered.

"Go fuck yurself, bro! An' yuh know I wanna be called Fang, not Otto," Fang said while glaring hatefully at Freddy.

The Trans-Am was pulling away from the trooper car. But the Trans-Am was shaking and the steering wasn't smooth. Charlie saw the rain water rising around the rear of the trooper's car and knew that the cop had the gas pedal floored.

Fang turned to Freddy and said, "Are the guns in the trunk?"

"Yeah. In the trunk, right where yuh wan'ed 'em and one there." Freddy answered, his eyes red and teary as he pointed to the glove compartment..

Fang opened the glove compartment and grabbed the .357 revolver. He caressed it like he would a young boy's penis or the labia of a young girl. He stroked the barrel as he turned and looked at Charlie.

Fang thought, The car's too much fer Freddy to handle. Freddy's reflexes be too slow an' awkward and his brain don't work as fast as it needsta ata time like this. He's too nervous, scared an' sweaty ta be behind the wheel. He swervin' in the road an' can barely keep the car in the right lane. An' I can't get out an' drive. Fuck me. I shoulda known better. Shit!

Out loud, Freddy said, "The Lord is my shepherd, I shall not want. He—"

Fang smacked Freddy on the back of the head, hard, and said, "Knock off that bullshit. Ain't no Lord, fool, but I be the shepherd an' yur one a my sheep, yuh wimpy, sorry-assed cry-baby."

Freddy was having an even harder time now that he had to look through a cascade of his tears and listen to humiliating insults and denigrating laughter.

Fang looked out the rear window. "Oh, shit. They drivin' one a them new Mustangs. Fuck! They's gainin' on us now. Soon they be right on are asses." He thought, in desperation, There must be a way out of this mess. We can't've planned an' waited months ta have it all go wrong like this. Then he saw it; a sign; a sign of hope. To him it was their only hope; maybe a way out of this fucking mess.

"Don't stop at the red light. Jus' turn right. Go through the fuckin' light an' turn inta the school parkin' lot. Step on it! Get movin'!" Fang screamed. "Them cops is still gainin' on us. They close 'nough ta see there're two of 'em in the front seat."

Freddy came to the intersection, his nerves tingling and adrenaline flowing. He was so scared he thought he would pee in his pants, but he didn't. The light had turned green— not that it made any difference. He rolled the steering wheel to much to the right and swerved around the corner, making a wide arc. The rear end fish-tailed and he lost control. He stomped the brakes and slid into the other lane with squealing tires. He smashed sideways into the lead car that was waiting at the red light, then stepped on the accelerator and sped away.

The troopers' siren grew louder and louder as the special, police edition Mustang gained rapidly on the Trans-Am.

Freddy was a nervous, trembling, sweaty mess. His hands and brow were wet. He could barely keep the car on the road. The sweat running down his forehead stung his eyes and made them water more. He wanted to wipe the sweat off his forehead, but didn't dare let go of the steering wheel, even with one hand.

Charlie yelled something about Fang's asshole, retarded brother.

Freddy seethed with anger and humiliation. "I ain't no retard!" he screamed.

The car engine roared, preventing anyone from hearing clearly.

Fang lost his clear thoughts to a hammer-like feeling of an oncoming migraine. Blood was whistling through his veins and arteries, supercharged with adrenaline. His heart pumped blood so powerfully that the veins in his temples and the arteries in his neck were twitching like little blue worms puffing themselves up and down, while Fang's large muscles tensed like coiled springs, aching for release.

Freddy cried pathetically, "I'm scared, Otto," though he slurred his words.

Upon hearing that, Charlie shook his head and said, "Fuckin'-A," to no one in particular.

"Who ain't, for Christ's sake," Fang responded to Freddy. "It's OK ta be scaret, baby brother. Yuh just can't stan' still while yur feelin' it.

Dead men stan' still jus' before they die. Yuh gotta keep movin' an' tryin' an' fightin'.'." To himself, he thought, I was so stupid ta ask him fer help. Shoulda kilt him years ago.

Fang looked back at the trooper car, then screamed at Freddy, "Go ta the far enda the parkin' lot an' stop close ta the back door. Quick. Then grab the key an' unlock the trunk. Then both a yuh get all the weapons an' ammo out an' run fer that back door while I cover yuh. Wait fer me inside the door. Don't go no place. We need ta stay tagether." Fang pulled out his hand-gun.

Charlie started to say something, but Fang cut him off by yelling, "Shut the fuck up an' jus' do what I tol' yuh!"

Charlie knew what that tone of voice meant. He wisely said nothing.

Freddy slammed on the brakes as he passed the tennis courts on his right. The car skidded to a stop at the end of the parking lot, then slid onto a patch of wet grass that was next to the swings and slides and other play-ground equipment The doors flew open.

The pewter sky cried rain that was constant, so now the puddles under each swing were so big that they were connecting to form what looked like a string of beads.

The troopers' Mustang pulled into the parking lot a few seconds behind them. Freddy was trying to open the trunk when the wet key slipped out of his trembling hand and fell to the ground.

Charlie made a finger-comb and pushed his drenched hair to the back of his head, then shoved Freddy out of the way with a sarcastic growl. Charlie picked up the key and unlocked the trunk. He and Freddy grabbed all the weapons: three AK-47 (Chinese made, but Russian designed) rifles (7.62x39 caliber), the kind that the NVA and Viet Cong used in Vietnam; two .357 caliber revolvers; two hunting knives (in sheaths); and plenty of ammo for both the rifles and handguns.

As the trooper car came streaking toward them, Fang took careful aim, with his handgun, at the driver's-side windshield. He wiped the rain out of his eyes. As he squeezed the trigger he could see the windshield wipers sweeping in front of the driver and passenger, making their faces clear for a second, then distorted as the rain streaked across the glass before the wiper could clear it away, again.

When the troopers saw Fang aiming at them, the driver braked hard. He must have realized that braking hard would simply put him into a forward skid toward Fang. His mind reacted automatically and he stomped on the accelerator in order to hit Fang. Fang fired his handgun rapidly, hitting the windshield with three out of six shots.

As they ran, Charlie's and Freddy's athletic shoes got soaked and felt as if there were wet sponges in each of them. They were half way to the school's back door when Fang fired the first shot into the cop car's windshield.

The trooper car abruptly veered into another parked car, the sound of collapsing, crunching, metal and shattering glass could be heard clearly in the damp air, like a thunder-clap.

The impact lifted the Mustang into the air; its front tires on the trunk of the other car, like a stallion on a mare. The Mustang settled there, motionless. Steam rose from the hood.

Fang ran for the school door.

The sound of metal crunching against metal made Fang look back as the Mustang slid off the other car with a huge cloud steam rising from the engine. Both front tires were flat and the passenger door was ajar. There was no movement from the troopers.

As Fang reached the door, Charlie pushed it open for him. Freddy sat on the steps scared and whimpering. He put his open hands together in prayer. "God is my savior now, Otto. I don't want ta do this. I was supposed ta just drive you ta a safe place, then I'd be done with helping you."

"Why the sad face? Yur cheek muscle goin' ta burst if yuh don't stop clenching yur teeth. Shit, man. Looks like yur constipated. Yur not tryin' ta take a crap on that step, are yuh?" Fang teased, oblivious to the pain and humiliation he had just caused.

Fang and Charlie smiled at each other. Their smiles shone like searchlights toward each other, in silent agreement. The violence sexually excited both of them. More importantly, Fang saw that there was a whole lot more to Charlie than he'd known. Charlie wasn't nervous or afraid and he knew how to follow orders.

At the same time, Charlie was thinking about independence and confidence and that he'd need payment of some sort to continue to be Fang's sex partner. But this ain't the time to think about that, he thought.

Charlie was pleased with the sexual tension and produced a dreamy smile.

Fang and Charlie had huge, warped egos, larger than the Chicxulub Crater.

Fang looked at his brother and said, "Where's yur savior now? Give 'im a prayer an' ask 'im ta rescue yuh."

Fang and Charlie smiled tauntingly. Fang said to Charlie, "Bring the weapons an' stuff." Fang ran ahead of them, up the stairs, to the second floor of the school.

Freddy and Charlie grabbed the weapons and took the steps to follow Fang.

At the top of the stairs, Fang peeked through the double-doors windows as he was waiting for Freddy and Charlie. Fang wanted the high ground and the advantage that it gave him. He knew about high ground being an advantage, but little else as far as tactics were concerned. And he certainly didn't know the man that he was about to meet; the fourth grade teacher who had seen all those disturbing things in Nam that they had missed, including hundreds of body bags being loaded onto Army UH-1 Hueys— helicopters. He knew all those things, saw all those things and hundreds more. His memories were all locked tightly in a remote section of his mind; maddening images in a locked box, a Pandora's box, a box he hoped to never open.

Fang didn't know Roman any more than most people know that Michelangelo's last name is Buonarroti. Most people thought of Mr. Wolfe as a quiet and solitary person. Fang, Charlie and Freddy didn't know that Roman had once been called "solo-lobo," or "lone wolf," or "ghost wolf" or simply "Wolf," and for good reason.

/.-../---/...-/./-.--/---/..-/.-./..-./.-/--/..././-.-./-.--/

6

★★★★

*"Nearly all men can stand adversity, but if you want
to test a man's character, give him power."*

Abraham Lincoln

FANG BURST THROUGH THE double doors at the extreme end of the
school hallway. The AK-47 pointing in a ready-to-fire position, its strap
running over his shoulder so the weapon could be aimed with only his
right hand on the grip, near the trigger guard.

Charlie and Freddy followed Fang into the hallway, the doors
slowly closing behind them, with a wheezing noise, like the hoarse
breathing of a dying emphysema patient.

Charlie had one of the .357 magnums. He felt like Billy the Kid
walking through bat-wing saloon doors, pistol drawn and looking
for action. That feeling of power resulted in a hard-on. Always the
pompous one, he considered his erection to be another one of his
weapons, like a cop's hidden, "holdout" gun.

Freddy carried the spare weapons bag and the ammunition bag.
He looked like a new Army enlistee who should have joined the Boy
Scouts instead. His face was red from the strain of carrying the heavy

equipment; his face saturated with fear and slick with sweat. His fear nearly choked him, so he inhaled heavily and gasped often. Now he regretted trying to show-off by helping his brother. He thought that this would be his chance to show Otto that he was brave and useful, to earn his respect. But he'd planned on an easy get-away, not this disaster. He was out on a thin limb and knew it. Even worse, he knew that Otto and Charlie knew it. He thought, I think that fag, Charlie, should be made to do this lifting and carrying. Shit! I'm not even more important than Otto's fag? He grimaced, then silently whispered, "Praise the Lord. God forgives all sins. Our father, who art in heaven, save me from evil." But Freddy never really thought much about the nature of *good and evil.* Naiveté caused him to like the frosting, yet know nothing about the cake.

Fang surveyed the hallway; his eyes snapping back and forth, sizing up the place. He could smell his brother's fear. It stank like vomit exiting his sweat glands. Fang was disgusted by the sight of Freddy and wished the little shit had something worthwhile to contribute. Fang thought, I'd hoped the jackass would have grown up while I was in prison.

Fang spied Charlie's strange cowboy act and wondered why he had never seen this weird, wild, sexually-excited-by-danger side of him inside the prison. In prison, Charlie acted withdrawn, timid, shy and helpless. He was like a cuddly puppy, cute and needing protection. Fang smiled, realizing you can never really know a person's true feelings.

Fang looked at his watch. It was mid-morning. The students and teachers were busy with their classes. The hallway was deserted. Muffled noises could be heard coming from the classrooms. The sound of teachers lecturing and/or demonstrating the lessons to their students was indistinct.

Fang, in brief flashes, remembered parts of his school days. He hated the thought, hated the prison-like look and sounds of school, hated the teachers, too. Teachers, to Fang, were simply know-it-all bastards and bitches who got their sexual thrills from the power that they had over kids. They were all bookish wimps who couldn't save their own asses without using a book or quoting from one. Fang thought, I'd like ta see those fancy words stop a bullet. Anyway, Fang thought, them teachers are perverts jus' like me, if their power over children sexually excites 'em. Fang laughed at his sudden revelation.

Fang whispered to Charlie and Freddy, "Teachers are like cannibals, yuh know. They feed on their students' helplessness, as if the kids are food. Classrooms are like a big melting pot. The teachers mix the male an' female students in their classroom pot, stir 'em with their pointing sticks, then use plenty a seasoning, mostly sarcasm and tests, add large 'mounts a humiliation, stir the pot, then put in large 'mounts a useless facts an' figures, then finally they add some secret stuff, that only teachers know 'bout, that stops any fun from happenin'. But it don't jus' stop the fun. It causes lots of strict discipline an', a course, they let all them things cook fer the whole school year an' then they've a tasty stew ta feed their egos durin' summer vacation. Probly most are fags or lesbos."

As Fang talked, Freddy wondered if Fang ever realized that his name was only one letter away from "fag." Take the "n" away and Fang is fag. Freddy giggled at the irony, but lacked the courage to say anything about it.

Fang pointed forward as an indication for Charlie and Freddy to follow him. Fang was like a shark, while Charlie and Freddy were the Remora attached to his side, feeding off left-over morsels cast aside for them by Fang. Fang walked cautiously past two classrooms. The classroom doors were closed so that no one noticed the armed trio.

Fang mumbled, "I don't wanna be next ta the stairs we jus' come up, an' I wanna take a classroom on the same side a the building as the parkin' lot. "We goin' ta have ta take this classroom here." He pointed toward the classroom across the hallway. The door nameplate said MR. WOLFE, ROOM 202.

Freddy was near total panic; his legs and arms were weak. He shivered from extreme fear, anxiety and nervousness. His body reeked from the odor of fear. Freddy said, in a hushed tone that crackled, "Wa. . . why . . . why the hell ah . . . are we goin' in there? Let's get outta here."

Fang replied, "How we gunna do that, bro?" Fang paused, then when no response came from Freddy, he said, "Shut up unless yuh 'ave a good idea." Then Fang thought, Yeah. Right. Like that's gonna happen.

Fang looked at Charlie, grinned at him, then said, "He's my brother, but I'm the one that been born with the brains an' the muscles. My bro be a waste of air and food."

When Freddy walked closer, Charlie wrinkled his nose in disgust, saying, "Jesus Christ, man. Yuh smell like shit. Yuh know what a shower is?"

Looking at Freddy's angry expression, Fang said, "In a couple a minutes this whole fuckin' place be surrounded by cops. We need ta take hostages in order ta stan' a chance a gettin' outta here." Fang raised his eyebrows, then smiled at Charlie, as they both stood and giggled conspiratorially in the dark shadow of Freddy's humiliation.

As Fang reached for the doorknob, he was startled when it suddenly turned, seemly by itself. He quickly withdrew his hand as the door opened inward into the classroom.

Framed by the doorway, like a picture frame, stood one of the fourth grade's prettiest and sweetest girls: Alyson Boyd. Even in shocked fear her face was beautiful. She was mature beyond her years, looking more like a sixth grader. She had her dark brown hair parted on the left side and slanted across her forehead. Her brown eyes dimmed with surprise; her flesh delicate and blemish free, with peach colored cheeks. A dainty, almost unnoticeable scar crossed the bridge of her nose, while a lovely, delicate, light-brown beauty mark sat at the left corner of her mouth. Her ear lobes glimmered with opal earrings. She wore a lavender pair of slacks with a matching lavender and white striped sweater, white socks and shiny black shoes.

Fang, then Charlie, noticed all those attractions; their pederast desires inflamed.

In a fraction of a second, Alyson's eyes showed alarm. She stepped backwards.

Then all hell broke lose. Screaming inundated the hallway with loud, shrill, fearful echoes. Some students, down the hallway, were going to the bathroom, as was Alyson, when they saw the men with weapons and panicked. They screamed as they turned around and ran back into their classrooms.

Roman Wolfe, Alyson's fourth grade teacher, came rushing toward his classroom door. Alyson was still holding the door partially open, frozen in that position. Fang smiled and stared at her, pleased with himself for selecting this particular room.

Roman drew the door completely open. Seeing Fang, he said, "What's going on?" as he pulled gently on Alyson's arm, pulling her away from the door. He told her to return to her desk and pushed her gently away from the door. Roman thought he saw more men so he tilted his head to look around Fang. His curiosity was dramatically interrupted as the barrel of Fang's AK-47 followed his head movement. Roman started to say something else, but at the first sign of lip movement, Fang pressed the barrel against Roman's upper lip. Roman could feel its circular coldness and could also feel the ridge of the front barrel sight against the septum of his nose. He could smell the combination of cleaning oil and burnt powder residue. His eyes immediately scanned the gun. He knew instantly what kind of rifle it was. His brain flashed with milli-second, synaptic images of Vietnam jungles, Viet Cong and NVA soldiers across the membrane of his mind. Without realizing what he was saying, his lips parted and he mumbled, "Shit! goddamnit. Not again!"

Fang sneered, saying, "Ferget about God, Asshole. There ain't no such animal, so yuh ain't gonna have any invisible means a support." Fang laughed loudly at his joke; a joke that had passed from prison cell to prison cell and brought some humor to the gloomy inmates. Fang shoved Roman backwards, into the classroom. "Now, back off Asshole or yur neck will get broke."

Roman cooperated immediately. He did as he was told, though he knew that the best chance of disarming someone is when they are close to you and an even better chance is when the weapon is in contact with your body. But there were twenty-four children to consider and a conservative reaction was the more prudent way to go, he thought. And since there appeared to be more men behind Fang, Roman backed off cooperatively, while visions of Nam and the Adirondacks mountains drifted, like vengeful ghosts and ruthless monsters across his mind. He thought of Stephen King who said, "Monsters are real and ghosts are real too; they live inside of us."

Charlie growled and contorted his face like a maniac at the curiosity seekers from other classrooms, who were now sticking their heads into the hallway. And when a couple of teachers stepped into the hallway to see what was happening, he brandished his handgun with delight and, again, felt the power of Billy-the-Kid surge through him. The hallway cleared in seconds. The quick-witted teachers had the sense to lock their doors immediately and call the office to report the incident to the principal.

Roman calmly told his students to remain in their seats and be quiet. They understood him, though his voice was slightly distorted by the pressure on his upper lip from the barrel of Fang's rifle.

Fang thought, The parking lot and the school will be crawling with cops soon, so he forced the barrel harder under Roman's nose, forcing it hard enough to make Roman grimace in pain as he was forced farther into the classroom.

Once Roman's students clearly saw what Roman had seen— not one intruder, but three— they grew fearful. Some moaned, some cried and some were silenced by shock and/or anxiety.

Fang yelled impatiently at Roman, "Lock the damn door, Teach, an' don't think a runnin' off or lots a little dead bodies will end up in the hallway." Fang removed the rifle barrel from Mr. Wolfe's lip.

"Please don't scare the kids," Roman said, as he took out his keys and locked the door. As he backed away from the door Fang told Roman to lean a long table, lengthwise, against the door to cover up the door's four feet tall by one foot wide window. The television stand was moved against the table to brace it.

There were many times when Fang grew sexually excited by the sounds of a crying child, but right now the moaning and the crying were getting on his nerves. "Shut up!" he growled loudly at the children, like a raging bear, then pointed the rifle at them and said, "Shut the fuck up, yuh damn babies," in order to quiet the kids and get their attention. But just the opposite happened when the kids heard Fang's growl. Instead of low moaning and crying, the kids began loudly crying, moaning and speaking incoherently to Mr. Wolfe.

Fang looked at Roman and snarled, "Shut 'em up! Now!"

Restraining his fury, Roman stated, "You can't shut them up by scaring them. You see what happens when you scare them?" Roman pointed to the students. "Be civil. Pretend if you need to, then they'll be calm and quiet."

Roman walked to the light switch and flicked the classroom lights off, then on. He repeated this action. It was a trick he'd used thousands of times to quiet the students. It's effect was Pavlovian. The students understood the signal, became quiet and, within a minute, all that could be heard and seen were a series of sniffles, some coughing, runny noses, and tearful eyes.

Roman walked to his desk, grabbed a box of tissues and gave them to the closest student, saying, "Take one, if you need it, then pass them around."

Fang was pleased. It was now relatively quiet in the classroom. He ordered Roman to sit in the chair by his desk. After Roman sat down, he said, in a normal voice, "Boys and girls, please stay quiet and calm. These men won't hurt you."

As Fang smiled at Roman, an announcement came over the school loudspeakers to evacuate the school for a fire-drill. Then the fire-drill horn blared through all the hallway loudspeakers.

Roman recognized Principal Howard's voice. Roman also recognized the strain in that voice. Mr. Howard's voice was clear, as usual, but the tone was not as confident as usual and the tension in each word was easily recognizable as having a slight tremor.

Mr. Howard said, "All students, teachers and staff should immediately evacuate the building by following the fire-drill exit procedures." There was a short pause, some indistinct whispering could be heard from the speakers, then Mr. Howard spoke again, "Attention all students, teachers, and staff: Please stay away from Mr. Wolfe's fourth grade classroom as you evacuate the building. If your normal fire drill route goes by his room, then change it and go a different way. Please do not attempt to go near that classroom, but leave your own classrooms immediately."

Roman thought, Good, everyone else will get out safely at least. But sinister, dark thoughts started to meander in Roman's head like slithering wraiths on the prowl. Roman rubbed his temples and thought, I try to be peaceful, but violence always intrudes. My life is too filled with violence, yet I can't escape it, not for long anyway. I've never been a "turn-the-other-cheek" kind of guy and when someone, like these guys, shatters my peace and quiet, scares the kids, performs some vile act, I need to repay them in kind. It's just the way my mind works, he said to himself— though he wondered if that was really what he believed. Yes, it's vengeance, but vengeance can be justice, especially when there's a miscarriage of justice.

After the noise stopped, Roman's classroom phone rang. Roman looked at Fang and Fang nodded, so Roman answered it. Roman listened, said, "OK," then handed the phone to Fang, saying, "It's for you."

A serious and highly authoritative female voice said, "Mr. Fangzahn, I'm Captain Lewis with the State Police. We're willing to negotiate with you as soon as everyone has departed the building. Please do not injure any innocent people. We will contact you again as soon as the whole building has been evacuated. Please be patient so that young, innocent lives can be spared. After that, I will listen to your demands. Will that be OK sir?"

Fang replied gruffly, "Sure, Sweetheart. I got plenty a time. This is much better than bein' in prison. I'm even lookin' forward ta lunch. Are yuh the waitress whose goin' ta take are order?" His savage laughter echoed into the right ear that was at the other end of the telephone line. Then there was the clicking sound of the telephone being hung up. Fang was still holding his phone to his ear and laughing when he heard the click. Then he wondered, Who the hell was that chick. Christ almighty! Did she say she's a Captain with the State Police? Damn! They let women do anything now-a-days.

Fang opened up the top compartment of the equipment bag. Then he unzipped the two side pocket zippers. He checked the ammo, stuck another .357 magnum into his belt, then strapped one hunting knife to his belt and gave the other knife to Charlie.

Freddy pushed his back against the wall as if he couldn't maintain his balance without it. Freddy was praying, "Praise the Lord. God's love is forever. Help me Lord for I have sinned." Tears rolled down his cheeks.

Fang whispered to Charlie, "Fuck the *love* shit. Fear's more powerful than love. I want fear, Charlie, an' yuh listen close, OK? Fear's 'bout havin' control, but love's 'bout givin' up control. That love bullshit must've been invented by bitches. So don't fall fer that crap. Yuh want control, Charlie? Then make the bitches fear yuh. Works on bastards, too."

Roman heard Freddy's prayer and thought of an Albert Einstein quote. "If people are good only because they fear punishment and hope for reward, then we are a sorry lot indeed."

Roman was at his desk when he heard the sound of those zippers. It unnerved him. The sound reminded him of all the olive green body bags that he had heard being zipped up in Nam. It's Nam and the Adirondack situation all over again, he thought. Sweat broke out on his forehead; his hands got clammy; his heart raced and all the while the projection screen in his brain flashed body bag after body bag at him; bodies in hundreds of bags; blood running down some of the green bags; blood oozing from closed zippers; the red blood on green body bags giving the impression of a mutilated frog. Roman saw severed arms and legs being placed into the bags, after the bodies had been loaded. He saw a severed head being pushed into a bloated body bag. All these terrible visions flashed across his mental projection screen in seconds. He squeezed his eyes closed, took a deep breath through his mouth then slowly exhaled from his nose.

Roman had only recently stopped cringing when he zipped up his own pants or coat. The sound of almost any zipper used to send chills up his spine and cause his face to break out in a cold sweat. His muscles would tense, his memories became vivid and his heart would race from the thoughts of his fallen comrades that were brought to consciousness by the simple sound of zippers.

His next vision was that of a white wolf, appearing out of a dense fog, then pacing back and forth, as if it were a sentry who was guarding something.

Roman was well acquainted with this ghost wolf and had given him the name Blizzard. Blizzard was Roman's spirit guide. Through the fog Blizzard howled, as if it was his way of honoring the dead soldiers in Roman's visions. The image of Blizzard made Roman feel more confident.

Roman remembered the first time that Blizzard had spoken to him via mental communication. The experience still shocked him as he thought of it. Blizzard said, "I am an ancient creature; a remnant of the ice-age. I don't fear Man, thought he fears me. I am feared because I can be vicious, yet mysterious. I am the ghost of ancient ancestors. I am wary of Man. Because of that I remain elusive. Man has nearly annihilated me, yet my spirit survives, a spirit that can see back to the ice-age as if it were yesterday. We white wolves have survived Man's evil and greedy onslaught, cloaked in our spirit world and committed to a few humans who, though certainly not perfect, represent our survival with a wildness of character, but one that is well disciplined. In return, for those worthy and extremely rare individuals, we grant our spiritual power to them.

"I am the color of ice-age snow. I am not pure of action and thought. I can be gentle; I can be violent. I can be a friend or an enemy. I can blend with the hoary frost, melt into a shadow or meld with fog and forest. I can always be with you, Roman, as your spirit wolf, if you will accept me and allow me to bond with your own spirit as I have done with many of my Native American friends in past centuries."

Then, in the vision, the fog disappeared and Blizzard walked regally in front of the black Vietnam Veterans Memorial Wall as if honoring the more than fifty-eight thousand dead Americans who died in Vietnam. Blizzard appeared in front of the Three Service Men's statue that stands near The Vietnam Wall. Roman's mind followed Blizzard. Blizzard stood on two back legs, its front legs propped on the base of the statue, where the soldier's feet are: one black man, one Hispanic and one white.

Blizzard had not appeared to Roman in a very long time. In a way Roman was glad to see him, but Roman knew that Blizzard usually appeared to him only in times of dire need, life-or-death situations, or unless Roman purposely called for him in times of great mental confusion or frustration. The vision of Blizzard turned to look directly into Roman's eyes, then vanished.

Roman felt guilty about not taking action immediately. He knew it was the best decision to wait, but the guilt nagged at him. The guilt had an added, disturbing effect because guilt isn't simply emotional. There's a distressing physical component to it, also, like large boulders that rest on each shoulder.

As Roman sat at his desk, looking at Fang, Charlie, and Freddy, a slight smile appeared on his face. He knew now what was happening to him; he knew what he was becoming; he knew that his conscious mind had sent out an SOS signal and that the long dormant animal in him was sprinting forward and that he'd be here soon. The soldier known as Solo-Lobo, Lone Wolf, Ghost Wolf and his mysterious white wolf companion would bring with him the honor, integrity, bravery and loyalty that he had promised Roman in Nam and in the Adirondack Mountains. And he would bring more, especially the skills, courage and resolve to defuse this dangerous situation.

Roman thought, sagely, Don't get cocky. Don't be overconfident. Be careful. Be smart . . . for the kids' sake. Be patient, like a stalking wolf, then pounce and sink your teeth in deeply.

Roman's face was his autobiography. Each line on his face told a story, each furrow on his forehead, each scar and each spark from those secretive, sensitive eyes had secrets and character written in them.

Roman was a reticent man who seldom revealed very much of himself and seldom allowed anyone to get close to him. He didn't laugh as easily as before the war and idle chatter bored him. He thought that all religions were false beliefs, non-existent hope, yet he seldom condemned religious beliefs in public because he saw that religion's false dogmas concerning a non-existent God actually helped a lot of people live happier lives, perhaps better lives, so Roman couldn't kick the crutch from under an injured person's arm. Religious beliefs were too contradictory for Roman. He remembered reading that Mohandas Gandhi said, "I like your Christ, but I do not like your Christians. Your Christians are so unlike your Christ."

Roman firmly believed that in another millennium, sincerely rational people will finally confront their own religious foolishness, fantasies and myths and place the present day religions and Gods into the same historical perspective as we currently view the ancient Roman and Greek (and others) religions and Gods.

Roman's daughter, Grace, once said to him, "Daddy, you should believe in God. It's like having an invisible, superman for another father. Angels are pretty neat, too." Roman thought about it, but not wanting to influence her with his atheistic beliefs he said, "Grace, don't you think it's incredible how invisible things look exactly like non-existent things? Just something to think about, Sweetheart." Grace then walked down the hallway to her bedroom as if she really had something confusing to think about and that's all Roman wanted from her.

But, Roman thought, if religious fantasy was doing more good than harm, he would remain silent about its lies. Besides, he was always out-numbered *plenty-to-one* when he informed others that he was an atheist.

The line separating good from evil passes through everyone's brain and heart. We are all part good and part evil. We all hope, for the sake of mankind, that the 'good' dominates the 'evil,' Roman thought. And before Roman and Blizzard took action, Roman needed to find out just how much evil resided in this trio, starting with Fang, who already appeared to be a despicable man.

Roman stood, smiled disarmingly and shuffle-stepped, like a frightened person, toward Fang. Outwardly Roman appeared calm, but inside he was a very tightly wrapped coil of spring steel, wound around knotted muscles, straining for control. Roman lowered his gaze to the floor as he walked. If the eyes are the windows to the soul, Roman thought— whatever a soul is or isn't— then Fang would see that his eyes were now the eyes of a lethally trained assassin.

As Roman walked to the front of the room, he felt something brush against his leg. Blizzard?

Roman's thoughts went to Nam and a Marine General who told him, "The men in our special forces, who voluntarily jump into a viper pit so they can rip the heads off poisonous snakes, then exit unharmed, are not just crazy and supremely weird, they are also desperately needed, especially at times when a Roy Bean sense of justice is called for."

/--./..-/.../../../--/-.--/-...//./.../-/..-./.-./../.-/-../

7

★★★★

*"I do not believe in a fate that falls on men however they act;
but I do believe in a fate that falls on them unless they act."*

Gilbert K. Chesterton

HER NAME IS BEVERLY Lewis, thirty-eight years old, gorgeous, and a cop. A New York State Trooper to be exact, and the captain of Troop B, to be even more precise. She's a rare commodity in the New York State Troopers. Seldom did one find a woman in a position with this much authority, in this overwhelmingly male dominated domain. It was like trying to find a man teaching kindergarten. There were a few, of course, but you'd have to search long and hard to find them.

She didn't get to this position by kissing asses either, or by letting her ass be kissed. She could be as tough as an absentee landlord's heart, if called for, and she was as competent and intelligent as she was pretty. Her rounded, triangular face was without blemishes, not even beauty marks. Her hair was a long, plush brown and had a natural sheen. Her mouth is wide and sensuous, highlighted by ivory white teeth. Above those Hollywood-perfect teeth were penetrating brown eyes; the skin at the corners slightly wrinkled from the stress of her job.

Long eyebrows and eyelashes hovered over those insightful eyes. From the neck downward she was a slim, hard-bodied woman with taught skin, toned muscles— from regular exercise— but well-developed in the places most men liked. However, she downplayed her looks by not wearing make-up or jewelry— other than a plain, non-expensive watch. Her hair was usually up in a stern-looking bun. She did not often wear tight clothing or expose cleavage, but when she did— at a party— her appearance was like that of the glamorous movie star, Catherine Zeta-Jones.

Captain Lewis's smile didn't shine like a crescent moon, either. You might say that her tight-lipped smile was thrifty, as if she were saving her best smiles for private occasions, more personal situations. Her public smile was restrained, but pleasant, though it did not usually escape the confines of her seriousness and seldom reached her eyes. In private, her open smile reached her eyes and radiated warmth. But she was known for her indelicate diplomacy, also, saying what needed to be said and doing what needed to be done. She had more guts than a slaughter-house.

After college, Captain Lewis attended Trooper school in Albany, New York. But, unlike most other troopers, she had finished at the top of her class in the overall rankings; a feat unheard of for a woman trooper and, to this day, unsurpassed.

She came in third, in her class of thirty-one, at the shooting range— accuracy compared to quickness of draw and the time it took to fire the first round— which made the men take her seriously. Her only weakness was a natural one, and to be expected. She wasn't built with the same amount of muscle mass that men have. So she faltered on tests of physical strength and the related area of physical combat. But that was only a weakness if compared to men, whom nature favored with larger musculature. If compared to the other women in her class, she was, again, at the top in the ratings.

She usually attracted attention, being pretty, tall, slender, and athletic looking. She played women's varsity basketball for the SUNY Binghamton (State University of N.Y. at Binghamton) and was not only the leading scorer, but the leading rebounder as well. At five feet, ten inches tall, she had a fade-away jump shot that was the envy of most guys on the men's varsity team. As a matter of fact, her college boyfriend was a varsity basketball player and they practiced against each other. They were evenly matched in shooting accuracy, but he was six feet, four inches tall and could easily out-rebound her. But she could dribble circles around him. She was so talented that the coach of the men's basketball team secretly wished that she'd get a sex change.

In her senior year, she and her boyfriend, Jason— he majored in Business Administration and minored in Marketing— had a serious, shocking (for Bev), and revealing discussion about getting married after they graduated. Jason wanted to settle down and have tons of kids. To accomplish his goal, he wanted Bev to be a stay-at-home mom— he didn't come right out and say it, but his idea of a good wife was one who stayed at home, having babies, preparing food and taking care of the house.

Bev's major, in college, was Police Sciences— her minor was American Literature. Her ambition was to become a cop, especially a state trooper. But Jason told her she'd have to settle down and act like a normal woman, stop showing-up the guys, take care of the house and kids and meals, and forget about being a cop. He said it was too dangerous for a woman and no wife of his would be a cop.

Bev realized that this revelation was something that he had deliberately concealed from her until he arrogantly thought that she was trapped into marrying him. It was then that she realized that love can easily blind a person's insight and reason, but it intensifies human senses, except maybe for common sense and that her deceitful boyfriend was a closet chauvinist and an overt hypocrite.

Bev Lewis vividly remembered her father telling her that the most important decision, affecting her entire adult life, would be choosing the man she married, if she married. "This is truly a Robert Frost decision," he told her. "Take all your other important decisions about yourself, combine them all and they still won't have equal importance to who you choose to marry," her father emphasized.

Bev remembered her dad talking about marital partnership, that partners often disagree and get angry, but in the end, if they truly love and respect one another, they persevere; they realized that they need to be there in their partner's time of need, with genuine concern for their spouse's welfare and happiness. They must help to console, support and offer advice, even if they disagree with their spouse's actions. A successful marriage, her dad emphasized, often means putting your partner's needs before your own. Caring about your spouse's and your children's needs quite often has to come before your own desires and wishes; not being subservient to them, of course, but realizing that their happiness also translates into your own happiness. But to make the marriage work, your spouse has to sincerely think the same way. And there's the rub because, sometimes, it's terribly difficult. She remembered her dad saying, "Honey, marriage isn't like a hobby or a career. Those are, relatively speaking, all short-term activities compared to nearly a lifetime of marriage. Whomever you choose to marry, you and he will act like a wheel with you and your husband at the hub and all the really important decisions projecting outward from the both of you, like the spokes in the wheel. So choose very carefully."

Bev remembered that talk between her and her dad, during the fall that she was going to start college— she thought the talk was going to be sex related and was grateful that the subject was different. Bev thanked her father for being candid and concerned. She thought her dad was a wise man.

Bev thought about that talk the whole day. The following day she immediately broke off her engagement and returned Jason's ring, as she stared defiantly into his stunned and startled eyes. She then applied for acceptance at the State Trooper Academy in Albany, New York. A month later she had an interview, then another one a week later. Two weeks later she received her acceptance letter and was asked to report for training in at the end of June— she would graduate from college in May. After her college graduation, she had a few weeks off, then officially enrolled at the trooper school. Now her ambition to be a trooper would become a reality.

For her last senior semester sociology class, with law enforcement in mind, she wrote a paper about a troubled, modern American society. There was one portion of her paper that really energized her with the idea that she could do good by being an excellent New York State Trooper.

She wrote: "Society is in great peril and few people seem concerned. Truth and reality are under attack by myriads of myopic religious fanatics and their lemming-like minions. Traditional values are spurned or simply ignored by recalcitrant youth, irresponsible adults and duplicitous politicians and generally ridiculed by the fringe population. Honesty and responsibility are considered archaic. Love, caring and concern for others are only thought of for the egotistical benefits they dole out, and not for genuine, sincere characteristics. The family structure and solidarity is crumbling quickly and parenthood is shunned more and more each year. The divorce rate is soaring, as well as most violent crimes. Hope for a better future is at an all-time low and clinical depression, anger, and violence are replacing good mental health, compassion, sympathy and logic. Our school system is failing our youth because the best and brightest won't allow themselves to be enslaved and humiliated by low pay and increased parental interference, which means that inferior teachers are filling the teacher job market. Police can't keep up with growing crime; serial killings are on the rise (serial killers aren't only men anymore, as in the past, because more women are getting involved). The frequency of sexual abuse is skyrocketing; suicides have increased dramatically and fewer and fewer responsible, conscientious adults are willing to be firefighters, police, nurses, teachers because of the huge sacrifices that are required of them, while men and women who play children's sports are paid multi-millions for each season six month season. Worst of all, nuclear weapons proliferate in rogue countries with borderline sane leaders who threaten the whole world.

"Society's downfall is glaringly apparent when a criminal's rights take priority over the victim's rights and asinine anti-gun fanatics think they can solve gun related crimes by taking guns away from citizens who have never committed a crime. How can you reduce crime by taking guns away from law-abiding citizens, but not getting them out of the criminals' hands? Legislators and police ignore the hundreds of laws that are also ignored by criminals because legislators have no solution for criminals using illegal guns. It's as if they think its logical to take all drivers' licenses away from persons who've never had an accident because a few drivers have killed people with their cars.

"Perhaps, the most controversial issue of all is rampant immigration. The early immigration of the Irish, Italians, Germans, Jews, Asians and many other cultures was one of the reasons that our country became great and so advanced. Our country, then, was built on immigration. Now, however, America is being torn apart by its liberal immigration policies and the increasing illegal alien population. Why should we be allowing immigrants who hate us, want to destroy us, into our country?

"Even the modern onslaught of the juggernaut of political correctness is muzzling our citizens' right to free speech. The Bill of Rights is slowly crumbling, which means that the traditional America that we once knew is crumbling like aged mortar."

Now, after many years of hard work, she is Captain Lewis: dedicated, career oriented, unmarried, no kids, but relatively happy. Her major commitments are to her job. She is stern, strict, forceful and decisive, yet sensible, reasonable and caring. But there's also an almost impenetrable veneer of toughness that covers her caring nature, like the bark on a tree. When necessary, her jaw locks and a steely stare comes over her eyes like someone has pulled a black curtain across a window.

She won't be bullied or intimidated by anyone, though she will listen to ideas and suggestions, as long as they are given respectfully and are cogent. She knows that the root of intimidation is basically about power and domination, about superior power and control over someone. She almost always tries to use her power judiciously.

She has a difficult time separating her demanding job from her personal life; seldom goes on dates, and doesn't pursue what, to her, had become romantic fantasies of marriage and children. She realized long ago that cops and marriage aren't a good mix. She also realized that she had probably sacrificed a family life to her career, yet she was only slightly disappointed because she found immense satisfaction in her career and with solid friendships.

However, when she had time, and was out of uniform, and off duty, around friends, she liked to have fun. Then she was humorous, relaxed and openly friendly. She usually shocked her rare dates and new friends with her robust, risqué jokes and conversation. One of her best friends once said of her, "She's so damn cheerful off duty that she should wear a clown costume to bed, just in case someone needed cheering-up in the middle of the night. She can also be as shocking as hearing the truth ejaculating from the mouth of Jesse Jackson."

She drank coffee heavily— heavy enough so that she should have invested in Starbucks. As a matter of fact she had a coffee mug on her office desk, for all to see, that said, "Men who call women 'sweetheart,' or 'baby,' or 'honey' should have their tiny, little peckers cut off." She caught many a male trooper staring at that coffee mug and had many private laughs over its effects on some of them.

* * * * * * *

Captain Lewis sized-up the school hostage situation in minutes, placed her men at strategic locations inside and outside of the school, asked the principal to give orders that everyone, but Mr. Wolfe's classroom, be evacuated and sent home, then she immediately called in a State Police SWAT team. But not just any Special Weapons And Tactics team. She wanted a certain team of men, commanded by a particular Lieutenant that she knew was a highly competent, experienced leader and close friend. She had the rank, drive and tenacity to get the SWAT team that she wanted and what she wanted was Lieutenant Joe Hawkey's team. She considered Joe and his team to be rigorously disciplined, having excellent skills and the best of the elite teams.

She knew that Joe was tough, knowledgeable, combat tested in Vietnam and a perfectionist— any major sloppiness or carelessness and you were off his team. She liked Joe a lot, though there was nothing romantic involved in their mutual respect and friendship.

/../.-/--/.--./.-./---/..-/-../---/...-./--/.-/.-./-.-/

8

★★★★

*"Two roads diverged in a wood, and I? I took the one less
traveled by, and that has made all the difference."*

Robert Frost

THE NEW YORK STATE Trooper SWAT teams handled the extra dangerous
situations involving armed criminal and/or hostage situations.

Lt. Hawkey received his phone call and authorization about an
hour after the hostage situation began. His specialized team was geared
up and ready to leave Henrietta— a suburb of Rochester— for the Kroy
School, in their special SWAT team van.

Lt. Hawkey, like Captain Lewis, was also a rare breed of trooper.
He rose through the ranks to the rank of Lieutenant, not on academic
achievements or classic intellectual prowess— not that he wasn't a very
intelligent person— but on his uncanny, superbly honed street smarts,
instincts, combat skills and his proficiency with weapons. He was a
man who got the job done. To look at his exemplary record, you'd
think that he didn't know how to fuck-up.

Because of his full-blooded, Native American, Mohawk heritage, Joe
appeared to have a sun tan even in mid-winter. Captain Lewis thought

that Joe looked like a young Burt Reynolds with his leather-colored flesh, roundish face, short brown hair and his medium muscular frame that rose to five feet eleven inches and filled out to about two-hundred pounds. His small waist and broad shoulders gave his torso the look of an inverted triangle.

Like Captain Lewis— who constantly fought female stereotyping— knew that Lt. Hawkey worked harder than most troopers because he had to constantly fight ages old Indian stereotyping: lazy, dumb, alcoholic and on welfare.

Lt Hawkeye was also a multi-decorated Vietnam Marine, a combat veteran who walked in the shadow of death several times in Nam. He joined the troopers shortly after his honorable discharge and not long after that he sky-rocketed to success and promotions in spite of his wise-guy, sometimes recalcitrant behaviors, his boyish arrogance and, disrespectful behavior. Normally, these traits would have been a great disadvantage when coming up for promotions, but getting the job done correctly took precedence over all of those characteristics. The troopers needed men like him, so his promotions came regularly and most certainly would continue as he traveled on his successful career path. He was now in a position of great responsibility. Protecting his men turned him into a much more serious leader and made him more respectful of his superiors, when on the job.

He was extremely competent as a SWAT team leader. His experiences in Nam gave him a tremendous advantage over other troopers who had more seniority and more college credits. And his Mohawk Indian training put him light years ahead of his competitors when it came to discipline, tactics, courage and hand-to-hand combat.

Lt. Hawkey had the knack for getting the job done and his superiors reveled in his successes because the spotlight of his successes shone brightly on them as well. Lieutenant Hawkey was a usually a happy person, the type of happy person who isn't happy because they have the best of everything, but because they make the most of everything that they do have.

Lieutenant Hawkey often told his troopers that really important SWAT decisions happen at three speeds: fast, faster and fastest. He said, "Men, most combat decisions, by necessity, occur at those speeds. That means that if you don't know who you are, what you value, what your goals are, what standards you use to rule your life, you'll miss most opportunities to better yourself, to do good things with your life, to protect your family, to hold chaos and panic at bay and to reach your full potential as a decent person and as a SWAT team member. Be decisive, but be smart."

Lieutenant Hawkey was, like most people in authoritative positions, envied, respected, loved and hated. Those who loved him were on his team. They totally trusted him. They knew that his knowledge, his experiences in Nam and his rigorous training, could save their lives, and that he wouldn't put them into foolish or irresponsible danger. He often fought by their sides; he didn't just give the go-ahead orders to the troops. He usually led them into combat— though his superiors, including Captain Lewis, requested that he not lead his men into combat for fear of an excellent leader and great asset being wounded or killed, and because he had a family. He was a man's man and not a single person on his team was afraid of any homosexual interpretations when they freely admitted that they loved this renegade Mohawk, that they'd fight along side of him even if he had to face the flaming legions of hell.

Those who hated him were the jealous ones, the ones who got passed over for the promotions and respect that Lieutenant Hawkey received. Sometimes it was simply just a case of bigotry or cultural bias. But now-a-days the bigots didn't spout their ethnic venom to his face, at least not since one night in a bar frequented by police, where two bigoted young troopers picked themselves up off the floor after only finishing half the sentence: "The only good Indian . . . "

Then there were those who loved him and hated him depending on whichever feeling served their purpose at the time. Those troopers who were his superiors loved him for the glory that his competence shined on them, but they hated him for his seemingly arrogant confidence and, sometimes, sarcastic humor and flippant attitudes. Hawkey was sure of himself, but occasionally stern and contradictory. He could be a PR man's nightmare as well as his fondest dream.

He'd been divorced for a few years. His ex-wife, Susan, loved him as a person. He was a good husband and father . . . when he was home. She loved him for giving her two wonderful children, a boy and a girl. But tension in their marriage quickly escalated when he would not take an easier, safer, less time-consuming job, so that he could be home more often. Susan could no longer deal with the constant worrying about his safety. It led to great friction, stress and the inevitable arguments, then finally to divorce. It was an amicable divorce. They remained good friends and neither remarried. Sue did not try to prevent Joe from seeing the children, she encouraged it. Sue resigned herself to the fact that Joe's mistress was his job and that his SWAT team was his family. Joe was unaware of the large volume of tears that his mistress and family caused Susan, yet she loved him.

Sometimes, usually under the stress of worrying about Joe's safety, Sue would think that she didn't really know Joe. On those occasions she would think, No matter how long you're married, once in awhile, just every now and then and spread out over the years, your spouse appears, talks or acts like a total stranger with a unknown face, an abnormal mood, a startling voice and piercing eyes. At those times, Susan would immediately shake her head, then thinking out loud, she'd say, "Enough of that masochistic crap."

She remembered how adamant Joe was to name their son, Roman, after telling her some fantastic, probably exaggerated, glory stories about some guy that saved his life a couple of times while both of them fought the Viet Cong and NVA soldiers, somewhere in the hellishly hot jungles of Vietnam.

She was genuinely surprised to hear Joe mention that there was someone, somewhere that he thought was tougher than himself because she knew that her husband was the toughest son-of-a-bitch that she'd ever known. Those stories peaked her curiosity about this character named Roman, especially when Joe referred to him as "Wolf" or "Ghost Wolf." She asked Joe for more details about Roman.

Joe remarks were sparse. He said that he and Roman had been separated in the panic and confusion after a battle had ended and hadn't heard from each other since then. But Joe never forgot Roman's intense face. They had shared an unspoken feeling of brotherhood and Joe, being a Native American, with extreme pride and honor, wanted to repay this man, somehow. Joe told Sue that one of the greatest disappointments of his life was that he'd lost touch with Roman so suddenly. They had had a special connection, as if they were brothers in a past life. Joe had even named his son after the guy. Joe's memories of the man were vivid— especially the white wolf sightings which he didn't mention to his wife— plus Wolf had saved Joe's life more than once. Even though he had also saved Roman's life, once, Joe felt honor bound to Roman because Roman saved his life more than once and with great danger to himself. If not for Roman, he told Sue, he'd never have survived Nam. Joe told her that Roman taught him how to survive, taught him that the code for survival in Nam was to *kill or be killed*, and then taught him how to do it.

Sue Hawkey loved her husband for introducing her to the Adirondacks Mountains, the traditional land of the Mohawk Nation. Joe always took the whole family there each summer for a couple of weeks. Joe visited with family members who all valued Sue and the children. Sue felt comfortable around them. They were warm, friendly people. Those summers were wonderful for her. She often thought, "Could there ever be a more wild and yet beautiful place on earth?"

Joe took her and the kids mountain climbing, canoeing, and hiking where few white people had ever been, where, in the distant past, thousands of Mohawk ancestors had travelled during hunting expeditions, or at war with the Algonquin tribes. She would miss the Adirondack vacations now that they were divorced. But she still thought fondly about Joe's relatives.

Joe's mother, father and grandparents kept the Mohawk traditions and history alive for him. The Mohawks, like the other Iroquois tribes, had no written language. They relied on good memory and the spoken word to pass on their cultural heritage. Joe's grandfather was his primary teacher in *the old ways* of the tribe. The oral lessons that stuck into and nagged at his mind the most were the teachings that concerned the sad history between the white, European settlers and the Iroquois tribes.

Joe often thought, "It's been over one hundred years since my people were placed on barren reservations, but the lot of most Native Americans hasn't changed much. They still exist on small, obscure reservations, many of them living on welfare. They have an exceptionally high alcoholic rate and are still tightly bound by that unyielding yoke of America's broken promises, broken treaties, broken hearts and minds." Joe wondered how he ever broke free— the military, he thought. But the pain of his people ate away at his insides like a voracious, monster. After his divorce he wondered how his wife had been able to stand him for as long as she did, with the dangers of his job, not being home much and with a misplaced hatred of what happened to his people. But, the biggest question for Joe, after his divorce, was, Why did I marry a white woman? Perhaps it was because she understood him and was willing to share the burden of his emotional pain— though always well hidden. But, realistically, she could only do that for so long, until the stress and anxiety conquered her own defenses.

Sadly, Joe and Sue divorced, but happily it was only then that Joe really set his dislike for white men aside, thinking how unfair it was to blame present-day white men for what their great, great, great, grandfathers did. Joe finally realized how wrong he was, with Susan's help. He and Sue had discussed the fact that he was actually becoming what he hated: a bigot, a hypocrite, and prejudiced.

Later Joe realized, with shame, that he had driven Sue away, so he reluctantly let his family go. Somehow he knew it was really for the best. He loved the kids, saw them as often as he could— which wasn't very often, according to Sue— and devoted himself to his job. He was sorry it had to be that way, but he loved his job, wouldn't think of leaving it, needed it, in fact, like an addict needs drugs. Nam had trained him for combat. That's what he knew best; that's what he wanted to do.

Lt. Hawkey also has a quiet, compassionate side that is a secret to most people. He has a weakness for kids, especially kids in trouble. A half-dozen times a year he visits— he brings his own children with him— some group of boys and girls and gives anti-smoking speeches and tells interesting, Native American stories and related history. Like his grandfather, Hawkey was a good storyteller, entertaining and educating children at the same time, especially with humor.

With children Hawkey was most popular for the demonstrations that he gave about shooting arrows with a traditional longbow, knife throwing, and tomahawk throwing. He has an uncanny ability with a bow and arrow. He called the system "instinctive reflex action." Joe told the children that he didn't really aim the bow, he simply focused on whatever he wanted to hit and let his brain, instinctively, compute the speed and distance for him. What he did was different, entertaining because it was unusual and exciting. Very few kids ever forgot him. And because of that, they remembered his lessons. Lieutenant Hawkey never mentions these off-duty activities to any of his trooper colleagues, though Captain Lewis knows, but also says nothing, at Joe's request.

Joe carries a quiet pride for having helped the kids. The crowning golden memory of all his demonstrations for kids happened on a recent trip to *Camp Happy Times*, a camp facility, near Rochester, for children who are terminally ill. As usual he demonstrated the use of the bow and arrow from many different positions: standing, running, sitting, and even the prone position. When standing, he could hit clay disks that were thrown into the air by camp counselors. It was a perfected skill that most hunters needed a shotgun to accomplish.

Just before he moved to the next demonstrations with knife and tomahawk-throwing, a sad and emotionally shattered ten year old boy with no legs approached him, struggling to push his wheel chair forward. When the boy got close to Hawkey, he looked up at him— it looked as if it were a strain to hold his head up— looked at his bow and arrows, tears rolling down his cheeks and spoke with an old-man's voice, "Mister, can you please teach me how?" Hawkey fought to stop his tears as he examined the lad, then told him in a cheerful voice, "Yep, I sure can. Right now. What's your name, Buddy?"

"Danny."

Hawkey picked up his short bow and an arrow. He knelt beside Danny and helped him hold the short-bow horizontally— since Danny was in a wheelchair— notched the arrow on the bow string and showed Danny how to aim the arrow. Joe looked over the kid's shoulder, helped him hold the bow, then guided Danny's hand on the bow, while helping him to draw the bow string back half-way. Joe instructed Danny to look along the arrow so the point looked like it was on the target, which had a large picture of a deer on it.

"I see it," Danny said. Hawkey made sure the arrow was pointing correctly and told Danny to let go of the string quickly. The arrow hit the deer's rear end— unintentionally— and caused a cacophony of laughter from the group. Everyone cheered for Danny, then applauded. Hawkeye looked at Danny and said, " Oops. The deer will have a hard time sitting at the dinner table tonight." Even louder laughter and applauding occurred, as Danny smiled for the first time in weeks. Danny's parents were crying.

Joe immediately, and very patiently, gave tips to Danny about how to correct the next shots, making the lad do as much as possible himself, until four shots later the elated boy had two more arrows in the target: one in the stomach and one in the chest. The other two arrows were in the target, but missed the deer picture. Hawkey praised Danny, smiled at him, patted him on the back and told him that he'd never taught anybody who learned as quickly as Danny learned to use the bow and arrow.

Danny, with the sparkling eyes of hero worship, stared at Hawkey, then laughed. Danny was so elated that he behaved as if it the event was several Christmases combined into one glorious event. Danny leaned over the wheel chair handle and grabbed Joe around the waist, then buried his face into Joe's belly until Joe's belly was wet with happy tears. Hawkey patted Danny's back, then kneeled down to Danny's level. He guided Danny's head to his shoulder. Hawkey's eyesight blurred from the sudden rush of uncontrollable tears. What Hawkey didn't see were the looks of admiration and respect that surrounded him.

Hawkey became so emotionally attached to Danny that he gave the boy his short bow and one arrow.

Danny was so proud and elated with his accomplishment and his souvenirs that two months later, his parents buried him with his precious bow and arrow after he had succumbed to his bone marrow cancer.

Hawkey was invited to the funeral. He went, of course, and he wept for Danny the same as he did for his Vietnam buddies who were KIA (killed in action) or for a trooper killed in the line of duty. He would never forget Danny and the happiness that he was able to share with him. He envisioned his son, Roman, being the one in that wheelchair; his eyes flooding and his chin trembling.

*   *   *   *   *   *   *

Whether loved or hated, few troopers, except for foolish novices, ever challenged Hawkey physically. Not only was he tall and strong, he was also a weapons expert with all sorts of rifles and handguns, knew how to use a knife and how to disarm someone with one. He was skilled in close quarters combat— thanks to Roman's training sessions in Nam. Many a criminal had seen his humor turn into their pain when they made the mistake of seeing Hawkey's humor as a weakness.

/-.--/---/..-/.-/.-./.-.-.-/-.-/---/---/-../-/---/-./-.--/

9

★★★★

*"It has been said that man is a rational animal. All my life I
have been searching for evidence which could support this.*

Bertrand Russell

FANG'S EYES WERE LASCIVIOUSLY glued to Alyson Boyd as Roman walked
toward him. Roman saw the sudden changes in Fang's facial expression:
the raised eyebrows, wide open eyes, a slight, open-lipped smile, then
licking his lips. Roman knew that look. He'd seen it in the Adirondacks
a couple of years ago. Roman could see the kind of hunger that Fang
had for little girls. Roman also knew that he had to distract Fang before
an innocent young girl got scarred mentally and/or physically for life.
Roman's primary responsibility now was to protect the kids, at any
cost.

Roman walked up to within a few feet of Fang. At five feet ten
inches and two-hundred forty pounds of muscle, Fang saw no threat
from a six feet two inch, one-hundred and eighty-five pound wimpy
teacher, especially one dressed in what he considered to be sissy clothes:
white shirt with cobalt-blue pin-stripes; a navy-blue silk tie held down
by what appeared to be a knife-shaped tie tack; black, neatly pressed

pants held up by a glossy black belt with a shiny silver buckle, and black wing-tip shoes. Probably a fag, Fang thought.

"We need to talk ," Roman, said as he stared directly into Fang's eyes.

Fang looked up at Roman's neatly combed hair and grinned. To Fang it looked like Roman thought he was Glen Campbell at the height of his career, with not a single strand of hair out of place. Fang's eyes slowly moved down the length of Roman's deceivingly slender body, examining his clothes. His eyes slowly rose back up to meet Roman's. Fang noticed a slight scar on Roman's upper left cheekbone, about an inch under the left eye. It looked like a cut, not a tear, but Fang didn't have an inkling that it came from a knife during hand-to-hand combat in the Adirondack Mountains— other scars, from Nam, were hidden by Roman's clothes. Fang's lips stretched into a contemptuous grin. He raised his right hand, stuck out his index finger and poked it forcefully into Roman's chest so that Roman was knocked a step backward. Roman could feel the power of that one finger, like a fireplace poker thrust against his chest, but Roman remained stoic. Nam had taught him to accept pain. He took a step forward and continued staring into the menacing eyes of Fang. Roman didn't fear for himself, but he was very fearful for the safety of his students who were currently sitting at their desks silently staring, terror radiating from their moist eyes and trembling lips.

"I'll let you know when we need to talk," Fang yelled, with a fierce growl, his chin jutted forward, eyes boring into Roman, trying to intimidate him into a more submissive posture.

Wanting to distract Fang's mind from Alyson, Roman's retort was, "Will that be when my lower lip starts to quiver and my knees begin to buckle from debilitating fear?"

Fang squinted his eyes. His eyes seemed to glow like red-hot magma deep within the bowels of the earth, ready to explode to the surface. Those eyes glared with rage when Fang saw that this wimpy teacher wouldn't back off, wouldn't be intimidated, wouldn't cower in the face of his brutishness.

Fang was not all brawn and no brains, however. He possessed a good deal of both, compared to his cohorts. He realized immediately that his first impression of this nerdy teacher could have been wrong, at least partially wrong, anyway. Either that or the teacher was a fool. But, none-the-less, Fang had a bad feeling about him. He thought that behind the weak-looking facade their was something rather peculiar, perhaps something dangerous. Fang was ready to shake off this feeling as absurd until he caught a spark in Roman's eyes, a spark that Fang did not want to become a fire. Fang wanted to break Roman in half, but thought it wasn't the appropriate time for that. Fang thought that Roman must be incredibly naïve or stupid to challenge him with his eyes, to stare into him like a drill-bit biting into wood. He didn't know that Roman's intent was to distract his mind from Alyson. The ploy had worked exceptionally well.

But, somehow, Fang's mind wouldn't let go of the idea that what he was looking at was a wimpy, faggy-looking teacher who was full of bluff and bluster. To him all teachers were chair dusters, paper prowlers and pencil pushers without much real value in the world. He thought, This creep's just being an asshole, putting on a show for his students, which, of course, he thought was par for the course. The pricks and prickettes, minus their books and red pens are mostly weaklings.

Fang hated all of his school teachers and thought of spreading the legs of some of those bitches, especially the JAP geometry teacher. Well . . . *Jap* is what he and the boys called her. To the boys, JAP was hotter than a preacher's teenage, hormonal daughter. Her real name was Judy Ann Perry. She liked to tease the teenage boys by sitting on the front of her desk, facing the students, wearing a skirt. Her knees would be close together, with her skirt reaching the tops of her knees. All the boys, Fang too, waited all period for her to get on or off the desk, make an errant leg move and spread her knees apart so they could have a glance at her panty pussy.

In the fall of Fang's junior year of high school— after daylight saving time, when it got darker earlier— he had kept a two week vigil on her house, watching her shadow move inside the house, keeping track of her routines, peering into her windows. It turned out, that on Thursday nights she brought the garbage can from the back of the house to the front sidewalk so the garbage collectors could pick it up early Friday morning.

The following Thursday, after school, he hurried home, full of excitement and shaved his pubic hairs, then put on a pair of boxer underwear. When his mom and dad got home, he pretended to feel sick, didn't want to eat and retired early to his bedroom where he turned on the radio a little louder than usual. He made a trip to the bathroom to pee and another trip to pretend to vomit. When his mom heard him and yelled up the stairs to see if he needed help, he said he didn't and that he was going to listen to his radio and try to fall asleep. He had already collected a pair of small, tightly fitting, cotton gloves; a condom; a small, bleach-soaked rag that he placed inside a plastic sandwich bag; two cotton ropes (a three feet length and a six feet length); an old, long-sleeve shirt; ragged socks; old pants; a solid, rubber ball, with a smallish, elastic rope through the center and exiting a foot on both sides of the ball and the ends tied (the ball was placed in the right pants pocket); an old pair of sneakers; a balaclava mask that he'd made from an old, stretched-out woolen hat that he'd cut holes into for the eyes and nose, but not a mouth hole so that his fang would not show; and, finally, a small container of Vicks VapoRub. Then, at dusk, he turned off his bedroom lights, dressed and kept the radio on so his mom and dad were sure to hear it. He placed a gob of Vicks on the back of both gloves, then stuck all his fingers into the container so that the tips of all his fingers were covered with Vicks. He closed the container and stuck it into his left pocket. He slowly tip-toed across the room and quietly opened his bedroom window, closing it just as carefully after he exited and climbed down the oak tree that was adjacent to the house. Then he carefully snuck to Miss Perry's house, staying away from roads and lights as much as possible. He cut through back yards when possible. A couple of dogs barked at him, but he was gone before they put up much of a fuss. When he got to JAP's house he hid around the corner from where her garbage can was resting.

Fang waited for his petite JAP geometry teacher to appear. When she did, he grabbed her, picked her up in the air— her shoes fell off— forced her farther into the dark back yard, threw her on her back, then slammed his knee into her stomach to knock the air out of her lungs so she couldn't scream. As she was trying to catch her breath, he rubbed the Vicks from the backs of his gloves into her eyes. Now her eyes burned and watered so badly that she couldn't see anything, and even if she could, it would be a teary, dark blur. Fang quickly choked her almost to unconsciousness, then stopped and let her breathe. When she caught her breath, he put his hands around her neck, again, whispering in a faked, hoarse voice, "Stay quiet or I'll do it again, but next time I won't stop. You understand me?" Fang was trying very hard to pronounce each word correctly because that was not his natural way of speaking. He liked his uneducated pronunciation of words because it frustrated his teachers. Miss Perry nodded her head which reeked of the thick, greasy Vicks.

With his left hand still on her neck, he whispered, "Open your mouth wide my sex slave. I've got something to put in it."

When she started to beg, up came his right hand with the rubber ball, jamming it into her mouth, effectively nullifying any further, undesired noises. He stretched the elastic rope around the back of her head so she could not tongue the ball out of her mouth. He rolled her over onto her stomach and used the short rope to tie her hands in back. With one end of the long rope he tied her ankles and used the extra length of that rope to make a slip knot noose which followed her spine up her back, then placed the loop around her neck. Now if she tried to straighten her legs, she'd pull on the neck rope, choking herself. This way, her hands would be out of his way, also. Then he rolled her onto her back so she was lying on her tied hands with her feet near her buttocks and her knees looking like the inverted letter "V."

"Now the fun starts, you cunt. I saw you in the grocery store and followed you home." A ruse. "I bet you're one of those teasing bitches, aren't you? I saw the J . . A . . P letters on your sweaters and blouses. Been stalking you for a long time, Missy. Checked your mail and even know what those initials mean." Another ruse. "We pounded those Japs in the war. Now I'm going to pound a JAP just like I would a whore. Hear that, my little lady whore? *War* and *whore* rhyme. So a poet is going to fuck you. Bet you wish I hadn't seen you so often in the grocery store . I bet you wish you hadn't opened your coat to show off your tits. "This was also a ruse to make her think that it wasn't any one from the school environment who was doing this to her.

As Fang slowly dragged his hand, starting at the knee, up her thigh, her skirt followed easily all the way to her panties. Fang was disappointed that he couldn't see the color of her panties. She squirmed and tried to talk, to beg, but it was futile. She felt her panties being ripped off, then the tug of her skirt being pulled down to her ankles.

She was like a trussed hog waiting to be slaughtered. The thought was so thrilling to Fang that he nearly ejaculated prematurely.

Fang ripped open her blouse and cut her bra between the cups. Now that she was totally naked, he finger fucked her repeatedly, seeing how many fingers she could take. He rubbed her clitoris sadistically hard, then middle fingered her G-spot roughly. After ten minutes of this torturous teasing and brutal foreplay, he lowered his pants, pulled his hammer-hard cock out the slit in his boxer underwear, slipped a condom on, then raped her repeatedly. In between rapes he'd rub more Vicks into her eyes while he waited to get his stamina back, using the time to also thoroughly lick and suck on her breasts and bite her nipples, leaving bruise-like hickey marks.

When he finished, she was barely conscious. He untied her, wiped her face, breasts and groin with the bleach-soaked rag— to prevent the analysis of blood or saliva, removed the ball and ropes, cut free and gathered her dress, blouse, panties, bra and shoes, then simply walked away and left her lying there, totally naked, immobile and semi-conscious.

He took a different way home, but he stuck to backyards and fields, dark, shadowed areas and wherever possible, avoiding lighted areas. One field led to the back of the pizza shop where there was a dumpster shared by two other stores. He removed all his old clothes except for the underwear, socks and sneakers, opened a black garbage bag that was already in the dumpster— among many others, since it was the end of the week and garbage day was tomorrow— and placed his and her clothes into the bag. He retied the bag with its twist-tie and buried it as far under the other bags as his arm length would allow.

He sprinted the remainder of the way home, climbed the tree, entered, closed and locked the window quietly, took off his sneakers and socks and hid them. Then he pretended to hurry to the bathroom while gagging. He faked vomiting. This time his father came up the stairs and opened the bathroom door a crack. Otto stood there in his underwear, wiping his mouth, while the sound of the flushing toilet combined with the radio to produce a very unusual symphony.

"You OK, son?"

"I feel better, now, Dad, but I feel sweaty and dirty. I'm going ta take a hot shower an' hit the sack, again. Really, my stomach feels much better now that I threw-up."

"Can't be your mom's cookin', son, 'cause your mom and me ain't sick."

"Nah. Must a been some bug I picked up at school today. Good night, Dad."

"Good night, son. Hope you feel better in the morning."

"I will."

Young Otto showered thoroughly. When he grabbed the soap and brought it close to his face, he noticed a weak smell of Vicks. He didn't think his dad had noticed or he would've said something. He soaped his entire body three times, doing his hands twice more, washed his hair twice, then poured drain cleaner down the shower drain to ruin any evidence that might have been down there— his favorite TV shows were the police, detective and forensic science shows, especially on cable TV where he learned a lot if fact-based information.

The next morning he also took a shower; no smell of Vicks remained. He felt very happy this morning. He attended school, of course— it might look suspicious if he didn't. When he arrived at school he was all smiles, but he didn't tell a single person what he had done— the only way two people can keep a secret is if one of them is dead. Miss Perry's class had a substitute teacher. The substitute teacher didn't say anything about Miss Perry's absence, probably didn't know about it, Otto thought and she's too embarrassed to report it. Otto's smile grew larger and so did his erection.

The garbage from the town businesses and residential homes was picked up that morning and carried away to a Rochester dump site. Evidence gone.

The following Monday, after class, and from then on, after all of Miss Perry's classes, he always stopped and said, "I hope you have an nice day and a relaxing night, Miss Perry." Then he'd smile and walk away, awash with glorious, evil satisfaction, though it turned out to be a minor mistake.

Miss Perry's suspicions were aroused, but she never did anything for fear of how she would be treated by the students and her colleagues. She never sat on the front of her desk again, and she always wore women's dress pants from then on. Not quite a year later she married the male algebra teacher, the biggest, strongest-looking man in the school. He looked tough, but he wasn't handsome. To Otto, he was too hairy and ape-like, while JAP was pretty. Why would she marry him? Otto figured that she had primarily married a body-guard, not a lover and husband. Otto desired control and, in his mind, he had even controlled whom JAP married.

*　*　*　*　*　*　*

Fang had been mentally unstable since his early years. Everything in life is filtered through a person's past experiences which contributes to the development of his self-concept. But if the filter, itself, is ineffective, tainted, dirty or sat in a polluted and shallow gene pool, then everything that passes through it is contaminated as well. Fang's academic intelligence was average, but his mental filter (e.g. feelings or lack of, behaviors, attitudes) was polluted. That caused him to misjudge the tall, skinny teacher standing before him.

Fang grinned and rubbed his chin with his left hand as Charlie reached for his knife.

Freddy was a blatant misfit in this situation, like sending a priest to fight in a war. In any physical confrontation, Freddy was useless, like a hammer with no head. But Freddy was trying to reform his criminal ways. However, brutal honesty showed that he was a frigid chill looking for a spine to crawl up. Freddy nervously backed away as he said, " Lord save me. For with God, nothing shall be impossible. Luke 1:37."

Roman, hearing Freddy's desperate plea for heavenly help, thought of a Christopher Hitchen's quote. "What can be asserted without proof can also be dismissed without proof."

Freddy's stomach churned from nervousness and worry. He was as jumpy as a startled frog. This was all supposed to be so simple, he thought. His intestines groaned. He felt the internal pressure of a large gas bubble running its course to its final exit point. He squeezed his buttocks together to stop the putrid cloud of flatus from being born, but, to his disappointment, out came the cloud of gas. He took the opportunity offered by Mr. Wolfe's distraction and walked to the back of the classroom, as he mumbled, "God is our refuge and strength, a very present help in troubled times. Palms 46:1."

Freddy's foul flatus must have been a tail-fart, like the tail on a kite. As he passed the students, they grimaced, some of them pinching their noses closed after their gag-reflex was activated, while others fanned the air in front of their noses with an open hand.

Standing in the back of the room, Freddy looked in fear at his brother and Charlie.

One of the students, Steven Blake, caught a whiff of the tail-fart and without thinking, turned, looked over his shoulder to the back of the room, stared at Freddy while pinching his nose closed and said, in a nasal voice that sounded as if he had a cold, "Man, you stink. You sure know how to cut-the-cheese."

Roman, hearing Steven's reaction to the smell, turned and looked, with concern, at Steven. Roman smiled, winked then placed his right index finger perpendicular to his lips— the universal sign for quiet. Steven nodded his head, an indication that he would obey, but stole another peek at Freddy who was staring back at him.

While in the process of turning back toward Fang, Roman wasn't aware of Fang's raised left hand, clenched into a fist, about to act like a piston. Fang's upper arm and shoulder muscles drove his piston-like fist into Roman's belly.

Despite Roman's karate exercises, which made his stomach muscles tight and hard, he was caught off guard. Air exploded from his lungs like air from a ruptured tire. The pain was excruciating. While desperately trying to catch his breath, he was hoping that no internal organs had been damaged.

The force of Fang's fist crashing into Roman's stomach was greater than anything he had ever experienced. The punch literally lifted him off the floor and threw him backward a few feet, making him stumble, lose his balance and fall on his back. Roman finally inhaled desperately, filling his lungs, breathing deeply and rapidly. He sat up, then pushed himself up from the floor slowly, still breathing deeply and quickly. Then he coughed, causing his stomach muscles to tighten, which caused more pain. He faked a smile for the kids, so they wouldn't worry as much.

"Not so brave now, are yuh?" Fang grinned.

Roman remained silent.

Roman noticed that a couple of the boys started to grin at him. They knew this game. Mr. Wolfe often let them punch him in the stomach as he teasingly said to them, "You can't hurt steel." But some of the boys had wondered what would happen if someone older and stronger had a chance to hit Mr. Wolfe in the stomach. Now, to their guarded delight, that question was answered and, for them, it took some of the fear out of their situation, allowing them to express guarded smiles.

Steven Blake yelled, "Yuh can't hurt steel."

Roman grimaced, wishing Steven had not said that. He looked at Steven, put a serious expression on his face, then shook his head back and forth slightly, indicating that he didn't want Steven to talk.

Taking the fear out of this situation was good for the children, but not for Roman. He thrived on fear and intimidation. He noticed the students smiling as his own anger increased. Fang glared at Roman, who was holding his stomach and loudly shouted, in a disgusted-sounding voice, "Steel, my ass, boy. Yuh ever seen steel gettin' bent, knocked back an' fallin' over. No, not steel, kid. More like that silver stuff yuh wrap food in . . . ah . . . 'lumnum foil."

In the back of his mind, however, Fang anxiously thought, No one had ever been able to take a blow to the stomach like this teacher had just done, even if he collapsed to the floor. He got up too quickly, as if he wasn't hurt seriously. When Fang had punched someone like that before, the guy didn't get up for quite a while because of internal damage. Fang thought, Maybe I should have punched the guy over his heart, thinking of the time he had killed a guy by punching the guy there. The punch literally broke the chest bones and drove them into the guy's heart. The heart ruptured and the guy was dead shortly after his limp body hit the ground. He fell limply to the ground, as if all his bones had turned into rubber bands.

Roman stepped toward Fang while taking another deep breath to inflate his lungs. He stared at Fang a moment before saying, "Listen, Fang. If you or your goons hurt any of these children, I'll make such a fuss that it'll attract the attention of the police and they'll be forced to come charging in here. Hurt me, not the children."

"Jus' did that, didn't I? That's not a threat, is it Slim? Sounds like suicide ta me," Fang ejaculated with gobs of saliva bursting from his mouth, like lava from an erupting volcano. "Yuh can't be that much a fool. Can yuh?"

"Suicide? What? You planning on killing yourself? Situations like these are like mini-wars. And in war, it's tacitly understood that one does not deliberately injure women and children. Better to be an honorable and civilized fool than a savage, contemptible and ignorant bully," Roman responded with venomous words.

There was a pause as Roman and Fang glared at each other.

Fang bunched his muscles, clenched his fists, then said, "Yuh goin' ta challenge me, Teach?"

Roman stood his ground, saying, "Only if you hurt any of my students."

Suddenly, Blizzard's thoughts entered Roman's mind and Roman knew that Charlie was coming up behind him. Roman could have easily rear-kicked him to take him out of action, but he decided against it. He didn't want to give away his karate knowledge and skills. It was to his advantage not to let them know that he was a black-belt in karate. Then a frightening thought occurred to him: What if the kids mentioned it? Then a further thought: What if Fang used the classroom television and the media mentioned it? That would take away any advantage that he had had and make this situation worse. Roman worried about the kids . Somehow he had to get the kids out or at least get some of them out of the classroom safely.

Roman was distracted by these urgent thoughts when he felt a sharp pain in his back.

Charlie stuck the point of his knife near Roman's lower spine.

Some children screamed. Roman looked at them and held up his hand to let them know it was okay.

To Fang, Roman whispered, "Tell your cock sucking chicken to back off."

Fang's anger flared. Like lightening he landed a vicious, but glancing right fist to Roman's jaw. Roman had rolled his head with the punch, unable to get his hands up in time to block it. Fang's fist was fast, for such a big man. Fang's follow-up left hook caught Roman on the upper lip and nose, knocking him backward into Charlie's knife point. The knife wound, Roman knew, would only be superficial. Roman's nose, however, was broken and his upper lip was cut. He did not dare to fight back. He staggered backward. He could feel and taste the stream of warm blood flowing down around the corner of his mouth and over his lips. He grimaced, then spit blood.

But despite the pain, he could still feel the presence of Charlie in back of him and as he spun around to make it look as if he were trying to catch his balance, he elbowed Charlie in the temple. Such a blow could be lethal due to the fragile nature of the skull at that part of the cranium. Shards of bone can be caused to ram into the brain causing hemorrhaging, swelling, pressure, then death. But Roman was, in fact, partly off balance and didn't intend for the elbow to be lethal. The knife popped out of Charlie's hand as he fell to the floor unconscious. Roman fell next to him and wondered if now was the time to unleash his fury on Fang.

Roman sat up, felt and saw the blur of white leap from his chest, then heard Blizzard's muffled growl. Blizzard, Roman's spirit guide, suddenly appeared to him. Roman looked around to see if anyone else had seen Blizzard. It was extremely rare for anyone but Roman to see Blizzard, but once in a great while someone did and that someone was usually a child. No one reacted to Blizzard's presence.

Roman and Blizzard communicated by a mysterious telepathic process. Thoughts were exchanged, like Monarch butterflies bursting from their brains, then speedily floating in a stream of vivid thoughts as if being delivered by a rainbow. In this way they could read each other's thoughts and observe the amazing process that took place, something only they could see, like owning a Picasso painting and hiding it so that only the owner can see it. So they spoke to each other in this manner, with Blizzard and Roman exchanging ideas, offering suggestions, advice and support which settled in each of their brains stems, then, in a millisecond, flashed to all the relevant nerve synapses and all the relevant receptors where they were translated into action, as if they were traveling at the speed of light, on the tracks of a cosmic train of thought.

Laughing hysterically, Fang said, "Did not think I hit yuh that hard. Guess yuh ain't as tough as yuh sound, little fella."

Roman stood, raised his two open hands and pressed them together, each on one side of his nose, then he snapped both hands in the opposite direction of the break. The crunch was audible— that's how Medics fixed broken noses when he and his fellow soldiers were in the jungle, days from their base of operation and doctors. Blood from his nose and lip trailed down the insides of his hands. Anger flushed his face and his eyes watered profusely. Continuous rivulets of tears streamed down his cheeks. He stood up as quickly as he could, but then realized that it was a mistake. Was this action be taken as rebellion or as an accident? he wondered.

"Yuh be very entertaining," Fang stated mirthfully, then thought, I could crush this guy like cotton candy, but the prick is right 'bout one thing. If I do that, then these babies would panic. No tellin' what they do, then I lose control of 'em an' they might do somethin' foolish ta attrac' the cops. He paused, then smiled. He had thought of something more effective that he could do.

Still on the floor, Charlie was stirring and mumbling. Fang kicked him lightly in the ribs and said, "Get up. I need yuh." Charlie did not respond.

Then Fang walked to Alyson Boyd, who sat in a front row desk. With his left hand he grabbed her by the neck, under the chin, lifted her out of her seat, then up and over her desk. He set her down in front of him as he one-handedly aimed his assault rifle at Roman.

Roman saw his students cringe and start whimpering.

"Stop that! You're scaring the kids," Roman yelled. Then Roman lied, saying, "I meant no harm. Knocking Charlie down was an accident. I tried to catch my balance and accidentally crashed into him, that's all." Roman made his voice and mannerisms sound and look contrite. "I mean you people no harm. I just want to keep the kids safe."

Alyson gasped, then rubbed her red, sore neck and wiped away her tears.

"Hell, I knows that," Fang responded as he lowered the rifle. "It be the part where yuh threaten me, an' thinks yuh has control, that bother me."

Freddy, hesitantly, came to the front of the room, bent over Charlie, reluctantly offering to help him, but Charlie was still unconscious, though he was moaning. Freddy stood up and looked at his brother with anger. "You beatin' up little girls now, brother? Our Lord only has so much patience, yuh know."

"Shut yur damn mouth with that Lordy bullshit, yuh sissy."

I'd rather have fanatically religious Freddy as a friend than a fiend like Fang, Roman thought. At least we could argue our religious positions without anyone being physically hurt.

Fang said to Roman, "Okay, Asshole. Now yuh listen careful. Yuh do what yur tol' an' back off before I start really hurtin' some kids." Then Fang dug his free hand into Alyson's hair, pulled upward and lifted Alyson's a foot off the ground. She screamed, her feet dangling in the air; her hands reaching desperately toward Fang's, attempting to relieve the pain. Her pretty face and smile became disfigured as her facial muscles contorted in anguish.

The students started squirming, mumbling and crying.

Roman held up both open hands, palms forward, in front of Fang and shouted, "Okay, okay, no more trouble," Roman said, then thought, I thought I'd have some leverage, but the bluff didn't work. "Please put Alyson down. Don't you think the kids are scared enough? The kids are scared by my blood and your rifle. May I go to the sink and wash up? And if you'll not aim that rifle at any of them, it'll help settle everybody down."

Fang lowered Alyson. "Go!" Fang growled fiercely, rage seeming to drip from his eyes like tears. "Sit yur ass down," Fang growled at Alyson, as he inspected the claw marks that Alyson had left on his forearm.

As Roman cleaned the blood off his face and hands, he could hear Charlie moaning and see him moving as he slowly regained consciousness.

At the same time, Fang was yelling at his brother for not helping out, for just standing by like a scared, little child. Fang slapped Freddy and Freddy pleaded with him not to do it again, but Fang did it again, twice. When Fang stopped slapping Freddy— Freddy's cheeks had turned red as ripe cherries— Freddy said, "Brother, please depart from evil and do good; seek peace and pursue it. Psalms 34:14."

Roman thought, Religion had to be the last vestige of Neanderthal superstition and like the human appendix, it still exists, despite being useless, purposeless and redundant. Most people are smart; why don't they understand the illogic of religion? Then Roman thought, Perhaps it's like Mark Twain said, "It isn't the parts of the Bible that I can't understand that bother me, it's the parts that I do understand."

After each Psalm recitation, Freddy appeared to enter a form of rapture that appeared as if it were self-hypnosis, in which he appeared to attain an orgasmic-like pleasure. "Otto . . . ah, Fang. Please. God will forgive all your sins, but you have to stop these evil ways. God loves you and will forgive you. I know that for a fact."

Fang turned away from Freddy, mumbling, "Useless fool."

Roman had frequently heard Freddy reciting religious nonsense and was thinking that ignorance is such fertile soil for the germination of a religious seeds. Plant those mythological seeds, watch them sprout, have the gardener praise them, nourish them, harvest them and distribute millions of those seeds, then watch new religions grow and claim mythological gods.

For some reason, the seeds of common sense were rare, but even if they weren't, they'd perish if planted in that soil of ignorance. That was probably why the most uncommon traits to be found in the world, when the subject is religion, are *reason*, *logic* and *common sense*. Roman thought of Mark Twain, again: "It ain't what you don't know that gets you into trouble. It's what you know for sure that just ain't so."

Fang looked at his brother and said, "Yur such a preachin' asshole. I liked yuh better before, when yuh didn't believe in fairy tales. Yuh always was a little, wimpy pain in my ass. I'm not yur momma or yur baby-sitter. Time ta grow up . . . or maybe yuh should sit down an' be one a them babies over there." Fang pointed to the students. "That or get yur head outta yur ass. Are yuh with us or against us?" Fang screamed at him.

Roman felt a sense of unrestrained evil in Fang's voice, like murky and infested swamp water, infested with multitudes of danger just below the surface.

Then, in what seemed to be an obvious contradiction, Fang gave the assault rifle to Freddy as he bent and helped Charlie get to his feet. Charlie was groggy and staggered as he held onto Fang's arm for support.

The room became as silent as a late night morgue.

Fang was thinking how good it felt to hold onto Alyson and how wonderful it would be to be standing over her as they were both naked, and what wonderful things he could force her to do to his naked body, if he could only get her alone somewhere. That thought aroused him, synapses fired like machine guns and nerve endings twitched. His groin stirred at the thought and he felt the pulsing of his heart behind his zipper. He looked at Alyson and smiled.

Freddy thought about the new hatred he had for Otto. How he had always been made to feel inferior to Otto, how he mistakenly thought that they could be equals if he collaborated with Otto by meeting him with the all-important, get-away car. But now he saw that his brother would always see him as a slow, lowly form of life, a slug, lower than whale shit. Psalm 1:1 filled his mind. "Blessed is the man who does not walk in the counsel of the wicked or stand in the way of sinners or sit in the seat of mockers." Then, much less forgiving, he thought, Otto isn't nearly as smart as he thinks he is. If there was a problem that someone said could be figured out by the simple process of elimination, Otto would be the first one to drop his pants and shit on the floor, then look a the turd to find the solution. Not bad thinking for a retard, Freddy thought proudly.

Charlie, who was now fully conscious and alert, was staring at Roman, suspiciously, and feeling that the elbow strike wasn't an accident.

Roman saw Charlie staring at him. "I'm sorry," Roman said to Charlie. "It was an accident. I was trying to catch my balance."

That's bullshit. I don't believe him, Charlie thought, as he glared at Roman.

To Charlie it wasn't worth the effort to differentiate between the two of them, except in a sort of lazy nonsense fashion. To him the result of a good coincidence was good luck and a the result of a bad coincidence was bad luck. He didn't know, and probably wouldn't give a shit, to learn that "luck" is a random occurrence that operates either for you or against you; whereas, "coincidence" is a random occurrence that brings two or more related circumstances together in the same space, and at the same time— so coincidence would be when a man's wife and mistress both unknowingly decide to visit him at his office at the same time of day, but luck is when his mistress gets a flat tire on the way and has to postpone her trip until another day. It's not knowing and not wanting to know things like this that held Charlie back during his whole life. He thought crime didn't take brains because he could simply steal the things he wanted from the people who had brains enough to earn nice stuff.

It wasn't that Charlie wasn't capable of such thoughts, he was just too lazy. If it didn't come easily, it wasn't worth going after. Being a thief and a pervert were easy. He wasn't aware of such sage advice as, *If you want to earn a lot of money, stay away from easy*. His simple thoughts— obsessions— were mostly of revenge and inflicting pain, especially when it came to his desires for perverted sexual gratification. Charlie's heart is cold, his mind is sadistic, his stomach full of ice and his eyes reflected those feelings. His eyes, now the color of blue ice, lacked civility, compassion and were devoid of even a remnant of remorse. His eyes looked as if an iceberg was floating in back of them, but an observer could only see the tip of his rage. And right now, the tip of his rage was aimed at Roman. Charlie picked up his knife, promising himself the ultimate revenge against Roman. Charlie thought, I'll savor the death of that teacher before this is over. I'll lick his blood off my knife, after I stab it deep into his guts, then rip him open like a gutted fish.

Charlie stared a Roman and laconically said five words. "You will pay for that." Then he silently mouthed the word "motherfucker" with a look of lethal portents.

Roman grinned, then responded; "Yeah. I know. You're a dangerous '*cereal*' killer, but do me a favor, OK? Please don't kill Mr. Cheerios. I really like him."

Charlie gave Roman the middle finger, then stuck his index finger out with his thumb up, while fisting the other fingers to show a finger-gun. He aimed it at Roman and mouthed the word *bang*.

*   *   *   *   *   *   *

Though the state police commander hadn't had a chance to read it yet, the prison psychiatrist's report concerning Charlie stated:

"As with adults, many long-abused teens, like Charlie, will injure or kill easily, the result of their overly and frequent aggressiveness, as well as their inability to control their rage. Those, like Charlie, are usually emotionally cold and lack feelings of remorse and compassion. They also tend to demonstrate explosive tempers and seem to find nourishment in revenge, sadism and perversions, especially when it's sexually related. Most of them will lash out after long-term victimization with a life dominating need for vengeance. Charlie may kill or maim because he has been traumatized and is simply unable to tolerate their own miserable existence. He feels worthless, hopeless and great anger, all of which, if prolonged, lead to dark and sinister thoughts and actions. Charlie is a classic case; he's dominated by immature and narcissistic behaviors which formed as the result of his prolonged abuse. His current personality traits are a reaction to his constant, prior abuse.

"Charlie is obsessed with certain sexual behaviors. For Charlie it appears to be domination of children, followed by oral sex, though in prison he's had to settle for adult oral sex and/or anal sex.

"Since he has been deprived of love and acceptance from early childhood, he feels justified with his own violent nature. He has stated in one of our therapy sessions that he shouldn't have to feel bad or have remorse because his violent nature and pedophilia were caused by his parents; therefore, they are to blame for his actions, not him.

"Less common, but often more dramatic are killings committed by the psychotic personality, those with disturbed, disordered, chaotic thoughts and delusions, with only a slim hold on reality. Though Charlie is not yet psychotic, he is highly susceptible to that condition in the future. (NOTE: Though Charlie has no record of killing anyone, I'd be very surprised if he hasn't done so already, but didn't get caught.)

"Psychotics use extreme violence because they say they hear voices that command them. Voices from gods, angels, saints, loved ones or even personal heroes. But psychopaths like Charlie (and his cell-mate, Otto) are different. They kill mostly for another reason. They relish the emotional ecstasy and thrill that it brings to them. It's like an orgasm to them. A psychopath's childhood is usually an appalling wreck, so the psychopath's learned behaviors are amoral, at best, immoral at worst, as well as anti-social to the point of being labeled a sociopath. Furthermore, a psychopath is often average to above average in intelligence (however, this particular trait varies more than the other traits), and shows no genuine shame or remorse for his premeditated crimes, even murder. They have the ability to separate their personal lives from their cruel actions, as if they were watching someone else commit violent acts in a movie.

"A person with a psychopathic personality, like Charlie, has few feelings that aren't somehow related to anger and rage. He sees people as unimportant objects to be used, like tools, and may, in fact, care much more deeply for objects (e.g. his car) than for human beings. The psychopath is also highly secretive about himself, his intentions and activities, and very often demonstrates mild to severe signs of paranoia. In many cases, like Charlie's, he can outwardly look and act quite normal. This allows for cold, calculated, well-planned and brutally sadistic behaviors that, in normal, everyday life, are well disguised. The psychotic wants to please the voices s/he hears, but the psychopath only wants to please himself, and, with Charlie, pleasure involves pain, sometimes his own pain, but usually it involves the pain of his sex partners or those that he abuses in other ways for the pleasure of watching their pain. It's what makes the normal appearing psychopath much more unpredictable and; therefore, much more dangerous than the delusional psychotic.

"Sometimes in life, for a few people at least, the pain of their past forges a painful and harsh destiny for them, a path that appears predetermined and nearly inescapable. For them that *path* becomes a dark, rough, sharply twisting and dangerously plunging psycho-*path* toward destructive behaviors and ultimately toward self-destruction."

*   *   *   *   *   *   *

The students were in a state of shock. They were all frightened to death of the three men with guns and knives. They felt helpless and confused, especially when they saw Mr. Wolfe's bloody face and badly bent nose. They thought of him as indestructible, a black-belt in karate who could beat-up these guys. They wondered why he didn't or wouldn't or couldn't. Some of them started doubting his bravery and his skill at karate, but mostly they were just confused, scared and stunned into a sort of numbness that wipes out logic as well as speech— which was good for Mr. Wolfe, since he didn't want any of the kids to talk about karate.

Roman absorbed Charlie's vengeful stare, knew that there would be a time of reckoning, but still felt pity for Charlie who must have had a life full of abuse, followed by rage, then tragic decisions. Roman thought, Charlie's life must resonated with mistreatment and blunders, like thunder and lightning from his past.

Then Roman's thoughts turned to Freddy. Roman felt a sad kind of pity for Freddy who was probably treated like shit all his life, experiencing abuse and the lack of love, then becoming a criminal turned deacon. Freddy was one of those cases where Roman thought that religion was useful, as a crutch for a handicapped person. Usually, though, Roman was against religious beliefs for many different reasons, but a simple reason was that Roman had similar thoughts to Richard Dawkins, who said, "I am against religion because it teaches us to be satisfied with not understanding the world." One has to temporality suspend reality and truth during the religious part of their lives, in order to blindly believe in the impossibilities and other nonsense contained in myths of religion."

Roman returned his concentration to Fang and thought, There would be a time of reckoning here, also, if he didn't get a shiv in the back from Charlie. Then he thought, How come I end up having to fight these big ass dudes? What the hell am I? A muscle magnet?

Besides keeping the kids safe, Roman's worse worry was how the students would view him after this incident was over. Could he ever again be an effective teacher? Would this incident, coupled with the Adirondack incident, combined with his Vietnam experiences, ruin his ability to be an effective teacher? Would parents, teachers and administrators fear him and feel uncomfortable around him? And worst of all, would the kids be traumatized if he had to use his combat skills in a lethal manner? Would he be seen as a menacing force by the kids, threatening their safety, making them unable to learn from him because they would be forever fearful of being punished or abused by him? Would he lose their respect? Would students, parents and school staff idolize him or ostracize him? Would he be banished from school for being a bad influence and a very poor role model? Roman felt discouraged.

Each question seemed to riddle Roman's body with painful holes just like many of the bodies he'd seen in Nam riddled by automatic weapons fire, knife wounds or shrapnel. He felt as if his life's blood was draining from him. He reached into his left front pocket and felt the Annie button that his daughter, Grace, had given to him a few years ago. It felt good in his hand. Roman took comfort in the worn smoothness of the button and the good memories that sprang from it as he rubbed it.

The simple feel of the button put him more at peace with himself. He thought of Grace and Sam. He loved them both tremendously and knew they'd always love him, too. He took comfort in that knowledge and fought off the advancing depression that he felt was slowly engulfing him, like an amoeba surrounding its food. The stress was releasing too much adrenaline into his blood stream and neutralizing the medication that he took for depression.

But Roman's heart and mind were uplifted when he saw Blizzard prowling in circles around the perimeter of the classroom. Blizzard looked so friendly and gentle . . . at this moment. He thought about how he and Blizzard were alike: gentle and sensitive when not threatened, but capable of much violence if threatened. It was as if both had the talent to change from cotton to iron.

How could such characteristics reside in one man or animal? Roman wanted to be nonviolent, but he was pushed or, perhaps, allowed himself to be pushed too far. The truth was, he wasn't as tough as many people thought he was. He never intended it to be that way, it just happened. There's a lot more cotton in him than most people would suspect. Only close family and friends would know that and he won't let outsiders get to know him. Actually, he's often scared, afraid that he won't be able to protect those who are closest to him, those who really do know him, though that's a very small group of people. He's afraid that he'll be in a combat situation with someone better, though it was hard to imagine anyone with superior skills. Roman knows that there's always someone better, especially a Dim Mak (death touch) master.

To Roman, reality meant the relationships between constant opposites (up-down, left-right, large-small. One can't exist without the other for comparison), which meant that there would always be winners because there are losers, even within the same person. He could lose a fight and not be bothered too much, but if losing that fight caused someone close to him great harm, that would bother him a great deal.

Sometimes Roman was even afraid of himself, what he might do or what he may not be able to control. He'd read an article given to him by Dr. Lash. The part that stuck heavily in his mind was the paragraph that stated: "Male depression is usually turned outward, to damage others with anger and violence, whereas depression in women is mostly turned inward, against themselves. Thus women are more likely to cut themselves, have eating disorders and other self-mutilating, self-destroying actions.

Roman's mind became peaceful and relaxed, as his thoughts drifted to his wife, Samantha. Sam's image appeared in his mind clearly and redolent from shampooed hair and perfumed skin. To him she was beautiful. He longed to lift the back of her luxuriant auburn hair, exposing the nape of her neck, then kiss that tender, sensitive skin, just at the hairline— Roman snapped out of than line of thought, saying, "Not now, stupid."

Roman shook his head and blinked his eyes to clear his mind. His thoughts focused on three things he had to do right away: First, he had to, somehow, tell all the kids not to mention his karate skills and not to mention Vietnam or the Adirondack Mountains incident. Secondly, he had to disable the television so that the media couldn't do the same things, if Fang decided to turn on the television. And, thirdly, he had to think of a way to get all, or as many of the kids as possible, out of this potentially explosive situation.

The bleeding from his lips and nose had stopped. His nose was straightened and would heal in time, but in order to stop it from bleeding he had to jam part of a tissue up one nostril. His left cheek was swelling and his left eye was turning black and blue and puffy, but the pain had subsided. He shook his head slowly, thoughtfully, and wondered how this would all end, then bowed his head and wondered why this type of incident kept happening to him. Coincidence? Bad luck? He thought, First Nam, then the Adirondack incident and now this school hostage situation. He shook his head in confusion and frustration. Shit happens, he thought.

All he wanted was peace, quiet, anonymity and the family he loved and that loved him, plus a rewarding job as a teacher of elementary school kids. He didn't want to be in the spotlight. He'd grown to hate that. He just wanted to blend in, to go unnoticed. But somehow fate wouldn't grant his wish for any great length of time. Sooner or later he was thrust into an unwanted spotlight and the danger that came with it.

Roman dried his face with a paper towel, then reached into his pocket to feel the Annie button. It felt warm and comforting like it had a life of its own. The thought of his daughter once again brought a comforting smile and hope to him.

Out of the blue, a memory came to him. He remembered reading somewhere about the stages of growth that a daughter goes through concerning her changing views of her father. Roman strained to think. He thought, It was something like: at age 1-2, Dad is the only man in her world; age 3-4, Dad knows everything; age 7-8, Dad knows almost everything; age 9-10, Dad doesn't know some things; age 11-12, Dad doesn't know a lot of things; age 13-14, Dad is really old and has weird ideas about kids; ages 15-17, Dad is so frustrating; ages 18-19, Dad is really stupid; ages 20-21, Maybe Dad isn't as stupid as I thought; ages 22-25, I should really ask Dad what he thinks before I do this; ages 26-35, I shouldn't make rash decisions. I need to check with Dad first; ages 36-50, Gee, I wonder what Dad would think? I'd better call him; ages 51-60, I'd give anything if dad wasn't so far away. I worry about him and how he's doing. He was so easy to talk to. He was so understanding and smart about everything; ages 61-90, Dad's been dead for a few years. What will I do without him and his advice? Dad was a wonderful father. Life will be so lonely without him.

Roman looked around the room. He thought about the look in everyone's eyes: the innocent and scared looks in the eyes of the children . . . and Freddy, the fire of hatred in Fang's eyes and the ice-like rage in Charlie's eyes. He wondered what shone in his own eyes. Sam had once told him that when he's angry or disturbed about something important, his eyes looked menacing, like pewter-colored storm clouds just before a heavy downpour of rain.

Roman came to a decision, then he strode meekly toward Fang, Roman's eyes and chin lowered to hide his fake nervousness. He swallowed, his Adam's apple bobbing up and down. He wanted to appear subservient to pacify Fang's need for domination and control.

As he approached Fang, he thought, What makes a brave person? His responding thought was that a brave person is simply an average person who sees what needs to be done and does it, regardless of the consequences or personal sacrifices. Roman knew that brave people seldom thought of themselves as brave until later when someone compliments them on how brave they were. But there are some brave people who were dull, bored and, perhaps, had been mentally stagnated by work and home routines that numbed their once sharp minds, but then acted bravely to surprise even themselves. Then there are those who act bravely because they were simply too afraid, too panicked to run away from danger. So they ran toward it and instinctually did something that was successful, making them appear to be brave when they were not.

As he got near Fang, Roman's anger rose. He didn't just remember his previous anger, he relearned it in all of its original intensity, power, force and emotion.

/-.--/---/..-/.-/.-./././..-./..-/-./-./-.--/--/../-.-/./

10

★★★★

*"What a distressing contrast there is between the radiant intelligence
of the child and the feeble mentality of the average adult."*

Sigmund Freud

CHARLIE WAS BORN TO parents who didn't love him or want him. He was
simply the unfortunate child of a primitive, biological and instinctive
sexual urge, enhanced by various liquids and drugs.

Charlie's very first memories of his early youth were of the Catholic
orphanage where he was placed when his father and mother got a
divorce. His father got custody because the mother skipped town, but
he had no idea what to do with Charlie. To Charlie's father, Charlie
was a serious inconvenience.

Charlie's father, Ignatius, was a contemptible bastard in more than
one sense of the word. He was minimally educated and worked as a
janitor for a computer company. He picked up trash that others threw
on the floor, emptied garbage cans, swept, mopped, served as a gofer
and usually went to work with a hangover. The loves of his life were
bars, beer and drugs. He was, at his roots, a repugnant, irresponsible,
immature man-child, devoid of love or concern for Charlie, though he

always brought Charlie home from the orphanage on weekends— for religious indoctrination. It was the Christian thing to do.

Charlie honestly, and bitterly, never remembered the man ever saying that he loved Charlie. Worse yet, he never gave Charlie the impression that he even liked him, though he let Charlie accompany him to one bar after another. Charlie's father simply brought him along because he knew of no one else who would take him. So Charlie got to stay up through the early morning hours to meet all his father's alcoholic, miscreant friends.

Charlie frequently laughed at his father's first name, Ignatius. He found that it was some Catholic saint's name. Iggy— the name Charlie used when he thought about his father— claimed to be a devout Catholic, but Charlie and Iggy's friends knew that, in truth, he was simply a devout hypocrite; his church was the local bar and his holy grail was a beer bottle. The only spirits he worshipped were beer and liquor. But he did go to church most Sundays. Iggy usually went to a late-morning mass so he could sleep through his drunken state of the night before, then he could appear at mass sober and not reeking of the smell of beer. After church he worshipped booze for the remainder of the day. Even after going to confession, he hurried away with little Charlie in tow. He'd leave Saint Anthony's Church with a brisk walk and spend the rest of the afternoon, late evening and early morning hours hopping, like a drunken rabbit, from one bar to another, sipping, guzzling, then gulping, one beer after another. Charlie, who was ten to thirteen years old during this time period. At the bars, Charlie was shoved into a dark, lonely, corner booth with popcorn and orange soda. If he was lucky he'd have a television to watch, though he often could not hear it above the roar of his dad's bellowing, boozer friends.

But, to Charlie, the television wasn't nearly as entertaining as his drunken father and his friends. Iggy and his drunken pals were hilarious entertainment for Charlie, usually much better than TV. He used to laugh silently at them, but deep down he was abysmally sad, being ashamed of, and hating his father. Since he had turned old enough to go to school, his hatred had grown each year. A knife plunged directly into his heart wouldn't have hurt him as much as having his father ignore him hour after hour, seldom coming to his booth— the bartender brought the eats and drinks to Charlie— never sitting with him, never a kind word— even when sober— never an arm around the shoulder, never a hug or a kiss and never a mention of the word "love."

The closest that Charlie ever came physically to his dad was when Charlie would do something or say something his dad didn't like. Then Charlie would get spanked. Most times the offenses he committed were mild infractions, like swearing, that he was being punished for. Actions that most parents wouldn't raise an eyebrow at or would just shrug a shoulder at or reprimand with a few words. But not Iggy. The booze made him over-sensitive and morally superior, paralleling his façade of rigorous religious faith. For punishment he made Charlie pull down his pants and underpants, then lie submissively across his father's lap. Then his father would spank Charlie's bare buttocks until Charlie cried. He wouldn't stop until he heard Charlie crying. Iggy was a saint in his own mind, but a faggot in Charlie's mind. Charlie lost complete respect for his father and didn't trust him any farther than he could throw Ayer's Rock.

Iggy constantly and inanely talked about religion, about God's will, about God's commands, the ten commandments, about immorality, about biblical references and how Charlie must always "follow the rules of Catholicism," or be plunged into the searing, agonizing and eternal flames of God's vengeful hell.

By Charlie's mid-teens he had read enough and learned enough to know that most people who behave themselves, seldom took risks that would make their lives better or change a bit of history— if even just family history— or benefit mankind. Charlie read about and thought of Copernicus, who said that the sun, not the earth, was the center of our solar system and, for that discovery, he was threatened with severe punishment and/or imprisonment. He was eventually placed under house arrest by the leaders of the his Catholic church who considered his discovery to be blasphemy and heresy.

As Charlie got older and wiser he realized that the warmth of Iggy's hand, as it came smashing down on the naked flesh of his buttocks, was the only warmth that his father had to offer him. It was the only familial warmth that he was ever going to receive from the guy. Shortly after that realization Charlie would act-up purposely in order to receive a spanking. Then, as he lay face-down across his father's lap, he would smile at the floor and wait for the warmth of that stinging, punishing hand. Charlie started enjoying the pain. He enjoyed hearing the slap of his father's hand, was excited by the tingling feeling that the harsh slap created on his fleshy buttocks. He relished the warmth and then the hotness of his flesh. He enjoyed the pain, but eventually faked his crying so he didn't let his secret become known. He did this for a few months, until he gained a solid, masochistic confidence. Then one Saturday morning he decided to surprise his daddy dearest.

Iggy lived in a small, one-room apartment over a bar/restaurant called The Coffee Pot— it should have been more appropriately called The Beer Barrel. The bar only served breakfasts. While Iggy and Charlie were eating breakfast that morning, Charlie purposefully spilled his orange juice. Iggy was moody. Charlie had learned to read his eyes, facial expressions, tone of voice and actions. He knew that he was going to get spanked when they went upstairs to Iggy's room. Charlie was delighted at the thought, but hid the gratifying smile that was anxious to burst forth from his lips. He could feel the pressure on his buttocks from the stool he was sitting on and the flattening of his buttocks aroused him enough to allow a slight, mischievous smile.

Iggy lit one of his usual, awful-smelling, stogie cigars, then paid for breakfast. He walked up the stairs to his room with thirteen year old Charlie following behind him, thinking that he wished his father was naked as he walked up the steps so that he could ram that stogie so far up his ass that it would burn a hole in his stomach. Charlie permitted himself a brief smile. He was thrilled by the thought and realized that sadism also aroused him. But he was even more excited about getting back to his father's room, even though it smelled as if it was a huge ashtray.

Iggy locked the door and placed the stogie in an ashtray that sat on an ancient and marred dresser. Iggy sat on the bed and waited for Charlie. Charlie knew the routine, but pretended to be reluctant as he slowly unbuckled his jeans and pulled them and his underwear down around his ankles. He thought about pissing in his father's lap. Even delaying the spanking was fun, he thought. Charlie could feel his scrotum pulling loose from the skin on his inner thighs, the scrotum skin tightening, shrinking, pulling his testicles up closer toward his crotch. He could feel his penis unbending and begin to stiffen as he lay across his father's lap. Iggy always placed his left hand on the small of Charlie's back, with his right hand resting on Charlie's buttocks— Charlie often wondered if his father was queer and got a perverted thrill out of the spankings. Iggy told Charlie that he was getting this spanking for spilling his juice. Charlie didn't answer, just waited for Iggy's right hand to rise slowly into the air, anticipating and savoring the moment.

Iggy's right hand rose from Charlie's soft, white mound of flesh and a second later came crashing down with a loud slapping noise. Charlie smiled and exhaled with delight, knowing that his father was totally unaware of the pleasure he was creating for him. Charlie remained quiet and waited. Then two more times Iggy's hand came smashing down, each of them harder than the previous one, but Charlie said nothing; he didn't even move. Surprise, daddy, he thought. Charlie's eyes closed as he felt the warmth, the heat, the pain, the intense pleasure, but no moaning or crying sounds exited his smiling mouth. Charlie had faked his crying long enough. Now he was taking a different approach to spanking, one that would frustrate and/or anger Iggy, but bring joy to his own mind and pleasure to his butt.

"Goddamnit!" Iggy bellowed with a nasty growl. "I guess I'm not hittin' you hard enough, huh? Well let's try this!" Then Iggy's open hand smashed downward upon Charlie's buttocks, twice; the sounds echoing in the small room.

Charlie smiled, his mind turning the pain to pleasure. Harder, harder, he thought, then said, "Daddy dearest? Is that all you got? You spank like a little girl. Is this really the best you got?"

"You've always been a good-for-nothing wiseass!" Iggy shouted.

Charlie remained silent, though a dreamy-eyed smile stretched across his face. He didn't think he had a wise ass. A hot, red, stinging ass, but nothing wise about it.

Iggy was frustrated with the continued silence and spanked even harder. Charlie lost all sense of punishment; the pleasure he felt was so great, so overwhelming that it hypnotized and numbed him into a dreamy, ecstatic silence.

The room, again, echoed with the rapid slapping of Iggy's hand on Charlie's bare, red and raw-looking buttocks. The thought of the pain that his father must be feeling in his hand made this an even more pleasurable experience for Charlie. Charlie remained as silent as a corpse and a limp as a flaccid penis. Even the smack, smack, smack noises could not intrude on his private, pleasurable thoughts.

Charlie knew then that he would never cry again. His father's hand stopped, to Charlie's disappointment, yet he was still feeling a residual pleasure, like no other pleasure he'd ever felt before. His whole body tingled with it, though now, it was concentrated within his groin. It was a pleasure so great that Charlie had to laugh loudly.

Iggy, in a gruff, frustrated voice said, "Get up, goddamnit!" Charlie got up, showing a face that was masked in ecstasy. Charlie stared at Iggy with glazed, dreamy eyes. He smiled at his father, then, again, burst out laughing manically when he bent and looked at his penis. The tumescence he had felt in his groin was very real. It was a living force that was pulsating with every heartbeat. Charlie's erection was so large that it didn't seem that it could belong to a thirteen year old boy. Iggy stared at and was shocked by the erection. Charlie continued to laugh and stare at Iggy. Then, to Iggy's horror, Charlie aimed his penis at him and ejaculated; the first spasm of thick, off-white, seminal fluid squirted out and landed on the knee of Iggy's pants, looking like a gob of Corn Huskers Hand Lotion. Successive spasms caused the remaining seminal fluid to land on the floor, then to run down the shaft of Charlie's penis, then onto his scrotum. Charlie was crazy with laughter and shouted, "Thanks for the spanking, Pop! We just had our first father/son sex experience." Charlie stared into Iggy's shocked eyes that radiated disgust. Iggy had been shocked into silence; no ridiculous, religious nonsense spilled out of his mouth like his usual vomit.

The pause continued, then Charlie said, "What's the matter, Pop? Cat got your tongue? How 'bout I give you a blow-job so I can return the favor?"

Iggy looked at Charlie in horror. Charlie looked back at Iggy with bright eyes and booming laughter. The laughter was deafening, as Iggy cupped his ears. Iggy looked into Charlie's vengeful eyes and made the religious sign-of-the-cross over his chest.

Charlie pulled up his underwear and jeans as his laughter quieted. Charlie stopped laughing completely when he saw his father's hypocritical sign-of-the-cross. It reminded Charlie of reading Lenny Bruce's biography, in which Lenny Bruce questioned why an instrument of Roman torture, a cross, crucifix, would become the universal symbol of Christianity. Lenny Bruce also wondered, "If Christianity just now had it's beginning, would its universal symbol be the electric chair? A hangman's noose? A firing squad? A needle?" Charlie sneered sarcastically. Too many of his family and friends thought he was stupid. No, he hadn't read any of the classics, couldn't even name any of them and didn't give a shit about them or what happened hundreds of years ago. So what if he wasn't good at math or science, he thought. He didn't think that that made him stupid. He was able to read, though slowly and had good comprehension. He could write well enough, though his spelling and punctuation were poor. He read books, but only those that interested him. He thought he had a creative imagination and was exploring his own perverted, dark side. You don't have to go to college to be smart, he thought. He smiled when he remembered an idea, concerning education, by Einstein. Einstein, who said something to the effect that, "Education is what remains after a person forgets what he has learned in school." Charlie thought that Einstein was referring to "street-smarts."

Iggy never spanked Charlie again, but Charlie never needed him to do it any more. Charlie found that his own curled fingers, a home-made whip for self-flagellation and a vivid imagination were even more pleasurable than his father's hand.

Charlie remembers that day as the day of his young manhood. The day he bested his father at his own perverted game. But, as Charlie remembered, the game still wasn't quite over because the unforgiving Iggy could still create emotional pain for Charlie, the kind of pain that came with guilt, shame and embarrassment.

Not many weeks after Charlie ejaculated on Iggy's pants, they both went into a bar and Iggy got full-blown drunk, like Charlie had never seem him do before. Usually Iggy had at least a little control of himself due to his high tolerance for beer. But this time Iggy was so stinking drunk that he nearly fell off the bar stool a couple of times. Iggy had started drinking at noon and it was now an hour past midnight. Iggy pointed to Charlie's booth, where Charlie sat watching him while drinking orange soda and eating pretzels. With a typical drunken slur to his speech Iggy began: "That's my sham . . . shame . . .ful son." Iggy pointed to Charlie. "He . . . he is . . .baaad. He a prob . . . lem fer (burp) . . . ever . . . buddy. . . . A qu . . . eer. A sin (hiccup) . . . sin-ner . . . (a coughing spasm) an' a devil . . . My son . . . su . . . such a embar . . . sment. Diso . . . disown him."

Iggy went on to say, in his slurred voice, that he wished Charlie was dead and out of his life and that Charlie should stay in the Catholic orphanage and that he would not take Charlie from the orphanage on weekends any more. The bartender and Iggy's semi-sober drinking pals had to stop him from continuing his venomous tirade when he began threatening violence toward Charlie.

No tears streamed down Charlie's face, as would have been normal a year or two prior to this incident. Instead, a bright, crescent moon smile flashed across his lips as he fingered the jack-knife in his pant's pocket. He knew that there could never be any love between him and his dad and that he had grown terminally tired of the man. So, looking directly at Iggy, he joyfully lied, "OK, Iggy. No more blow-jobs for you. I can't keep it a secret any more. You guys know that we give each other blow-jobs? We swallow too. Don't let him fool you, he loves it an' keeps asking for more."

Iggy's pals stared at Charlie, then at Iggy, wondering if it was true.

"Fuckin' bas . . . turd. Li . . . liar!" Iggy screamed with rage. He picked up an empty beer bottle and staggered toward Charlie.

Charlie stood up, grasped the jack-knife more firmly, still in his pocket, until Iggy's pals stopped him, held him back.

However, when Charlie stood up, he was not worried in the slightest. He wanted to stab his father, kill him and be able to call it self-defense, but Iggy's pals saved him.

Though outwardly calm, Charlie felt much differently in his private thoughts. His body warmth vanished, to be replaced by a cold chill. His face, drained of blood and gave a ghostly impression. His stomach churned. From that point on Charlie knew that there was no turning back, no healing of wounds, no forgiveness. He permanently hated his father from that moment on and granted him his barroom wish: Charlie would no longer be a part of his father's life. And from that point on he avoided his father in any way possible.

Shortly thereafter, Iggy decided that he wanted Charlie to be far away, so Iggy took Charlie out of the local orphanage and sent Charlie away to live in another state with Charlie's older brother, Larry, his sister-in-law, Fran, and their children, for as long as it might last. During those years Iggy and Charlie only saw each other during Thanksgiving dinner when Iggy drove to Larry's house. Iggy and Charlie both liked that arrangement and never spoke to each other and never sat close to each other again. Their relationship was ice-cold, with Charlie showing up at the dinner table a couple of minutes before dinner and usually departing before anyone else was done. Then Charlie usually could not be found until Iggy's Ford Edsel drove away.

To everyone's surprise, Charlie and his brother's family got along very well. Charlie didn't want to be a problem because then he would be sent back to the orphanage or to a foster-home or, perhaps, to a juvenile correctional facility. Larry and Fran tried to do the best they could while raising Charlie through his rough teenage years and though Charlie enjoyed his new family, especially his nephews and niece whom he bonded with, he knew that an ominous die had already been cast for his future.

*   *   *   *   *   *   *

Iggy died of a stroke one night as he lay thoroughly inebriated in bed. It happened in August, a month after Charlie's eighteenth birthday. Charlie celebrates that date every year by stripping off his pants and underwear, then beating his buttocks raw with his whip. He doesn't stop until he gets an erection, then he masturbates until he has an orgasm. He's ecstatic as he watches his seminal fluid squirt into the air, like a feeble shot from a water gun. Now, years after Iggy's death, Iggy is vicariously giving Charlie sexual pleasure.

However, in a way, Charlie felt cheated by Iggy's death. Charlie wanted the man to suffer long and hard before he died. But, somehow, Iggy got off easily— much too easily— thought Charlie. A stroke was much too quick for such a hypocritical bastard, Charlie mused. He would have liked to have killed the man himself, up close and personal. Find the rib separation that's adjacent to the heart and slowly— very slowly— slip an ice pick into that separation, a fourth of an inch at a time, watching the blood drip as the ice pick penetrated slowly, but deeply, while he delightedly watched Iggy's eyes and body react in terror. Charlie wouldn't gag the man; he wanted to hear the pathetic begging, the futile pleading, the painful crying, the desperate promises and apologies. Charlie thought it would make him feel like a kid on Christmas morning.

At Iggy's funeral Charlie sauntered down the aisle to his father's casket as people on each side of him turned and stared. Charlie wondered how a man such as Iggy could have so many friends. Then he thought, Must have treated them a hell-of-a-lot better than he treated me. Must have pretended to be a nice, fun-loving guy, or he bought them enough beer to make them feel obliged.

Charlie stood alone in front of the casket and peered downward at the man he had grown to hate. Iggy was dressed in a black suit, quite appropriate, Charlie thought, for the black hearted bastard. Iggy's face had been shaved and make-up had been applied. His thick, salt and pepper hair had been combed nicely. Charlie thought he looked better dead than alive. He glared at Iggy's arms folded across his stomach with rosary beads in his fingers. Hypocrisy, Charlie thought, but at least now it was silent hypocrisy. "Praise the Lord," Charlie whispered to Iggy, sarcastically, then giggled as he added, "You good-for-nothing bastard. I'm so glad you're finally dead." Charlie wouldn't touch Iggy, his clothes or even the casket. Charlie couldn't forgive Iggy, nor pray for him. Pray to what? Charlie thought, if there's a God, he must be vengeful, mean and sadistic if he could create, in his own image, men and women like his father, mother and himself. Charlie would not kneel; it seemed inappropriate. A sneer slowly stretched his lips, a venomous sneer. Charlie whispered, again, to his father, "Good riddance, asshole, and may you feel the agony of hell forever." Then Charlie pulled both his hands up close to the front of his chest, thus well hidden, and gave his dad a double, middle-finger salute, while whispering, "Fuck you, Father. I hope you know that whenever I anal fuck a boy or man, it'll be you that I'm fucking and when I anal fuck a girl or a women, it'll be Mother that I'm really fucking. And I intend to fuck the both of you a whole lot."

Charlie startled the other mourners by spinning around swiftly and walking briskly away from the casket, his heels clicking on the wooden floor, his face displaying a broad, happy smile. As he exited the funeral parlor, he mused, The world is a fucked-up place and its carpenter must have been a drunken fool. Charlie thought, God must have created the earth and people so he could enjoy their pain, then created hell so he could enjoy their agony, or maybe earth *is* hell and was created for his own sadistic enjoyment. Perhaps there isn't a God, no heaven and no hell and the Bible is simply a two thousand year old children's book of pure nonsense. Hell, I like that idea, thought Charlie, enthusiastically.

That same night, after Charlie's simple revelation, he became a *bitter atheist*, not a *thoughtful atheist* who uses research, reasoning and logic to form a conclusion, but an atheist formed by a reaction to a tragic and abusive childhood, with frequent punitive experiences that resulted in self-hatred, hopelessness, paranoia and aggressive anger toward others, a sociopath— though in prison he controlled himself because he got what he wanted and needed from Fang. Fang didn't know what Charlie was thinking any more than a woman knows what a man is thinking while his erection is inside of her.

That was also the first night that Charlie encountered the toilet snakes. In the middle of the night he felt a bowel movement coming and went into the bathroom to take a dump. He locked the bathroom door, pulled his pants and underwear down around his ankles and sat on the toilet. He spread his cheeks apart using the friction of the toilet seat to keep them apart He started straining while looking between his thighs at the toilet water. Abruptly, he stopped straining and jumped up off the toilet seat as if he was a tightly-coiled jack-in-the-box. He looked down into the toilet water and saw a snake. It looked as if it were patiently waiting for him to sit back down. Charlie closed his eyes, rubbed them vigorously, then looked again. No snake. Must have been my imagination, he thought. Immediately following that thought, came another thought, Hell, why not? Could feel good.

Charlie sat back on the toilet and had his bowel movement. He wiped himself and flushed the toilet, but stayed seated. He closed his eyes to heighten his imagination. He heard rippling noises in the water, which made him smile. Then he felt the snake poke its head into his anus. The snake squirmed around in his colon, to Charlie's surprise and pleasure. When Charlie opened his eyes, he found his hand wrapped around his erection. He could feel his own heartbeat in his hand. As his anal pleasure continued, he spit several times into his hand, then stroked his erection gently, caressing it with a loose, saliva-lubricated grip that repeatedly moved up and down his engorged penis. Just before climax he aimed his penis into the toilet and ejaculated into the water. Charlie imagined the snake swallowing his ejaculate before disappearing down the toilet bowl. Charlie felt such bliss that he yanked-up his underwear and started to flush the toilet to rid it of his ejaculate . . . but none of it was there. How could it be gone? he thought. The snake? He unlocked the bathroom door and walked out. He was still hard.

∗   ∗   ∗   ∗   ∗   ∗   ∗

Charlie's mother was nearly as bad as his father. She'd had polio as a child which affected her right leg movements and made her limp—behind her back he called her Gimpy. Charlie figured it also must have affected her mind. She only had a second grade education, couldn't write enough to sign her own name, couldn't read and couldn't do simple, basic math. Charlie was embarrassed by her illiteracy and hated her almost as much as he hated his father, though not so much because she punished him, but rather because she had deserted him, abandoned him to his father and the cruel nuns at a Catholic orphanage.

She and Iggy had divorced when Charlie was four. Gimpy remarried and moved from New York State to Florida and, because of the distance and the disinterest, Charlie didn't see much of her, sometimes not for years. That's the way she wanted it, though, Charlie reasoned or she would have stuck around. She was a child-like cripple, both physically and mentally, in an old lady's body, Charlie often thought. She professed to love young Charlie, but her words were rarely followed by meaningful actions. She used her professed love for Charlie to make him feel guilty, which led to a few gifts and some money from him. That's the impression that Charlie got on those rare occasions that he saw her or when he received a letter that had to be written by her second husband. Charlie desperately needed his mother to genuinely love him, to make up for the hate and bitterness that existed between him and his father. But it wasn't to be, so Charlie shut her out of his life, too. After that, not even residual guilt remained in Charlie. He felt at least one positive thought about her: She hadn't, because he only saw her twice in ten years, burdened him with religious dogma, or a lot of overwhelmingly, negative memories like Iggy had. In his earlier years Charlie was a little more sympathetic towards his mother, not because he loved her or even liked her, but rather because he hated her less than he hated his father. After all, he thought, he was constantly abused by his dad, but his mom had only abandoned him to the care of others who could then abuse him. It did, however, seem ironic to Charlie that one of the rare positive things that he could say about his own mother was the fact that perhaps she felt less negative about him than Iggy did. Charlie's mother embarrassed him, so he felt no guilt when he told his friends: "Light travels faster than sound and that's the reason why his mother might appear smart, until she opened her mouth and spoke.

Charlie had a recurring vision of his mother limping in a backyard garden, then going down on her knees to pick weeds. Right where she belonged, Charlie thought. He was pleased that he was not the near moron that his mother was— by comparison, he felt superior and proud of it. He thought, As least I made it through high school— although just barely and by taking the easiest courses available to get a local diploma, which was much easier that trying to earn a New York State Regents diploma. He was overly proud of himself because he didn't have to have someone write a letter for him. He could read, write and think well enough, he thought.

But life was a continuously negative experience for Charlie, being thrown away and tossed about like garbage, by loveless, ignorant parents, then being embraced by an unrelenting loneliness and a barely contained rage. He felt as if he were sliding down a greased pole, into Satan's lair, into boiling oil, into an eternal conflagration of pain. But he acted resigned to his fate because he thought that that's where he belonged . . . in Hell.

*　*　*　*　*　*　*

Charlie had labored to read the book, *Helter Skelter*. He had become fascinated with Charles Manson and had grown to revere Manson and his gang. In that book, Manson said, "No sense makes sense." Charlie thought that if that was true then his mom's stupidity must "make sense" because he believed she sure as hell had "no sense." He thought he was being clever and felt proud.

Charles Milles Manson's name often popped up in Charlie's mind. As Charlie got older he thought about the man more and more. He wished that he could go to Folsom Prison to visit Manson. Charlie took great pleasure in having the same first name as Manson, like somehow it meant that they were kin. Charlie felt a special closeness to Manson after reading about Manson's similar early family life, his diminutive stature, and because of his search for power and opportunities to vent his rage.

Charlie wanted to make others suffer more than he had suffered, just like Manson. If he could make others suffer more than he had, then, by comparison, he felt better because he could say, "Man, I'm sure glad I wasn't abused that much or abused in those ways." Charlie had a great need to share and disperse his pain by inflicting it on others, like bad seeds thrown into the wind. He wanted to know that others understood his pain first-hand, by experiencing that pain. He felt that causing pain in others lessened his own pain and increased his pleasure. He learned this from the Manson book and soon started thinking like Manson, who thought that, by hurting people, he had really helped them and by killing them in painful ways, he was actually setting them free. But how does hurting and killing people help them and what does it set them free from? Those were two questions that Charlie didn't have answers for. He wished that he could ask Manson personally. He knew that Manson would surely have the perfect answers.

Perhaps, some day, he mused, he'd get a chance to talk to Manson. But better yet, perhaps some day he'd out-do Manson's deeds, over-shadow him, take his place in the limelight of criminal history, steal his reputation and fame. Given a chance, Charlie thought, he could do it. He had the genes for it. He definitely knew he had the right genes. Manson and his family of outlaws liked knives. They liked to stab, slice, chop and sever flesh. Charlie liked knives, too. Knives were hard, cold, sharp, just as he thought of himself, plus they killed up close and personal. Manson was mean, aggressive, forceful, and it led to power, control, domination. Charlie wanted power, too. Given a chance, he'd make something of his life. He'd have power. He'd rid himself of the putrid memories of his mother and father. Given a chance, he'd make Manson proud, too. Some day, Charlie thought, Manson might be the one who wants to meet me. "No sense makes sense," Charlie thought, with a cruel twist of his lips.

/../.-../---/...-/./.--./.-./../.-./.-../.-../../.-../---/.-./../

11

★★★★

"There are a thousand hacking at the branches of evil to one who is striking at the root."

Henry David Thoreau

FANG PEEKED OUT OF the classroom door. He observed an empty hallway. He stepped back into the room, then quickly stuck his head through the doorway again to see if he could spot anybody who may have been hiding. Nothing. He yelled out, "I don't see you assholes, but I know you're there, hiding like scared puppies under a porch."

"Charlie. Freddy. Step out here a minute," Fang ordered, as he pointed towards the hallway. As they stepped into the hallway, Fang made sure that Charlie and Freddy were unsuspectingly shielding him from possible gunfire. This was his way of seeing if the cops would shoot at them. If they did, then he would know that negotiations would not occur and killing a kid would be necessary to gain their attention and cooperation.

When the door closed behind them, Roman wished that he could lock them out, but the dolts would go wild, shoot out the window by the doorknob or break it out with a rifle butt or even threaten the kids with harm if he didn't open the door. Then it would have been all for nothing and he would've angered all of them and increased the danger to his students. Roman resisted the impulse to take action and this inaction infuriated him.

But a different, more fruitful thought prodded him into action. He quickly stepped to the classroom television and removed the cable from the back of it. Without it, there could be no television reception That's exactly what Roman wanted: no TV, no media coverage to see and no news-hounds excitedly reporting every detail about his past, all of which would be detrimental to his students' welfare.

"Shit! I have to get my transistor radio out of here, too," Roman mumbled.

Roman hurriedly carried the TV cable to his desk. He opened his bottom drawer and took out the transistor radio. Walking fast, he brought both of them to the window, opened it and threw them out. The falling objects startled two roving policemen. One of them picked the objects up, while the other aimed his weapon at the classroom window as a precaution. Then they both walked to Captain Lewis and gave the objects to her. She knew immediately why the teacher had thrown those particular objects out of the window. She grinned, then mumbled, "Smart."

Roman turned toward the children. They were all watching him. They didn't hear the thump of the radio or TV cable as it fell two stories to the grass that fringed the parking lot.

Quickly, but in a soft voice, Roman said, "Don't talk about my karate. Don't say anything about Vietnam or what happened in the mountains last year. It might make them mad and extra mean." Roman didn't want to scare the children any more than they already were, so he didn't say they might hurt some of them or himself. "Don't ask me why you shouldn't talk about me. I don't have time to explain. Just trust me and do as I say. Then we'll all get out safely. I'll protect you. Believe me. Be brave and—"

Roman was interrupted when Fang heavy-handedly opened the door, straining the hinges. The three men entered the room. Fang smiled, apparently satisfied about something that Roman couldn't fathom— there was no shooting, which meant that the cops would negotiate with Fang. Fang and Charlie strode side-by-side, both laughing. Freddy forced a grin. Fang and Charlie stopped laughing, but grinned, as if the whole world was theirs and all they had to do was spin it in any direction they wanted.

Observing their grins, Roman's internal voice spoke sarcastically. "I bet that if I gave them both a penny for their thoughts, I wouldn't get my money's worth."

Fang stared at Roman, knowing that he must've been talking to the kids because they all had been looking at their teacher when he walked into the classroom. Fang wondered what Roman had said. "So. What yuh been up to? What were yuh talkin' 'bout, Teach?"

"I've just been trying to calm them and assure them that if they behaved themselves that they wouldn't be hurt," Roman lied. "Please don't get upset. I'm helping you out here. I'm just keeping them calm so they don't bother you. I told them that you'd be gone soon and that they should be brave and do what you tell them to do. Then everything will be OK." Roman thought that he'd sounded convincing.

Charlie, looking at Fang said, "He's lyin'. Maybe he ain't as stupid as he looks." Charlie laughed, but his face appeared sinister, with bad teeth showing against pale-pink gums. He wanted to plunge his knife into the teacher's belly. Subconsciously, Charlie knew the sexual symbolism of his knife. It was a classic phallic symbol that he used to penetrate the people he hated or people who had harmed him, regardless of gender.

Fang peered at Roman, suspiciously, then at Charlie and whispered, "Yeah. That what worries me. Keep yur eyes on 'im." Fang glared at Roman, again. Then he turned to Freddy, asking, "Whaddaya think, Freddy? Is he tellin' the truth?"

"Sounds ta me like whata teacher would do. Don't yuh think?"

Roman thought, Yep. You tell 'em Freddy. I need more time. Time heals all wounds, but time also wounds all heels. Sometime soon, Fang and Charlie will be under my heel. But, I might be able to save you, Freddy. If religion can change you from a criminal to a moral, caring person, then you're worth saving.

Charlie glared at Roman. "What yuh thinkin' Teach?" Don't be thinkin' about doin' something stupid. Don't wanna hear any insults either. Didn't come here ta be insulted by some shit-fer-brains teacher."

"Really? Where do you usually go?" Roman asked, sarcastically, then regretted it.

There was a silence in the room, but the menacing stares between Roman and Charlie were interrupted by Freddy's prayer. "Lord forgive us our trespasses as we forgive those who trespass against us." Can't remember what psalm that is, Freddy thought. "He that loveth not, knoweth not God; for God is love. John 4:8."

"Will yuh shut the fuck up, asshole? Christ almighty! That God crap's sickenin'."

Freddy cringed at the words *Christ almighty*.

Freddy looked extremely nervous. He was on the hot spot. He hated it. He hated having to make decisions. He thought that he'd be better off in the Army or even in jail, where life's trivial and complex decisions would be made for him. He said. "I think he's probly telling the truth, Otto. What's he got ta lie about? He's afraid for the kids."

Fang reached and grabbed Freddy by the hair, nearly yanking a patch of it out by the roots, then said, "Yuh know I don't like ta be called Otto, not even by me baby brother. Yuh call me Fang. Understand?" Fang's lip got caught on his tooth. It frustrated him to have to contort his face to unhook it, especially if he had to reach up and unhook it with a finger.

Fang let go of Freddy just as Freddy started squealing in pain. Freddy put both hands up to rub his painful scalp. His face was red, there were tears in his eyes as he said, "Yeah, OK, sure. You know I'm used to callin' yuh Otto. I didn't mean no harm." Then he made the mistake of preaching to Fang, "Brother, please listen. Blessed are the peacemakers. God will look down upon us with wrath in his eyes. There will be a judgment day. You will be punished for your wicked ways."

Not if I get to Fang first, Roman thought. Roman had an idea: What if I had Blizzard spook them, mildly scare them? Would it do more harm that good? He knew that Fang wouldn't be spooked, but if Blizzard could scare Charlie and Freddy, it might cause enough pressure on Fang to surrender. I doubt it, but it's a risk that I should take.

Fang looked disgustedly at his brother, showing his anger by slapping him. Freddy lifted his hand to cover his stinging cheek and ear.

Fang emphatically stated, "Yuh damn fool! There ain't no God. Look at the people around the world, the misery, the suffering, the poor people, the disease an' all the other bad stuff out there. If yuh think there be a God, then it be a cruel, miserable son-of-a-bitch, and if yuh think there be an all-good God, then where does all the bad stuff come from? All the suffering, pain an' misery? If there be a God that created everything, then he created all the evil too. See, Freddy? Then yur God be a cruel, fuckin' monster. Can't be no God, yuh jerk-off. Damn, Freddy, can't believe yuh still thinks like a child. Probly still believe in Santa Claus, too, don'tcha?"

"God works in mysterious ways," Freddy retorted defiantly.

"Yur such a damn fool, Freddy. Yur hopeless."

There it is, Roman thought sarcastically. That pathetic *mysterious ways*, bullshit answer. Something's a mystery and can't be explained, or the explanation is rejected, so there must be an invisible God lurking around the corner creating all the mysteries. It must be just a coincidence that the *invisible* looks exactly like the *non-existent*. Mysteries defy logic and defying logic is exactly what is required to believe in an illogical myth. Roman thought, "Where knowledge ends, religion begins." (Benjamin Disraeli). "Faith means not wanting to know what is true." (Friedrich Nietzsche).

For a much needed distraction, Freddy self-consciously said, "How many of you kids need ta use the bathroom? Raise yur hand if you do."

An alarm shot up Roman's back, like a current of high-voltage electricity traveling upward inside his spinal cord, all the way to his brain stem.

"Hey. Finally a good idea, Freddy. OK, then," Fang smiled, having an ulterior motive. "I take the girls an' Charlie, here, takes the boys. But we do it one at a time so's there ain't so much confusion. Don't want no one runnin' away an gettin' hurt, do we?"

Roman's ears were ringing from distress. Those perverts alone in the bathrooms with the children? One at a time? No fuckin' way is that going to happen. Roman felt his rage building instantly. His face flushed from anger and anxiety.

Roman knew that in real life, when push comes to shove, many of the biggest braggarts, and often the biggest men, end up on their asses looking up at the person who finally put them down. Bullies almost always think that they're the best. Then they're shocked at what some smaller, innocent-looking guy, did to them. They should know that there's always someone better, someone faster, stronger, more cunning, with better fighting skills and better weapons.

Roman looked around the room, wondering if now was the time for action. Get to them fast. Start with Fang, do it fast, disable him, then put the others down viciously. Roman felt Blizzard's spirit howling, then stirring within him. It was a hopeful feeling.

A painful roaring, like Niagara Falls, filled Roman's ears. Blizzard. Roman's skin tingled, his fingers and fingernails felt as if they were elongating, though he couldn't see the change. His sense of hearing and smell intensified tremendously. Roman's inner voice spoke to Blizzard. "We must do it now."

*   *   *   *   *   *   *

Roman's chest tingled as Blizzard leaped out of it. Roman didn't want the children to see Blizzard for fear of scaring them, so Blizzard remained invisible as he stalked Freddy and Charlie. Fang was preoccupied glancing out the door and down the hallway. Blizzard streaked toward Freddy and Charlie as they both turned. They thought they heard a noise. Then Blizzard showed himself as a transparent, white fog, his teeth bared.

To Charlie and Freddy, there was no question that the fog appeared to be in the shape of a growling, white wolf. Both surprised men sucked in air as their eyes protruded in horror, then terror. They saw Blizzard streak at them, launching himself with his mouth agape, teeth ready to puncture their faces, then rip and tear their flesh. They moved backward, instinctively, pulled their hands up to protect their faces, then screamed and fell against the blackboard, whimpering.

Fang didn't see what happened, so he concluded that they were clowning around. "Stop the crap," he reprimanded. "Get off the floor. Why yuh two screamin' an' whimperin' like babies?"

"Didn't yuh see the ghost wolf? A white wolf. We saw it. It jumped at us. Really," Charlie said in a serious tone of voice.

"Yeah, Otto . . . ah, I mean Fang. I saw it too," Freddy offered.

Fang starred at them with disgust painted on his face. "Christ, Charlie. I thought I could depend on yuh. Now yur tellin' make-believe stories like my bro. Sheee it."

Then Fang stared at Roman. "Did yuh see anythin'?"

"No. Didn't see anything and I was looking right at them," Roman lied, then looked at the two men and smiled brightly.

Roman could tell that Charlie wanted to kill him. Freddy, however, just sulked, looking at his shoes as if they had holy pictures pasted on them.

This hostage situation is somewhat like Nam, Roman thought. It's basically the same, except for the kids. Life and death, success and failure depended on arriving at a successful solution or action before the enemy did the same thing. Quick, decisive, direct and brutal action was called for, just like in combat. Arriving at a successful solution to a problem, however, required time to think, but in war, on the battlefield, there's often no time to think, just act, or react, with instinctive or reflexive actions that'll save your life and, perhaps, someone else's life.

Isn't it ironic, Roman asked himself, that, with so many people, their victories and successes seem to wash away as easily as dirt in flowing water, while their failures, guilt and negative memories become dark shadows that seek their attention, trip them constantly, harass them, lay heavy hands on their shoulders by day and haunt their dreams by night.

Roman's mind wandered to a conversation that he once had with his friend, Joe, in Vietnam. It was after their patrol had surprised a Viet Cong campsite. The men spread themselves into a 150 degree arc—encircling the enemy would risk shooting their own men on the other side of the circle. His platoon killed every enemy soldier in the camp. Roman remembered most of the conversation:

Joe: "Does the killing ever bother you? Haunt you with guilt? Do you ever think about the sanity of war and the value of human life? Or becoming judge, jury and executioner? Do morality and ethics come into play at any time?"

Roman remembered staring at Joe to make sure he was serious. He was.

Roman: "Kill or be killed, Joe. You wanna stay alive in a war? Then forget the morality, ethics and guilt bullshit. Save it for civilian life where it belongs. There's no time for it when you're being shot at, bombed or trying not to step on land mines and other lethal traps."

Joe: "OK. I understand that. But, Wolfe, don't you think we're acting like savages, being reduced to beasts, cheering the sight of the enemy's blood and guts, sometimes even if they're women and kids? It bothers me."

Roman: "Joe, killing is one of man's primal instincts. We haven't outgrown it, we've just camouflage it in a dense forest of laws, rules, etiquette, talk of morality and ethics and the facade of advanced civilization. Under that grand facade of civilized behavior, man is still a hunter, a killer. He still destroys, only his weapons are better now, much more destructive. And one thing that hasn't changed in thousands of years is that the strong prey on the weak. The irony of inequality is that until everyone is equal, has the same things, believes the same things, and thinks the same way, thus creating few differences between peoples, there will always be conflict between the *haves* and the *have-nots*. Inequality causes friction, friction causes heat (anger), anger leads to conflict and conflict, if large enough, ends up in civil or world wars. Since there almost always will be inequality, plus disparate and rigid beliefs, then conflicts between the haves and have-nots, and varying belief systems, especially differing governments and religions, there will almost certainly always be personal conflicts, battles and wars.

"All that stuff used to bother me, sometimes keeping me awake, but I don't let it bother me any more. As a matter of fact, in wartime, any of those things will almost certainly get you killed. If you value life, then put all that theorizing and philosophizing crap on hold. If you really value life, then save your own life first. You can't help others to stay alive and you can't help change the inequalities, the injustices of the world, if you're dead. Think of it that way."

Joe: "Hard not to think of the value of human life and the rules and laws, and such, that make life safer and satisfying, don't yuh think?"

Roman: "War and conflict are inherently ugly. War is when the human primal instinct for killing is no longer disguised by the decorative facade of civilization, but rather, exposed in all its naked ugliness and waste of human life. During war there are few rules and laws that bind you. But, it all comes down to kill or be killed, Joe. Right now killing is my government job. I'm required to kill the enemy. Kill for my country and kill to stay alive. Do I sleep well? Hell, no, but I'm alive to complain about it."

Joe: "Maybe the guilt is good, in a way. If you feel guilt and regret for what you're doing, then you're probably a mostly good person. But when someone can kill easily and sleep well, perhaps his morality is questionable. Does the guilt ever get to you?"

Roman: "Joe, I care deeply about my country and Americans, especially American soldiers here in Nam. If I killed thousands of the enemy because of blood-lust, or I got a thrill out of killing and really enjoyed it, then I'd be a true killer. But I'm already overburdened with guilt. I have no choice. To stay alive and get home to my wife and daughter, I need to kill. It always comes down to that, Joe. You kill or you get killed, sometimes both. I happen to be fighting for my country, even though I disagree with it. But, primarily, I kill to save myself and those who are with me in this war. I don't believe in this war. It sucks, all right? To tell you the truth, I don't really give a damn about how poor the Cong are, or if they're homeless or not, or whether or not they get some form of democracy. If the Commies want this shit-hole country, and the people won't defend it themselves, then fuck it. Let the Commies have it. What are they going to get out of it? Some extra rice, hot sauce and terrible monsoons and debilitating heat? What I care about is American lives and because of that I'll keep killing the enemy. Hell, whoever wants this backward, puke-hole can have it, for all I care. Let the people do what they want with their lives and their country. To me, it's simply not worth the loss of American lives. I simply want to get out of here alive and go back to my family. And how do I do that, Joe? I do that by stopping myself from thinking about guilt, morality, shame, laws, right and wrong and focus on the basics of staying alive. And what's the most basic of the basics? Kill or be killed."

Joe: "Yeah. I guess I understand. I wish I could rub a bottle and have God pop out, like a genie and fix things."

Roman: "You'd be rubbing an empty bottle, Joe. No offense intended."

Joe: "Huh? Oh, yeah, I forgot you're an atheist. No offense taken. Hell, I think almost the same way. Many of my people still worship the earth and the natural environment, similar to a the Wicca religion. I prefer the old ways, the old spirits."

Roman: "You mentioned a bottle and my mind drifted off, Joe. My wife and I have a song that we like. The title is: *Time in a Bottle*, a song by Jim Croce. It's about how precious time is, perhaps the most precious thing in life."

Joe: "That's for damn sure."

That night, when Joe was trying to sleep, he couldn't help thinking of Roman. Wolfe certainly wasn't perfect and could be a hard, stoic person, both physically and mentally. He had a strong character, kind of like granite— solid despite the imperfections. But it's those imperfections that are keeping him alive in this hell-hole. They also give him a sort of uniqueness. He radiates a palpable sense of extreme danger, too. That's why the other guys usually stay away from him. I wonder why he likes me? I'm just one of the guys, but he accepts me. Is that good or bad luck? Wait a minute. I wonder if those lines of imperfection in his tough, rock-like hardness are really faults created by his admitted imperfections. Shit, how would I know? I'm no damn psychologist. He does appear to be restrained when he needs to be and savage when he needs to be, though looking at him, he sometimes appears to be dynamite with an unlit fuse.

Joe adjusted his backpack, which was serving as his pillow, then turned from his back to his side. He could hardly see his own hands, it was so dark under the thick canopy of jungle foliage. His thoughts about Wolfe continued. It seemed to Joe that Roman was carrying the seeds of his own destruction within himself, buried deeply, and Roman's struggle is to never allow fertile soil to exist for those seeds to grow. If that happened, Joe wondered if Roman's toughness and hardness would rupture like an earthquake ruptures the hardness of the earth's surface. Probably not, Joe concluded. Joe thought that underneath the "kill or be killed" character there lies a decent human being. He hoped so, anyway. One thing's for sure, he sure knows how to stay alive.

It turned out that these particular thoughts were the impetus for Joe's continued curiosity, which led to frequent future conversations with Roman. Joe thought of another conversation he and Wolfe had a few weeks later.

Joe rolled back over onto his back leaving patches of sweat on the waterproof ground mat. He remembered when some young ass Lieutenant hassled Roman. Later, after Roman visited the base-camp store, Roman got the Lieutenant's shampoo bottle and replaced the Lieutenant's shampoo with Nair hair remover. Goddamn, that was funny, Joe thought. The whole camp was laughing when the Lieutenant's hair started falling out, little by little. The next day his head was patches of baldness in between patches of hair. After that the Loo wore his hat all day and never took it off until bedtime. The Loo never found out who did it, but he had his suspicions, although, without proof, he couldn't do anything about it. The Lieutenant stayed away from Wolfe after that.

Joe continued the conversation with himself. Jesus. I remember when Wolfe told me that he wasn't as tough as people thought he was. God, now that was a shock. My jaw dropped so low that I probably could've kissed my own dick without bending over. When I told Wolfe about my thoughts of comparing him to iron and cotton, he shocked me again by saying that he was sometimes afraid when in battle, and that he didn't understand why the guys thought that he was fearless. Wolfe said that he was afraid that he wouldn't be able to protect those closest to him, afraid he'd meet someone better, meaner, more violent and more skilled. Wolfe is afraid of getting killed, leaving his family defenseless. I remember him saying that he's not, by nature, a violent person, but as society becomes more and more violent he needs to be more alert, more vigilant and prepared to defend himself and his family from violence.

/..¸/.-../---/.¸.-/./-.¸--/---/..-/.¸.-¸/.-¸/.-/-¸/

12

★★★★

*"You will never do anything in this world without courage.
It is the greatest quality of the mind, next to honor."*

Aristotle

THE SUN HAD PEAKED when they entered the school parking lot. They made few noises, no sirens, nor horns, and no flashing lights. They arrived quietly in a large State Police mobile command-post vehicle. It lumbered along smoothly, though it gave the impression of an army tank: solid, heavy, slow, ominous; a rolling fortress. The walls, roof and floor were made of reinforced steel. The windows on the back doors were slightly olive-colored due to the large amount of metal baked into the glass. All this, of course, making the vehicle and glass bulletproof. The tandem rear wheels supported its heaviness. The vehicle pulled to the end of the parking lot and came to a quiet stop, no tire screeching, no sliding on gravel like you see in the inaccurate, hyperbole-laden cop movies. This vehicle could survive a bomb blast equivalent to the power of five grenades. "The Tank," as the guys called it, came to a stop like a dinosaur dying in slow-motion.

Inside the Tank were other weapons, such as tear gas, shock grenades, extra ammunition, and an M72 Light Anti-Tank Weapon, also referred to as the LAW. The LAW is a portable, shoulder mounted, one shot, 66 mm anti-tank weapon, operated by one person It can penetrate heavy armor— the need for it in this situation was extremely remote.

The "Tank" swayed on its ultra heavy-duty, shock-absorbers, releasing a groaning sound, giving the impression that the vehicle was alive. The groaning sounds were actually caused by the unseen occupants who were moving around inside, causing weight to shift and the shock absorbers to groan. The double back doors, like elephant ears, swung open. Ninja-looking State Troopers, specially dressed in their battle-rattle, came bursting out, immediately searching for snipers, smelling the air for trouble, sizing up the situation in a few seconds.

Their honed sense of situational awareness was taught to them by Lieutenant Hawkey, their SWAT team leader. He'd taught them to always be aware of what was around them, pay attention to small details, focus, and survey their surrounding. "The key to survival," Lieutenant Hawkey often stated, "is to be paranoid. Don't trust anyone unless you are absolutely sure of them; keep a constant eye and ear open for hidden or potential danger. There are only two types of SWAT team members," he would say, "those who act temporarily paranoid and use it to their advantage, and whose every sense is alert to danger, and then there are those who are now crippled or dead."

The Tank could fit twelve SWAT members, in full gear, six on each of two opposing metal benches, although today there were only six men and one woman. The Tank was all black with huge white letters that boldly read STATE POLICE SWAT.

Each member of the SWAT team wore between thirty and forty pounds of equipment, starting with a Web belt and a ballistic helmet; goggles; black cotton gloves; a mike-mounted portable radio; two sets of matte black, metal cuffs; hard plastic flex-cuffs; black, flexible steel-sole and steel-toed boots; a Beretta handgun in a hip holster with an extra, fully loaded magazine containing fifteen bullets, that hung from a shoulder rig; a can of Mace; a Level III tactical vest, that would stop common caliber bullets and, finally, their primary weapon, which could be one of three weapons: (1) a shoulder mounted MP-5 assault gun—the Heckler and Koch, 9 mm, submachine gun— (2) a cut-down, 12 gauge Remington shotgun or (3) a high quality, police model, sniper rifle— a bolt-action, high-tech, McMillan TAC-308, in .308 caliber. This sniper rifle was specially made, with a heavy duty, match grade, free-floating barrel. It included a bipod for stabilization and was matte black to prevent the reflection of light. The sniper rifle was topped with a Leupold VX-II, 4-12X50 scope, also with a black matte finish.

But the thing the SWAT team wore most noticeably was their grim expressions. It was a deadly business for them. Their lives were on the line each and every second and some of them had families to go home to. Lieutenant Hawkey trained his men well; they each knew their job perfectly. The jokes and humor that covered up their anxieties and fears left inside the command vehicle. In combat situations, some men fight hard, while others hardly fight, but Lieutenant Hawkey's team fought harder than most because Lieutenant Hawkey, himself, was harder than most people in this business.

Captain Lewis hurried to Lieutenant Hawkey, as she held the fourth grade classroom students' pictures that the school principal had given to her. It was a five-by-eight inch card with twenty-two individual student pictures, plus a picture of the teacher and the principal. Each picture was small, about one inch long by three-fourths of an inch wide. She handed the picture card to Joe who glanced at the faces quickly. Something about the pictures snagged his curiosity, like a jagged fingernail catching on a thread of a sweater. But he wasn't sure what it was. He handed the card back to Captain Lewis.

"Joe," Captain Lewis said, "there're three of them. Two escaped from prison and the third provided the transportation and the outside connections. They've taken this whole classroom hostage." She pointed at the picture. "Twenty-two kids and one teacher. Teacher's male. That may be helpful later on, depending on what kind of guy he is and the size of his cojones. Principal says he's over six feet tall, about one-eighty to one-ninety pounds. Very quiet. The type that keeps to himself, a loner, but very good with kids." She handed the picture card to Joe, while mumbling, "Three cock suckers."

Joe smirked at Bev's cussing, then raised his eyebrows and smiled at her.

"Don't say a damn word, Joe," Bev responded with a friendly smile.

Joe used his rifle sling to place his weapon over his left shoulder. He took a closer look at the picture card as a breeze flapped it up and down like a single bird wing. Twelve boys, ten girls. Nice looking kids, he thought. Again, something caught his eye. He studied the picture, as Captain Lewis stood silently next to him. Something vague stirred in his brain, a nebulous memory, a ghost in a fog. He couldn't quite grasp it, couldn't make the right connection. Something about the pictures. The kids? . . . no, not the kids. Something about the teacher, maybe, . . . a male teacher . . . tall and slim . . . his eyes? Something about the teacher's eyes.. He focused on the teacher's face, squinting at it, trying to recall something . . . but what? He closed his eyes in concentration. Memories swirled in his mind like stirred oil in a caldron.

Suddenly, the memory was born. His eyelids shot open. He inhaled so quickly that it sounded like a gasp. He stared directly into Bev's eyes, put his right hand onto her left shoulder and said, "What's his name, Bev? The teacher's name." He said it with authority, impatience and a touch of excitement. Captain Lewis was startled by Joe's loud almost fierce response. She didn't like his tone of voice, but she knew it wasn't like Hawkey to speak to her like that either. Something was afoot. She searched his face, looking for a clue, but only saw the faintest curve of a smile and wide open eyes that appeared to have more mirth in them than on his lips. It didn't make sense, but she'd known Hawkey for a long time and trusted him. She put her initial feeling aside and trusted him now, too.

"It's on the card, Joe. Small letters. Right here. Look." She pointed to the center of the card where both the principal's and the teacher's names were printed. Captain Lewis said, "The principal's name is Mr. Howard and the teacher's name is Mr. Wolfe."

"Bev, it's very important. I need to know the teacher's first name," Joe stated adamantly as he took his hand off Captain Lewis's shoulder. Her heart was pounding, but Captain Lewis wasn't aware of it yet. She did know, by the expression on Joe's face and the tone of his voice, that something extremely important was bothering him. She also knew that very few things bothered Joe Hawkey. He was usually the coolest cube of ice around. But now there was a sense of explosive motion and impatience about him, as if he were a bullet waiting for the firing pin to strike its primer. Now she worried as she became aware of the pounding and pain in her chest, as if a badger was pounding and clawing its way out.

Captain Lewis pushed the button on her microphone and talked to a trooper who was with the school principal. He was to ask the principal what Mr. Wolfe's first name is. There was a short pause, then she received the answer. Bev asked Joe, "What's so damn important about the guy's first name?" When Joe stared impatiently at her, she whispered, "Christ almighty, Joe. What's going on? She stopped immediately and listened to the radioed answer, then stated, "His name's Roman. Roman Wolfe. Now tell me what the hell's goin' on," in her own stern, impatient voice of authority.

Joe stared at the picture, smiled broadly, then said, "DAM!," as he rubbed his index finger over the teacher's picture, as if to make it clearer and capture the man's spirit. "DAM!" he repeated, followed by, "His face is so clean shaven, no dirt, no smudges, no camouflage paint, no long hair, just a little older, but it's him. Jesus, Bev, it's him."

Captain Lewis moved closer to Joe and placed her hand gently on Joe's shoulder. "Who, Joe? Now settle down and tell me what's happening with you. What the hell is it? What do you know that I don't?" she asked, while holding back her frustration.

"Bev, if I'm right, this guy is the guy who saved my life more than once in Nam, especially during the siege of Khe Sahn. The other guys called him all sorts of respectful names, Bev. Some guys called him Solo-lobo, meaning, Lone Wolf. Some called him Ghost Wolf or Wolf Man, while others simply called him Wolf, referring to the animal, not his last name. But you know as well as I do that when a nickname sticks and sticks immediately, it's a sign of a much deeper truth. The deeper truth here is that Roman's nicknames are not misnomers. They're mirrors reflecting the truth. They're a reality, substantiated and corroborated. And the reality of Roman, in Nam, was that he had one hell of a reputation for killing the VC and NVA troops in a special way. He specialized in stealth and nighttime killing, usually with a knife, but sometimes with a garrote. We sometimes also called him DAM." Hawkey spelled the letters for Bev, "D . . . A . . . M. The letters meant DEATH AT MIDNIGHT. Bev, this guy would sneak out of our safety perimeter after midnight to kill as many of the enemy as he could before dawn arrived. About an hour before dawn he's sneak back in. We'd know it was him approaching the perimeter because he would howl like a wolf as he returned to our perimeter.

"When the two-months long siege at Khe Sahn ended, we found almost as many enemy deaths by knife-wounds as there were deaths by bullets and/or explosives.

"Wolf went after the enemy that were positioned by the mortar tubes and those who were snipers. At night the snipers would be out of the trees so Wolf simply looked for rifles with scopes, then killed the enemy who had that rifle. The VC found their dead comrades with their throats cut or their lungs or kidneys punctured. The VC were a superstitious people. They probably could have over-run us with a mass assault, but we believed that they didn't do that because they were frightened by the mysterious, phantom-like killings.

"Later on we heard that the VC thought there was some sort of demon helping us. There were sightings of a white, ghost-like animal, so when the VC soldiers discovered wolf foot prints, they thought that an American evil spirit was sent out at night to kill them. Eventually they got so seriously spooked that they packed up and left, but the rumor of the white wolf traveled like gun powder in the wind.

"That isn't all, Bev. One time he went out at night to do his killing with his usual weapons: the Ka-Bar knife and garrote. But in addition to those weapons, he brought a Hush-Puppy with him. That's a pistol with a silencer which was originally used to kill enemy guard dogs. He also had a radio/GPS. Well the crazy bastard got cut off from his own perimeter when the enemy unexpectedly moved forward during the night, passing right by his hidden position. That meant that he couldn't easily get back to the safety of our fortified perimeter. He knew there was no way that his three weapons could handle the overwhelming numbers of VC.

"According to Wolfe, a VC sniper spotted him and sounded the warning. Wolfe ran, bullets plunging into the ground all around him, splashing dirt upward like rain drops hitting dust. He found a place that offered temporary protection and returned fire with an ineffective, silenced handgun. He radioed us saying he knew he'd be surrounded and overwhelmed soon. So what's the crazy guy do? He radios the artillery base, gives them his own coordinates, from his GPS and asks for a *Danger Close*. A Danger Close is practically a suicide request. It's seldom used except when the enemy has you out-numbered, surrounded and they are closing in for the kill, your situation looks hopeless and being captured alive to be tortured was not an option."

"Danger Close is only called for when you're certain you'll die, so you might as well take as many of the enemy with you as you can.

"The artillery base, which was miles away, fired high caliber projectiles, more like bombs, at his position. Can you believe that? He called a *Danger Close* right on top of his own damn position, Bev."

"Lt. Hawkey," Captain Lewis whispered, trying to calm him down, "Don't piss down my leg and expect me to believe its raining."

Hawkey lowered his voice and replied, "I'm not lying or exaggerating, Bev. I'm telling you that Wolfe was surrounded by VC, so he gave his exact coordinates to the nearby artillery base and called for a bombardment on and around his own position. His *own position*, for Christ's sake. In a few minutes we all heard the whistling shells passing over us and blowing the crap out of everything around Wolfe's area. We waited, and waited, but saw nothing to give us hope. Another five minutes and we gave up on him surviving that hell fire. I volunteered to go get him or what was left of him, but my request was denied. Then, suddenly, we see the SOB with a branch held high in the air and a white surrender handkerchief waving from it. The guy's face is so black and dirty that the black guys in our platoon thought the VC had a "brother" fighting with them. When that SOB smiled, his teeth looked like a glowing, white, neon sign at midnight. Then Wolfe yells, 'Their gone!' —meaning the VC. Wolfe's clothes were charred and smoking. He looked like walking chimney, a crispy critter, except he had this really wide, shit-eatin' grin on his face. He wasn't a guy to smile very often, but at that moment he had a sort of childishly, arrogant smile. Then he started howling like a wolf over and over and in between howls he's laughing hysterically. The damn fool was in the middle of Hell, Bev, and he came out laughing as smoke wafted off his charred clothes. Later he told us that he found a fall-down tree, dug as deeply under it as he could and pushed his body into the shallow hole, directly under the fallen tree trunk. The only place he was injured was on his back which took some shrapnel, but nothing serious. His hair was singed, his eyebrows and eyelashes were burned off and he had some burns. That's all.

"The guy gets himself cleaned up, but off and on, he's giggling quietly. After a few minutes of this, I asked him what the hell he was giggling about. He says to me, 'Well, Hawk Eye, my friend, when the artillery shells were raining down all around me, I had some sudden muscle spasms that caused me to squeeze out a huge fart. And that got me to thinkin' about the Aussie guys in the division. So when we get back to base camp, I'm going to ask them if they know what an Australian fart is called. That's why I'm laughing.'

'An Australian fart? You almost get killed and you're thinking of a fart joke?'

'Don't worry. I'm OK. Now, back to the Australian fart. Like I said, I farted and it made my mind wonder, or maybe wander from the stench. But, you see, at the time I needed a distraction and that fart did it. Damn! I almost wanted to die right then and there, the damn thing smelled so bad. You don't know what an Australian fart is called, do you Hawk Eye?'

'Hell no, but you're going to tell me, right?'

'Of course I am," Wolf said. "An Australian fart is *thunder, from down under.*'

"Wolfe was usually so serious, but now the guy's being funny and weird, like he was in shock. Really kind of out of character, for him. Actually, the medic checked him and said Wolfe was acting like that due to a concussion from the Danger Close bombing."

"Joe, are you sure it's him? People can change drastically over a few years."

"Well, he's my friend, unless he acts terribly stupid. He's still the guy that saved my life more than once, so I'll give him the benefit of the doubt. You don't have to change friends as long as you realize that friends change, Bev. All friends change. I hope he has changed for the better and has left the violence and killing back in Nam. And, yes, I'm quite sure it's him. Why do you ask?" Joe responded curiously.

"For the simple reason, Joe, that in my experiences, men in a crisis tend to act like Neanderthals, not knife-wielding Platos." Captain Lewis grinned. "Also, there could be many men with the name *Roman*."

"OK, then quickly name two living men with the name Roman?"

Caught off guard, Bev responded, "Uh . . . I'm thinking . . . Wait . . . Shit! You're right. I don't know any men named Roman. Have your ever come across the man's name, Roman, except for this teacher?"

"The only other Roman I've ever heard of, in modern times, is the ex-football quarterback for the Los Angeles Rams and that was way back when I was a kid. Guy's name was Roman Gabriel. But even if the name, Roman, was much used, you'll not come across eyes like his but maybe once or twice in a lifetime. Look at his eyes. I know those eyes, Bev. It's Wolfe all right. We were very close for a short time. I fought with him and shook hands with him and went into the boonies to do some nighttime stalking. I've seen the reddish, star-shaped, keloid scars on his forearm, chest, back and on one leg. And speaking of shaking hands, when I first shook his right hand, I felt a lump and wondered what it was. He said it was a hard callus at the base of his index finger, where the handle of his knife applies the most pressure. He said the more someone uses a knife the harder and larger the callus gets. Then he says, with a sly grin, 'Chefs have them, too, but if there were any here in Nam, they'd probably *cut* and run.' Hawkey laughed.

I got drunk with him more than once. A surprising guy. Not really strong in the brute-strength sense of bodybuilder muscles, but still tough and extremely quick."

There was a lull in the action. Everything was temporarily quiet. Fang wouldn't answer the phone and SWAT hadn't gotten approval to take action. Bev and Hawkey wanted to talk to Fang. See if this situation could be resolved without gunfire.

Joe said, "Bev, did you know that my family name isn't really 'Hawkey?' It's 'Hawk Eye.'"

"Yeah, I read it in your personnel folder. Just figured you didn't want it known."

"I study peoples' eyes. I see things that others readily miss. My ancestors were like that, too, thus the name 'Hawk Eye,' which was changed to Hawkey to fit into the white world. Insight is my family trait, Bev, and I remember Wolfe's eyes real well. There was an unstoppable, fierce determination in them. It made up for his lack of muscle mass. I've seen him look at bigger, stronger men and those men back off after looking into his eyes. The guy's a black belt in karate and as devastating with karate as he is with a knife. Oh, I forgot to tell you. He's also ambidextrous and fighting him would be like standing nude in a razor-blade hurricane. When he's calm, he's the eye of a hurricane, but in a fight, he's the hurricane. And sometimes he's dark-hearted, with the soberness of a stoic funeral director. And Bev, the guys didn't call him Wolf because of his last name. They called him Wolf because he hunted like one, acted like one, sometimes even looked and sounded like one. But the most mysterious thing of all about Wolfe is that sometimes a white wolf was actually seen in the same vicinity as he was. Even though we were as close as two friends can get in a short period of time, he wouldn't discuss these ghost-wolf sightings that others swear they had seen."

"It's a long way from Nam to the classroom," Bev said, as she looked skeptically as well as seriously into Joe's eyes. "Would he be dangerous to the students?"

"I seriously doubt it."

Bev's radio activated; she talked to someone at headquarters. She said, "They haven't made their demands known yet. We'll sit tight until they do; they always do." She listened again, then responded, "Sure. Of course. I'll call and let you know. Out." Then, to Joe, she said, "So, what else do you know about the guy?"

Joe smiled at Bev. "He told me that he was from New York State, not the city. Somewhere near one of the Great Lakes, though I don't remember which one. Said he wanted to be a teacher. Said he enjoyed working with kids. Said that his early experiences with his nephews and niece made him interested in teaching as a career. Bev, he wouldn't hurt those kids."

"Could just be a coincidence, you know. Same name. Same look. A doppelganger."

"A what 'ganger?'"

Joe peered into Bev's eyes, laughed, the said, "OK. Go ahead, smart ass, and increase my vocabulary."

Bev grinned. A *look-alike*. You know how it's said that everyone has a twin some where in the world. Someone who has an uncanny resemblance . . . a doppelganger."

"OK. I'll remember that, but to answer your question, no, I don't think he's a doppelganger and in our work, Bev, we are always suspicious of coincidence.

"He was a loner back then, too, didn't want the Nam guys around him. At first some of the guys thought he was unfriendly. But that wasn't it, Bev. He knew the VC and NVA had a bounty on him. They had his picture on posters. The VC and NVA wanted him badly, dead or alive, preferably alive, so they could torture him, publicly. Make an example of him.

"Roman knew about the bounty, the torture, and decided that he wouldn't allow himself to be taken alive, but he also didn't want anybody getting killed because they were standing or sitting next to him. The guy really did care. He was brutal with the enemy, but he cared enough about his fellow jar-heads to keep them away from him, no matter how they interpreted his actions. I spread the word about the real reason that he didn't want the guys near him. All the guys understood.

"The night before his last day in Nam he didn't come to my tent like he usually did. I walked to his tent. It was raining in buckets that night, but I wanted to see him one more time, to thank him, you know. I walked in the darkness, through the steady downpour and, Bev, I swear to God, I thought I saw a white wolf standing next to him. I could even smell, or I thought I did, that wet-dog smell. But then when I blinked my eyes, the wolf was gone, just faded away, or it was an illusion. Couldn't be an illusion though. Other people had reported seeing it and that's not the first time I'd seen it. When I got close enough to his tent to see him clearly, he was standing in front of his tent, naked, staring up at the sky, hands raised as if trying to pick a star, like he was plucking a cherry from a tree. The rain matted his hair and poured over his body. I didn't think he saw me in the dark. I should've known better. As I turned to walk away, he spoke to me. He called me by my Mohawk family name. He's the only guy outside my family that I ever let call me 'Hawk Eye.' He still just stood there naked, unashamed, and asked me what I needed. I told him I wanted to say goodbye and thanks for everything.

"He was momentarily silent, looking at his hands as if he really had plucked a star from the sky. He said he was glad he could help, glad that we were friends. Said he must look funny standing there naked. Said he was standing in the rain to get clean, wash off the blood and dirt. Said he had to get rid of the smell of death before the chopper came in the morning to remove him from the combat. Said he had to get out of Nam, had to stop killing and had to get home to his wife and daughter. Said he owed them more than he owed Uncle Sam. Said I was the only one he really felt close to in Nam and he wished me luck and hoped he might see me again, some day. We shook hands. You shake hands with this guy, Bev, and you can feel his energy. I don't mean a powerful grip. That's not it. The feeling is more like he's got stored lightening in his fingers and the electricity makes your fingers tingle. Five minutes later, you can still feel it.

"In the early morning," Joe continued, "the chopper noise woke me up. It landed, then seemed to leave almost immediately. As the helicopter flew away, I heard a wolf howling. I'm serious, Bev. I've not seen him again, until now.

"Bev, I'll tell you something else. I've never been afraid of hand-to-hand combat with anybody . . . nobody . . . not until I met him. His skill, speed and ferocity are very deceptive. I've seen muscle-bound guys in the Nam, weighing over two-hundred pounds who wouldn't mess with him. For him, retreat is not an option.

"But once off the battlefield he'd act lethargic, didn't want to fight or horse-around. Just wanted to relax in a peaceful environment. Christ, he didn't even want to fight or brawl in bars when we had the chance to blow off some steam. He didn't want to join the special forces, didn't want medals, didn't want the recognition, didn't want publicity, didn't want the notoriety, just wanted to serve his country, kill the enemy, then get out of Nam and back to his family and his career goals.

"Actually, I don't even know why he was in the Marines, being married and with a daughter. When I asked him, he got angry and growled, 'Some kind of goddamn, military fuck-up.' I think it may have had something to do with his Military Reserve status. Don't know why he had to leave Nam so suddenly either. He still had time left to serve. Maybe an early discharge came because he was married. I do know that the whole platoon missed him, even most of the officers. He was kind of like our reticent security blanket, our confidence captain." Joe grinned sheepishly. "Yeah, I know, it sounds corny. Guess you had to be there to understand."

"So what makes you think that a person like that can change so much? Pretty hard for that type of person to make it through college and be a teacher for this long without some psychological problems following him like a diseased tail. Like you, for example," said Bev with a teasing smile.

"Ahh . . . Real funny, Bev. Best I can say is that it was his indomitable spirit and determination and the fact that he didn't enjoy killing. He only killed because he felt that he had to do it to save not only himself, but his fellow Marines. He did what was necessary on a battlefield, Bev, just as the rest of us had to do."

Joe whispered, "I doubt that anyone in the community knows about Wolfe's Nam experiences. The parents might freak-out with that knowledge. So it's probably best, Bev, if we refer to him as Mr. Wolfe or Roman or teacher. Don't go into his Nam experiences or his atheism, OK?" Joe said, rhetorically. "And please keep in mind that Wolfe's not dangerous to us or the kids. I'd bet my life on that. I'm saying that I think we can worry about the kids in his classroom a lot less with him there than without him there. We're all down here worrying about those kids getting hurt and, if I'm right about this situation, it's the unsuspecting jackasses in his classroom that are more likely to get hurt than the kids."

Lt. Joe Hawkey laughed out loud, then muffled the laughter with his hand.

"Well, I certainly hope so," Bev said, "Laugh if you want to, but think about this Joe. Even if this is the same guy, what makes you so sure he hasn't changed completely over the years? What if the son-of-a-bitch is the same as the way he was in Nam? What if he still has a killer mentality and attitude, but it's buried superficially? That's not impossible, Joe. As a matter of fact, given the circumstances of him being a teacher and not getting into any kind of trouble, as his records indicate, it might be highly logical to assume that he is the same, but is smart enough to have a good disguise as a shy, mild-mannered teacher. Joe, he could be a Jekyll and Hyde personality, dangerous underneath a thin facade of teacher goodness."

All humor drained out of Joe's face as he realized that Bev might be right. As a matter of fact her logic seemed reasonable, especially if Roman went home with PTSD— post traumatic stress disorder. Then Joe thought of a counter argument.

"Shit," said Joe, "You may be right about that, but I still doubt it. The principal's description of him didn't indicate any trouble. Not even a hint. It's been years since Nam. A lot of time to adapt, to come to grips with that experience. And instead of thinking that he's hiding his rage, what if his mild manner, shyness, no trouble, no record of post-Nam violence, what if all that indicates that he has learned to deal with his violence? Instead of his mild, shy manner being an indication of his disguise, what if it's genuine and an indication of his ability to adapt to a relatively normal civilian life?"

Captain Lewis smiled. " Yeah, I see your side of it too. Shit!" she said, mad at herself. "I almost forgot something."

"What's that?"

"Damn it! The teacher was smart enough to throw that radio and TV cable out the window so Fang couldn't get any news reports, but I wasn't smart enough to stop the media from getting that Nam information on this guy. I'll take care of shutting out the press. That way we can keep this incendiary information away from the parents who may panic, then all come here wanting their kids right away, and swarming the principal, wanting to know how such a killer could even be hired. We've got enough trouble already. No use asking for more. OK, the media doesn't get any information unless it's through me and I'll sanitize any information they do get. Let's keep this between you and me and our men, OK? You inform your team and I'll notify my team."

Joe nodded his agreement, then added, "Excellent idea, Bev, but we'll have to resolve this situation soon. The sooner the better because no matter how well we keep the reporters at bay, no matter how much you sanitize the information you give them, they always keep on digging, and sooner or later they'll dig up this guy's past. Then it'll be all over town and all over the airways. We'll have to work cautiously and quickly."

Bev paused, looking at Joe. He seemed to want to say more.

"Bev, I forgot to mention something else." Joe smiled broadly as he stared at Bev.

"Yeah? And what might that be, Hotshot?"

Joe's smile broadened as he said, "I named my son after that guy, so I sure hope you're wrong about him."

"Wait a minute. I know you call your son 'Ro,' but I thought it was short for Roger, or Robert, or something like that."

"Nope. Short for Roman," Joe said with a toothy grin.

/.-../.-/.-./.-./.-./-.--/../.../.-/.-/--./---/---/-../--/.-/-./

13

★★★★

"When morning brings mourning, brave men won't sleep, brave men won't weep, brave men will fight, to make things right, then be vigilant at night, so morning never again brings mourning."

Liam Anthony

SAMANTHA WOLFE, ROMAN'S WIFE— he called her Sam— brought her first graders to an early lunch at Pavlon Central School. When her students were settled at their tables she walked to the teachers' room to eat her own lunch. Few teachers were there due to Sam's early lunch schedule, so she ate as she thought of her daughter, Grace.

Grace was at school, also— Grace, Sam and Roman all went to different schools. Sam thought that her *Bugs*— her nickname for Grace— was growing up too fast. She was ten years old and sprouting as if life itself was her fertilizer. She wore her hair long, a couple inches below her shoulders. Her naturally rosy cheeks gave the appearance of light rouge, and when she smiled, two shallow dimples appeared, like beauty-mark companions. Her smooth, unblemished skin encircled pearl-white teeth. Her brown eyes normally sparkled with happiness. She was mature for her years, both responsible and trustworthy, so

Roman and Sam gave her a key to the house. Now, instead of getting off the school bus at the babysitter's house, Grace rode the bus straight home.

When Grace arrived home, she usually retreated to her bedroom, a fifteen by twenty feet corner room with a dark blue rug and egg-shell white walls. Her queen size bed, with a book shelf for a headboard, dominated the room's space. The room was well lighted by day with two large windows framed by pale blue curtains. When Grace arrived at her bedroom she'd sit at her white desk, or sometimes on the bed, or on the floor, then complete her homework so she could, read, watch TV, or just talk to friends on her phone during the evening.

Sam smiled. She was so proud of Grace.

Sam envisioned Grace's two cats, Apricot and Licorice, playing on the green, living room carpet, then scampering under the dining room table, enjoying mock chases and fights. The cats playfully chased each other around the legs of the chairs, then stopped and licked each other's fur. Sam broke out laughing when she thought about the awful faces Grace made the first time she saw Licorice (female) lick her anus and Apricot (male) lick his testicles.

Sam was in a pleasant daydream about her family. She was so grateful that they were happy and enjoyed each other and that Roman spent a lot of time with Grace, kind of like her playmate. She remembered the time when Grace saw her dad watching a New York Yankee baseball game. The announcer, with a wildly excited voice said that the bases were *loaded* and Grace had walked up to her dad and asked if that meant that the bases were *drunk*.

Sam's pleasant, lunchroom daydream turned into a nightmare when Linda— Sam's guidance counselor friend— came rushing into the teachers' room.

"Samantha." An ominous tone of voice. "Samantha. I was just in the office. The secretary and the principal were staring at the radio, so I listened. It's about Roman."

"Oh no, Linda. What happened?"

"Joan and Karen thought I should be the one to tell you. Roman and his whole classroom have been taken hostage. They're trapped in Roman's classroom with some convicts."

Disbelievingly, Sam replied, "Are you sure it's not a mistake? Sounds like an inner-city kind of thing."

"Jesus, Samantha, it was just on the radio. I heard most of it myself. Roman and his whole classroom are being held hostage by three escaped convicts." That's how the initial news reports were given, though Freddy was not an escaped convict. "According to the reports, those guys have guns. Joan wants you to come to the office. She wants to have a substitute teacher take your class so you can go and do whatever you need to do."

After a shocking moment, Sam answered, "Yeah, OK."

Sam felt dazed, her head feeling light and her brain changing to a shrunken, cotton ball. Her thoughts became fuzzy. The same words kept flashing in her mind, like a blood-red, neon sign. The words appeared to her over and over: ADIRONDACK MOUNTAINS . . ADIRONDACK MOUNTAINS. The Adirondack Mountains, in northeastern New York State, where Roman and Grace were taken after they were kidnapped two years ago by a violent, criminal family.

In a nearly panicked voice, Sam stated, "Do you know anything else about it, Linda?"

"Well, only that the whole school has been evacuated, except for Roman's classroom. Apparently all the other kids, teachers and staff are out and the State Police have the school surrounded. The radio reporter said that the parking lot looked like the school was holding a State Police convention. It must be on TV by now. Christ, Samantha, I'm sorry to be the bearer of such bad news. I—"

Sam interrupted Linda. Her thoughts were becoming clear now. Sam said, "No, No, Linda, don't worry about that. You did the right thing. It's what a good friend would do. Will you pick up Grace after school and bring her to your house? She'll be at home."

"Of course I will."

"Be sure to say the word *French* to her. She won't go with you unless she hears that word. It's our secret word that permits someone else taking Grace with them in an unusual situation."

Sam stared at Linda. "Grace will want to know what has happened. Just tell her that her dad had some trouble with a gang coming to his school and that I went to his school to see if I could help him. You have my cell phone number. Call if you need to."

Before Linda could respond, Sam left the room and headed to the office, leaving her lunch on the table. Linda was crying, with her face in her hands, as other teachers entered the room for their lunch break and asked, "What happened? What's going on?"

The substitute teacher arrived quickly. Sam got in her car and left immediately. Once on the road she screamed, "Dammit!" and slammed the steering wheel with her right hand. Then she spoke to herself, or was it supposed to be to her God? With her teeth clenched in anger, she yelled, "First Vietnam, then the goddamned Adirondacks. Now this. What the hell is going on? Why him? Why always him?" Gushing rivulets of tears washed down her cheeks, dripping onto her white blouse, making temporary, wet stains.

She drove the remainder of the way with her agitated brain on automatic. She didn't notice the trees and building that appeared to be flashing by her windows.

When Sam arrived at the Kroy school, she had to park quite a distance away, due to the traffic congestion. She walked to the closest trooper. He saw her coming and held up his hand to stop her from going past the yellow tape, his territory to guard.

"You can't go any farther ma'am," he said, as he stood directly in front of her.

Sam looked up at the tall trooper. Her voice was calm, but there was a subtle edge to it that caught the trooper's attention. He listened.

Sam said, "I'm Samantha Wolfe, officer. I'm the wife of the teacher that's being held hostage with that classroom full of fourth graders. I want to talk to whomever is in charge here." Sam used sibilant "Ss" for emphasis, catching the officers full attention with those hissing sounds.

The trooper stared at her. Nice looking woman, he thought, but a snooty *whomever*. Well la-dee-da for her, he thought, sarcastically. Nice and tall, though. He wondered, Is she good in the sack? He smiled at her, then, in an official voice said, "Please wait here. I'll have to check. Be right back." He turned and jogged toward Captain Lewis, who was in charge of this whole operation. Well, he thought, with a sardonic smirk, One loud-mouthed, good-looking bitch is sending me to see another loud-mouthed, good-looking bitch. Shee-it! Today seems to be my day to be a bitch sandwich. Go ahead ladies. Eat me or, preferably, suck on me. He smiled, thinking himself to be witty.

Trooper Jones was full of himself, over-confident for a rookie and arrogant. He graduated last, academically, in his trooper academy class, but first in both pistol and rifle shooting. He bored his classmates with his constant comparison of himself to Tom Knapp— the civilian, extreme marksman with a successful percentage of 99% at hitting what seemed like impossible shots with targets thrown into the air or at ground targets. Jones was so proud and so arrogant that he actually thought that being the best pistol/rifle shot over-ruled the academic part of the course. He considered himself the best prepared student in that class, despite the fact that a vast majority of police officers go through a whole twenty to thirty year career without ever firing their weapon at someone.

When Trooper Jones reached Captain Lewis, he said, as he pointed, "Captain, there's a lady over there who claims to be the wife of that teacher. Says her name's Samantha Wolfe. She wants to talk to you."

Captain Lewis was tired. She'd been there nearly all morning, supervising every action, giving most of the orders, trying to calm the parents of the kids in that classroom. Her weary eyes locked on Trooper Jones. She cleared her throat. "Bring her here, please," she said, laconically, but with a veneer of frustration.

Captain Lewis figured that Samantha Wolfe got her information from the radio or TV reports. It was inevitable and probably also inaccurate. Captain Lewis could withhold certain facts about the teacher's background, but she certainly couldn't withhold the teacher's name and the fact that there was a hostage situation. She saw Samantha out of the corner of her eye and turned slowly towards her as Sam approached. Captain Lewis offered a strained smile, then reached out and shook hands with Samantha. Bev said, "Hi, I'm Captain Lewis. I'm in charge. Trooper Jones already told me that you're Mr. Wolfe's wife. How may I help you?"

Trooper Jones was not dismissed so he stood by in case he had to escort Sam somewhere, plus he wanted to know what she said. But primarily he wanted to look at this Wolfe lady a little more closely. After all, he was young and single, and not coveting thy neighbor's wife had little meaning for him. Actually, he enjoyed the view of both women as the two ladies talked. All he saw were sex-objects.

Sam, full of bottled-up anxiety responded, "You can help me in the obvious way,"— Sam recognized that she sounded demanding, but was unable to control her tone— "You can get my husband and those kids out of there safely and quickly." There was a note of impatience in Sam's voice. Captain Lewis was irritated and challenged by it.

Normally Captain Lewis had plenty of patience. She was used to being challenged, though it normally came from chauvinistic men. But she was tired and took an immediate dislike for this woman who seemed to be challenging her, especially with Trooper Jones standing beside her.

Captain Lewis's reaction was hostile. "You don't belong here, Mrs. Wolfe. Let us do our jobs without interference. We're doing the best we can under the circumstances. However, if you can answer one question for me, I'd appreciate it. Does your husband have violent tendencies? I'm concerned for his students."

"Does Roman have violent tendencies?" Sam repeated sarcastically. "He was in jungle warfare in Vietnam, killing people for his country. Then a couple years ago he survived a brutal hostage situation in the Adirondack Mountains and saved the life of our daughter. How do you suppose he did that, Captain? You think he read the Bible to his enemies, his kidnappers and then they miraculously became peaceful and full of love? He used violence. For Christ's sake! Of course he has violent tendencies. You threaten him, his family, his students or friends and he'll react violently and with deadly force, if need be. But he would never hurt any of his students. Now let me ask you a question. Don't you have violent tendencies? If not, why the gun, the mace, the handcuffs? Does your SWAT team have violent tendencies? You use violence in order to keep the community and state safe, right? The only human not having violent tendencies is a corpse. We all have violent tendencies if the right buttons are pushed. And violence doesn't have to be a bad thing. It can save lives like your SWAT team tries to do. Violence is just a tool, like a gun or a hammer. How it's used determines if it's good or bad. Have you ever heard the quote: 'The very atmosphere of firearms anywhere and everywhere restrains evil interference. They deserve a place of honor with all that's good.' You know who said that?"

Captain Lewis turned her head to indicate that she didn't.

"It's an exact quote from none other than George Washington."

Both women sized each other up. They stared at each other. Neither backed down, neither shifted their eyes. Their eyes seemed to flash laser beams into each other's heads.

"Captain, shall I escort her out of here?" Trooper Jones said, smiling.

Sam, turning away from Captain Lewis and responding to Trooper Jones's remark, said, "Trooper! You lay even one finger on me and I'll kick your balls so far up into your body that they'll squirt out your nose and dangle there like plums." Sam paused and stared at Trooper Jones whose jaw dropped slightly and whose face suddenly transformed into a very ripe tomato. Then Sam returned her stern gaze back to Captain Lewis.

Trooper Jones felt a painful chill pass through his body. His hands instinctively went to his crotch. He hadn't ever taken physical threats from women seriously before. But there was something about Mrs. Wolfe. The way she talked, the scowl, the glare in her eyes, her tall stature, and her defiant stance, but most of all, her challenging Captain Lewis. The chill passed through his groin and he shivered. He could feel his scrotum shriveling, pushing his testicles up closer to his body. Wisely, he did not step toward, or touch Sam.

Captain Lewis broke eye contact with Sam and impatiently said, "Trooper Jones. Go back to your post."

Trooper Jones, thoroughly embarrassed, turned and walked to his guard post, whispering curses, while looking over his shoulder at the two women.

Captain Lewis waited a couple of seconds for Trooper Jones to walk out of hearing range. She looked back at Sam. It was still a case of dueling eyeballs between the two women. However, when Captain Lewis smiled at this feisty lady, who was still staring at her, she said, "OK, Mrs. Wolfe. You've proved your concern. I can respect that, so let's start over with a more friendly note, OK?"

"Sure . . . Sounds good . . . I'm sorry," Sam said, and she meant it. Sam smiled, then stated, "Please call me Samantha or Sam."

As they shook hands, again, Captain Lewis appreciated Sam's genuine smile. It created less tension. Maybe this woman wasn't the bitch she had originally thought she was, thought Captain Lewis.

"Samantha, I've learned much about your husband. The information about some of his duties in Vietnam, his military evaluations and combat records, have all been passed to me." Captain Lewis didn't mention the psychological evaluation that Roman had while he was waiting for his final DD-214 discharge papers. Her mind flashed through that report, which stated:

"Through his violent war experiences, in particular having killing become routine, the subject has, to a high degree, become desensitized to violence. He speaks in terms of violence or some aspect of violence being an accepted part of his daily life. Therefore, it is unlikely that what transpired in the jungles of Vietnam can be totally eradicated from his cognitive and physical behaviors. Continued behavior modification therapy in civilian life may have a favorable impact on him, if he chooses to attend therapy. However, he does not impress me as the sort of man who will accept therapy, at least, not for a sustained period of time. He is too independent, recalcitrant and a 'lone wolf.' Should he again be placed in any similar situation where he thinks that violence is the only option, then, in my opinion, even sustained therapy will not act as a psychological deterrent to resist his ingrained violent impulses. If he feels he must act with deadly force, in order to protect himself and others, I believe he will be quite able to act immediately to correct the situation, as he perceives it. He is highly skilled (black belt in karate, a master at offensive and defensive knife fighting) and will not hesitate to act with deadly force if he senses that it's required. However, with a little help, perhaps judicious medication, he could display enough self-control to live a normal life, as long as he is not subject to high levels of stress, anxiety and/or depression.

"The subject has a normal functioning conscience in that he feels guilty, and/or shameful when he has used violence and/or deadly force, even on the enemy. Subject has communicated that he will use his own genuine guilt feelings to control himself, to insulate himself against the dangerous and violent reactions to stress, anxiety and depression. Subject experiences guilt-ridden nightmares which often leave him tired from lack of sleep. When nights like that become cumulative, fighting off stress, anxiety and depression will be much more difficult. The prognosis for a good night's sleep probably will not be positive for a long while, making support from his family and a therapist very important.

"Subject demonstrates higher than average intelligence. He enjoys philosophy and likes to discuss philosophical conundrums like Maxwell's Demon, Schrodinger's Cat, Lucretius's Lance, and Russell's paradox amongst many other debatable subjects, such as atheism, for which the answers are difficult, speculative and varied.

"An unresolved issue that is disturbing to both this therapist and the subject is that the subject has a strong feeling of loss without knowing what he's lost. Perhaps it is not as mysterious as it sounds, but my findings are inconclusive. Perhaps what is really lost is an unrecognizable part of himself. Which part and the details are the real mystery along with the fact that whatever was lost was important and valuable to the subject, or he wouldn't have thought of it with such intense feeling."

Captain Lewis's thoughts returned to the present. "And I was also given the information about what happened to him and your daughter in the Adirondack Mountains. That must be an awful strain on you. I'm truly sorry. I promise you that I'll do my best to get everyone out safely." She flashed her own genuine smile at Sam, then continued, "I've read all the facts given to me about him. Now, can you humanize those facts for me? Put some flesh on them so I know what kind of man we're dealing with?"

Captain Lewis shouted to Lieutenant Hawkey and waved her arm and hand, gesturing for him to come to her. Sam was introduced to Lieutenant Hawkey. He didn't tell Sam that he had known her husband in Nam. He studied Sam as she began to talk.

"I can tell you that he's a loving husband, a wonderful father, and a dedicated teacher. He's strong, in a very quiet way, unless physically provoked. Normally he's good natured and likes to joke around. He has a great sense of humor, except on the day after a nightmare. He says weird, but funny things, like he'll say he has a checkered past that's composed mostly of the black squares— like on a checker board— or he'll ask me, 'How come Goofy can talk, but Pluto can't?' He jokes that he wants to eat *whey* for breakfast so that he can have his *way* with me.' Hawk Eye and Bev smiled. "He makes Grace and I; Grace is our daughter, feel wanted, needed, and loved. But there's also a sadness about him, too; a sadness that he conceals as best he can, especially from Grace. He doesn't like to talk about Vietnam. Sometimes when I look into his eyes I can't detect anything. Nothing appears to come out of them. They're like the black holes in outer space. Things get sucked into them, but nothing comes out. You know what I mean?

"You know how with some guys you can look into their eyes and tell that they're not only dangerous, but you can sense or scent, like an animal, that they've killed people and that, if need be, they can easily kill again. I mean *easily*, in the sense that they have the skills to do it, not in the sense that the person is eager to kill. Guys like that don't brag, they may not look tough, they may even be shy and reticent, but somehow you can feel that they are unusual . . . extremely unusual. That's Roman. So when he's with me, I feel like I'm the safest woman in the world."

Lt. Hawkey moved his head up and down. He'd seen Wolfe's eyes in Nam.

"He's had problems with depression, stress and anxiety since coming home from Vietnam. He's still taking medication for his bouts of depression. Vietnam took a lot away from him; the disturbing memories still torment him. He still has nightmares and yet he protects his family from them, not burdening us with their ugliness. I asked him once why he wouldn't talk to me, let me help. He said that his memories of Vietnam are like the Agent Orange chemical and he doesn't want to contaminate me with its cancer causing effects.

"He has a mini-gym area in the cellar. He practices his karate; he's a black belt, you must know that already. He also knows a lot of knife combat stuff, but he won't talk about it. Not to me, anyway. He's in excellent physical shape. He works out a lot.

"For Roman, Vietnam's still an open and infected, mental wound, not a scar; a scar involves healing. His problems are psychological: the war, the grief, the anger, the guilt, the killing. It's all trapped inside his mind, like a starving rat roaming around in his brain, eating away at it. The torment is buried deeply inside of him, but he keeps the lid on it. He deals with it in his own secretive ways. He's strong that way, but years of pressure can crack even the hardest of men. Sometimes he still has nightmares, but one particular one must have been especially tragic. Some guy named Billy was involved. Roman talks in his sleep. He says, 'I'm sorry Billy. I'm so sorry. It was an accident. An accident.' Sometimes he suddenly sits up in bed and whispers, 'the black wall, fifty-eight thousand' a few times. It took me a long while to figure it out. He was referring the Vietnam Veterans' Memorial wall in Washington, D.C. Those dreams occurred mainly for a few months after we visited that wall with over fifty-eight thousand names of dead soldiers.

"He can be as hard as his tempered steel knives, but it's surprising how remarkably gentle he can be, too. Sensitive and caring."

Lt. Hawkey shook his head in nearly complete agreement, but remained silent. He disagreed with her, somewhat, when Sam said that sometimes she saw nothing in Roman's eyes. She just couldn't see what was there because what was there was too dark, like trying to see a black cat in a black room. However, Hawkey could and had seen into Wolfe's eyes in Nam. Not much could be hidden from the "hawk's eyes."

"And something else," Sam said. "He likes kids. Actually, he'd rather be around kids than around most adults. So you need to get those three prisoners out of there because if any of them hurts a kid, there'll be hell to pay . . . and blood to clean up."

Captain Lewis informed Sam that there were two prison escapees and a third man, whom they didn't know, but who was apparently the outside contact and the get-away car driver. Then Captain Lewis encouraged Sam to continue.

"Well, when he came home, after his tour of duty, he had long periods of deep depression that were usually haunted by violent dreams. Insomnia followed as his mind acted defensively, not wanting to sleep to avoid the terrors that awaited him in dreams. His doctor said that his mind was trying to repress the guilt and anxiety he felt about the terrors of war, about all he'd seen and done to survive in Nam.

"He's like an eagle with no place to land. He's lonely in the midst of all the beauty he sees, alone amongst all the other birds; he soars alone, though he could be surrounded by people. He likes being a loner, while in another way it cripples him. Grace and I are always there for him, though. We wait in the nest for him to come to us.

Eventually he does. He's our life; we both love him. The good news is that he's improved a lot since his discharge.

"But, don't get me wrong, he's no angel. Sometimes he's not easy to love. Sometimes he's hard or, perhaps, *harsh* is a better word. He gets ice-cold, sometimes. He has sought love all his life and so many people have left him out in the cold, depriving him of love's warmth, comfort, and security. So he's grown suspicious of love and is, to this very day, somewhat suspicious of those who try to grant it to him, especially if they are the same people who deprived him of their love in his youth. In the beginning he didn't trust my love either. He told me once that he thinks a man desires a woman, but that a woman only desires a man's desire for her. It took months to gain his trust. Basically, he only fully accepts and trusts the love that's offered by me and Grace. He refuses to kiss anyone but Grace, me, and Lori, his niece. He's most comfortable around his nephews, Mark, Tony and Mike, but not around most people.

"Sometimes he even draws away from us, like an iceberg slowly drifting away from the shoreline into a vast sea. And, like an iceberg, there's a lot hidden beneath the surface. He believes that his aloneness, somehow, was meant to be. He tells me, sometimes, that he needs to be alone. He says his mind craves solitude for it's peace and tranquility. That solitude is his body's energizing force. He says that solitude brings him solace, that it rejuvenates his energy, refreshes him as if it's a battery charger.

"But this doesn't mean he wants to be permanently alone. He realizes that he needs some people; he needs to be needed, to feel valued. But, he says, he only needs friendship on a limited basis. He often says he doesn't need, nor does he want dozens of acquaintances when a couple good friends will do. He tells Grace and I, quite often, how much he needs us and appreciates us.

"Before Vietnam, he always had confidence that adversity would make him stronger because one way or another he would always overcome it. But Vietnam tore him apart. It ripped the fabric of his self-confidence and his sense of humor.

"You already know about his karate and his knife-fighting skills. When he practices karate he's like a cyclone of various hand techniques, dynamite kicks, and explosive knife slashes and thrusts. I don't watch him do the knife stuff any more. It's too disturbing. He's very confident, perhaps overly confident, in hand-to-hand combat situations.

"When he's upset, he gets a certain set to his jaw, you know. His teeth lock, his jaw muscles bulge, his eyes squint slightly as they stare deeply into you. Then his body tenses and takes a subtle posture, like a panther getting ready to spring on its prey. Don't get me wrong though. He's not a deliberately cruel person, doesn't enjoy hurting others, though he knows it's sometimes necessary. His harshness, however, is softened by a velvet cloak of ethics and honor that are comprised of many moral fibers, which usually surprises those who discover that he's an atheist. He's not some immoral, bestial Satanist just because he's an atheist. Actually he's probably more honest, caring, considerate and kind than the majority of supposedly-avid religious people.

"Roman's a man capable of much tenderness and love for Grace and me, plus a few friends and certain relatives. He's capable of vast amounts of inner strength and determination, which belies his appearance. He gets depressed by memories of childhood rejection and with their resulting loneliness, self-doubt and insecurity.

"His family support system and affection were tragically faulty. He was not close to his mother or father, he spent a year in a Catholic orphanage, then life with an aunt and uncle. After that he and his older sister went to live in an apartment above a bar with their alcoholic father. After his sister got married he went to live with her and his brother-in-law. Life with his sister and brother-in-law finally offered him stability, but irreparable damage had already been done to his psyche. His sister became his surrogate mother. He has three nephews and a niece, his sister's kids, that he adores.

"He's a very determined person. Perhaps *indomitable* is a better word. Once, a significant family member told him that he was stupid to quit his good job at I.B.M. to go to college. He did it anyway and that rebuke furnished him with the incentive to receive a Bachelor of Science degree in education, a Bachelor of Arts degree in psychology and a Masters degree in educational theory.

"I don't think it's a big-deal that he's an atheist, though I'm sure that some of his relatives would. He simply thinks that logic and reason contradict any purported Christian God with supernatural powers. I guess you could call him a Cartesian or a rational empiricist because, for him, things don't exist unless his senses or legitimate science can offer conclusive evidence. He enjoys reading philosophy and he enjoys the search for new information, new ideas and new thoughts, as long as they're logical, reasonable and not contradictory or obviously foolish.

"He's built an invisible shield around himself and he only allows a few adults and kids to penetrate it. All others, he feels, brush against the shield and simply ricochet off it in an insignificant way.

"But, you know, there was this Native American guy, a Mohawk Indian, I think, in Vietnam with him, that he liked a lot and sometimes talks about with unusual fondness, but Roman lost track of him.

Sam paused, not knowing if she should go on. "Shall I go on? Is this too boring, too much irrelevant information? Am I telling you what you need to know?" Sam looked into two pairs of eyes that seemed mesmerized by her words.

"No. No. Don't stop. Please continue. We need to know as much as you can tell us," said Lieutenant Hawkey, delighted to hear that Wolfe liked that Mohawk Indian guy, who was, of course, himself.

"He's certainly no coward, but he says that there are times when it's prudent to act like a coward would act. He says that a smart person knows when to be a coward, to simply walk away, you know? Like not walking into a gun fight with a knife. He gets pessimistic, sometimes, but he seldom quits unless he feels its the logical thing to do. He says that sometimes prudently quitting is the most intelligent thing to do.

"He'll protect those kids with his life, you know, or die trying," Sam said, suddenly changing the direction of her information about Roman.

Sam's eyes glazed over with tears, again, at the sound and hotness she felt while saying the words *die trying*. "But," she continued. "if those men get violent with the kids or with Roman, something bad will happen. He'll undoubtedly have flashbacks of Nam and act accordingly. He . . . he ah . . . he changes. This is strange. Have you ever watched one of those nature TV shows and seen a wolf's eyes when it stalks it's prey?" Sam didn't wait for a response, but continued, "Well, that's what his eyes look like, sometimes." Sam eyes opened wide, as if she thought of something else that made her afraid, but she remained mute about it, then said, "Please get him and those kids out of there.

"Well, that's about all I can tell you, Captain Lewis. It's all I can think of anyway, unless you want to ask specific questions."

Captain Lewis hugged her, then said, "Call me Bev, please." Then she took Sam to her car, where Sam could sit down and collect her thoughts and emotions.

Lt. Hawkey followed them to the car. Once seated, he asked Sam, "Did your husband ever say where he was in Vietnam, ma'am? You know, did he say the names of any places that he'd been in Vietnam?"

"He won't talk about Vietnam, Lieutenant. But he used to have a lot of bad dreams, earlier in our marriage and he used to say the name of a person or a place that sounded like 'Kay's son.' Something about a siege, a lot of deaths. He wakes me up when he rubs his hands vigorously on the bed cover. I thought he was rubbing off the sweat. I asked him why he was doing that and he said one word, 'blood.' He wouldn't explain himself and went back to sleep."

Lt. Hawkey bent down and whispered to Sam. "Ma'am," he said, "Is he still in control of his skills . . . I mean . . . is he really in control of himself? What I'm trying to say is, do we have to worry about him up there . . . you know . . . with the kids?"

Sam gave Lieutenant Hawkey a grim stare so he knew that she didn't like the implications of that question, then said, "He's a black belt in karate, Lieutenant. He still practices. He's a good man, a person who truly loves kids. He does not hurt kids. You don't have to worry about him that way. He'll do the right thing. But there's a fine line somewhere in his head. You can't push him beyond that line or he transforms. He becomes all adrenaline and spring steel. His body turns into one whole weapon: feet, shins, knees, elbows, forearms, fists, fingers, even his forehead, all working together, all skillfully coordinated like the pistons in the engine of a sports car. And its all under control, Lieutenant," she said harshly, still glaring at him.

"Lieutenant Hawkey. Roman's got that old KA-BAR marine combat knife at home. And just the way he looks at it, you can see his sadness and regret. It used to scare me, the way he looked at that knife, but it doesn't any more. I know him much better now. He would never hurt me, or Grace, or any of his students.

"He's probably more sane than the three of us combined. The final proof of that, for me, is that I know how much hurting people really bothers him. It bothers him tremendously, though, on the surface you might not notice. I've heard him cry at night for the people he had to kill in Vietnam and for his dead buddies. He also says that in this world you often have to do what you 'can' do instead of what you 'should' do. He says that sometimes good people have to do bad things to prevent worse things from happening. Does that answer your question, Lieutenant?"

"Yes. It sure does, Ma'am, and please, call me Joe."

"OK, Joe," Sam said with a smile, "Why don't you call me Samantha or Sam." Then Sam looked carefully into his eyes. She hadn't noticed them before. She paused, then said, "You know Joe, you have eyes similar to Roman's. Were you in Vietnam?"

"Yes, Sam, I was. As a matter of fact, I think I'm that Indian friend that you said Roman liked. I served with him. I fought with him at a place called Khe Sanh. We struck up a good friendship in a short period of time, then one day he was gone."

Captain Lewis and Lieutenant Hawkey walked away from the car and Sam. Once out of ear-shot Lieutenant Hawkey looked at Captain Lewis and said, "He's definitely our man. Mr. Wolfe is the guy from Khe Sanh. That's Wolf all right, the guy who saved my bacon."

"Guess you had it pegged right. She's pretty tough, too, isn't she?" Captain Lewis's eyes shifted in Sam's direction.

"Yeah. You got that right. She's some woman. Some guys have all the luck. I bet she's the only person Roman fears. She reminds me of you, Bev."

Joe smiled at Bev, then teasingly winked at her.

"That's bullshit, Joe. Don't bullshit with a bull-shitter," Captain Lewis said with a wicked smile.

"So, who's bull-shitting, Bev?" Joe said, as he turned and walked away with a shit-eating grin hidden from Bev.

Bev's eyes followed him for a few steps. She whispered, "Good man, that one."

/../.-../---/...-/./.-.-/---/..-/--/.-/.-./.-/--./---/.-../.-../

14

★★★★

*"I say quite deliberately that the Christian religion,
as organized in its churches, has been and still is the
principal enemy of moral progress in the world."*

Bertrand Russell

FANG STARED LASCIVIOUSLY AT Alyson Boyd. He desired her with the hot intensity of a bonfire. The corners of his mouth turned upward into a ravenous grin when he looked at her and thought, It's been a long time since I had me somethin' like that. To Fang, she was a sexual delight, a pre-pubescent sex toy.

Fang wanted to be with her . . . alone. He wanted to see her naked body, bare of any pubic hair and only minor buds for breasts. He wanted to delight in all the sensations that came along with being between her legs and very tightly inside of her.

Fang's penis stood erect. He made no attempt to hide the bulge behind his zipper, though the kids did not notice.

Roman noticed and was disgusted. Anger, like steam, built pressure within him.

Roman's mind drifted into darkness. He remembered the C-47 aircraft he'd seen on a Nam airport runway, its cargo consisting entirely of shiny silver caskets. He thought of all those reluctant heroes. He thought, Show me a hero and I'll show you a tragedy (F. Scott Fitzgerald). Then his thoughts segued as he imagined just one coffin, a tarnished, battered and soiled one. The one that Fang should be lying in. The one with punctured holes in it that would be kicked out of the plane, at a high altitude, dropped into the brinish, ocean water. The casket would slowly fill and slip under the water, with Fang's screams unheard and the salt instantly beginning the process of pickling him for eternity.

Roman's guilt festered. He reluctantly looked deeply within himself, saw his own anger and bitterness and felt it rise in his throat like sour bile. He wondered what had happened to the young men, most of them not even out of their teens, who left high school with big dreams, but were then drafted and sent to Vietnam. What had happened to their dreams of independence, peace, a good job and a family? They lay to rest in those coffins, also; the dreams ripped from them by the specter of death.

Roman thought about how much he had changed since high school; he didn't like many of those changes. He tried not to think of those thoughts, and received coincidental assistance from Fang's thunderous voice.

"Charlie. Freddy. Get yur asses over here!"

When they arrived, they stood in a tight triangle; all Roman could hear was the rumbling mumble of Fang's deep voice, followed by a joyful giggle from Charlie and a nervous giggle from Freddy. The three of them turned around, their faces plastered into huge perverted grins, though Freddy's grin looked false, his eyes hesitant. Both fear and guilt dominated his body language.

"It's 'bout time we have a toilet break," Fang said, his face radiant with a deceitful grin. Fang raised his voice and continued, "Now we take one kid at a time. I take a girl ta the toilet an' Charlie takes a boy, an' we keep doin' that 'til everyone has a chance ta do what they need ta do."

Most of the kids had to use the toilet and were anxious to go. Some of them even raised their hands, out of habit, to indicate that they wanted to go first. Fang and Charlie flashed conspiratorial smiles to each other.

Fang looked in the direction of Roman and said, "Freddy, here, can watch the Teach when we bring the kiddies ta the toilet."

Roman knew what they were up to. It didn't take the New York State Police Violent Felony Squad psychiatrist to recognize a pedophile. Roman knew that he needed to act fast. He couldn't allow any of these men to escort a child to the bathroom. His mind churned out ideas like a short automatic burst from an M-16.

"Alyson, Honey. You'll be first. Come with me," Fang said. Then he nodded his head at Charlie.

Charlie pointed at Davey and said, less sweetly than Fang, "Come here, boy. You can be the first boy to relieve yourself." Charlie crooked his right index finger, hand palm upward, then bent and straightened that finger to indicated that Davey should come to him.

Roman knew that the first two people to get relieved were going to be Fang and Charlie and it had nothing to do with emptying their urinary bladders.

Roman stood and calmly said, "You're being pretty stupid about this you know. A couple of Einsteins, you're not. That's for certain."

Roman was taking a calculated risk. He was deliberately provoking Fang. He wanted to anger Fang. He knew that anger was the father of carelessness and that carelessness, like a disease, breeds self-destruction in combat. Roman wanted Fang out of the picture; he wanted Fang neutralized quickly. Roman knew that the longer he waited, the more dangerous Fang would become and he was already too dangerous.

Fang and Charlie dropped their smiles, and their tumescence as well, when Roman distracted them by calling them stupid.

But while Fang was shocked to hear the Teach showing some balls, it was Charlie who spoke first. "What the fuck yuh talking about, Asswipe?"

"You smart enough to even know who Einstein is? You know his theory of relativity and other insights into the nature of the universe?"

"Don't be an asshole, Asshole. A course I heard of him. So what!" Charlie shouted.

"So you know that he was an exceptionally smart man, right? Well Einstein said, 'There are only two things that are infinite in this world; one is the universe.'"

"Yeah, yeah. Jesus! Is there a point to yur nonsense?"

"Sure. The other infinite thing that Einstein named is 'human stupidity.' You two are a perfect example."

Charlie's face turned red and hot. He walked toward Roman, until Fang grabbed his arm and pulled him back.

"Well, if you both didn't have your mind on other things," Roman smiled knowingly at Fang, "you'd stop and think with the object above your neck instead of the object below your belt." Roman was being cryptic to spare the children blatant sexual references." Then you could be more logical. Perhaps, with some effort, you might even realize that you're putting yourselves in a life-threatening situation by attempting to take the kids to the toilet. Anyway, I know it's not relieving kid's bladders that you want. Your girlie giggles gave your intentions away. "

Roman had talked to Fang and Charlie as if they were a infants.

Fang became embarrassed, then furious as he took a threatening step toward Roman with his fists clenched into large, solid knots. He was so furious that he didn't speak, but his randy feeling faded into fury as he glared at Roman.

Fang simmered, nearly going into a boiling rage at Roman's reference to him being like an infant. He thought, That bastard called me a baby. Fang's thought immediately drifted into the polluted fog of his childhood.

Fang's family background was much like Charlie's. The lack of love and comfort from his parents, the continual rejections. Life became a cruel experience for him very early, especially when his father constantly, physically abused him, beat him, kicked him, slammed him against walls. Black eyes, bruises, cuts were the usual result. A couple of times it was broken bones. He was young then, not big and strong. His father beat him, but not Freddy. Freddy was too young and his father couldn't stand Freddy's crying, so he usually left Freddy alone. It was the oldest son, Otto, who had suffered frequent physical abuse. Otto wouldn't give his father the satisfaction of crying and, strangely enough, that, in itself, created further abuse.

Fang exited his thoughts when he heard Roman speaking.

"An' 'nother thang, Massa Fang," Roman said, teasingly, as if he were a black slave, "please don' be usin, dat kine o' foul langage 'round deese kids. Dey might be thinkin' dat yuh be some sort o' bad person an' den not coperate wid yuh an' yur two igits." Roman's voice abruptly changed to a deadly serious tone as he finished. "And let me tell you that a room full of twenty-four uncooperative kids, all yelling, crying, screaming and running around, is no kind of fun. It's positively distracting and nerve-wracking . . . Massa Fang."

Charlie, with his knife in his hand, rushed toward Roman.

Roman was going to break his arm to create a pressing need for negotiations, but Fang stuck out his long, huge arm, like the long wooden arms that swing down at railroad crossings, and blocked Charlie. When Charlie ran into the arm, he bounced back, as if he'd hit a wall.

Fang had a bad feeling that Roman was trying to goad him into making a mistake by using a black man's old slang, slavery expressions, like "Massa" instead of "Mister," or "Master," and calling his partners "igits" instead of "idiots."

But what kind of mistake could this wimp be thinking of, Fang wondered. Perhaps there was more to this teacher than he'd supposed. This insight irritated him like a sharp pebble in his shoe. Unexpectedly the pebble took on a face, not the face of the teacher, but the face of Otto's father.

*   *   *   *   *   *   *

Otto's father punished Otto even for trivial infractions, like shoelaces untied, a button unbuttoned on his shirt, dirty hands, but especially for bed wetting. Otto was once punished for bed wetting lying belly-down and having his arms and legs tied to the four corners of his bed, while lying all day in his foul-smelling urine. After that young Otto slept naked in the cold bathtub to avoid wetting the bed. Otto was also punished by being locked in a dark closet, without food and water for two days.

When Otto was a young teenager, he was fired from several jobs because of his obsession with cleanliness. He'd spend so much time in the bathroom washing his hands that he didn't get much work done. A cook, in a kitchen where Otto was a dishwasher, reported to the owners that Otto chewed gum obsessively. The cook said that Otto only chewed the gum two-hundred times exactly— Otto told him— and he counted each chew out loud, getting on other people's nerves. Then Otto put the chewed gum in the gum wrapper and threw it in the garbage. Otto would take out another stick of gum, repeating his chewing routine over and over, unless he ran out of gum. This, all the hand washing, and ugly bruises and nasty looking cuts and scabs that patrons noticed and asked about, falling behind in his work, plus other weird quirks, got him fired after only a month.

Fang's father was fanatically religious, despite the huge conflict and contradiction between his handling of family members and his religious beliefs. Otto's father, a perfectionist with OCD (Obsessive Compulsive Disorder), made sure that his wife, Freddy and Otto went to their fundamentalist church every Sunday. The Bible was the only book in their house. The mother was forced to conduct prayer sessions every evening for an hour, while her husband and sons listened and prayed. Otto's father combined credulous, religious superstitions with personal interpretations of biblical text. The father's superstitions included a crucifix in each room. Each crucifix had to be kissed before retiring to bed at night (to show love and respect for God and obedience to his words), black cats must be killed (they were Satan's followers in disguise). Holy water was made by placing a crucifix in tap water for twenty-four hours. Before dinner the silverware and dishes had to be washed in the holy water. The interior walls of the house had to be painted white, for purity and his wife had to wash them each day. No pork could be eaten. In the master bedroom, over the bed, hung a symbolic, phallic crucifix that the wife had to kiss each night. To Otto's father, the full moon represented the opening of the vagina, so in the darkness of the bedroom, during a full moon, his wife had to open herself to her husband as many times as he wished.

In extreme anger, when Otto swore and used the words "Jesus and/ or Christ, or mother-fucker, etc., Otto was considered to have given his soul to the devil and his father would force Otto into anal intercourse to symbolically drive the dirty, foul devil from Otto's body.

But young Otto wasn't the only tragedy in the Fang house. Otto's older sister, whom he didn't like, was being methodically raped by her father; the mother knew about it, but could do nothing. She was too terrified to try to put an end to it. Otto's sister saw the terror in her mother's eyes and, like a contagious disease, that terror came to reside in her eyes as well. She saw no hope in struggling against her abuse so she let it happen while she mentally went to another place.

Otto witnessed the power and authority that this terror put in his dad's hands and he wanted it for himself or, at least, to share it. Soon young Otto, at thirteen years of age, was also finding his way to his fifteen year old sister's bedroom, in the middle of the night, where he would tell his sister that dad said he could do it to her, too. She was too terrified to go against her father, plus Otto was now physically powerful enough to overpower her. Otto saw the terror in his sister's eyes, again and again and enjoyed it more each time. It empowered him. The pleasure of her pain was only surpassed by his volcanic orgasms. Soon, with a young man's sexual appetite, he was raping his sister more often than his father was. Otto's sister finally realized that having hope, wishing and praying were useless and could be the worst of all evils, since they prolonged her torment and terror.

She committed suicide shortly after her seventeenth birthday. Fang was angry at her; now he'd have to masturbate. His father was frustrated and irate, too, so he began forcing his wife to pleasure him with oral sex and anal sex when vaginal sex got boring for him. He also started taking out more of his anger on Otto and began punishing Freddy. Thus, Freddy was initiated into the circle of abuse. To the boys, the punishments became unbearable, especially after their mother ran away and disappeared.

At fourteen, Otto started lifting weights after school, in the school's weight room. After two years of weight lifting, Otto was strong and violent because his newly gained strength gave him power and power meant that he could control others. He needed to have control over others. Power and control were now his drugs. But, despite the pleasure of his power, he lived a life of concealed rage, with moments of insanely murderous visions, alternating with moments of thoughtful, deceiving calmness.

*   *   *   *   *   *   *

Fang stopped flexing his massive muscles, settled down emotionally and focused for a few seconds. The Teach could have a good point, he thought. Then he said, "Whaddaya think would be so dangerous 'bout goin' ta the toilet, Teach?"

"Well Fang, bullets, you know, are kind of dangerous. Pesky little things, aren't they? Of course a bullet needs a target to hit, a soft, full-size, adult human target is best. And a nice, big human target like you is even better. You being four times bigger than Charlie, I guess it would be natural for the SWAT snipers to shoot you first." Now Roman added the bluff. "So why don't you step out into the hallway with Charlie and be a nice big target for a flesh-pulverizing rifle bullet. We've been here a long time, Fang. That hallway isn't empty. I know that, so why is it that you don't seem to know it? You're really going to walk out there and be an easy target, or are you going to shove Freddy or Charlie out first to see if they get shot? Maybe you can bully Freddy into going first."

Charlie and Freddy appeared awestruck by Roman's statement.

Roman smiled at Charlie and Freddy. "Hey, Charlie. Freddy. You're going into the hallway, first. That way, when you get blown apart, Fang here." Roman pointed to Fang, "will definitely know that the hallway is a lethal place to be. Whaddaya think about that?"

Roman's sardonic smile widened as he stared at Charlie, then at Freddy.

Charlie, doubt and suspicion etched into his face, looked at Fang, then back at Roman.

Fang, speaking to Charlie, said, "Don't let 'im spook yuh, Charlie." But at the same time, Fang knew that Roman was telling the truth. It was very likely that there were snipers from the state police SWAT team out there. He hated to admit it, but the Teach was right and he had almost walked into danger, allowing his dick to lead him astray.

"Of course," added Roman, "There's an easy solution to that toilet problem." Roman stood, then stared at Fang, Freddy and Charlie.

"Yeah? An' what might that be, Teach?" said Fang.

"Simple," Roman said with a relaxed smile that irritated both Fang and Charlie— Freddy looked shameful. "Just send me out there to take the kids to the bathroom. The cops'll know what I look like. The scopes on their rifles will give them an up-close view of my face. They'll know I'm the teacher and they won't shoot me. I can stand outside, between the bathroom doors to the girls' and boys' bathrooms to direct traffic. And what if they did shoot me? So what. You'd still have all your hostages. It's a win-win solution."

"Yur a smart-ass bastard aren't yuh, Teach?" blurted Fang.

Swiftly Roman spoke with a rough, strychnine edge to his voice. "Fang, I keep my brains a lot higher than you and Charlie. You ought to try it sometime. It works nicely. But you know I'm right. If you walk out there it'll be difficult to protect that body of yours from being punctured by one, perhaps several bullets. And from the look of Charlie's face, you aren't going to get him to volunteer to test the water for you. I guess you could shove Freddy out there, right?"

Freddy cringed.

Fang knew, Charlie knew and Freddy suddenly realized that Roman was right. Only Roman didn't know if he *was* right and if he was about to accomplish an extraordinarily, good bluff.

"Do it, Asshole. Do it fast," Fang snarled.

"OK, boys and girls. I'll take you to the bathroom."

Roman took the kids to the bathroom, a few at a time. He would casually glance up and down the long hallway every few seconds. He saw two, dark, thin-looking, round pieces of metal jutting out at the corner walls from both ends of the hallway. The ends of those rifle barrels looked like black dots. They were Parkerized, non-reflective rifle barrels. SWAT team snipers, he thought. Probably state police. He smiled. His bluff turned out to be the truth. He had saved the kids from sexual molestation, but lost some of his advantageous, wimp-like characteristics to the criminals. Fang and Charlie could have been blown away and he could have handled Freddy easily, armed or unarmed. But he had saved some of the kids from sexual abuse and trauma. He considered that a fair trade-off. He knew that there was an obvious solution to this hostage problem, but it involved killing in front of the children. Roman didn't like that option, though he knew that it may come down to that. He hoped it didn't involve tragedy for any of the children.

Maybe seeing the hopelessness of the situation would cause them to give up, he thought. Fang's two sidekicks didn't have the maniacal bravado to carry this through to the bitter end, but Fang. Charlie and Freddy would follow Fang's lead, except, perhaps, for Freddy. Freddy might be salvageable. Fang would squash them if they didn't obey him.

Fang ruled, and was ruled, by fear. But fear was a force that Roman usually dealt with successfully, at least in the past. And Roman knew that anybody can act cowardly. He knew that the line separating the brave from the cowards was as frail as one thread in a spider web.

Roman also knew that there were three types of people, with reference to bravery and cowardice. First, there are the timid, shy, insecure persons who are intensely frightened and will run away at any hint of danger. Second, there are the persons who are so afraid, in the face of danger, that they freeze and the third kind are the brave persons who do whatever needs to be done and are frightened only after they realize what they have successfully accomplished and the importance of it. All three types of people will be fearful, but all three react in different ways.

Roman also knew, via his karate training, that where there is too much fear, there is defeat. Fear distracts, paralyzes, dilutes skills and saps energy. To be the victor, Roman thought, he must keep his fear under control, then do whatever is necessary for that particular situation. Roman controlled his fear via discipline, concentration, training and had done so, in the past, while facing overwhelming odds.

Roman asked himself, "How do I solve this problem? There has to be another way out." But Roman didn't know what it was, not yet. He stood in the hallway, between the bathroom doors and projected good humor and confidence to his students. But in his mind, a picture of Fang was forming. Fang's over-inflated ego was blowing him up like a huge balloon full of hot air . . . and Roman was holding a needle.

/../.--/.-/...)./.-/--/.-/--./../.-.-./../.-/-./

15

★★★★

*"The world needs anger. The world often continues
to allow evil because it isn't angry enough."*

Bede Jarrett

EVERY STUDENT HAD A chance to use their bathroom. Roman was the
last to use the boys' room. As he stood at the urinal a warm grin spread
across his face like butter being spread across hot toast. He was not
only physically relieved, but emotionally relieved as well. Then the grin
disappeared, like a coin from a magician's fingers, as he thought about
what may happen next. He zipped-up quickly, did not wash his hands
and rushed back to the classroom.

As Roman hurried back to the classroom, he saw Fang looking
around the doorway, his pistol pointing at him. Roman had no fear of
being shot, not yet, anyway. If they shot him, they'd have a little less to
bargain with, negotiations might fail and the cops could come storming
into the school. When Roman got to the doorway, Fang grabbed him
around the neck. Roman acted meek and submissive, though he could
have gotten free of Fang's grip. Roman allowed Fang to manhandle
him as he thought, It would be bad timing to fight Fang now. The kids

were his responsibility, so he offered no resistance, not even verbally, though he gritted his teeth and grunted from the pressure on his throat from Fang's one-arm grip. Fang pushed Roman head-first and Roman stumbled forward, into the classroom.

"What took yuh so long!" Fang growled.

"Had to pee," Roman responded, laconically.

The children giggled at the word *pee*.

Fang glared at Roman, sneered at the kids, then grabbed a long table and used it as a shield as he walked toward the boys' room. He set the table down so it stood up vertically to shield him and his men while they used the toilet, one at a time— the table was not a shield against a bullet, it was a shield that prevented the snipers from knowing which of the men was using the bathroom.

Charlie's face expressed insolent disappointment. He had had more than just peeing on his mind and Roman had ruined his anticipated pleasure. But worst of all, the table could have been brought out there before and they wouldn't have had to use the teacher.

"Christ!" Charlie said to Fang, through clenched teeth. "Why didn't yuh think of that sooner?"

"Don't know. You so smart, why didn't yuh think if it?"

Charlie sulked like a first grader, knowing he couldn't challenge Fang.

Roman peered at Freddy and didn't get the impression that Freddy wanted to participate in Fang's and Charlie's perversions. Roman thought, It was probably the peer pressure that made Freddy act like he wanted to do what Otto and Charlie had suggested.

After Fang, Charlie and Freddy used the bathroom, one of the less fearful kids said, "X-Y-Z," and pointed to Freddy.

"What's that mean?" Freddy asked the boy, then turned to Roman.

Charlie and the other students laughed at Freddy.

Roman told Freddy, "It just means that your zipper is down."

The children laughed more loudly.

Charlie laughed harder and said, "Hey, Freddy, what's on yur mind?"

"Asshole," Freddy mumbled as he turned his back to the kids, then zipped up. Freddy's face was an oversized, ripe cherry when he turned back to face the students.

The sound of Freddy's zipper triggered images of body-bags to Roman. The sound gnawed and squealed at him. It was like someone running their fingernails across a blackboard. Roman tried to cast off the horrible image of all those body bags.

Rage blurred Roman's vision, then total darkness engulfed his mind. To Roman, the darkness was like being in a cave at midnight.

If you could see into the tar-black tunnel in each of Roman's pupils, you would see tortured, grotesque images straining against chains and metal doors. These creatures of Roman's post-Vietnam guilt and shame were locked up in strong mental and physical restraints, not allowed to exit into the light of the outside world. Roman's demons created fierce pressure. Roman shook his head to clear his mind, to let the light in. He would not give in to the strong urge to let these personal demons escape his mental jail, to become fully detailed, alive and nourished by creating havoc in the outside world. Roman worried because the demons sometimes had a will of their own and got into a battle with Roman's will. This battle of wills created friction and the friction created intense heat which felt like it would fry Roman's brain.

Roman's vision cleared when he heard Fang's heavy-footed steps.

Roman decided that he would do well not to underestimate Fang. It was much safer that way; it allowed for less chance of a fatal mistake. Fang may, Roman thought, combine both the brawn and brains of an Arnold Schwarzenegger— though Roman was still skeptical of the "brains" part. But Roman knew that Fang was more intelligent than he looked, or that his criminal records may have indicated. It was easy to think Fang was all muscle and no brain, especially with his extremely poor grammar, an indication of very poor primary school learning or, perhaps, the absence of much formal education at all.

Charlie handed the rifle to Fang, then casually walked to Roman's chair. Quickly he drew out his knife, the blade gleaming from the overhead lights. Charlie held the point of the knife slightly inside one nostril of Roman's nose. It was an intensely intimidating position and being close to the eyes made it even worse. Charlie had learned some lessons well when it came to intimidation with a knife.

Most untrained, inexperienced people would have been frozen with fear. Roman felt intimidated even though he knew that intimidation was Charlie's goal. Roman figured Charlie had no intention of using the knife in a serious manner, not now anyway. Roman also thought, Fang wouldn't want him being hurt before their escape because the Teach controlled the kids and that was very important to Fang.

Roman observed Charlie's sadistic grin as they stared at each other. Roman saw Charlie's extended right arm, almost sticking straight out towards Roman's face. With Charlie's arm extending straight out like that and with the element of surprise, plus the knife pointing at such a small target, Roman knew he could disarm Charlie easily with a simple backward flick of his head, an open-hand arm block to deflect the blade, then an arm-lock, a knee to the groin, an elbow to the face and, as Charlie sagged to the floor, the coup de grace joint-break at the elbow. Roman could visualize the moves clearly. He had practiced them hundreds of times and performed them a few dozen times in combat. It would only take a couple of seconds and it would be all over. But if he did it, then his charade as a wise-ass, overconfident, wimpy teacher would be blown. He'd lose the element of surprise that could be crucial later on. No . . . as much as the urge to lash-out had a strong grip on him, he held back. The wise-ass teacher facade is what was needed, he thought, especially the weak, wimpy part of it.

Instead, Roman looked straight into Charlie's eyes and whispered, so his students wouldn't hear, "Are you as good with that blade as you must be at stroking your dick? I'll bet you get a lot of practice when you're alone, huh?"

Charlie heard both Fang and Freddy snicker behind his back.

Fang said, "Don't be careless with the blade. We need 'im."

Fury contorted Charlie's face, the blade trembling in his hand as he stepped closer to Roman and applied more pressure to the blade in Roman's nostril. Roman thought the blade was going to tear through the nostril, but it didn't. Charlie's lips parted slowly and Roman could see the sticky, frothy saliva at the corners of his mouth and strands of it forming fragile, web-like columns between his slightly parted lips. Roman was reminded of the rabid, Adirondack Mountain coyote, frothing at the mouth.

"Put that knife down an' get over 'ere," Fang ordered Charlie.

"I oughta jam this blade right up yur nose and inta yur brain." The blade still trembled in Charlie's hand, accidentally cutting Roman's upper lip enough to send a trickle of blood flowing to the corner of his mouth.

Roman heard Blizzard's growl. Roman felt the release of pressure from his chest. He saw a flash of white fur and ivory teeth exit his chest.

Charlie dropped his knife as blood dripped from two puncture wounds on his wrist. Charlie grabbed his right wrist with his left hand, trying to stop the bleeding. Instead, blood drizzled out from between his fingers as he looked bug-eyed at the blood.

"You should be more careful with that knife," Roman taunted.

Fang interjected, "Goddamnit! Charlie, I tole yuh ta put that knife away. Now what did yuh do? Cut yurself?"

"No, dammit. I was bitten. Look," pleaded Charlie.

Fang looked. "The Teach bit you? Jesus. I guess he's got some balls, though they can't be any bigger than grains a rice," Fang responded, with a grin.

Freddy laughed heartily, delighted to have a chance to laugh at Charlie.

"Look! Goddamnit!" Charlie shouted, while holding his wrist out for Fang to see.

"Sure looks like a dog bite. Then the Teach didn't bite yuh, yuh dummy."

"Didn't say he did. Just said I got bit. I saw somethin' white, too. Somethin' weird's goin' on in here."

"Yeah. It's you. If yuh have a dog bite an' there ain't no dog, then yuh ain't just weird. Yur crazy, too. Hey Teach? Yuh got any large band-aids?"

"Yeah. Above the sink, in the cabinet." Then Roman reached for a tissue to clean the blood on his upper lip. He applied pressure and the cut coagulated, leaving a red line running diagonally from under his right nostril to the septum of his nose, as if drawn on his lip with a red marker pen.

Charlie mumbled angrily to himself at the sink as he ran water over the wound. "Damn Teach. Fuckin' bastard. Shit! Calm down, don't be stupid. Grab a paper towel. Still, I should kill that son of a bitch."

A tugging, tearing sound announced Charlie pulling out a paper towel from its canister. Then the squeak of the cabinet door and the tearing open of two band-aids. Finally an "Ouch!" drifted from the back of the room. Then Charlie hurried to Roman's desk.

Charlie spit on Roman, saliva spraying onto Roman's shirt. Charlie shouted, "Yuh goddamn mother-fucker! I should kill yuh right now. I'm going ta . . . !"

A gauzy, white flash jumped in front of Charlie's face. Blizzard.

Charlie suddenly stopped his tirade. He looked all around himself. Seeing nothing, but feeling a spinal chill. He leaned his body backwards without moving his feet. Fear captured Charlie and held him prisoner. He heard a growl and felt as if he had been released from something, though he still couldn't move.

Roman laughed at Charlie, only feeling mild pain and burning on his upper lip.

While laughing, but looking, Roman was unexpectedly introduced to Charlie's fist.

Roman stopped laughing, blinked and gritted his teeth in pain. His upper lip started bleeding again, only worse this time. He felt the trickle of warm blood running over his lips and chin, then dripping onto his shirt. Roman started laughing, again, his white teeth turning red as if he'd eaten a lot of red licorice. The red teeth made him look like a vampire who had just sucked fresh blood.

Blizzard, unseen, nipped Charlie's calf.

Roman smiled.

Charlie felt pain, looked surprised and backed up a step. He screamed, "What the fuck's goin' on?"

The children started crying. Fang acted quickly. He grabbed Charlie's arm and said, "That's 'nough, boy. Kids're cryin' an' that'll make the folks outside nervous. Nervous cops will start thinkin' of stormin' the building. Git back over there by Freddy."

Charlie reluctantly turned and limped away, though, over his shoulder, he glared at Roman, then faced Fang and protested, "There's something wrong in here. I think I saw a white dog. I know it sounds crazy. Look. I got bit again on my calf. Only my pants stopped the skin from getting' cut again."

"Shut up, Charlie. I'm tired of yur crazy whining. Jus' shut up."

Roman stood and walked past Fang toward the sink at the back of the room. Just as he passed Fang his vision suddenly turned black, then the blackness filled with tiny sparkles, as if his mind was full of the night sky. He dropped on both knees, catching his breath, only then realizing that Fang had kidney punched him. He placed his hands on the floor for stability, then shook his head to clear the night sky and stars away. He looked up at Fang. "Going to the sink to wash off the blood. Kids get scared when they see blood."

"Next time git permission. Yuh go nowhere unless I say so, unnerstand?"

"Sure. Of course. May I go to the sink . . . please?"

"Yeah and stop those babies from crying," Fang said, angrily.

"Boys and girls. I'm not hurt very badly and the blood will wash off easily. I may look worse than I really am. So now I want everyone to stop crying, OK? Please help me and stop crying. That's the best thing you can do for me right now."

Roman continued to the sink, ran the water on a paper towel, then washed off the blood. He dried his lip, then using another dry paper towel he applied constant pressure to the wound. He grabbed a couple more paper towels, walked back to his desk and sat down, his lower back still very painful.

Roman started to open his top desk drawer to retrieve a band-aid, but stopped. He looked up to see Fang, holding a cocked pistol. Fang aimed it at Roman's chest.

"Sorry. Forgot. I have band-aids in here, too. May I get a band-aid out of the drawer?" Roman asked.

"Yur hand comes outta that drawer with somethin' other than a band-aid an' I shoot yuh. Don't care what the cops do. When yuh got the band-aid, take yur hand out very slowly." Fang continued to glare at Roman.

Roman reached into the drawer and brought out a band-aid. He removed the paper towel then applied the band-aid to the cut. Then, speaking to his students, he said, "See? I'm fine, people. Nothing to worry about." Roman smiled broadly, not showing the pain as his smile stretched the wound.

When Fang wasn't looking, Roman gave Charlie the middle-finger salute.

Freddy was, again, delighted, but said nothing.

Charlie saw it as he was rubbing the pain in his calf. If looks could kill, Roman would have died a horrible death.

Fang checked the door to make sure it was locked. The vertical window in the door wasn't a problem. It measured about nine inches wide and was about two feet long. It was set into the middle of the door.

Fang grabbed a chair. He jammed the back of a chair under the classroom door knob. "Just in case," he mumbled. He looked out the door window, again, and smiled. Across the hallway was another door. It had a black, plastic tag on it and four white letters etched into it that said, ROOF. Fang's brain started churning out possibilities as his smile widened. As he turned around, his face turned stern and ugly. Then he saw Charlie walking towards Roman, brandishing a knife.

Fang took a giant step forward, reached his branch-like arm out to Charlie and grabbed the collar of Charlie's shirt. When Fang yanked Charlie backward, Charlie looked as if he had been shot backwards from a circus cannon. He crashed into Fang's chest. Fang squeezed his knife-hand wrist. Charlie felt excruciating pain, as if his wrist bones would break. The puncture wounds on his wrist screamed at him, so he immediately dropped the knife.

Fang growled menacingly at Charlie, "Put that knife away," he said. "Don't want yuh scarin' the kids. I tol' yuh that already. Can't stand their whimpering and cryin'."

Fang released Charlie. Charlie picked up the knife and placed it back into its belt sheath. He started to walk back to Freddy when Fang grabbed him again, speaking low, "Yuh pull anythin' like that again, without checkin' wi' me first, I cut yur balls off. Unnerstand?"

Charlie was humiliated, a line of sweat ran along his upper lip. He nodded his head submissively to indicate compliance with Fang's command.

Charlie turned to stare at Roman. It was a chilling stare that seemed to cool the whole room as if an air-conditioner had just been turned on.

A few of the children, who witnessed the stare, thought they saw frosty white puffs of vapor escaping from Charlie's mouth. But the weird thing was that there was puffy, white vapor around Charlie's legs, as if he could breathe through his knee caps.

Freddy sat on the counter by the windows, seemingly daydreaming, oblivious to the fact that he could be shot easily.

"Give me the key ta yur door," Fang demand of Roman.

Roman squinted his eyes, wrinkled his brow and shrugged his shoulders indicating that he didn't understand, then replied. "What key? I don't have a key to the door."

"Don't screw with me, Teach. I wan' the key. I wan' it now an' I won't waste time word-dancin' with yuh. I got over twenty kids here. Which one da yuh wan' me ta hurt first? Blondie, there?" He pointed to Alyson, then started to lower his pistol in the general direction of Alyson Boyd. The children froze with fear as the gun was aimed toward them. They buried their heads in their arms and started crying, again.

"I thought you didn't want the kids to cry? You just started them crying. Make up your mind."

Shit, Fang chastised himself. He put the gun away, then whispered to Roman, "I'll hurt that girl. Now give me the key."

Roman couldn't take the chance. Fang was too ruthless. Quickly Roman said, "OK. Don't scare the kids. Here's the key." He reached into his right front pocket and removed the door key from his key ring and gave it to Fang. Fang, as quick as a cobra, snatched all the keys. "Just in case," he said. Then Fang locked the door

"So, yur smarter than yuh look. Good ta know. Good fer the kids, too." There was a harsh, impatient, savageness in Fang's voice so Roman didn't want to push him too far, not yet. He'd had second thoughts about trying to goad Fang into a fight. Not in the classroom, he thought to himself. Three to one with the kids safety at stake are not good odds. Damn, how to get out of this, Roman wondered.

Fang yelled, "Freddy! Get yur ass away from the windows. They got snipers down the hall, an' probly some outside, too."

Freddy nearly fell off the counter when he tried to get off it too quickly. He lost his balance and stumbled. Before he stabilized himself, his mouth formed an "O" and his eyes bugged out with surprise.

"Why yuh didn't say somethin' sooner?" Freddy asked.

"Didn't think yuh were that stupid," Fang replied.

Fang stared at the children. "OK, brats. I want all the girls to sit on the counter, by the windows . . . Wait! Freddy, pull down all them shades. All the way down."

Freddy glanced at Otto fearfully.

"Just do it, Goddamnit!" Fang growled.

"Yuh really don't give a shit about me, do yuh?" Freddy whimpered.

"Yuh damn cry baby. Do like I say."

Once Freddy's job was completed, Fang ordered all the girls to sit on the counter in front of the windows that faced the parking lot. But there were too few girls to fill the entire counter-top area, so Fang selected a few of the smaller boys to sit there, too. They would all act as little, flesh and blood shields in case a sniper tried to fire at them through the windows. The half-dozen bigger boys that remained, he ordered, gruffly, to come to the door, where he stood. Everybody wondered what he was up to. Fang unlocked the door. "OK, the rest a yuh boys I want yuh ta take all the desks an' stack 'em up out in the hall so we can make a blockade. Put a line a desks all the way 'cross the hall, 'bout ten feet down from this door. Then block off the space unner the desks with the flat surfaces of some tipped-over desks. Then put more desks on top a the original line a desks so that we has a wall a desks. Teach, yuh can help 'em. An' don't get any crazy ideas 'bout escaping. Yuh know what'll happen, right?" Fang made a gun with his fingers, pointed it at one of the boys, dropped his thumb down and said, "Boom. Ya get my meanin'?"

"Yeah, I get it. No problems. Promise," Roman responded.

"OK then. Now yuh help the boys with the wall a desks."

As Roman walked toward the doorway he thought he saw white flakes, then more and more of them until it looked like an indoor blizzard. He had started calling Wolf, Blizzard. Out of the blizzard that only he could see, came a voice, "Be patient. Be strong. Your time will come." Roman smiled. He refocused his eyes. No one else looked as if they'd seen or heard anything unusual.

Roman and the boys built the wall of desks about ten feet down the hallway from the classroom door. When they ran out of desks, they took more from the classroom across the hallway. Fang ordered them to barricade the double doors that they had come through in order to get to the classroom. Now the normal routes to the classroom were blocked. The barricades were frail, but would act as shields and as an alarm system. If they were tampered with and squeaked or fell to the floor, they would make plenty of warning noise. Roman had to admit that it was a good idea. He and the boys returned to the classroom.

Next, Fang took the AK-47 rifle from Freddy and walked across the hallway— he was now shielded by the desks from the snipers whom he thought were at the end of the hallway. He tried Roman's room key on the roof door lock. It didn't work. In anger, he grabbed the door knob with both hands, gave a mighty yank and pulled the dead-bolt through the door frame, with a cracking, ripping sound, resulting in an open door and easy access to the roof. But were there cops up there? he wondered. He'd have to risk it and find out.

Roman saw what Fang had accomplished with shear muscle power and felt intimidated by such a grand show of strength.

Now Fang has access to the roof, Roman thought. That meant that, strategically, he would control the high ground. It was sound military strategy; he who controls the high ground controls his enemy. Roman swore under his breath because Fang appeared to know what he was doing and it worried him. But Roman calmed himself and remained resolute in his own abilities.

After a short time Fang returned to the classroom, then closed and locked the door. The door was now automatically locked the outside. He ordered the boys, who had made the wall of desks, to stand by the door window. He shoved them in two rows, each parallel to the door. Any direct, violent assault through the windows or through the door, would end up with the loss of children's lives.

Roman shook his head, then swore silently. The thought of any of his students being hurt sent shards of pain though his head. He realized that this situation would not be easily resolved. It would be damn tough to get all the kids to safety now that Fang showed himself to be a cunning foe, rather than just a muscle-bound rube.

Steven Blake whispered something that must have been derogatory because the other boys smirked and hid their mouths with their hands to muffle giggles and hide smiles.

Charlie slapped Steven across the head. Steven fell backwards, but his friends caught him.

Roman picked up a roll of tape and threw it at Charlie, hitting him on the shoulder. Charlie turned and charged at Roman, a flurry of arms in motion like a windmill. Fang couldn't stop him this time. Roman kicked him in the balls and Charlie sank to the ground, on his knees, holding both hands over his crotch.

Looking angrily at Fang, Roman stated, "I told you I'd raise hell if you or your partners hurt any of the kids. The only way to stop me is to shoot me and you can't do that. Face it. Your hope for escape all depends on the children's safety."

Fang glared at Roman, wondering how he was going to handle this teacher.

"Charlie. Freddy. No hurting any kids," Fang commanded, then, to Roman, "We won't hurt any kids, but that don't mean I can't hurt you," Fang growled to Roman.

"It surprises me that you caught that subtle difference. Guess you're not a retard after all."

Freddy looked ecstatic upon hearing Roman use the word *retard* to his brother.

Fang noticed and growled, "Wipe that smile off a yur face or I cut it off."

Then Fang pushed Roman into his desk chair and slapped him repeatedly, thinking of ways to handle this rebellious teacher. Roman's cheeks were red and swollen like small red balloons.

Roman felt discouraged by a lack of opportunity to strike a lethal or crippling blow at Fang and his minions. Roman thought of Grace and Sam. He reached into his pocket and felt Grace's Annie button. He imagined the soft, velvet touch of Sam's kisses as he was being slapped. Thinking of Sam and Grace seemed to cushion the blows. He looked up at Fang. Fang returned the look, a vicious gleam in his eyes.

Neither man broke eye contact. Each man searching the other, probing for weaknesses and strengths. Fang, Roman realized, was not one to give up easily. In Fang's mind, this situation condensed to: Get free or die trying.

Fang suddenly looked away when his peripheral vision caught Charlie getting up off the floor, still holding his crotch, but in much less pain. Fang turned and walked to Charlie, as if to help him walk. Instead he put his left hand around Charlie's throat, while his right hand grabbed Charlie's crotch, then lifted him up and threw him half way across the room where his head hit the wall. The hard landing knocked Charlie out cold.

Fang mumbled, "Stupid mother fucker."

/../.-/--/.-/-.../.-../.-/-.-./-.-/-.../.-/-.../.-../.-..-/-/

16

★★★★

"It is possible that mankind is on the threshold of a golden age; but, if so, it will be necessary first to slay the dragon that guards the door, and this dragon is religion."

Bertrand Russell

THE RIPPING AND SPLINTERING noises that had been created by Fang yanking the dead-bolt completely through the wooden frame of the roof-top door, echoed up and down the hard-tile hallway and into the open door of the classroom. It caught everyone by surprise, including Charlie and Freddy who both had snapped their necks toward the door like everyone else in the room. They were thinking that the SWAT team was coming.

Charlie grabbed his AK-47 from its shoulder sling and ran, flicking the safety catch to the "off" position and placing his finger on the trigger as he approached the door.

Roman noticed Charlie's index finger on the trigger. Roman thought the word *fool*. One never runs with one's finger on the trigger. Accidents happen, runners trip, stumble or fall, then friends or innocent by-standers die. But Roman supposed that Charlie didn't give-a-shit about that. Protecting *numero uno* was the only thing that was ultimately important to him.

Freddy didn't approach the door. He stayed by the children who sat by the windows. His back leaned against the wall, not a window. He looked like one of the scared children.

Roman heard Freddy say, "Psalm 3:3, My Lord and savior; you are a shield around me. O Lord, you bestow glory on me and lift up my head."

When Charlie stared at Freddy angrily, Freddy continued, but did so silently, though Roman could see his lips moving.

After hearing Freddy's psalm, Roman thought of Kurt Vonnegut's quote: "Say what you will about the sweet miracle of unquestioning faith; I consider a capacity for it to be terrifying and absolutely vile."

For some inexplicable reason, Roman felt sorry for Freddy, whom he supposed went through agonizing familial abuse, societal torment and, worst, rejection by his big brother. Roman thought, Freddy probably had no idea what he was getting himself into when he decided to help Fang. Freddy was easily manipulated and was probably told that the escape plan would be a quick, easy get-away, nothing to it and then he'd be done. Freddy probably saw a chance to restore his friendship with Fang, so he must have jumped at the chance to redeem himself in Fang's eyes. So it wouldn't have taken much convincing to talk Freddy into providing the get-away car. It was obvious to Roman that Freddy needed acceptance desperately, as well as the appearance of being useful, needed and valued, so he'd most likely do just about anything that Fang asked of him, even though he'd found religion and seemed sincere about it.

The kids who saw Charlie rush toward the door started crying; others were too scared to cry. Fear had paralyzed some of them; mental trauma solidified in their brains like dried super glue. Roman did his best to comfort and quiet them. What worked best was Roman's assuring smile, plus his confident tone when stating, "Shhh, I'll get you all out of here safe and sound, but you need to be quiet and trust me. The crying and whimpering makes that big guy angry. We don't want to make him angry at you. Let him be angry at me, OK?" Most heads moved up and down nervously, then the students gradually became quiet.

When Roman turned around, the sight of the AK-47 in Charlie's hand caused Roman's mind to switch to unpleasant battlefield images of fire-fights, tracer-bullets, sieges, snipers, oriental faces and slashed throats. The images danced through his mind like ice-picks tap dancing on his brain. His mind conjured up the familiar AK-47 sound, allowing the black, horrible creatures and shadows in his mind loose from the mental chains that had held them captive for so long. Roman struggled against his own panic, his own mental collapse. He blinked his eyes rapidly to clear them, as if those images were outside his body. His hands went to his ears, trying to shut out the sound of the AK-47, which was only accomplished because it was replaced by the diabolical tone of Fang's laughter. The laughter reminded Roman of the Adirondack Mountains ordeal and Jake's taunting and tormenting laughter. Roman's thoughts focused on his actions of self-preservation, the killing of three men to save himself and his daughter, Grace. He felt pleased to have saved Grace, but haunted by what all his killing said about his flawed character.

When Charlie peered out the door and saw what Fang was up to, Charlie wanted to join the fun. However, Fang waved him back to the room. But that didn't stop Charlie from shouting "Bang! Bang! Bang!" while waving the rifle around the room.

Roman cleared his head, stood up from his desk and walked to the windows to calm the children. Some were shouting, "Stop!" while others were pleading for Mr. Wolfe. Nearly all of them had their fingers stuck into their ears to assuage the anticipated noise when a rifle is fired in a confined area.

"Put the damn safety on and take your finger off the trigger, you idiot. You accidentally shoot one of the kids and I'll kill you," Roman shouted.

"Sure you will. You think yur skinny ass will stop a bullet?" responded Charlie.

Freddy said, "Please stop this. It's wrong, Charlie. 'Blessed are the peacemakers.'"

Roman thought, Peacemakers? Come to think of it, where are all the peacemakers in the biblical stories? There's very few words about peacemakers, very few Paladins mentioned, but bad deeds and characters abound.

"That's total bullshit, so shut the fuck up, retard!" Charlie screamed at Freddy.

Freddy responded with, "Matthew 22:14, For many are called, but few are chosen."

Roman was a fountain of quotes that disparaged religions. They stuck in his mind like ants in honey. "Lighthouses are more helpful than churches," said Ben Franklin.

Charlie didn't respond verbally, but looked at Freddy with contempt.

Roman noticed Alyson's tears and her trembling body, though she was quiet.

She was staring at him much like a puppy would look at its master when it desperately needed protection and security. Roman walked to Alyson, who was sitting by the window as one of Fang's human shields.

"Get back to your desk!" screamed Charlie.

"Or what, sissy britches?" Roman spat out the words with disdain flowing thickly off his tongue, forcing spittle to fly into the air.

"Or? Or I'll give yuh a new asshole." Charlie aimed the rifle at Roman.

"I've already acquired three more assholes when you guys walked in here," Roman lashed out, sarcastically.

Roman noticed that Freddy didn't offer any support to Charlie. He looked as scared as the kids. Freddy seemed to be studying the floor and mumbling, probably more Psalms. Roman couldn't see Freddy's eyes, but realized that stress, anxiety and nervousness were ripping him apart.

Roman thought, Freddy's superstitions couldn't help him no matter how many he quoted, no matter how frequently he verbalized them, no matter how deeply he believed them. Roman still felt sorry for him. Roman pondered, When the strength of reality meets the false hopes of superstition, it's like a strong wind meeting an insubstantial fog. The fog simply cannot stand against the wind.

A loud crunching sound came from the hallway. It sounded like Fang had now ripped the door completely off its hinges.

Roman and Charlie glanced at the hallway, again, but couldn't see Fang, so they returned their vision to each other.

Roman could usually tell what a person would do just by looking at his facial gestures and body language. Charlie looked like he might just be crazy enough to shoot. His finger was still against the trigger and Roman could see that it was not held loosely. Roman thought it best to let Charlie win this contest of wills, so he looked away. He turned, stepped toward Alyson, gently brushing the damp hair off her tear-tracked cheeks then hugged her reassuringly.

Roman heard talking from the doorway. He heard Fang tell Charlie, "Not now. Kids are cryin'. " Roman heard a smacking noise as Fang slapped Charlie on the back of the head. Roman glanced over his shoulder and saw that Fang had taken Charlie's AK-47 away from him. Charlie's face was aglow with pent up rage.

Roman continued walking around the room comforting the kids, hugging them, patting them on the shoulder or back, giving them words of encouragement and a gentle smile, while refusing to mention the smell of urine so as not to embarrass any child.

Then a loud noise forced everyone to look toward the windows.

Some one was using a bullhorn outside, but Roman couldn't understand what was being said; there was too much noise in the classroom.

As Roman made his way around the room, the classroom phone rang. Fang walked into the room, stared at it for awhile, as if not sure whether to answer it or not. But he needed to talk to negotiate, so now was a good chance to talk. He picked up the phone and gruffly said, "What?"

"Mr. Fang, this is Captain Lewis, State Police captain in charge. We haven't done anything to provoke you. May I ask what the noise, from the hallway, is about?"

Fang recognized a feminine voice and said, "Woman, ha? Got listenin' devices and men in the hallway, have yuh? Only way yuh could know 'bout the door noise. Well listen, bitch. We're gettin' hungry up here an' we thought we'd have ourselves a hostage bar-be-cue. Some young, tender meat, yuh know, unless we be gettin' some food from yuh. So, whatcha think, Captain Lew?" Fang was trying to make Captain Lewis angry, maybe lose control. The psychological warfare between the two continued, "Any real cops down there I can talk ta? An' I don't mean no pussy in uniform."

Lieutenant Hawkey was listening on another line while standing near Captain Lewis. Occasionally their shoulders touched as they shifted their weight. Joe was wondering how Bev would handle the extreme, sexist insults and the food request.

"You mean a male police officer? There are plenty of them, Mr. Fang. Unfortunately, they aren't in charge of this operation. I am. You'll have to deal with me. No compromise on that. This whole situation is difficult for all of us Mr. Fang, so— "

"Jesus! Jus' call me Fang, liddle lady," he interrupted. "Mister don't fit my image. Yuh know *twat* I mean? Guess you claimin' *squatter's rights* out there. What's yur name, again?"

"Call me Captain Lewis."

"OK, Capee-tan Lew. Don't y'all worry, now, Honey Buns. None a them babies was hurt. Jus' a door rippin' an' crunchin', Babe." Fang laughed tauntingly.

"If that's true, then I want to hear it from Mr. Wolfe. Put him on to verify what you said about the door and that no students were hurt."

Faking a sardonic southern drawl, Fang said, "Shore thing, Mistress Sweet Cheeks."

Fang handed the phone to Roman, saying, "Don't tell 'er which door it was or yuh be gettin' a fist in the kidneys. Sweet liddle Capee-tan Lew wants ta know if any a them babies is hurt." Fang shoved the phone into Roman's chest, making a hollow thump, then commanded, "Tell 'er."

But when Roman held the phone to his ear, what he heard was not a female voice, but a somewhat familiar male voice. He was confused to hear, "Wolf? Don't talk yet. Don't show surprise, if you can help it. It's Joe, from Nam. I'm a state trooper now. Don't acknowledge me by name. If all the students are uninjured, say, 'No one is hurt, Lieutenant Lewis.' She's the Captain in charge here. But if you say Lieutenant then I'll know you aren't being forced to say things."

"Yes, that's correct, Lieutenant Lewis. No one is hurt. They're scared, though."

"We think that there's only three men holding you hostage. Make something up with a number in it to indicate how many there are."

"I'm sorry, Lieutenant Lewis. We do have three students that look sick and— "

Fang snatched the phone away from Roman and said, "That's enough! Talk to me, Honey. Thought yuh said you's a Captain?"

During the pause, Roman glowed inwardly, thinking, "There's the ray of sunshine peeking through the blackness that I needed. It's Joe. I'll be damned. It's Hawk Eye."

When Lieutenant Hawkey heard Fang's voice, he quickly handed the phone to Captain Lewis who said, "Mr. Wolf simply made a mistake. I'm here to help resolve this situation without anyone getting hurt, you or the kids. So, let's help each other. What can we do to get the hostages freed? The longer you keep those kids, the more likely that one will get hurt or seriously sick or even killed. Then the situation and, of course the consequences, will escalate into the tragic, no-further-negotiation zone. Let's both cut through the bombastic fat, Fang, and get right to the bone. How can we help each other?"

"Well, Lew, speakin' a getting ta the bone; I got me a boner. Yuh can sure help me get rid of it. Yuh sound so sexy on the phone. Hows 'bout you an' I negotiating for some pussy? Hope yuh's on the thin side 'cause, yuh know the old sayin', 'the closer ta the bone, the sweeter the meat.' Watcha think, Lew?"

"Fang, this is a serious situation and it requires that those in charge be serious. You and I are in charge so let's negotiate seriously."

"First, I ain't afraid to die, liddle lady. Are you?" Fang snapped.

"Yes, I am, Fang. But I don't want anyone to die. Let's work something out."

Freddy said, "Proverbs 29:11; A fool uttereth all his mind, but a wise man keepeth it in till afterwards. I have complete faith in thee, my Lord."

"Faith means not wanting to know what is true." Friedrich Nietzsche, Roman thought.

Roman could not hear who Fang was talking to, but it had to be Captain Lewis. He knew that Joe must have quickly given the phone to a woman, that she must be in charge and that she must be in the elementary or high school office because that's where the only switchboards were for a landline connection. A woman trooper in charge? She must be damn good, he thought, and that thought comforted him, but not nearly as much as knowing that Hawk Eye was out there. "Damn. Where'd he come from?" Roman wondered as he smiled.

Roman assumed that the SWAT team had surrounded the building long ago. It was early afternoon, now, and that made him think of food, so when Fang paused on the phone. as if to collect his thoughts, and then turned toward Roman, Roman made the motion of pushing food into his mouth with his fingers. Fang nodded his head to indicate that he understood.

"We need food for all of us, Lew. Lots of it, 'specially for me. I'm still a growin' boy. Matter a fact, Missy, jus' hearing yur voice is makin' a part of me grow right now," Fang said as he laughed.

Captain Lewis pulled the phone away from her ear, not wanting Fang's loud laughter to puncture an eardrum. When the laughter stopped she said, "We can send food up there in about an hour or two, but there's too many mouths to feed, Fang. Let ten of the kids go as a show of good faith. That way you've got fewer kids to watch, fewer that can get hurt, fewer to feed and we'll all know that you're serious about negotiations and not just some crazy lunatic. It'll show us that you're a reasonable person who's willing to cooperate with us. That's not too much to ask for, Fang. That leaves you with Mr. Wolfe and over half the class. We won't do anything foolish if you don't do anything foolish. Sound reasonable to you?"

The classroom was as quiet as a mouse that's hiding from a cat. Everyone's attention was on Fang even though he was the only one who could hear Captain Lewis.

Fang talked and Roman listened while he strolled around the room whispering assurances, calming emotions and keeping the children quiet. He'd been moving about without permission, but it was worth it if it helped the children and it did.

Fang did want to get rid of some of the goddamn brats. He really hated kids. He figured that the only good kid was one who would submit to being sexually abused. Fuckin' liddle brats, he thought, an' worse then New Year's Eve noise makers.

Fang's lips brushed the mouth-piece on the phone as he said, "OK, Capee-tan. Can we slice through the psychology bullshit? Yuh got things twisted in yur liddle head, liddle lady. See, I want— great emphasis on *want*— yuh ta know that I'm a uncooperative, unreasonably, crazy lunatic. An' if yuh don't do 'xactly as I say, Honey Buns, yur thoughts will come true, an' I'll send some kids out ta yuh, all right. Only they won't be alive, Sweetheart. Now yuh send the fucken' food up in a hour an' maybe, jus' maybe, the food will bring this here lunatic back ta his senses, an' maybe I will or maybe I won't, send out five girls an' five boys. Maybe. But yuh listen real good, bitch," Fang paused and the tone of his voice changed dramatically, as if some demon had taken over his body. He continued with a deep, bass and growling loudly, "Yuh cross me, Sweet Cheeks . . . yuh pull anythin' funny an' yuh'll need ten, small body-bags. Yuh unnerstand that clear 'nough or do I need ta pistol-whip one a these babies an' send 'im out all bloody or dead?"

After Fang's outburst, Freddy forcefully squeezed his groin muscles so he wouldn't pee his pants. Then he stated: "Daniel 5:27, Otto, thou art weighed in the balances and art found wanting."

Roman's thoughts were far from biblical ethics. He was thinking: Some men need killing, despite the doctrines of religions and the laws of civilizations. And, he thought, there's nothing wrong with admitting this because there are uncivilized, savage beasts roaming amongst us, beasts who need to be killed, like a rabid dog, to protect the dozens of innocents that they will eventually harm or kill.

Then Roman was distracted by Freddy's biblical statement. Roman looked frustrated with all of Freddy's hypercritical, hyperbolic myths. It was Voltaire who came to Roman's mind, "On religion, many are destined to reason wrongly; others not to reason at all, and still others to persecute those who reason correctly."

Captain Lewis felt cold. It was the threatening chill in Fang's voice with its brutal sincerity. "I know exactly what you're saying, Fang. No tricks, but you must understand that the same rules apply to you. Understand?"

Fang, somewhat caught off guard by Captain Lewis's boldness said, "And what the fuck does that mean, Missy?"

Meanwhile, Charlie got Roman's attention, pointed at him, then swung his arm so it pointed at the teacher's chair. Roman understood that he was being ordered to go to his chair and be seated. He did.

"It means," Captain Lewis said in a calm, but stern voice, "that if you fuck with the rules, mister, if you cross me in any way, if any kids or the teacher get hurt or if any more of my people get shot, that will indicate that there can be no further negotiations. Negotiations are based on trust and compromise, Fang. Agreed?"

Captain Lewis knew that 'compromise' was necessary, but 'trust'? That was smooth-talking bullshit. You just don't trust criminals, especially criminals with guns and hostages.

Fang laughed into the phone. "Well, shore thing, Darlin'. I agree," Fang replied.

Lt. Hawkey wanted to tell Captain Lewis something so she told Fang to stay on the phone, then pressed the phone against her stomach so Fang couldn't hear Lieutenant Hawkey. Joe whispered in Captain Lewis's ear. "Tell him you'll send him a walkie-talkie, a police Pro Walkie-Talkie, so we can communicate with him from anywhere on the school grounds." Bev smiled at the good idea, then she put the phone back to her lips.

"One more thing, Fang. We'll send up a walkie-talkie with the food so you can communicate with us at any time, and not need the phone. Is that okay?"

Fang hesitated, wondering if it was some sort of trick. Captain Lewis anticipated his thoughts. "No, Fang. There's no trick. Just a plain, police walkie-talkie for convenience. No tricks. No gimmicks. You can trust me."

"OK," Fang answered, "an' how 'bout yuh bringin' up the food fer us?"

"No can do, Fang. Wouldn't do any good for this situation for me to get taken hostage, too, would it?"

"Well, where's all the trust yuh were talkin' 'bout, Captain Lew?"

"Nothing wrong with trust, Fang, but blatant stupidity is a different story. Neither of us can afford to be stupid in this delicate and volatile situation, can we?"

"Oh. Course not," Fang responded, "but I won't allow a man ta bring the food up here. Yuh send a woman. A nice, gentle, unarmed woman, with 'er arms full a food an' everythin' in plain sight. That way are trust an' compromise will go smoothly an' no one gets hurt, OK?"

"I agree. I'll be in touch in an hour or so."

"In an hour. No *or so*."

"You know damn well that ordering several pizzas will take more than an hour. Along with trust comes *reason*. Don't make demands that are impossible. The food will arrive as soon as possible. I'll tell the pizza place to rush the order."

"OK. OK. I can be reasonable. Hell, I can jus' get one a the girls an' eat at the "Y," if yuh know what I mean, Sweetheart."

"You're disgusting and bluffing. You touch any of those children and Mr. Wolfe will force your hand. You'll shoot him, then we'll storm through the doors and windows. You'll leave us no choice. So keep your taunting and disgusting perversions to yourself and Charlie." Bev heard Fang laughing hysterically.

After that exchange of insults, taunts and bluffs, the classroom became silent, except for Freddy who was saying, "Don't be overcome by evil. Overcome evil with good. Romans 12:21."

Roman's mind spoke to him, saying the words of Bertrand Russell: "Many people would sooner die than think; in fact, they do so."

*   *   *   *   *   *   *

Fang walked to the windows, found Alyson Boyd, grabbed her by the upper arm then roughly pulled her off the counter. As she screamed, he dragged her to Charlie before Roman could act.

"Charlie," Fang said determinedly, "yuh hold yur knife ta her throat an' if the wise-ass Wolfy gets outta his chair, yuh cut 'er throat. Unnerstand?"

Startled, Charlie said, "For real?"

"Goddamn right, fer real. I ain't goin' back ta prison. No way. No how. We be free or we die. But let me warn yuh, Charlie, if yuh hurt her and the Teach was not outta his chair? I'll kill yuh."

Both Charlie and Alyson froze in fear. Tears boiled out of Alyson's closed eyelids. The other children followed suit. Roman saw Charlie remove his knife from its belt sheath. Charlie grabbed Alyson by the hair and pulled hard to make her squirm and scream in more pain, as if to dare Roman to get up from his desk. Roman remained seated and thought, Oh, fuck. Charlie was smiling. Alyson cried louder as Charlie needlessly pulled her hair harder.

"Yuh shut 'er up," Fang said, pointing at Roman.

Roman yelled, "Don't be so damn stupid. You got the cops over a barrel now, so you let Charlie pull her hair and make her scream? What if the cops panic and come charging in here because she's screaming? Charlie needlessly causes her pain and instead of telling Charlie to stop, you tell me to keep her quiet. You want her quiet? Talk to the resident idiot. Talk to Charlie!"

Fang, angered at Roman's eruption, knew that he was right. "Don't grab 'er hair so tight, Charlie. I wan' it quiet in here. Pull the knife away from 'er neck, but keep it in yur hand. The big, bad wolf man happens ta be right."

Roman breathed a sigh of relief.

Charlie loosened his grip on Alyson's hair and lowered the knife to his thigh. The screaming stopped, but Charlie still had a tight grip on Alyson's long hair, though he wasn't pulling as he had been doing before.

Fang told Freddy to close the door and keep the six boys in front of it until he got back from the roof. Freddy moved slowly as if he were hypnotized. Fang slapped his cheek, then shook his brother's shoulders and slapped him again, telling him, "Wake-up an' be useful, yuh religious nut case." Freddy stared at Fang in shock. To Freddy, Fang had just committed the ultimate betrayal.

Fang paid no more attention to Freddy, he simply took the AK-47 and headed for the roof. He was only gone twenty minutes when the door unlocked and startled everyone as he re-entered the classroom noisily, bumping the door into the boys. Roman almost stood up, but relaxed quickly as Charlie's hand tensed around the handle of his knife. Roman was the first to notice the worried expression on Fang's face.

"Let 'er go, now," Fang said to Charlie.

Charlie let go of Alyson's hair. She coughed and rubbed her head and sore arm as she ran to Roman. Roman could see the tears running down her cheeks and the hurt in her eyes. Alyson trembled as Roman held her. Alyson reminded him so much of his own daughter. That's why, he supposed, he felt so partial to her. That's why he felt her pain so intensely. His rage increased two-fold, but he restrained it.

He thought of Grace and her unique sense of humor. He remembered once, at the dinner table, she put pitted black olives on each fingers and made funny motions with her hands. He and Sam cracked-up laughing at this antic. Then one day Grace looked closely at Sam's breasts, after Sam had taken a shower. Grace thought Sam's nipples looked like mouse noses and when Sam told Roman about it, they both laughed again. Later, Roman had whispered into Sam's ear, "I really do love kissing mouse noses."

Fang ordered Alyson to return to the windows and sit. Roman let go of her.

Roman smiled at the happy memories of Grace, then got up from his chair, picked it up and attacked Fang with it. He smashed the chair into Fang's head and when the chair fell, he kicked it into Fang's knees. Fang had bent over when hit on the head, so Roman punched him in the side of the neck, to no effect. Roman knew that he couldn't use karate on him or it would give away just the thing that was needed to escape with the kids, when the situation was right. Again, Roman kicked the chair hard into Fang's legs, tripping Fang, causing him to stumble, then fall onto his back.

Noises caused Roman to swivel around just in time to see Charlie's knife coming at him— the noise came from the kids who had been yelling a warning to him. Roman blocked Charlie's stabbing, right arm, with his left arm, then grabbed the arm at almost the same time. As Roman was pulling Charlie toward him with his left arm, he reached out with his right hand, grabbing Charlie by the throat and pulling Charlie toward him. Then, as Charlie was pulled into Roman, Roman kneed him in the balls. When Charlie bent forward in agony, Roman elbowed him in the back of the neck. Charlie fell like a house-of-cards in a hurricane, dropping the knife to the floor. But Roman now had his back toward Fang.

Fang was on his feet and punched Roman in the kidneys. Roman bent forward in pain, facing away from Fang, then immediately sensed Fang's boot coming up between his legs. Roman made double fists, crossed his forearms to make an "X," then placed the "X" under his balls and pushed downward, trapping, cushioning and protecting his testicles. Since Roman was facing away from Fang, Roman back-kicked Fang in the knee cap, stopping him in mid-stride. Spinning around quickly, Roman said, "I told you if you hurt any of the kids I'd make a fuss. I meant it and this was just an example. No kids get hurt!" Roman screamed at Fang, who was trying to catch his breath. "And don't threaten to beat me up or shoot me because one loud yell or one shot from this room and you'll be in an impossible FUBAR situation, with the possibility of negotiations gone and the SWAT team crashing through doors and windows. And you can't gag me, either. There are listening devices and if they don't hear my voice, they'll know something's wrong. And something you don't know, hotshot, is that there's a secret way that I can communicate with them and if I do it, they'll all come storming in here." Roman was bluffing, but he was a damn good bluffer.

The boys at the door were fidgety, shuffling their feet, showing nervous faces, glossy with sweat. Some were moaning and rocking side to side. Others were rocking back an forth on imaginary rocking chairs. Then some burst out crying.

"Shudup!" Fang yelled, then said, "What the hell's a *fool bar*?"

"Not fool bar." Roman spelled it, "F-U-B-A-R. It's a term used during the Vietnam war. Roman turned his back to the children and whispered to Fang, "It means Fucked Up Beyond All Repair."

Fang stared at Roman as a lion stares at its prey, intense, focused and hungry. Fang shifted his eyes to the children, who were standing by the door, then screamed at them, "Goddamnit! You babies go sit by the brats at the windows and shut the fuck up!" The children were terrorized. They moved away from the door quickly, wanting to get as far away from Fang as they could.

"May I ask that you please refrain from using the F-word," Roman requested.

Roman watched Fang as he put his left hand on his temple and rubbed— his right hand held the rifle.

Roman knew that rubbing the temple could mean that someone is getting a headache or, perhaps, because of stress or anxiety or a migraine. So, it could mean that Fang was starting to crack under the pressure.

Fang approached Roman and whispered, "Fuck you, Asshole."

Fang got himself, Charlie and Freddy together in a tight triangle and started whispering to them about what he had learned while on the roof. Roman couldn't clearly hear what Fang was telling Charlie and Freddy.

Fang told Charlie and Freddy that one of the cops in the car that they shot at, in the parking lot, was dead and the other one was in the hospital in serious condition. He told them that he'd overheard one cop yelling this information to another cop who was across the parking lot. Fang told them that they were, from that point on, considered to be cop-killers, so they had to be real careful because once someone was classified a "cop-killer," his life was in mortal danger from any vengeful cop. It makes surrendering much more dangerous, though Fang had no intention of surrendering. Fang told them that they'd have to negotiate for a helicopter if they hoped to have any chance of getting away.

Fang put his right arm around Freddy's neck in an unusually and suspiciously friendly and brotherly gesture and said, "Freddy, I'm sorry fer yelling at yuh. I'm unner a lot a pressure an' said things I didn't mean." Actually, his brother repulsed him, but Fang needed Freddy for a special job, so getting back into Freddy's good graces was necessary.

Freddy looked sympathetically, but suspiciously at Otto, trying to understand him, trying to change him, wishing and hoping for no more violence. He pleaded with Fang, "My brother, 'depart from evil and do good; seek peace and pursue it.' Psalm 34:14. Your sins can be forgiven, Otto." Freddy's eyes begged Otto, but when he saw no affect on Fang, he said, "Vengeance is mine sayeth the Lord."

Roman mumbled to himself, "Only if that myth gets there before me."

Fang told Freddy, "Please, Freddy, no more a that God stuff. Keep it ta yurself. Listen, I want yuh ta be are look-out on the roof. It's a important job. I'm trusting yuh ta do somethin' really important. It will be a great help ta us, OK?"

Freddy, of course, didn't know that, just as a canary did for the long-ago coal miners, Fang was now asking him to do. "Don't let the cops in the parking lot see yuh, if yuh can help it. Jus' keep an eye on the roof. Make sure no cops come up there. And if they do, yuh get down here fast to—"

"Christ almighty. What was that?" Charlie interrupted, then stared at the floor with horror and fear in his eyes.

Freddy was silent, but kept turning in circles trying to see whatever Charlie had seen. Freddy turned in frantic circles, like a frolicsome dog chasing its own tail.

All three of them looked down at the floor, then at each other. They all agreed that they had seen something white, a blur that brushed up against their legs, as it circled them, leaving a tingling sensation and the tiny remnants of a fading echo from a frightening growl.

Roman giggled, then said, "Why are you guys looking at the floor like it was an unflushed toilet?"

"Asshole," Charlie said.

"Did you see it, too?" Fang asked Roman.

"See what? You guys seeing things?" Roman said seriously, so he wouldn't antagonize them needlessly. Then, not being able to prevent his impulse, he looked at Fang and Charlie with a grim, basilisk stare. Then Roman had to look away, desperately trying not to laugh. When he felt he could not resist laughter, he coughed to cover it up. The coughing created a tickle in his throat, forcing him to really cough, but his coughing came from deep in his throat, like that of a growling canine.

"Goddamnit! It was somethin' white, shaggy, kind of like blurred white fur. Somethin' rubbed against me leg," Fang said to Roman. Then to Charlie and Freddy, he said, "Yuh feel a tingle in yur leg?"

Both Charlie and Freddy nodded their heads up and down as their disbelieving eyes bugged out. They were spooked, as if the classroom had suddenly become part of a haunted house.

The children stared, too, but saw nothing and looked thoroughly confused.

Roman said, "You talking about white fur that's moving? You mean like a snowshoe rabbit or maybe a polar bear?" Roman grinned slightly.

"No, wise-ass. Like a dog," Fang spat.

"This repartee is interesting," Roman said. Then added, "I seriously doubt that there's a white dog in my classroom. Maybe it was a white elephant. Of course that's about as likely as a lighthouse in the desert. Don'tcha think?" Roman grinned.

"Time will come when yur smart mouth will git yuh killed, Teach," Fang said angrily, with an intimidating stare and grinding teeth.

"It was nothin' guys," Fang spoke to Charlie and Freddy. "Ferget about it."

"Freddy, my liddle brother, yuh understand what yur important job is on the roof?" Fang asked, feigning a friendly smile.

Freddy knew now that his brother was lying to him; he was too overly friendly, but there was nothing he could do about it. Otto was hopeless, Freddy decided. Freddy smiled insincerely at his brother, saying, "Sure. I know what ta do." Then he walked out of the classroom door and climbed the stairs to the roof to act as a sentry. He felt hopeless and begged God for help, saying, "Psalm 5:2. Listen to my cry for help, my King and my God, for to you I pray."

Freddy's was deeply depressed; the black hole of hopelessness had sucked him inside an abyss. But neither did he realize that his brother had given him the most dangerous job. In Fang's eyes, Freddy was the one who was the most expendable.

*   *   *   *   *   *   *

Roman got permission to walk around the room to console the children. Keeping them quiet and hopeful was important to Roman.

Roman approached Alyson. Roman bent over so she could whisper in his ear, "I saw it, too, Mr. Wolfe."

"You saw what, Alyson?"

"A big, white dog. I saw it. Didn't you see it?"

Roman positioned himself close to Alyson's ear, then whispered, "Yes, Alyson. I saw it. But don't talk about it to anyone, but me. It might start more trouble than we are in already, OK? And it might scare the other children who didn't see it. The dog won't hurt children. You are all safe."

"It's our secret?"

"You bet, Sweety. It'll be our secret until this is over, then it's not a secret any more, if you want to tell."

"I can tell someone, later? It was beautiful, Mr. Wolfe. The prettiest white dog I ever saw."

"I know, Alyson. It's very handsome. Sure, you can tell whomever you want after we are all safe, OK? But remember, some people, probably most people, won't believe you. Don't get mad at them. It's just that they didn't see it, so they won't believe you. Only certain, very special people can see it and you're a very special person."

/../.-/--/.-/.--/.-./../-/.-./

17

★★★★

"Only two things are infinite. The universe and human stupidity."

Albert Einstein

CAPTAIN LEWIS AND LIEUTENANT Hawkey both paused, looked at each other with shoulder shrugs of uncertainty, then both started walking toward Mrs. Wolfe.

"You think it's a good idea to ask her to do it?" Hawkey asked. He walked with his hands in his pockets and head bowed, as if studying the shine on his boots. He could feel the crunch of pebbles beneath the flexible metal soles of his boots.

Bev focused on Sam, trying to analyze her as a doctor might do with an X-ray. Bev wanted to see inside this woman's head, see what she was really made of. Was she as tough inside as she appeared to be on the outside?

Bev walked quickly, trying to keep pace with Joe's long strides. Bev glanced to her left, looking up at Hawkey, waiting for a reply.

"Yeah," Bev replied, "I think she has what it takes, but we don't have much choice. I can't do it. Fang's not the cretin we thought he might be. The SOB's vicious, but smart. He'll take me hostage. Even if

I tried to fool him and wore civilian clothes, he'd recognize my voice. He'd take me and then have even more leverage. Can't get another female cop out here quick enough. Don't think I can go by the book on this one. If anything goes wrong, my goose is cooked."

"Awe, shucks, Bev. You needn't worry about that. I can always give you a goose," Hawkey said, in a teasing tone of voice and a little boy's mischievous smile.

Captain Lewis intentionally didn't look at Hawkey. She continued walking and looked straight ahead, saying, "Down, boy. Now's not the time or place. Save your strength. You may need it later. That Fang character's a bad one, and he's mighty big and desperate. Big and desperate, plus guns, is an equation for tragedy. You read the information on all three of 'em, right?"

"Yeah, I read it. One's a wimp, one's a chimp, and one's no shrimp. Fang won't be easy to take. His record's written in blood. He may not want to be taken alive. If so, then he's a triple, lethal threat. He's King Kong, a mountain of muscle with a vicious reputation, in or out of prison. Not all brawn either. The guy's got brains. Nothing superior, but compared to the other two dolts, Fang's a genius. Don't know if Wolfe can take him even if he gets the chance. Wolfe might have gone soft since Nam." Joe felt disappointment in himself for denigrating Roman. "You'd probably need to put a bullet in his brain to stop Fang, anyway."

Bev whispered, "I'd like to be the one to do that. Another good reason for me not to go up there, I guess." Captain Lewis frowned as she peered into Lieutenant Hawkey's eyes. "You read the part about Fang giving the enema?"

Hawkey lips drooped at the corners. "Yeah. I read it. The girl wouldn't do what he wanted so Fang knocked her out, then gave her a boiling water enema. Shit! . . . Poor kid was only ten years old. I don't understand that. How could anyone, if they're human, do something like that? It even sounds as if it would be a perversion to a pervert. The world's become such a brutal place, especially for kids. Fang's a megalomaniac with delusions of competence. Probably loves nature, too, despite the awful things it's done to 'im."

"Well, aren't you full of wisdom today. But, yes, there's no understanding the brutal, ultra-sadistic ones," said Captain Lewis.

"Even if you tried to understand, you probably couldn't. They just wouldn't make sense to anyone who's sane."

Hawkey mused, "This guy's not just tough and smart, he's an uncivilized, brutal, remorseless beast. Can we really risk sending Sam up there?"

"All you can do is ask. She can always say no. Then we think of something else," Bev stated.

Their conversation ended abruptly as they took their last few steps to reach Sam.

Samantha saw them approaching her and saw the intense concern on both their faces. She stood her ground and when they stopped in front of her, she searched their eyes. Neither seemed to want to speak first, so Sam spoke. "If you've got something to tell me, just say it." Sam looked sternly at the both of them, trying to sandwich her fear between thick slices of inner bravery and outer stoicism.

Hawkey grinned, then thought, What a woman. Hawkey said, "Sam, I haven't told you, because I wanted to be certain. I fought side by side with your husband in Nam. He was one hell-of-a fighting soldier, too."

" So you're that Mohawk friend that he liked? Well, then you know he hated it, Joe."

"Yeah. I know. Most of us did. But that's also why he was so good. He wanted to help end it. He got caught up in it, though. He figured that the more Americans he helped keep alive and the more enemy soldiers that he killed, the better the chances for him and his buddies to make it back to the World. I never met anybody better at hand-to-hand combat, Sam. He tell you much? I mean, about Nam?"

Captain Lewis decided to listen and see where the natural flow of the conversation went. Sam Wolfe interested her and became the center of her attention while Joe talked.

"No," Sam said laconically to Joe. "He's usually pretty closed-mouthed about Vietnam. And when he does say something, it's vague or a generalization, no specifics or details. We went to the 'Wall' in Washington, D.C. awhile back. I saw him cry for the very first time, but he still didn't say much. You might know that side of him better than I. What can you tell me about him in Vietnam?"

"We were remarkably close for a short time. I know that he saved hundreds of lives by killing as many Viet Cong and North Vietnamese Army soldiers as he could. He was bold, daring, courageous, maybe even obsessive . . . and definitely crazy. But above all, he was the best at what he did. Everybody, including me, was concentrating on death; our own. We all killed when we had to and we were all brimming with terror. Nam was a year of death-saturated thoughts and actions, but Wolf . . . ah . . . I mean Roman—."

"That's OK, Joe. I'm used to his multiple sobriquets now."

Hawkey, diverted his eyes toward Bev, thinking, "*sobriquet?*"

Bev smiled and thought, "English teacher?"

Sam kept talking. "I know now that he was good with a knife, as well as karate." Joe didn't want to mention the garrote. Sam smiled at Joe and their expressions both softened. She felt comfortable with Joe. She was going to like him because he reminded her of Roman and Roman had talked so admirably about Joe.

"You know, Roman still sleeps with his Marine Ka-Bar in a drawer next to his side of the bed." Her grin was strained when she said, "That used to scare me."

Joe grinned back at her as Bev stayed focused on Sam's conversation and facial expressions, to see if she could gather any insights into Sam's character and thoughts.

"Anyway," Joe said, "It seemed like Wolfe's thoughts, at least on the surface, weren't death-saturated like the rest of us. His thoughts were of you and staying alive to get back home to you. You know what he'd say when he returned from his solitary, nighttime stalking? He'd say he just saved more American lives. Roman's ambidextrous. You know that, of course. The guy's equally good with both feet, too. He's unbelievable to watch in action, unless you're the enemy. And his 'situational awareness' is instinctive. He has an uncanny awareness of where he is, what dangers are present, who is around him, foe or friend, and even how close they are. The guys in the Special Forces are trained for months and years to develop what Roman already had.

"He was good; I mean really good. The ROKs . . . ah, the R...O... Ks," Joe spelled it. "The ROKs, that's the Republic of South Korea. Their special forces soldiers were considered to be the toughest troops in Nam, after the Navy Seals, and much tougher than the average

American soldier. The ROK *regular* army soldiers weren't worth much, but those special forces guys, almost all of them were involved in martial arts since they were little kids. They were so fierce that captured documents indicated that the VC and NVA were ordered to avoid contact with the ROK Special Forces teams.

"Don't know if you know this, but sometime in late 1967 or early 1968, Roman got transferred to one of the ROK outfits for a few months prior to his discharge. Roman's reputation had grown so much that the ROK special forces wanted to train with him. So Roman taught and trained the ROKs in silent, nighttime stalking and silent killing techniques. He learned some of their specialized techniques, also, especially the various uses and techniques of strangulation that the ROK special forces commander had learned when he was stationed in India. India, in the 18th and 19th centuries had a murderous cult named Thuggee— the English word 'thug' is derived from the name of the cult. The Thuggees were a group of killers who specialized in the art of strangulation, then offered the victim to their god Kali.

"Roman earned the respect of the ROK Special Forces and that's no easy task. Given these circumstances, Sam, I'd say that those guys that tried to kill your husband and daughter in the Adirondacks never really had a chance. And, if I read the report correctly, the big guy, what's his name . . . Jake? He got taken out with a garrote that Roman made from a couple pieces of a branch and some goddamn braided lengths of dental floss. He sure didn't forget his training. When I first met him he was very reticent. The really good ones— the strong, self-confident types— they keep to themselves, don't say much, but they observe a lot.

"We spent many hours together before he opened up a little and let me get to know him on more than a superficial level. The boredom and anxiety of waiting can sometimes be almost as bad as the battle so we had time to talk. When we talked, the boredom evaporated. I didn't know him long, but I got to know him better than most. He seemed fascinated with me being a Mohawk. Perhaps that's why he opened up to me.

"He reluctantly thought about doing another tour of duty in Nam, you know." Joe glanced into Sam's eyes and saw shock and question marks.

"No, I didn't know that. Roman never mentioned it," Sam said with a note of surprise and disappointment. Sam leaned toward Joe and Bev as if her message was private, then whispered, "He can be quite stubborn once he gets an idea in his head. So, why didn't he stay?"

Captain Lewis moved in closer to Sam to make a tight circle, each person being mesmerized by their own anticipation, like scientists fascinated by a new discovery and not wanting anything to break their team concentration, blocking everything else out, focusing their attention only on each other.

Joe continued, "Some guys have a death wish, you know, and they stay for two or three tours or they stay because there's nothing waiting for them back home or they're running away from something back home. Some simply enjoy the adrenaline rush they get from killing. They have the power of life and death so they stay. But Roman? No, he wasn't like that, no death wish, no taste for killing, not power hungry, you know. As a matter of fact, now I don't know how true this is, but I heard that the only single criticism of Roman's abilities from the ROKs was that he didn't relish killing the enemy as much as they did. He had no taste for it like the ROKs had. They savored killing communists.

"I heard that some of the ROKs were a match for Roman, in daylight, with their martial arts combat skills, but at night, when they had simulated nighttime combat to demonstrate stealth skills, Roman had no peers. The ROKs were amazed with his ability. The ROKs didn't like fighting at night. There was some taboo or superstition that made them balk at nighttime combat. Wolf—"

Joe was getting away from the original question so Sam interrupted him. "He's not afraid of the dark at all. I know that. He often goes out at night without a shred of fear. I've noticed that about him. He likes to walk in the dark. It looks as if he actually embraces it," she added.

Joe persisted. "Some of the guys did drugs in Nam. I tried some, but didn't want to fu . . . ah, I didn't want to mess myself up with them, so I stopped. But Roman never touched 'em. Didn't need to. He simply waited for the darkness of night and had a natural high from stalking the enemy."

Sam, somewhat frustrated by Joe's non-answer to her question of why Roman didn't stay a second tour, decided to let it go . . . for now.

Bev thought it was time for getting back to the present. She looked at Sam and said, "It's been some years since Nam. I don't know how your husband will react to this situation. This guy, Fang, is worse than his record indicates. He's a real, cold-hearted, sadistic bastard. His coldness towards the rights, concerns, and wishes of others is a common thread throughout all his criminal records. His heart is as cold as a grave in January and his personality has a severe case of frost-bite. With Fang, joy comes from causing pain in others; pleasure comes from violence or perversion; laughter comes from cruelty and human abuse or death becomes his ultimate pleasure. We have to deal with this guy. But we need to know how you feel your husband will deal with him. Is Roman still a fighter? How do you think he's reacting to those three guys?"

Joe and Bev stared at Sam, expectantly.

"Bev," Sam said, staring into the Captain's eyes. "Roman will probably kill anybody that attempts to hurt any of those children. He may even be thinking that he can defuse this explosive situation by removing Fang permanently. Roman sometimes says, 'You cut off the head and the body dies.' Roman's probably thinking that removing Fang will automatically remove the other two guys. Without Fang, those two guys cease to function. However, I doubt that he'll do anything in front of his students unless any children are abused or if he has an upsetting flashback to Vietnam."

Lt. Hawkey smiled.

"You mean, for Christ's sake, that you think he might try to solve the problem himself by killing Fang?" Bev asked a little too loudly, as if startled by Sam's response.

"If you can't put Fang in a canvas blazer with wrap-around arms, soon, there'll be serious trouble. But he won't just kill indiscriminately, Captain. He will think and plan and consider alternatives. He's not a mindless robot programmed to kill, you know. He will probably be extra careful, maybe hesitant, because of the kids. But I'm telling you that he probably will come to the conclusion that he'll have to remove Fang, and the longer it takes to get them all out of there, the more likely he'll come to the conclusion that he has to solve the problem himself. If he can end it by breaking an arm or leg or knocking someone out, he'll do that, but if he's backed into a corner— "Sam didn't finish the sentence, but continued to stare into Bev's eyes.

Lt. Hawkey's faint smile couldn't be readily detected. It rested mostly in his eyes. He was right about how Sam would answer Bev's questions. It was still Solo-Lobo up there in that classroom. Joe cocked his head upward, looking at the classroom windows. "See you soon, Lone Wolf," he mumbled.

"She's right," Lieutenant Hawkey interjected. "Over the years he's probably become like a dormant volcano. The 'Ghost Wolf' part of him is now all internalized. But when danger approaches and the threat becomes physical, like a volcano eruption."

Lt. Hawkey looked at Sam. "Are you aware of any violent behaviors that Roman has demonstrated since Nam?"

"No, except for the Adirondack situation," answered Sam.

"Good," responded Joe.

"Jesus Christ," Bev whispered. "I don't want him to do anything until we've had a chance to try to resolve this peacefully, via negotiations, Sam. Will you help us get a message to Roman to hold off on any action that he may have planned?"

"He's no goddamned diplomat, Bev. He doesn't say nasty things in a nice way. What is it that you think I can do to help? How am I supposed to get a message to him?" Sam asked Bev.

"The school is surrounded by Joe's SWAT team and my regular troopers." She swept her arm the length of the school for effect. "Nobody's going anyplace," she said. "But we agreed to send food to the classroom. Shortly, we'll have a few boxes of pizza and soda to send up there. Will you consider delivering the message to Roman when the pizza comes? Fang won't allow any men up there. He wants a woman to deliver the food. I can't do it myself. He may take me hostage and I don't have any women troopers in my division. Joe can't use his female SWAT member due to department regulations. It'll take too long to get one out here from Rochester. If you could deliver the food, Fang'll probably make Roman take it, as a precautionary measure and then you can pass along the message. And, for Christ's sake, tell him to be patient. We can solve this thing, but we need time and we don't need a show of force from anyone. Not right now, anyway. What do you think? Can you help us?"

"Yes," Sam replied.

Bev and Joe were both surprised by Sam's quick response.

Sam stared at them, then said, "Sure, I'll help, but I want you to know that Roman isn't some trouble-making, violence-oriented, closet maniac, Bev. He'll do the best he can under the circumstances that he faces, just as you would. But he's not you and he may have different interpretations that may lead to different decisions than you might make. To put it bluntly, Bev, Roman and I have talked about this many times. He's sick and tired of the bad guys going free on technicalities or plea bargaining or reduced sentences and early parole. He's tired of seeing the victims getting screwed while the criminals sit back and use the laws to avoid being punished for their crimes or going to cushy prisons. You capture these bastards and they either get off or get reduced sentences due to some technicality or some phony plea of temporary insanity or plea bargaining or they blame murder and rape on their bad environmental upbringing. People are getting tired of that, Bev, and that makes them quicker to take action on their own, especially with those who have military combat experience. People are starting to trust their own instincts rather that rely on our castrated laws and our perverted justice system that favor the criminals and humiliates and/or emotionally destroys the victims."

Captain Lewis knew she'd made a mistake by attacking Roman's character. She didn't mean for it to come out like that. But she was frustrated and took a bad shot at a good guy instead of taking a good shot at a bad guy. Bev looked at Sam, an apology written in her eyes.

Sam said, If negotiations and compromise fail, or will place added danger in the situation, I believe Roman will take action. Bev, if you can see past the glare of suspicion in his eyes, if you can hear beyond the strychnine edge to his voice, if you can understand his need for privacy and solitude, if you can understand the fact that trouble seems to follow him, if you can accept his skill at meeting evil directly, head-on, and defeating it, if you can understand his love of kids and of his family, then you'll understand him better than most people.

"He's really one of the good guys, despite his flaws. You simply don't know that yet because you don't know him. Roman isn't your normal straight arrow. He prefers the path least taken and that path is usually serpentine. He may be fierce in battle, but he's gentle in friendship and comforting in love, a good husband and father, though there usually seems to be some sort of internal battle going on in him and, most likely, it's Vietnam related."

Captain Lewis looked apologetically at Sam, then at Lieutenant Hawkey, who was bobbing his head up and down in agreement with what Sam had said. Lieutenant Hawkey knew firsthand about Roman's good side. Roman had put his own life at risk for Joe.

Sam continued, "Roman and I were talking once and he said that when he was real young, he used to admire smart people; when he was a teenager he admired strong, tough, aggressive people, but now that he's approaching middle age, after having himself been called both clever and aggressive, he finds himself admiring kind, gentle people with average competitive attitudes, those who value friendships and love their families.

"But he's no pacifist, Bev," Sam stated, with a giggle. "Sure, he's much more gentle than when he was in Vietnam, but when physical force is needed, he's got all the tools necessary for the job. He avoids physical force as much as possible, not because he has a weakness, but because he's aware of the damage that he can do and is reluctant to do so. A *pacifist*? No way. Before this is over, he'll probably *pass-a-fist* into some noses."

Joe looked at his boots and smiled at Sam's pun.

Captain Lewis focused on Sam and whispered, "I'm sorry, Sam." They hugged each other like long lost sisters, finding comfort in each other's embrace, which surprised the both of them. When they separated, they smiled. Something nice was developing between them—understanding, compassion, friendship.

Sam thought of Bev. Nice woman behind a tough veneer.

Captain Lewis thought of Sam. "Sure had her figured wrong. Her husband too."

Joe thought about pizza and, as if he had magically commanded it, the pizza delivery car arrived.

/-../.-/.-/.-../.../.-../-.--/.-/.-.../.-../.../.-../---/-./././

18

★★★★

"Cowards die many times before their deaths; the
valiant never taste of death but once."

William Shakespeare

ROMAN GAVE OF HIMSELF to his daughter, even many times when he was nearly exhausted from a day of teaching and/or doing yard work. Grace knew it, delighted in it and appreciated it. A child's eyes see much deeper than you can ever imagine and they remember more than you'll ever guess.

While waiting for her parents, Grace walked into the back yard of her home and approached the swings. She looked down as if acknowledging the softness of the lush, green blades of grass, the sponginess of the moist soil. She raised her chin to the sky and saw a small bird diving speedily at a gliding hawk, pestering the much less maneuverable bird until its concentration on a nest with eggs, or on any unsuspecting prey was lost, then hurriedly moved on.

Grace still stared at the orange-yellow orb of the descending sun, its fading warmth still comforting, giving her a sense of security. That feeling reminded her of her parents. She thought of the comforting warmth of their embrace, how secure she felt with them, how much she loved and appreciated them. She was troubled by her dad's lateness. He was a man of routine and habit.

She sat stationary on the swing. She leaned forward, placing her elbows on her thighs, her head staring at the ground and the grass poking up around the edges and outlining her athletic shoes; her long hair fell like a light brown curtain, shielding her face from the low-angled rays of the sun. Tears dripped from the inside corners of her eyes and then from her nose. The tears dripped onto the patch of grass between her shoes, making the verdant blades of grass glisten with the ebbing rays of the setting sun.

She was experiencing the terrible feeling that her dad was in trouble . . . again. She could feel his pain, though she couldn't share the intensity of it as she did during the Adirondack Mountains ordeal. She felt his pain in a way that she found difficult to explain. When he got hurt, working around the house, she felt it physically in the form of a vague, uncomfortable pressure in her chest as if her lungs had overly inflated. When something was bothering him, she felt it mentally as a vibration that resonated with tones of sadness, like the sad effect of many country songs. Somehow she knew, had always known, that she was in tune with her Papa. It was usually a very loving, special and strong connection, like warm, golden links in a priceless chain of emotion. She liked having her dad's attention and when he gave it to her, which was often, she lapped it up like a kitten at a bowl of cream. It was as if his attention nourished her.

She pushed her feet away from her, just enough to fully extend her legs so that she gently swung in a minimal arc. She leaned back, holding tightly to the swing chains, peered at the sky and glided back and forth as she concentrated on her dad.

Some far off war had changed him, she knew that because her mom had told her. Once she heard her papa talking to her mom about the war he was in. Her Papa was whispering his thoughts to her mom, trying not to let her hear. But her hearing was good, like her mom's, and she heard fragments of the conversation. She remembered the tone of her Papa's voice, a whisper, deep with haunting sadness.

Her eyes were sharp, too, and she sometimes noticed her Papa reading a book, or a magazine article, or seeing a movie about that far off war. Then she would see the tears streaming down his cheeks as he sat on his reclining chair, his feet jutting straight out as he reclined.

He would use the book, magazine or the TV guide as a shield to hide his tears, not because he was ashamed to cry, but because he wanted to protect Grace from his own sadness and depression. But Grace felt the sadness, anyway, and saw him wiping the tears away, saw the dark, tear-spots on his shirt.

Papa loved her. She never doubted that. She'd been through that horrible Adirondack kidnapping with him. He'd saved her life, though he had to kill the three kidnappers in the process. She felt his sadness about the killings for months, but that was a minor sadness because she secretly, and with much guilt, was thankful that her dad had killed them. She didn't like thinking of what those men might have done to both of them, had they been captured. Maybe her dad was correct, she thought, there were some people who, like cancer, needed to be killed, though her guilt prevented her from voicing that opinion to anyone, but her father. She used to feel major guilt about her dad having to kill. Killing was supposed to be the worst thing a person could do. But her guilt became minor when she talked to her dad and mom about it being permissible in times of self-defense, when you were sure that your life or someone else's life was in danger.

The sun still spread a soothing, comfortable warmth on her, like warm butter spreading across warm toast. Papa was like that too, she thought. He was kind and warm— though he had his bad moods. He lighted her life with happiness and made her feel so comfortable, so secure, so needed, valued and loved.

But Grace knew— she suspected that her mother did too— that her Papa had a dark side. Not dark as in "unknown," but dark as in "scary." She saw some of his combat skills in the Adirondacks. She knew what he was capable of doing, if threatened or attacked. She had seen his deceptive strength and quickness. She sometimes watched him practice his karate techniques. And she knew what he could do with that scary knife. To Grace, the Marine Ka-Bar combat knife looked like a spear with a seven inch, razor-sharp, black blade and five inches of grooved, grip-tight, leather handle. When she saw it the last time, she had wondered why the first two inches of the top of the blade, from the point of the knife, was also razor sharp. She figured that if she didn't want to hear a scary truth, then she shouldn't ask. She knew that he kept it in the top drawer of his night stand and that knowledge was scary to her, especially when her mom said that she was never to touch it, as if some unknown evil resided within it.

Seen through the innocence of a child's eyes, that knife was a symbol of her Papa's dark side. But that realization wasn't the only conundrum that she had faced when she had concluded that the knife was an instrument of evil. Now she was faced with the question, "Is the user of that knife also an instrument of evil? If he no longer uses the knife, is he reformed? Did he shed the evil, like a snake skin?" Grace wondered, "Maybe it's not evil if it's used to protect lives." That's what her mom had told her. Grace felt relieved at that thought because now she could conclude that her dad was not a bad person, nor was the knife evil any more than a pencil is evil. Plus, her Papa had told her, as her mom did later on, that whether or not something is evil or good is determined by how and why it is used in a particular way. She believed that that explanation was correct. She trusted and believed her mom and papa, though there still exited a lingering discomfort.

What no one else realized— with the possible exception of Joe and Blizzard— was that the Ka-Bar wasn't simply a *knife in Roman's hand*. To Roman, it was an extension of his arm, his wrist, his fingers. Like in a sci-fi movie, Roman's skin, like roots, invisibly grew around the handle. Roman's muscles, tendons and cartilage felt as if they grew directly and securely into the blade handle and that, to Roman, made the blade feel like a natural extension of his arm, exactly like a branch is a natural extension of a tree trunk.

Grace wiped the last tear off the end of her nose, then used the back of her hand to dry her eyes. Now that her eyes were dry, the blades of grass were not blurry. She could distinctly see each green blade. Blades of grass reminded her of Papa because she knew his penchant for referring to a *knife* as a *blade*.

What kind of trouble awaited him now? she wondered. All he wanted was peace and quiet, and to be left alone. But something always came along to break his search for that peace and quiet. She could feel his pain, again. She knew that her papa liked being around kids. Kids were innocent, honest, accepting of him. She knew that her Papa didn't have to strain so hard to conceal his past, as he did with adults. He could relax when he was with kids. He found it much easier to be gentle, patient and less frustrated when he was with kids. He liked being gentle. For him, gentleness was the salve on the cavernous wound of his past.

Children accepted him and genuinely liked him, unlike many prying adults who wanted to overturn the rocks in his past and then condemn him when something hideous or repulsive crawled out. Kids left those rocks in place. They sensed that those rocks shouldn't be overturned. They knew instinctively that they should skip over them as if they were part of a game.

Grace remembered going to school one day with her papa. One of the older boys told her that she was lucky to have him for a dad because, unlike most parents and most teachers, he didn't constantly tell kids what to be, how to think and what to do or not to do. Instead, he would tell kids what they could be if they did this or that or what would happen if they did this or that. The boy went on to tell Grace that her dad, unlike most teachers, joked around with kids, did interesting things and let them have playtime after lunch. He made kids feel good about themselves. The boy also said that Mr. Wolfe made his students feel important.

Grace knew many things, surprising things, that came to her young mind, then shown through her bright eyes as epiphanies. One night Grace saw her mom and papa watching the movie *To Kill A Mockingbird*— one of her papa's favorite movies. Gregory Peck plays the lawyer father, Addicus Finch. His son, Jem, and his daughter, Scout, want to know why it is a sin to kill a mockingbird. "It's a sin," Addicus tells them, "because Mockingbirds do no wrong, they just make beautiful sounds and lovely music that everyone can freely enjoy."

Roman often thought of himself as a more simple, mental version of Addicus Finch, but with many more physical, offensive and defensive, self-defense skills. And when Roman thought of Scout, it was Grace that he pictured. Addicus read to Scout at night, talked honestly and lovingly to her, explained things with infinite patience and treated her like a delicate angel.

Roman, like Addicus Finch, radiated calmness, peacefulness and logic. Like Addicus, Roman had hidden mental resources of strength making him look like a pacifist, but Roman would wage a personal war to protect Grace. Have pity for the person who hurts this object of his love because behind the calm, peaceful eyes glows a hidden and intense ember that would burst forth like a flame-thrower to destroy any evil that would dared attempt to injure her.

Even more profound are the words of Addicus's neighbor, Maude, who tells both Jem and Scout that, "Some men, like your father, are put on this earth to do the dirty work for others; those unpleasant but necessary jobs that some people can't do for themselves." Addicus and Roman, given those circumstances, could be kin, though Addicus used ideas, concepts and the law as his weapons, while Roman used physical attributes, martial arts and a blade. But, perhaps the biggest difference was that Roman did not feel absolutely bound by the law which he sometimes skirted.

Addicus and Roman were both self-assured, courageous and caring. It wasn't a temporary, blustery confidence. It was innate, something adults sometimes missed or misinterpreted, yet children spotted it as if it were an elephant in a bathtub.

A child's eyes can see so much more than they're given credit for. There's insight behind the innocence, there's love behind the occasional tantrums and recalcitrant behaviors and there's understanding and appreciation when explanations are given with patience and sincerity.

/../.-../---/...-/./-/...././-.../---/-/..../

19
★★★★

"Question with boldness even the existence of a God, because, if there be one, he must more approve of the homage of reason, than that of blind-folded fear."

Thomas Jefferson

NAGGING DOUBTS ARE SO much more cruel than destructive lies or hurtful truths. It's the doubts that gnaw at a conscientious person, eating their insides like acid, making them indecisive, confused and mentally off balance. Captain Lewis felt those doubts, like fishhooks dangling all around her, waiting to snag her. She wasn't sure what she was dealing with and wasn't sure that Lieutenant Hawkey, as much as she admired him, was correct about not sending in the SWAT team as long as Roman was still in the picture.

"Our best bet is with the Wolf," Lieutenant Hawkey advised her. It startled her at first because so many times before he and she had agreed that, given a situation where negotiation and compromise dragged on, like the situation that they were currently in, the SWAT team was their best bet for a quick resolution. But she also knew that using the SWAT team always had its severe risks, sometimes casualties, so her nagging doubts continued to gnaw at her. And the kids? It was the kids that made her doubt herself.

She and Hawkey had seen Freddy on the roof with a rifle, though Freddy was trying to conceal himself. Bev had given orders not to fire unless fired upon. She prayed that Freddy wouldn't use the rifle. Through binoculars, it looked as if he'd been crying. His lips were always moving as if he was talking to himself.

"He's an odd one," said Captain Lewis. "He doesn't look like he fits in this situation. Looks scared to death. Whaddaya think?"

"Exactly," Lieutenant Hawkey replied. "Looks definitely scared. No bravado. He's the weak link and I'll bet the Wolf has already been talking to him."

Bev looked sideways at Hawkey. "Yeah? You think Roman can turn him on the others?"

"Not turn him on the others. He's too scared for that, but Wolfe may convince him to do something helpful for us."

Freddy peeked at the parking lot again.

With a hand-held, portable loudspeaker, Captain Lewis again warned Freddy not to attempt to use the weapon because the school was surrounded and he SWAT team personnel had their weapons trained on him, though, at present they were ordered not to fire unless fired upon. Then Captain Lewis calmly advised him to place the weapon on the roof in order to reduce the tension in the minds and trigger-fingers of the troopers.

Freddy, being timid, was frightened easily and set the rifle on the roof where it was out of sight. However, his head could now and then be seen bobbing up and down behind the low brick wall that outlined the perimeter of the roof.

Lt. Hawkey had three snipers positioned on the ground and strategically around the three sides of the school roof— the fourth side was inaccessible due to a high brick wall that was part of a new addition to the school. The snipers were discreetly hidden: one in a tree directly opposite Mr. Wolfe's classroom windows, one behind parked vehicles, another behind a garbage dumpster and one in school. If anything could be seen of them, it was just the barrels of their high powered rifles or, perhaps, a brief reflective flash off the lens of their Leupold Premium scopes.

When Bev and Joe hadn't seen Freddy's head bobbing behind the wall for a while, they were speculating whether or not he was still up there, or if he was staying in one place instead of roaming the rooftop as he had been doing.

Lt. Hawkey heard the footsteps coming up behind him long before Captain Lewis heard them. As a matter of fact Captain Lewis was still focusing on the roof as Lieutenant Hawkey, with residual instincts from Nam, swung around to see who was coming up behind them.

It was the same trooper that had delivered Mrs. Wolfe a couple of hours ago. Lieutenant Hawkey saw the snide grin on the trooper's face, as if this situation were some sort of game to him, as if he'd planned to sneak up on Lieutenant Hawkey just to see how close he could get without detection, to test himself against a man of Lieutenant Hawkey's caliber and reputation. But, most of all, Hawkey saw a smart-ass who should have been washed-out of the academy program. One of these days, thought Joe, that smart-ass will get someone killed. He'd talk to Bev, about the guy, after this situation was resolved.

Lt. Hawkey's motion had alerted Captain Lewis. She turned and saw the grinning rookie trooper. She didn't like his naïve arrogance and made a mental note to talk to him about it. She had also noticed Lieutenant Hawkey's irritation with the young trooper.

Coming up behind the young trooper was a short, portly man whose appearance was very dignified. His serious countenance, his short, well-trimmed, black beard and moustache with splashes of salt that the years had sprinkled on him, plus his black glasses made him appear very intelligent. He wore polished, black shoes, light blue pants and suit coat, with a salmon colored shirt and a dark blue tie with alternating diagonal stripes of blue and salmon colors. He looked like a college professor. His stern expression changed to a friendly grin. He said nothing, waiting for the young trooper to introduce him.

Rookie trooper Casey Jones caught Captain Lewis's attention with his irritating smile, then said, "Sorry to disturb you, again, Captain, but this is Doctor Lash. He's the prison psychiatrist that you wanted to speak to."

Captain Lewis aimed a cold stare at Jones, then turned to Doctor Lash, saying, "Glad to meet you, Dr. Lash. It was good of you to come so quickly."

Captain Lewis shook hands with Dr. Lash. Then she motioned to Hawkey and said. "Dr. Lash, I'd like you to meet Lieutenant Hawkey." Hawkey and the doctor shook hands.

Captain Lewis noticed Trooper Jones still standing next to Dr. Lash instead of returning to his post. She placed an asterisk, for emphasis, next to her mental note about not only talking to Jones, but to reprimand him, too. She said, "Trooper Jones. Your job is done. You may return to your post."

Trooper Jones didn't like the way he was dismissed. He was no one's servant, he thought. He had high hopes of making a name for himself soon, so that he could scoot up the ladder of success and receive those promotions that it normally took many years to earn. He replied, "Yes ma'am," with a tone of insolence, then departed.

Captain Lewis and Lieutenant Hawkey both noted Jones's insolent attitude, but ignored it . . . for now.

Captain Lewis's abrupt dismissal of him was embarrassing. It made Jones feel like a child, just as he had felt all through middle school and high school when kids teased him about his name. They'd always called him "Choo-Choo" because Casey Jones was some asshole who worked on a railroad, long ago, or something like that. He disliked his given name, but hated the Choo-Choo nickname. He never openly mentioned it, but some day he hoped to have the opportunity to even the score with some his tormentors.

Knowing they were in a time bind, Captain Lewis bluntly stated, "So, what can you tell us about these escaped prisoners, Miller and the other one who likes to be called Fang?"

"What I can tell you right off, Captain Lewis, is that these two are serious trouble, especially Otto . . . uh, you know, Fang, who is triple trouble, even in prison. However, I know nothing about Fang's brother Freddy, except that, since he's Fang's brother, he's probably really traumatized, psychologically. And don't be deceived by Miller. He's a particularly vicious person, though he lacks the physique of Fang. They should both probably have been placed in Attica, but the crimes they were caught at and convicted of were much less severe than some other crimes they've probably committed, but haven't been brought to trial for. Lack of evidence, I suppose. The scuttle-butt around the prison is that they have both murdered people. Eventually, they'll end up in Attica where they belong and where the other hard core cases are."

"So you're saying that Otto and Miller are brighter than the impression they give?" asked Captain Lewis.

"No. Not so much Miller. He's been lucky so far. He's pretty straight forward. He's simple, but sadistic and hide it very well, plus, he hasn't needed to get sneaky mean because Otto is his prison protector, as long as Miller consistently gives Otto sexual favors. But don't let him fool you. He's dangerous.

"Otto's another story entirely. I gave them both IQ tests. Miller scored in the low-average range, while Otto scored in the above-average range. The guy's fairly bright and he's mean, vicious actually and can be cunning. Don't let his speech pattern fool you. It's probably genuine, but don't let it make you believe that he's obtuse. He'll be a huge problem, no pun intended. He's like an Arnold Schwarzenegger gone terribly bad.

"Fang possesses incredible strength and is an unusual specimen of a man who's overly aggressive and possesses raw savagery. But what really makes them both so dangerous, in this situation, is that Otto is a pedophile and Miller is a child molester."

Captain Lewis glanced at Lieutenant Hawkey. Both sighed at the atrocious news.

Hawkey took this cue and said, "The better we understand these guys the more informed we are about their attitudes, personalities and foibles, the better we'll be able to understand them and deal with them. So tell us whatever you can about them, Doctor. Anything that'll help increase our chances of dealing with them successfully."

"Well, first of all, do you know the difference between a pedophile and a child molester?" Dr. Lash asked.

"Pretend that we don't and explain everything," responded Captain Lewis.

"OK. Pedophilia, which is a psychological disorder, is a distinct sexual preference for pre-pubescent children. The *Diagnostic and Statistical Manual of Mental Disorders,* commonly referred to as DSM 111-R, which is published by the *American Psychological Association,* supplies this definition of pedophilia: Quote: It's recurrent and intense sexual urges and sexual arousing fantasies of at least six months duration, involving sexual activity with a pre-pubescent child. Unquote. It's specifically referred to in DSM, volume three, 1987. Generally, however, this usually means that the target of the fantasy will typically be less than twelve years old. But notice here, Captain Lewis and Lieutenant Hawkey, that this definition does not require the person to actually engage in a sexual act. Pedophilia, being a psychological disorder, does not require, and usually does not involve, a criminal act because it is not acted upon by the pederast. Most pedophiles keep their desires a secret. A pedophile may never go public or share his fantasies with anyone. He may have control of it and has never actually physically engaged in it. At times pedophiles will marry a woman with children to gain access to her children. Pedophiles can be very determined and single-minded in their efforts to stay close to children. Maintaining access to children at all costs is one of the defining trademarks of pedophilia. Fang, of course is a blatant pedophiliac. He openly brags about the aromatic wonders of hairless pussy . . . ahh . . . excuse my French, and the supreme turn-on that he gets from it. He says a lot of other gross and disgusting stuff, too, but there's no need to go into it. So now—"

"And child molesters?" Lieutenant Lewis interrupted, short on patience.

"I was just about to get to that. So, how are child molesters different than pedophiles? It's the fact that child molesters can have many different motivations for molesting children and their motives, surprisingly, do not have to be sexual in origin. For example, a child molester may not feel normal, loving arousal when engaged in an act of sex with a adolescent. He may simply by sadistic actions, enjoying inflecting pain or humiliation on the child or the child's parents and this sense of power, domination, arouses him. Perhaps the sexual abuse is used to gain leverage, for revenge, or simply to show-off for friends in order to be accepted into a gang, for example. It could be the simple fact that some pedophiles find that orgasm is the only release for the pent up tension, stress, anxieties, or, perhaps it's an uncontrollable obsession."

"So, you're telling us that Fang . . . ah, Otto, is the sadistic pedophile, while Miller is the sadistic child molester? Is that it? There's got to be more to it," Lieutenant Hawkey stated.

"Oh, you bet there's more," Dr. Lash said while looking from one person to the other, as if he was about to spring a surprise on them.

"OK, so what else can you tell us?" Captain Lewis added.

"I'll start with Fang," stated Dr. Lash, in a matter of fact tone of voice. "He likes to abuse little kids, especially young girls between eight and ten years old, usually, and occasionally young boys that same age. Like I said, he doesn't deny his predisposition for pre-pubescent girls and is rather proud of it, as a matter of fact. No real young kids in prison to satisfy him, no girls, so young Miller takes care of his sexual needs. Miller attempts to look and act much younger that he really is in order to please Otto. Miller even shaves off his pubic hair, underarm hair and leg hair to please Otto.

"Otto told me once, in a counseling session, that kids should be seen naked and not heard, that they should be groped and not listened to, that kids were for an adult's sexual pleasure. He has an enormous need for power and control. He's a megalomaniac who never gets challenged by his peers and seldom gets caught by the law. So it's that much easier for him to take advantage of helpless children. If a parent tries to press charges, Otto sends a buddy to do the dirty deed, again, to that child. And another will follow after that, until the parents withdraw the charges. If they still don't withdraw the charges, then the wife and/or husband get raped. I feel like taking a shower every time he leaves my office. It makes me—"

"Jesus, doctor! Are you saying that Otto may not even want sex with adults?" interrupted Captain Lewis.

"Hell no! Not at all. It's just his way of finding sexual satisfaction with the least chance of confrontation. Of course he's not concerned with confrontation, itself. It's the confrontation that spoils his mood. He's got certain ideas of what he wants to do, and how to do them. He doesn't want confrontation to distract him, thus he chooses kids because they are so much easier, plus he enjoys them more than an adult. He gets much more pleasure out of a little girl than from an adult woman or man, so why bother with men or women when kids are powerless? And, before you ask, yes he's a tempered homosexual. He'll fuck men, but rarely for pleasure. Mostly for punishment and humiliation, or to keep someone in line, keep them obedient. He's a dedicated and very vocal misogynist. So dominating children saves him energy and time. You see, for him, it's a lucky two-some. It's not only the most pleasurable for him to force sex with children, it's also much easier. He told me that power and control are all about one thing. He smiled at me mischievously, then told me that— without the bad grammar— 'Power and control are all about ass. You're either the ass fucker and the ass kicker, or you're the ass licker and the ass fucker's sweetheart.' He burst into uproarious laughter and added that he was the ass kicker and the ass fucker, which gave him all the power and control he needs. It was frightening just listening to his laughter. It was as if the savagery in his body had been released into the air and the air became contaminated and foul, like a long dead corpse in a confined room. It was like trying to breathe sewage. It made me glad that two guards with stun-batons were regularly stationed outside my door, looking through the door window in case of trouble."

Captain Lewis asked, "Would you go back to the pedophilia and shine more light in that area, Doctor?"

"Sure," he responded, "pedophiles, are the group of sex offenders most likely to use force to perpetrate their deviate behavior which may take the form of verbal threats or physical restraint, and in most cases leads to the severe physical and emotional injury of the child.

"Also, pedophiles need young girls or boys because they have a strange need for absolute control and to see and feel an immature, supple, unwrinkled, hairless genital area. Fang is constantly informing me that he likes his fruit under-ripe. Pedophiles want immediate obedience and those things come much more readily from children, but, surprisingly, that's not the major issue with them. If possible, they hope to touch virgin, unblemished skin, have innocent, pale legs to spread and many of them demand compliance or they use violence. Some bribe or blackmail for it, still others are logical and manipulative, that is, they can talk the kid into doing what they want. As idiotic as it seems, they want to trick or force the child to be respectful and willing, but that approach has a reduced success rate due to the fact that the kids are suspicious and; therefore, scared. Then force is used instead. Like I said before, pedophiles crave youth, no pubic hair and no breasts, which shows an antipathy for adult women. Something in their past, something traumatic turned them against natural, normal love with mature women.

"Furthermore, many pedophiles feel grossly inadequate in their dealings with peers of the opposite sex and feel an intense fear of rejection and humiliation. These inadequate and emotionally immature individuals focus their attention on children as the safest means of meeting their sexual needs and avoiding failure and self-concept devaluation. Pedophiles are usually men who are unable to establish normal interpersonal relationships with people of their own age, or to find a satisfying role in their community, due to psychopathic behaviors, so they turn their hostility, aggressive and sexual gratification needs towards children who are much less threatening to a pedophile's ultra-fragile ego and their own physical strength. Think about it. Even a weakly adult can overpower a pre-pubescent child. Naturally they don't want to take a chance that their victim is stronger than they are, so children make an ideal target for them. But there are all sorts of variations on this theme. Each pedophile is a little different, and some are often a lot different than the classic cases that I've just presented to you.

"As a matter of fact, Otto is not a classic case. He always seems to be changing form, like an amoeba. He's cunning, confusing, inconsistent and supremely arrogant. He taunts me constantly during our psychology sessions, saying that half of him wants to confuse me by being inconsistent and the other half of him wants to be partially honest and dishonest because he gets so much pleasure out of its frustrating effects on me. You can't figure him out because of his inconsistencies, lies and mind games. You never know when you've heard the truth from him. Of course, that's exactly the way he wants it. He toys with people because that's another way that he can demonstrate his power and control over them.

"So, it's extremely rare to be able to help someone like him or Miller. To help someone, they have to want help, they have to want to change. Otto doesn't want help, doesn't want to change. I certainly couldn't force him to cooperate. People normally come to me because they want to be helped, but, unfortunately, he was forced to come to me, so our sessions were like a poker game where he held all the aces. To him I was just the Joker. The threat of guards or isolation or delayed parole or even rejected parole didn't phase him at all. You couldn't really threaten him with anything to make him cooperate. He's hard to the core. I always hate to admit this, but he's unsalvageable.

"In further sessions, Otto continued with his egotistical monologues and I couldn't get a word in edge-wise. I couldn't stop him. He kept talking rapidly, using words like a boxer uses his fists. Finally, as I was about to call the guards, he settled down. His face and demeanor grew calm, so I relaxed, too. I didn't realize until after he left the session that he had controlled nearly the whole session and during the parts he didn't control, he had me so distracted and frustrated that I couldn't get back to trying to help him. It's hard to get me frustrated, but, like I said, he's a hard man. He was staunchly incorrigible. We had more sessions with the same results, so I dropped him from my patient list.

"During our final session I told him that he wouldn't be coming any more. I got up from my desk to indicate that the session was over and Otto smiled as he rose from his chair. He towered over me and said we could have had more fun if I had been a good therapist. I asked him what a good therapist would do. He cupped his hand over his crotch and said it would be easy to figure out if I looked at the word 'therapist' carefully."

"The rapist," Captain Lewis and Lieutenant Hawkey blurted in unison.

"Exactly. Does that help?" asked the doctor.

"Was he a Satanist, Doctor?" inquired Captain Lewis.

"No. He said he was an atheist, so Satan couldn't exist either. No God also meant no Satan to him. I never asked him to explain it. Probably I should've, but I was simply tired of him at the time and wanted him out of my office. He's irritating in the extreme."

Captain Lewis and Lieutenant shook their heads. Both were thinking the same thing: How do we deal with a guy like this? Fang was violent, inconsistent, immoral, sadistic, arrogant and the fucker was also intelligent in the sense that he thought about things logically and there, Bev thought, is the clue to why he hasn't been caught at the most serious crimes he's committed.

"What about Miller?" asked Captain Lewis, almost not wanting to know.

"Another form of psychopathology," said Dr. Lash, instantly, "but different from classic cases in some ways. He demonstrates a clear-cut case of father rejection. More truthfully, he has an intense hatred and rage for his father. He's still a teenager and very much a dangerous delinquent. You see," continued Dr. Lash as he cleaned underneath one fingernail with another fingernail, "delinquent boys almost always feel that they have been rejected by their fathers. Normally a child wants to behave in ways that meet with parental approval, especially boys with their fathers. Of course, this is the basis for a child's beginnings at socialization. But if the boy is actually rejected or he just feels rejected or is treated inconsistently, which causes confusion and mental disillusionment, then he has little need to behave in approved ways since there are no clearly defined guidelines for controlling and modeling his behaviors. So, what does he do? He makes his own guidelines or follows the guidelines of a friend, a gang or of someone else who gives him attention.

"In other words he does what he wants, or he does what his peers say to do. Unfortunately the peers he associated with were also neglected, violent, aggressive, immoral types, so they served as his models for developing adult behaviors.

"And the problem with father rejection," said Dr. Lash, "is exacerbated by the fact that in this type of pathogenic family set-up, the father is usually physically and emotionally abusive with his disciplinary methods, thus increasing the hostility already felt by the boy toward his father, which, of course, increases, and then solidifies his rejection of his father. The tragic result is a boy, and later a young man, who is extremely hostile, defiant, inadequately socialized, lacks normal internal behavioral controls and tends to be overly aggressive, without compassion and, at times, terribly violent.

"Miller's homosexual tendencies may also be attributed to the fact that he can seek revenge on a non-threatening male symbol of his father. So if he has anal intercourse with a young boy, he may deliberately make it a painful experience for the boy, thus, symbolically hurting his father and satisfying his need to seek revenge on him. However, Miller, like Fang, has a duality about him. Miller is not truly consistent in this respect because he can enjoy anal and oral sex. He doesn't always use it as a symbolic father punishment. He can enjoy it personally. He enjoys pleasing those people whom he respects or likes and takes pride in being able to expertly bring them to climax. In so doing he has power and control over them which doubles his pleasure. Unlike Otto, however, Miller also desires acceptance through these sexual acts.

"But, you know, both have many demon-driven memories of certain people in their pasts on whom they need to seek revenge, symbolically or up close and personal, especially Otto who likes to mentally torment, then physically punish his enemies, mano-a-mano. They can both be extremely abusive, both physically and sexually to both sexes, to varying age groups, but especially pre-teen children.

"However, for pure physical rage toward anyone that crosses him, Otto's the most punitive and dangerous subject I've ever come across. His psychopathic personality is like a maze full of traps and inconsistencies, horrible experiences, terrorizing memories, deviate behaviors and terrible emotional and physical pain. The way his warped mind works is that, since he can feel all that pain, then it's only fair that he should share it with other people. It's pseudo-pleasure derived from pain for the psychopath, but agony for his victims."

Doctor Lash paused, took a deep breath and smiled, though the smile never reached his eyes. Then he said, "I think that's about all I can tell you. Oh, almost forgot." Doctor Lash handed a packet of papers to Captain Lewis. "This is information about that teacher."

Dr. Lash handed a large, but thin manila envelope to Captain Lewis.

"Where'd you get this," she asked, curiously, "especially so damn fast?"

"It sure as hell wasn't easy, Captain, but between my status as a psychiatrist and having a personal friend who works there, plus a conference call that your commanding officer agreed to make, we had the combined influence to have Mr. Wolfe's school and military records faxed to your commander. I was coming here, anyway, so I was asked to pick up the records from your commander and bring them to you."

"OK, but one more question, Doctor. Do you think they would use extreme violence to get themselves out of this situation? In other words, if you had to rate the chances of them using violence to get out of this situation, even though we have them surrounded, how would you rate it? Let's say on a scale of one-to-ten, with one, meaning no violence and ten meaning extreme violence," added Captain Lewis.

Doctor Lash's face turned grim as he replied, "Ten for Otto, Captain, and perhaps seven for Miller. I can't speculate on the other fellow. I don't envy you, Captain."

"Thanks, Doctor," Captain Lewis replied.

Doctor Lash said, "You know that fellow that brought me to you? That young trooper? Something's not right with him. You should check him out. Anyway, good-bye and good luck to both of you." He shook hands with Captain Lewis and Lieutenant Hawkey, then turned and departed briskly.

Captain Lewis and Lieutenant Hawkey watched their harbinger of bad news as he walked away, hoping that he was wrong about Fang and Miller, as well as Trooper Jones. Captain Lewis and Lieutenant Hawkey were disturbed because their worst fears had just been corroborated by a professional.

*   *   *   *   *   *   *

Bev and Joe checked with their men, asked them some questions, asked them to give reports, checked for messages, then returned to each other, with Bev immediately opening the folder. They both started reading.

HIGH SCHOOL RECORD SUMMARY

C O N F I D E N T I A L

A. STUDENT: Roman Wolfe

B. SCHOOL: Maine-Endwell Sr. High School, Endwell, New York.

1. Date of graduation: June, 1964

2. Graduated in the top third of a class of 302 students.

3. Grades much higher than the peer group he associated with. Guidance Counselor reports that student did not apply himself to demonstrate his full potential. (Guidance Counselor's note: Students

with very good grades were often ostracized; therefore, being an underachiever is advantageous to some students).

4. <u>Tenth grade</u>: Grades in geometry average, yet on N.Y.S. Regents exam he outscored everyone in all of the school's geometry classes. The following year, in algebra, he finished third in all algebra classes.

C. Student initially appears to be an <u>underachiever</u> (performs at a level lower than expected) during most of the school year, then becomes an over-achiever (performs at a level higher than expected) on his end-of-year exams. <u>Probable causes</u>: Wanting to fit in with his close friends or a poor self-concept or being unmotivated, or a combination of some of these factors, despite an IQ of 146.

D. <u>Academic strengths</u>, in descending order: History, English, Literature and Science.

E. <u>Academic Weaknesses</u>: Math (difficulty with calculus and trigonometry (Did not apply himself, or did not understand material? Probably both). English grammar: poor at recognizing the more complex parts of speech, thus difficulty with diagramming sentences, etc.

F. <u>Subject desires a college education</u>, but outlook not good for a young man, who appears to have fluctuating motivation, whose behavior has been problematic, whose mother only reached 4th grade, whose father only reached 6th grade, and whose family financial resources are very limited.

1. <u>Solution to above college acceptance problem</u>? Student intends to join the U. S. Navy for the expressed purpose of sacrificing four years of his life to gain four years of paid college tuition using the G.I. Bill. (<u>NOTE</u>: Subject verbalizes great determination, motivation and maturity, plus the ability to sacrifice in the present to gain future rewards.)

G. Idiosyncrasies: Avoids seriousness with humor (class clown). Has fascination with wolves. Says he dreams about a white wolf.

H. Logical thinker, but will often fight much bigger opponents even if the likelihood of winning is negligible and, thus, illogical.

1. Despite being logical, he is often careless, reckless and daring. Told Counselor that he doesn't care if he wins or loses, as long as he damages his opponent enough to make him think twice before confronting him again (guidance counseling was ineffective with correcting this mind-set of determined counter-aggression. Student may end up being expelled if violence continues). NOTE: Student was already spared expulsion, mostly due to the fact that the current high school principal was his biology and chemistry teacher, who saw something in the student that he liked. NOTE: Principal's comment: "Student doesn't start trouble, but gets blamed for defending himself and others. He will not retreat from this position and I sympathize with him in spite of school policy. He's a better person than all of you think he is. The future, I'm sure, will verify this." (Mr. Phillips, the principal, was speaking to the school superintendent and the Board of Education.)

I. Student likes sports. Played H.S. soccer (goalie), football (split-end), baseball (center field, switch hitter), and track (mile relay team, high jump). Excelled at track and soccer; average in other sports.

J. Jobs: Student worked after school, as a janitor and a "go-fer" at a Japanese karate dojo (school), where he used his salary to pay for his karate training. He also worked, on weekends, in a restaurant as a bus boy and dishwasher.

K. Accomplishments: Awarded a New York State Regents diploma and earned a first degree, black belt at the end of his senior year. (NOTE: He didn't get into a fight, on school property, during his entire senior year.)

Captain Lewis flipped through the pages to read Roman's military record.

U. S. MARINE CORP.
RECORD SUMMARY

SECRET

1. <u>Originally enlisted in the U.S. Navy in August of 1964.</u> Subject entered boot camp at the Great Lakes Naval Training Center, Lake Michigan.

(a). Rebelled against "asinine" (his word) jobs such as hanging-up washed clothes with shoestring, size cords, that had to be tied with a special knot, instead of using clothes pins.

(b). As retribution and as a joke, "rumors" were that he got up late one night and squirted piles of shaving cream on both sides of the sleeping dormitory leader's pillow so that when his head moved, it had to go into the shaving cream. Apparently, cream was also spread on the part of the sheet that covered the dorm leader's crotch area so that in the morning a stain appeared that made the dried shaving cream look like dried semen, as if the dorm leader had been masturbating or had a wet-dream. No one would come forward as a witness so no official charges could be made; therefore, no official disciplinary action could be taken.

(c). Dorm leader unofficially assigned subject extra marching and extra jobs: kitchen duty, dormitory clean-up duty and physical exercise. <u>Results</u>: It did not stop subject from playing practical jokes, thus, the other recruits in the dorm liked and protected him by not supporting the dorm leader's future accusations. (<u>NOTE</u>: the above information is supposition, not fact based, since no one would be an eye-witness, nor would anyone give information. The above example is used to show this recruit's persistence, determination and leadership skills, in spite of the minor, negative nature of some of his acts.

(d). When questioned by a Navy officer, this recruit was reported to have said, "Sir, humor is a morale booster for me and my classmates. Whoever is playing the practical jokes, therefore, is actually helping us by lifting our morale and patriotism, which is increasing our motivation to perform better here at boot camp. "NOTE: When privately questioned by his superior, this officer stated that he agreed with this unusual recruit and had to quickly walk away from him so the recruit could not see him laughing.

2. <u>Excelled in all physical activities and exercises.</u>

   (a). Vision: 20/20

   (b). Height: 6'2"

   (c). Weight: 185 lbs.

   (d). Basic hand-to-hand combat skills: Excellent.

   (e). One mile run: 4 min., 47 sec. (best in his class).

   (f). <u>Target range</u>: skills are beyond marksman and sharp-shooter designations with rifle (<u>Note</u>: possible sniper ability) and with Colt .45, model 1911 handgun, this recruit earned an expert classification. (<u>Note</u>: Subject was a member of a rifle and pistol league prior to his Naval enlistment). <u>ATTENTION</u>: Recruit possesses unusually good skills in self-defense and with the rifle and pistol. <u>Marines</u> should be alerted for possible transfer.

3. <u>On completion of Navy boot camp</u>, and recognizing his unusual skills, this recruit was approached and interviewed by Navy Master Chief Robert "Bud" McDermott and Marine Master Gunnery

Sergeant Gustov "Gus" Kovalik with reference to his voluntarily transferring from the Navy to the Marine Corp.

(a). Subject was very interested in transferring to the Marines, but had one condition. He wanted four years of the G.I. Bill for two years of his Marine Corp enlistment. Unusual request was approved.

(b). Subject jumped at the offer, saying, "I should have done that in the first place, but I wanted to travel to see the world." Then recruit immediately agreed to transfer to the Marine Corp, saying that he now sees that it would be a better fit for him. Master Gunnery Sergeant Kovalik had recruit pack his belongings. Reportedly, on his way out of the dorm, this recruit, in front of everyone, sprayed a whole can of shaving cream under the top sheet of the dorm leader's bed (<u>NOTE</u>: Rumor has it that, later that day, Sergeant Kovalik, with friends, could not stop themselves from laughing at the story).

(c). Subject was immediately transferred to Beaufort, South Carolina for Parris Island, the Marine boot camp training facility.

4. <u>Parris Island</u>:

(a). Recruit excelled in all areas of training, except for discipline. Had minor discipline aberrations (mostly pranks and practical jokes, laughing at officers whom he thought had oversized egos and minimal abilities).

(b). This recruit, as a prank, did not inform his instructors of his karate knowledge until he bested his training Master Sergeant at unarmed hand-to-hand combat. He apologized to the Master Sergeant, and the apology was accepted. Later, the other two instructors helped the Master Sergeant to teach this recruit a lesson by pummeling him with fists, but not badly hurting him. The class (except for Wolfe) had been ordered to plug their ears and to turn their backs to the practice area, so they could not be witnesses. Recruit did not press charges, but reportedly said, "Damn! Guess I deserved that," then laughed as he wiped his bloody nose and held onto his bruised ribs. <u>Recruit's reasoning</u>? He said he thought that taking the Sarge to the ground would be humorous. <u>Results</u>? A punitive, five mile run with an eighty pound backpack. No pranks occurred for a week.

(c). Awarded expert level badge with rifle and pistol, but weapon of choice is a Ka-Bar, Marine combat knife (has unusual fascination with edged weapons).

(d). Excels at stealth nighttime combat. (<u>NOTE</u>: The top ten Marines at boot camp were tested in all areas of E and E (escape and evade). To pass the test they had to remain undetected, in a forest, for 24 hours. They were given a six hour head start). Recruit, Wolfe was the only one to pass the test. How? He ingeniously made a camouflage Ghillie Suit out of weeds, brush, twigs, leaves, mud and dirt. Knowledgeable Marine trackers walked within ten feet of him, three times, and did not spot him. (<u>NOTE</u>: The test is usually based upon "hours," i.e. who lasts the longest without being detected. It's extremely rare for a recruit to remain undetected for 24 hours. Recruit learned about Ghillie Suit because of his interest in survivalist techniques.

5. <u>Idiosyncrasies</u>:

(a). Rejected suggestion to join special forces. Reason unknown.

(b). Rejected Officer Training School. Reason unknown.

(c). Minor recalcitrant behaviors and unpredictable.

(d). Sometimes a hair-trigger temper, though usually tightly controlled.

(e). Has obsession with protecting recruits from bullies (bullies tend to make him shed his tightly controlled temper). Appears to be a residual behavior from High School. Obsessively talks about wolves, for no apparent reason. He wants to know what and how they think.

6. <u>Weaknesses</u>:

(a). Overly compassionate for a war-time soldier. Makes for undesired vulnerability.

(b). Too willing to take unnecessary risks; careless, reckless, sometimes.

(c). Overconfident. Puts himself and friends at risk.

(d). Thinks rationally about orders. Reviews them, criticizes them instead of following them immediately. Not your typical sequacious, pliable soldier. (<u>NOTE</u>: Most officers will not feel comfortable with him.

7. <u>Strengths</u>:

(a). Extremely patriotic. Usually acts as a good role model for others; a morale booster for other recruits.

(b). Extreme loyalty to members of his squad, platoon, etc. Willing to help them with their military training deficiencies.

(c). Non-linear thinker. Thinks "outside the box" to come up with practical, logical, but unusual and creative ideas and solutions to problems. (<u>NOTE</u>: Troops will form a firm attachment to him, but the typical officer will not). (<u>RECOMMENDATION</u>: Recruit should be placed with a young, but competent officer who is not militarily over-bearing and is willing to sincerely listen to conflicting opinions. That officer should not possess a rigid, "gung-ho" temperament.

(d). Reliable and responsible, but sometimes recalcitrant.

8. Psychiatric Evaluation:

(a). No Axis 1 or Axis 2 disorders.

(b). Admits to bouts of depression (controlled by meds). Without meds some minor anti-social behavior is demonstrated.

(c). Susceptible to father/mother role model influences, due to lack of father/mother role models in youth.

(d). At end of Vietnam tour of duty, subject was hostile to the suggestion of re-enlisting in the Marine Corp., even though rewards such as going to officer training school, promotions and pay raises (when he became an officer) were offered. Reason given? Family obligations and college ambitions.

(e). Bouts of insecurity (though well concealed), presumably due to traumatic childhood memories and/or other unknown events.

(f). Strong, sometimes rigid adherence to personal values, ethics, etc.

(g). Facial and verbal expressions indicate intense control over emotions and actions. Very reserved, almost stoic, at times, but no abnormal lack of appropriate emotions and has a clear knowledge of right and wrong.

(h). School records indicate some adolescent and teenage behavior problems, especially frequent fighting with peers and getting into trouble with teachers due to practical jokes and class clown behaviors.

9. Personal:

(a). Occasionally sleep-disturbed (nightmares) due to Vietnam experiences. Some negative emotions. Rarely did it interfere with duties or performance.

(b). No history of drug usage or alcohol abuse.

(c). Childhood family atmosphere unstable. Father and mother divorced. Subject and older sister sent to Catholic orphanage, at young ages, in Binghamton, New York. Then they were separated and each went to live with a separate aunt.

(d). Mother remarried and relocated to Florida. Subject rarely heard from her or saw her from age 10 to age 20. Subject feels that mother is a stranger. Subject embarrassed by mother's illiteracy.

(e). Subject's father never remarried. Father is an alcoholic, but took subject and his sister from their aunts to live with him in apartment above a bar. Subject does not have a normal relationship with father, or mother.

(f). About age 8 or 9, subject's sister marries. Sister and brother-in-law become subject's surrogate mother and father so he would not have to live with his alcoholic father, or be made a ward of the state (foster homes).

(g). Insecurities grew large when sister (as a behavior control method) threatened to send subject back to Catholic orphanage (where the nuns punished him by hitting him with a teacher's pointer-stick if he did not follow their strict rules and inflexible, illogical religious dogmas. Subject reports that some nuns would often wait until he was done taking a bath, and naked, to apply their pointer-stick punishment).

10. <u>Religion</u>: Subject says he is a "knowledgeable atheist" (as compared to a "reactionary atheist" who becomes an atheist simply out of some sort of rebellion or trauma and is not knowledgeable concerning the logical and philosophical reasons for being an atheist).

11. <u>Family Relationships</u>:

(a) Relationship with three (3) nephews and one (1) niece, his sister's children, is excellent. Talks proudly about them and often brags about their personalities and accomplishments. Subject feels as if he is their older brother.

12. <u>Vietnam Veteran. Discharge Status: (DD-214) Honorable</u>.

(a). Vietnam Duties and special assignments: TOP SECRET (For further information, contact with the Department of Defense National Security Office, Washington, D.C., is required).

/---/..-./-.--/---/..-/...-/./.-./-.--/--/..-/-.-./..../

20
★★★★

"You can't shake hands with a clenched fist."

Indira Gandhi

WHEREAS FANG WAS GUILTY of many crimes but felt no guilt, Roman wasn't legally guilty of any, but felt much guilt. Roman felt guilty about things he had done in Nam, mostly. But now he was feeling guilt that rose from his own recognition that he and Fang shared something: their ability to master violence and to dole out pain, injury and death. Roman abhorred the comparison and instantly wished he hadn't thought of it. But it remained with him, nagging at him, nibbling at him like a cautious fish at bait. As always, he dealt with it in a half successful manner, trying to maintain his own morality despite the savagery that was an intimate part of him. Every day he fought diligently to control this veiled savagery, while at the same time seeing, hearing and reading about similar savagery that was spreading throughout his own country, his own state and town.

But guilt has a way of obliterating the obvious and while there were some similarities between Roman and Fang, the differences between them were as great as the Grand Canyon is wide. But Roman's guilt blinded him to these differences. Perhaps that's how moral people punish themselves: they minimize the myriad number of good things they've done and exaggerate the number of bad things they've done. Thankfully, Roman knew that there was hope. And with each passing year his guilt lessened and the attrition was welcomed. Roman kept his more savage, uncivilized abilities locked away, securely, in the remote Pandora's Box that was buried deeply in his mind.

Fang, in contrast to Roman, increased his savagery; he needed it and looked for ways to release it. He would never admit it, but it was due to a misguided sense of his own masculinity and because it made him feel part of, or in control of, his violence oriented peer group. Fang willingly ruled his life with a *might is right* philosophy.

But Roman's guilt has, in many ways, made him a better person, more conscientious and concerned about how other people are treated, more sympathetic to their pains and problems. Unfortunately, some of his attitudes and actions forced him to remain directionless, adrift in a rough immoral sea, struggling not to capsize.

By contrast, Fang had long ago sunk to the depths of that, frigid, turbulent and depraved sea. He sank in this foul sea as if it were in his nature to instantly seek out the darkness in his environment, to establish his evil dominance in that darkness, to rule men's lives in a place where crime is a badge of courage, where the violent use of strength makes you a celebrity and where murder catapults you to a hero's status.

*   *   *   *   *   *   *

As the sun dove toward the horizon, the weary students whimpered from hunger pains. Some were holding or rubbing their stomachs, but, fearing Fang and Miller, none of them dared to complain. Some couldn't help emitting a few moans and groans of discomfort. Mr. Wolfe did his best to distract them.

Roman heard a ringing noise and looked at his watch, as if his watch had an alarm; it didn't. He noticed that the time was just past six a clock. Then, when the ringing noise repeated itself, he realized that the sound was coming from the wall phone.

Fang approached the phone, then roughly grabbed it off its cradle.

"Yeah!" Fang barked as he put the phone to his sneering mouth.

"Fang," Captain Lewis said, recognizing his canine growl, "the pizzas and soda for your dinners are here. There's plenty for everybody. May we send them up?"

Before Fang could reply, he heard Freddy's prearranged knock on the locked door, three hard and two soft knocks. Fang covered the mouthpiece of the phone, by pressing it against his stomach, so Captain Lewis couldn't hear, then asked who was at the door— in case Freddy was somehow captured and had given-up their prearranged signal. The reply was, "It's me. Freddy."

Fang said, into the phone. "Hold on a minute." He, again, pressed the mouthpiece on his stomach, then pushed the children away from the front of the door and opened it carefully, peering at Freddy, then checking the hallway.

Freddy entered the room, saying, "I need to talk ta you. It's important."

The urgency in his brother's voice nearly made Fang laugh. The seriousness made Freddy sound as if he knew what he was doing and Fang knew that that wasn't possible. Fang's brow wrinkled; a frown of contempt for Freddy. Fang shot a middle finger at Freddy before saying, "Dammit Freddy. Not now. Are food's comin'."

Freddy started to interrupt him, but Fang held up his left hand like a policeman halting traffic and Freddy knew it was no use saying anything else. OK. Have it your way, Freddy thought.

Freddy sulked, then said, "Depart from evil and do good; seek peace and pursue it. Psalms 34:14."

Fang said, "Bullshit," to Freddy, then thought, Stupid shithead's been sniffin' glue.

Freddy walked to the corner, the one farthest away from everyone and bowed his head. His eyes filled with tears in spite of his efforts to hold back. He stared at his brother, then mumbled: "The words of his mouth were smoother than butter, but war was in his heart; his words were smoother than oil, yet were as drawn swords. Psalm . . . Shit. I can't remember the chapter and verse numbers. Doesn't matter any more. We'll die here."

Fang turned his attention back to the phone. "Yeah, Sweetheart," Fang said, mockingly, to Captain Lewis, "I'm back. So yuh have some food fur us, huh? Well, how yuh plan on gettin' it up 'ere so none a these nice, young brats gets hurt?"

Captain Lewis ignored the "Sweetheart" taunt and stated, "We've got a civilian lady, not a cop, who will bring it to your door. She's not, I repeat, not a cop. And she's unarmed. Besides the pizza and drinks, she'll be carrying a walkie-talkie which she'll give to you so you can communicate with us without the phone. Don't mistake it for a weapon, please. No harm should come to her, Fang. Is that clear?"

"Oh, well, a course I unnerstand, Sweetheart. Whatever yuh say," uttered Fang in a belittling and defiant tone of voice.

Lt. Hawkey cringed at the sound of the second "Sweetheart."

Fang knew and enjoyed the anger level that he thought must be building within the Captain. He supposed that she was one of those modern broads that hated sexism. He could imagine her fighting for self-control and being only partly successful.

"Do you need anything else?" said Captain Lewis, keeping her voice calm.

"Just a helicopter, Honey," answered Fang. "I want a damn helicopter. Yuh know, a chopper, a whirlybird. Get one out 'ere quick, Captain, so's I don't have ta show yuh how it looks ta see a kid flying outta a window."

Fang's voice was not mockingly playful any more. It was deadly serious and impatient. A terrible silence spread out from both phones.

"I can't do that, Fang. It's strictly against state police policy. Besides that, our Rochester based State Police helicopter took a VIP to Albany this morning and won't be back for a couple of days," Captain Lewis lied, hoping it was convincing.

Fang pressed his lips into the phone, his teeth scraping the plastic mouthpiece, then yelled, "Don't fuck with me, bitch! Yuh get a helicopter, any helicopter, an' yuh do it quick or I start throwin' kids outta the window, one at a time. You think I'm stupid? Fuckin' Rochester airport is only twenty-five mile away. Airports have helicopters, private an' commercial. So no more bullshit. Now, I hope I made myself perfectly clear, little lady. Don't waste any more time. Jus' get it done."

Lt. Hawkey was listening to the conversation. He remained silent, knowing he should only talk if the Captain signaled him to do so. She was an excellent leader and he liked working with her— though his wife had once expressed reservations about him working with such an attractive, single woman.

"I'll get you a helicopter, Fang," said Captain Lewis. The no frills directness of that statement startled Fang, as well as Lieutenant Hawkey.

After a momentary pause, Fang replied, "Honey, that's good. Do it quick."

"Not so fast, Fang. We make a deal and I'll get the helicopter for you. I don't just hand it over 'cause you ordered me to. You let half those kids go when the pizza is delivered and I'll have a helicopter here in an hour or two after their release. No kids, no helicopter, Fang. You help me and I help you. That's the way it always works and that's a damn good deal, mister. What do you say?"

Fang looked at the children. Some of them were always whining, crying, sniffling and moaning. It irritated him. He knew that soon there would be more teary eyes, whining voices, pathetic moaning and sniffling noses. He hated that, hated tears, hated kids, hated crybabies no matter what their age. They were all weaklings and he found it thoroughly disgusting. But the bitch Captain didn't know that, he thought. He could get rid of half these snot-nosed brats and get the helicopter all in one stroke, though it would be a terrible waste to have them and not to fondle some of them.

"Deal," Fang shouted into the phone. "Yuh have that servant bitch a yurs deliver the pizza. Then I let a dozen a these brats go, an' yuh get me a helicopter. An' if it don't work out that way, some a these brats are gonna wish they had wings."

"Sure, Fang. I understand. Would you like the pizza now or do you prefer to keep up this cute repartee and impress me some more?"

"Re-par-tay?"— Fang exaggerated the syllables. "Wow! A butch bitch with an awesome vo-cab-u-lary. Yuh sure do impress me." Then, sardonically, Fang stated, "Oh, yah, massa. I do obeys yuh every word. Please massa, don' whip me. I does always worship at yoo feet." Between bouts of laughter, Fang shouted, "Sen' the crap up an' remember, the brats'll be eatin' it first, so there better not be anything in it that shouldn't be in it. Better not be no trick with that walkie-talkie either."

"The pizza's clean, so's the walkie-talkie," replied Captain Lewis— they were.

"So send the Dago shit up 'ere," said Fang, replacing the phone in its cradle.

Freddy approached Fang and spoke so softly that no one else could hear him. Fang listened intently, then smiled at Freddy and patted him on the back with obvious delight. Freddy couldn't remember how many years it had been since he'd seen Fang smile at him or had given him a brotherly pat on the back.

Fang told Freddy to wait in the classroom for a few more minutes so he could get some pizza before he returned to the roof. The kids who were standing by the door were ordered to join the other children who were sitting by the row of windows.

Fang then selected seven of the fourteen boys and five of the ten girls— the worst whiners— and told them to wait by the door with Freddy. Alyson Boyd was not one of the girls selected to leave, nor was Steven Blake. Fang motioned to Miller to follow him into the hallway where they'd meet the pizza lady.

$$* \quad * \quad * \quad * \quad * \quad * \quad *$$

Roman seized this opportunity to leave his chair and hurriedly walk to Freddy. As Roman approached, Freddy raised the barrel of the AK-47 so it pointed at Roman's belly. The rifle was shaking in Freddy's nervous hands

"Don't come any closer . . . I don't want to shoot anyone," Freddy blurted.

Roman stopped a few feet away from Freddy, not wanting to make him more nervous than he already was. "Just want to talk to you, Freddy," Roman said calmly.

Freddy was unconvinced and anxiously said, "Yuh best go to your chair and sit down or I'll have to shoot. I don't want to have to hurt no one, but Otto will kill me if you take this rifle," he said hesitantly, while backing away a step and wishing he hadn't been left alone. He felt for the safety switch on the rifle, but then realized, even if he found it, he couldn't tell if it was on or off.

Roman saw Freddy swipe at the beads of perspiration that were rapidly forming on his brow, some of those beads acting like prisms, flashing rainbow colors. A nervous man with a gun was a serious danger to everyone, so Roman halted, casually taking a step backward, but keeping eye contact with Freddy. Freddy's body relaxed.

"Freddy, I won't hurt you. I won't try anything, I promise. I just want to talk, please. It could save your life, our lives. Just give me a couple minutes."

Freddy thought of his young life and how little he'd enjoyed it. But he certainly didn't wish to die. He felt himself wanting to grab onto Roman's words like a drowning man grabs for a life-preserver. He wanted to live, but he knew that this was a bad situation that was getting worse and he was scared. He gradually lowered the rifle so it aimed at the floor, then looked at Roman with eyes that begged for help.

"You're going to get hurt, maybe die," Roman whispered. "You don't want to be here. I can see that. Your brother is using you. He doesn't like you as a good brother should. I can see the contempt he has for you. Miller's just as bad. He doesn't give a crap about you either. You have to escape. Get out of here and turn yourself in. Somebody's going to get hurt or killed and, if it's any of these kids, you'll pay the penalty just like the one who pulls the trigger or the one who throws someone out a window. Fang's crazy and desperate. Your only hope is to get away from him the first chance you get. Don't go back on the roof. Go downstairs and surrender."

Freddy froze. Being scared, nervous, anxious was too stressful for him. His mind and body were starting to shut down, but he was still listening to Roman.

"If Fang or Charlie shoots me or harms a child in any way, then you'll be just as guilty as they are, but not if you get out now. Otto's losing control fast. Can't you see that? He's getting frustrated, angry, desperate. When he panics, he'll do something stupid and Charlie will follow right along with him. Then you'll be an accessory to an even more serious crime. If you're an accessory to a felony, you get treated the same as the person who actually performs the crime. You understand what I'm saying? Your brother's not going to get you out of this. You can see that, right? This place is surrounded and the cops aren't simply going to hand over a helicopter without a good plan to capture or kill all of you. Listen to reason, Freddy. You profess to be a *born-again* Christian. so shun your old ways and turn to God. Do what you've been telling Fang to do. Ask yourself, Is this something God would approve of? Get out of this while you can."

Freddy looked helpless. "The cop'll shoot me anyway. I never asked for this. I try to lead a better life now. Preacher Adams is helping me. He's gonna get me a job an' help me find a place ta live. I don't want no part of this. It wasn't supposed ta happen like this. I'm afraid of my own brother and Miller. I don't wanna go back on the roof. I'm scared up there . . . and not just of the cops. There's somethin' up there. Somethin' spooky white, yuh know? Like a ghost or somethin'. I felt it brush against my leg, then I felt like I gotta bee sting, but when I looked, it wasn't no bee sting. Somethin' bit me. Look."

Freddy pulled up his left pant leg to show his calf. "Looks like a dog bite, though it ain't deep. Hardly broke the skin."

"Sure looks like dog bite marks, Freddy. Maybe it's a warning or an omen. Something's trying to tell you to get away."

"If it's a dog, then it must be a damn ghost dog. I'm tellin' yuh that it's haunted up there," Freddy said, then tried to nervously laugh away his confusion and fear. Freddy asked, "You a man of God, mister?"

"No, Freddy, I'm not. If there was a God, Freddy, he'd have to be the greatest underachiever in the entire history of the universe. He'd have to be extremely shameful and embarrassed about the tremendously poor job he did with the creation of Mankind. But let's assume there is a God and that you're serious about all those Biblical Psalms and your belief in God as your savior. If you're truly a man of God, do you think your God would want you to be doing this? Being a part of murdering a cop? Holding children as hostages? You think your God might require positive action from you and not simply all those easily memorized and recited religious words? You're at the crossroads of good and evil, Freddy. You have a chance to prove yourself to your God, to show that you know right from wrong and that you've really changed for the better. If your God is watching you Freddy, then he's probably thinking, 'Put up or shut up.'"

Freddy bowed, then said, "Oh Lord my God, I take refuge in you; save and deliver me from all who pursue me. That's psalm 7:1. Preacher Adams has been teachin' me the Bible. I like the Psalms the best. I go every Saturday night ta learn stuff and I always go ta church on Sunday. I read the Bible at the church shelter every day. Otto hates for me to even talk about it. The devil has taken his soul."

"I'm the worst person you want to talk with about religion, but if you truly believe what your preacher is telling you and you believe it makes you a better man, then follow that path, but being with and helping your brother and Charlie will lead you down a path to hell. You think about that, Freddy."

Roman felt sorry for Freddy. All the years of trying to measure up to his big brother, trying to earn big brother's friendship and respect, and failing miserably. He didn't want to hurt Freddy any more than he was already hurting, but he had no choice— not with the safety of the kids at stake.

Roman continued, "Freddy, listen carefully. Your brother sent you on the roof because you're the least important person. He would rather lose you than Miller. That's why Miller stays safely in this room with him. Fang knows that you're easy pickings on that roof. Miller's more valuable to your brother than you are. Charlie's more useful to Fang and Fang would rather sacrifice you, his own brother, rather than Miller. It's the truth, Freddy. You've got to see it and get the hell out of here. Don't stand by your brother any more or you'll take the big fall right along with him. Death by lethal injection or the electric chair is just around the corner for you if you don't get out of this quickly. Save yourself and get out of this mess the first chance you get."

Roman could see the tears forming in Freddy's eyes as he looked downward and silently backed away from Roman while lowering the rifle barrel so it touched the floor. Then Freddy returned to the door where the twelve children were standing. Freddy stared at Roman for a few seconds and Roman could see the confusion and misery in those lonely eyes, eyes that reflected a life of emotional torment, of hopelessness and a lack of love, until he found religion. People have the right to believe what they wish, even if they believe in fantasies and myths, Roman mused.

Freddy wiped his tears with his shirt sleeve, then, looking at Roman with a pathetic gaze, said. "Your wife is bringin' the food. I told Fang who she is. I seen her. Some stupid trooper was talkin' about it so loud I couldn't help but hear 'im. I'm sorry now that I done that, but it's too late now, I guess."

Roman's heart rocketed into his throat and gagged him. His immediate anger set fire to his lungs. He sucked air into his lungs and still felt short of breath. He'd been holding onto a metal desk drawer handle. The handle bent, snapped, then was pulled off the drawer as if it were made of aluminum. Roman stood up as he heard the knocking signal on the door. Freddy backed away from Roman and opened the door.

In walked Miller, then Sam with the boxes of pizza and several six-packs containing a variety of soda. Then Fang's bulk filled the doorway, his AK-47 in one hand, the walkie-talkie in the other. The .357 magnum and a sheathed knife were hooked to his belt. He stared at Roman, a sadistic smile of overt contempt etched on his face.

Roman's heart thumped like a hammer on an anvil.

21

"Success in not final, failure is not fatal: it is the courage to continue that counts."

Winston Churchill

FANG TURNED ON THE walkie-talkie, after closing the classroom door, then said, "Hey, Babe. Yuh listenin'?"

Captain Lewis grimaced. "I'm here, Fang. Send the kids down now."

"They'll be down soon," responded Fang, as if trying to bait Captain Lewis.

Lt. Hawkey looked concerned. He caught Captain Lewis's eyes with his and mouthed a silent message to her.

Captain Lewis looked alarmed. She placed her mouth to the walkie-talkie, again, and in a tone of voice, with a rough edge to it, she stated, "Fang, where's the woman who delivered the pizza?"

There was a momentary pause, then a chuckle, before Fang said, "Oh, I forgot ta tell yuh that Mrs. Wolfe suddenly decided ta stay an' visit with her husband. A course we take good care a her. So, my Sweety-Pie, do yuh want some kids in exchange fer a helicopter? I got 'em all lined up here an' ready ta go, if yuh still want 'em. But it's a shame ta waste the pizza, or ta let it get cold, so I'll let 'em eat first. I'm a generous guy. No use starvin' the kiddies. Fang was really grinding in the sarcasm. "Whaddaya say? The helicopter coming? We still gotta deal, don't we, Babe?"

"The deal was, you let half the kids come out, *then* I call for the helicopter."

"Wow, yuh should see 'em devour that pizza. Yuh catch that word *devour,* Little Lady? Almos' as impressive as *repartee,* don'tcha think? But yur so much smarter than me, so I has ta give up on dat contest." Taunting, sardonic, loud laughter caused Captain Lewis to move her walkie-talkie away from her ear. "Damn brats sure is hungry. Can't let 'em go away hungry, now, can I? That be too cruel."

Captain Lewis turned off the walkie-talkie and looked at Lieutenant Hawkey. She said, "Now the bastard's got Samantha, in addition to all those kids. Shit!" she cursed, "How the hell did he find out? Jesus, fucking Christ! Maybe Wolfe's students knew what she looked like. Damn I was stupid. I never should've let her go up there."

Lt. Hawkey hooked the walkie-talkie to his belt, then raised both hands, palms together, like a church steeple, with his index fingers touching his nose and his thumbs under his chin. He closed his eyes and in frustration mumbled "Fuck!"

Captain Lewis and Lieutenant Hawkey paced nervously. Then Bev asked Joe to check with his men. "Make sure they're all in position."

As Joe did that, Bev looked at her men. Everything looked good.

Captain Lewis then said, "As I see it, we still have to go along with the deal to release the kids in exchange for the helicopter. He's playing with me by postponing the release, that's all. He knows he has to release the kids before he'll get the things he needs. Now that he has Sam, he can afford to release the kids. That shouldn't be a problem. I hope. Of course we have to stop him, somehow, from getting away in the helicopter, but if it will get half the kids out, then we'll have to go along with it. That's twelve less kids who can get hurt if we have to go in there and take them by force. So, I'd better call the helicopter for him and consummate the deal. Do you agree, Joe? Don't hold back on me. Whaddaya really think?"

"Not much choice here, Bev. I agree."

Captain Lewis, showing her frustration, said. "Christ, Joe. This teacher's your friend. What the hell's he waiting for? We've been here all afternoon. Didn't you figure he'd make a move by now?"

"Yeah. Actually I did, but this situation is sort of like a mini-war, Bev. It's hours and hours of horrendous boredom, interrupted by a few seconds of deadly terror. But that was Roman's specialty. Sneaking into the blackness of the night jungle, prowling silently for hours, patiently waiting for his opportunity to kill the enemy without a sound. You gotta give him credit, though. He's got a couple dozen kids to protect and it's three against one. Maybe he doesn't have a good plan. Maybe he has a plan, but is waiting for the right opportunity to put it into action. Of course, maybe he's changed dramatically and we're shit-out-of-luck hoping to get help from him, though I really can't see that happening."

"Yeah, well maybe he's just not the same person you knew. He could've sublimated all his violent Vietnam skills with his gentle teaching skills. Those are just little kids up there. I think maybe your friend's lost it, you know?

Lt. Hawkey smiled and said, "Maybe, Bev, but I doubt it." Then, in a moment of self-doubt, Hawkey shook his head, saying, "Damn! I sure hope I'm right."

"From what you say, I know he earned his fearsome reputation, but it's been a few years since you've seen him, right? People change, Joe," added Captain Lewis, raising her eyebrows for emphasis. Then, "You know the saying, *You don't need to change friends as long as you realize that friends change*?

"Yeah. I know, but I'm not giving up on this guy, Bev. I guess you had to know him to know what I mean. Besides, just because he hasn't acted yet doesn't mean he's turned chicken. Anyway, the Wolf was never blood-thirsty, but always patient. He's certainly not timid either and, by God, he's no coward. He needs time to work it out himself. Something's preventing him from acting and it's probably that there are too many of them to risk being careless. Give him more time. He's thinking of those kids. He's looking for the right moment and it just hasn't happened yet. Of course, now that his wife is a hostage, too, he'll be even more careful about his actions. If it were only his own personal safety at stake, hell, this situation would have been over hours ago.

Ease up on the guy, Bev. I vouch for him. We fought together. We had a deep connection, so if you trust me then you gotta trust him."

Captain Lewis smiled at Lieutenant Hawkey. There was a softness in her eyes now. They were less tense. She said, "I didn't say anything about Mr. Wolfe being a chicken or a coward. I don't think either one. But thanks, Joe. I'll keep that under advisement and take your word about this guy. I just hope he doesn't let you . . . us down."

Captain Lewis brought the walkie-talkie to her lips and called Fang. When he responded, she said, "Send the twelve kids down now and I'll call for the helicopter as soon as the last one walks out the door. No tricks, I promise. Then I'll give the command for the helicopter to be on its way here."

Fang, having a change of heart said, "No. Don't think so. When I see the helicopter, I'll send the kids, Honey."

Captain Lewis's face flushed hot with anger. She spat. "That's not the deal we had, mister. You stick to the original deal or I don't even call for the helicopter at all. You understand?"

Fang laughed into the walkie-talkie. "Yeah, yeah, sure, Babe. Look, don't get yur tits in a uproar, OK? Speakin' a tits, I bet yur nipples are hard right now, right? Sure would like to have my mouth on 'em. Can even taste them—

"Stop talking like that in front of the kids!" Captain Lewis blurted.

"Damn. You women get so 'motional. OK, the kids'll be comin' down now, even though they not finished eatin'. Then yuh call that helicopter."

"When I see twelve kids out here in the parking lot, unharmed, then, and only then, will I make that call, so send them now," she demanded, impatience in her voice.

"Finally got yuh upset, hey, baby girl?" Fang laughed, then disconnected.

The last thing Captain Lewis heard on the walkie-talkie was the sound of Fang's taunting laughter.

Captain Lewis's face blushed, again. Her guts simmered like a teapot.

Fang yelled, "Freddy! Get yur ass over 'ere."

Freddy, who had wandered to the back of the classroom, walked to Fang.

"Freddy, yuh bring these brats down ta the back door. Yuh don't go out, just let the brats go ta the parkin' lot. Then get yur ass back up 'ere, pronto."

"Why me?" asked Freddy. "Why not Miller? I could get shot bringin' the kids down there."

Fang grabbed the front of Freddy's shirt and pulled Freddy's face to within inches of his own face. Freddy not only turned his head aside from fear, but also away from his brother's fetid breath. Fang growled, through clenched teeth, "Cause, I say so, yuh cowardly, wimp. When I tell yuh ta do somethin', goddamnit, yuh do it. No questions. An' when I say 'jump,' yuh oughtta be askin', 'How high?' So jump damn yuh."

Freddy could feel the blast of fowl hot air and the droplets of spittle spray on his face. When his brother let him go, Freddy snuck a peek toward Roman.

Roman had an expression on his face that Freddy read as disappointment. Then he saw Roman's lips form the word, "Go" and knew exactly what was meant.

Freddy looked at the floor as if he was ashamed of himself for defying Otto. He knew it would always be this way with Otto, always being intimidated and humiliated by him. He glanced at his brother and said, "Sorry. Sure, I'll bring 'em down whenever you say." But, when he turned away from Otto, there was a satisfying curvature on his lips and a mischievous sparkle in his eyes. Roman noticed both and sighed with relief.

"Move! Goddamnit," spat Fang, his eyes still radiating flames of anger over a disgusted tone of voice. "An' take the Teach with yuh, too."

Freddy, Miller and Sam were shocked by Fang's statement. Roman knew that Fang had something evil on his mind. When Sam walked into the room, Fang had given Roman a broad, yellow-teeth, sadistic countenance as his snaggletooth caught on his upper lip. He knew then, but not when, Fang was going to do something unexpected, so Roman wasn't stunned by Fang's statement that he could leave with Freddie.

Roman stared at Fang and calmly stated, "That's out of the question." Then tersely added, " The remainder of my students, my wife and I will not be separated," and he said it with such finality that Fang gave him a hot, second glance.

Freddy interrupted, saying, "Otto….. um, Fang. Please believe me. This will get us all killed. Seek guidance from the Lord. 'I sought the Lord and he answered me.' Psalm 34:4."

"Yuh asshole. Yuh still spoutin' that crap. I oughtta heave yuh out the window. I don't understand yuh at all. Never have. Jesus, yuh piss me off."

"Isahia 7:9," Freddy responded, "Unless you believe, you will not understand."

Roman felt empathy with Freddy. He definitely wasn't the brightest bulb in the room, but at least he gave the effort to do the right thing. If false beliefs help a person to do the right thing, so be it. "Where knowledge ends, religion begins. Benjamin Disraeli," Roman mumbled to himself.

Fang had detected a minute change in Roman, like a storm cloud passing over his eyes or the way he cocked his shoulders. Whatever it was, it bothered Fang. It seemed to be a renewed anger and a growing confidence. There also seemed to be a reservoir of strength behind the teacher's occasionally defiant voice and it made Fang feel uneasy. Being ill at ease was an alien feeling for him and he was irritated by it.

Fang figured it was a psychological game; he could play that game, too. So, not letting his voice or face give him away, he said, "Shit, man. Yuh want ta stay, stay. It's yur ass that's in a sling. Yuh wanna keep it where it can get some extra holes? Be my guest. Knew yuh were a fool right from the get-go."

Roman stared at Fang without offering so much as one word in response, just a mysteriously ominous stare.

Fang still felt strange about this teacher; he was becoming a major irritant, an unknown factor, a possible threat. Fang realized his frustration was mounting. Something odd was happening inside of him. Something was crumbling. He could feel it, like a brick wall with the mortar weakening. He looked at Sam, who was standing near Roman. Fang's eyes darted to Roman who was still staring at him. Fang finally admitted to himself that those eyes had grown cold, though there was a flicker of searing hatred there, too. He asked himself, "What the hell've I got here? Some damn Jekyll an' Hyde? That's too exaggerated, he thought. Can't be. The asshole looks like a classic wimp." But his doubts lingered . . . and began to fester.

Fang grew furious due to this unexpected source of intimidation. He felt like his insides were being gnawed, as if there was a hungry rat prowling around in his guts, biting off chunks of organs and intestines. Outwardly, he tried to remain calm, but Roman's stare riled him and to make matters worse, he knew that Roman knew it. Fang tore his eyes away from Roman's glare, slapped Freddy's head, then ordered Freddy to leave the room with the kids, saying, "Take the Goddamn brats outta here. Jesus Christ! I can't stan' there pathetic whining an' crying."

Freddy looked alarmed. "Thou shalt not take the name of the Lord Thy God in vain," he said to his brother.

"How can yuh keep vomitin' that garbage, Freddy? Yuh know how stupid yuh sound?"

"I sought the Lord and the Lord answered me. Otto.... ah, Fang, you must seek the Lord for answers, too."

"Yuh know I don't believe that shit. It's fairy tales little brother!" Fang screamed.

"John 3:16, For God so loved the world that he sent his only begotten son and whosoever believeth in him shall have eternal life. You can still be saved, Otto."

"Oh, fuck yuh, asshole. Here's my God," he said, then looked at his straining biceps that were positioned like a body-builder might do at a contest. "That's my God and here's my Lord," Fang uttered as he grabbed his crotch as if he were Michael Jackson.

"God will understand and forgive your mistakes. God is fair. The Bible, God's words, tells us that God wants justice and happiness for all his children," Freddy pleaded.

Roman listened to Freddy and thought of Isaac Asimov who stated, "Properly read, the Bible is the most potent force for atheism ever conceived."

Roman asked himself, Hasn't Freddy ever read the part of the Bible (Exodus 20:5) that states: "I am a jealous God, visiting the iniquity of the fathers onto his children, to the third and fourth generations of those who hate me." Roman shook his head in disgust, thinking, Now, is that a rational, just and fair God? Would a just and benevolent God punish innocent children for what their great, great, great grandfather's thought or did? That's not a benevolent God; it's an absurd, fairy-tale demon buried inside the pages of a Marvel comic-book.

Freddy turned toward the door, opened it, then looked over his shoulder at Roman before he departed with the twelve lucky kids who would be free in a few seconds.

Roman knew what the smile meant, of course, but Fang was confused by it, disturbed by it, but his anger distracted him as it built like steam in a pressure cooker.

As Freddy and the kids left the room, pizzas in hand, some of the other children started to cry. They wanted to go, too. Sam and Roman walked to the windows, where the other children were sitting and comforted them.

Freddy brought the children down the stairs and to the exit door. The children walked out, single file, their pizzas flapping up and down like puppy ears. Their smiles red with tomato sauce, making them look like they were wearing sloppy lipstick.

Fang looked displeased and agitated. He ordered Roman back to his desk. Roman refused, still comforting his students. Fang pulled the gun out of his belt and aimed it at Roman. Roman looked over his shoulder at Fang. Sam immediately grabbed Roman by the arm and pulled him back towards the desk. She could feel the ripple of tense, slender muscles, like thin steel cables. Roman reluctantly allowed her to steer him, never taking his glaring eyes off Fang.

Miller, seeing the tension and worrying about a confrontation, withdrew his handgun as well, but not knowing quite where to aim it, he let the barrel hang at his thigh, towards the floor. Sam was talking soothingly to Roman, trying to get him to relax, when the walkie-talkie came alive.

"Fang. This is Captain Lewis. Acknowledge, please."

Fang reluctantly broke eye contact with Roman and responded. "Acknowledge? Wow! Aint yuh something of a worksmith. I ack-now-ledge. Whaddaya want?"

"Just wanted to let you know the kids arrived safely. And, the word is not *worksmith*, but *wordsmith*, with the letter *d,* instead of a *k; word,* not *work.*" She didn't mention the surprise.

"Screw yuh an' them damn kids, Bitch. When's the chopper gettin' here?"

"Soon," she responded. "They have to refuel and go over a standard safety check list whenever they are about to take off. An hour, perhaps."

As soon as Captain Lewis had the kids, she asked Lieutenant Hawkey to call Trooper-One— a Bell Jet Ranger helicopter. Lieutenant Hawkey used the mobile UHF radio and did as requested, while Captain Lewis ordered someone to bring all the children to the ambulance to be checked.

She was thoroughly surprised when Freddy walked out behind the children with his hands up and no weapon visible. Freddy was then handcuffed and taken into custody by one of Captain Lewis's men. But before he left, he told Captain Lewis to tell his brother to, "Go fuck himself because he never appreciated me and always treated me like shit and I don't owe Otto anything, any more. I surrendered 'cause what they're doing is wrong. Like Job 28:18 said, 'The price of wisdom is above rubies.'"

Captain Lewis stared at Freddy, but didn't respond.

"The helicopter's on its way. Should be here soon, Fang."

"Yuh better not be playing any tricks, Bitch. I still got twelve more kids, the Teach and his pretty wifey," Fang said, with a slight, but ominous giggle in his voice.

"Got a message for you, too, Fang. From your brother. Wanna here it?"

"Yuh got my brother!" Fang screamed. "Yuh'll pay dearly fer that, Bitch!"

Captain Lewis grinned at the sound of Fang's crackling, nervous and angry voice before saying, "You know the old saying, Fang? *What goes around, comes around.* You broke the deal by taking Mr. Wolfe's wife and now we have your brother. Actually, we didn't grab him, Fang. You'll love this part. He just walked out with the kids and gave himself up. Said to tell you that you should go screw yourself because you never liked him, never treated him right or appreciated him. He says he doesn't owe you anything any more. Damn! Your brother's sure a lot smarter than you are."

"That's a damn lie! Yuh don't really have 'im, do yuh? That's a goddamn lie! I know it is. Freddy wouldn't have the balls ta do that. He wouldn't do that ta me." Then Fang remembered the smile that passed from his brother to Roman, just before Freddy left with the kids. Christ, he thought, it was true. His own brother had deserted him. The thought of his own brother's defiance made him nearly boil with rage.

Something inside Fang snapped as he took a few quick steps, grabbed Alyson Boyd by her long hair, then told Sam to follow him out the door as Alyson screamed.

Roman started walking quickly, straight at Fang.

Fang quickly put the barrel of the magnum .357 to Alyson's temple and said. "OK, hero. This one'll be dead before yuh reach me . . . . Come on, asshole! Come get me! An' watch 'er die."

Sam screamed, then looked at Roman.

Roman stepped backward toward Sam.

Fang pointed to Roman and ordered, "Sit down." Then Fang yelled at Miller. "Yuh shoot the bastard if he leaves that chair. An' watch the rest a those brats till I get back. I'm headed fer the roof. I'll show 'em a thing or two. They'll learn who's boss real quick."

With the handgun in his left hand and dragging a screaming Alyson by the hair with his right hand, he departed the classroom.

Alyson continued screaming and struggling to get free. She clutched Fang's fingers, scratched them and tried to pry them apart.

Sam yelled, "At least let her walk, or her screaming will force the cops to come."

When Fang ignored her, Sam went berserk and before Miller or Roman could react, Sam leaped on Fang like a lion on a gazelle. Sam slapped, kicked and clawed at Fang's face as she screamed, "You bastard. Let her go!"

Fang ducked his head to avoid the slaps and clawing, tucked the gun into his belt, at his belly, then viciously grabbed Sam's hair, saying, "OK, bitch. You can come to the roof, too." Fang dragged Sam and Alyson out the door.

Fang's brain was racing, distracted, preoccupied. His face was a ripe tomato; the blood vessels in his temple, throat and arms jumped with each pulse of his thumping heartbeat. He had only one thing on his mind and was so focused on it that he didn't hear Sam and Alyson screaming as they were dragged by their hair.

The classroom door slowly closed. Roman could hear the screams growing fainter and fainter, each scream feeling like an ice-pick in his heart. He didn't feel brave any longer; he felt weak, helpless and tortured as Miller laughed at him.

Roman stared at Miller, his contempt for the man was obvious. It's not three against one now, he thought. He sat as his desk and continued to glare at Miller.

Then he did something strange. He began stroking the air next to the arm of his chair. He buried his fingers into the invisible, thick, white fur. He looked downward and very softly he whispered, "Go to the roof."

*   *   *   *   *   *   *

Youth and inexperience breed over-confidence, arrogance and carelessness. Trooper Jones was young, inexperienced, over-confident and definitely arrogant. He saw how easily Freddy gave himself up, so Trooper Jones was convinced, without a shadow of a doubt, that these Fang and Miller characters couldn't be nearly as much of a problem as the Captain and the Lieutenant seemed to think they were. And from what little he'd heard, when they talked to that prison psychiatrist, those two guys were just a couple of whackos, especially the one named Fang. Fang, he thought, jokingly, I'll give the guy a tooth ache that he won't forget. Why be so damn cautious with whackos and perverts? I could go in there and nail them to the wall with bullets and be the hero.

Trooper Jones, being a megalomaniac himself, completely missed the fact that he was more like Fang than anyone else in this hostage situation. He seriously believed that it was his destiny to rise in rank to the top of the State Trooper power structure during his early career, as if it were written in stone tablets ages ago. He also believed that shortcuts were part of his destiny because shortcuts were the hallmark of ambitious people who've accomplished great success and this hostage situation was must be one of those short-cuts to his destiny. He had a high risk, high gain outlook on life.

Trooper Jones decided that if he could single-handedly capture Fang or Miller, or both, then promotions would be easily gained. His path would not be a sidewalk to success; it would be a race track to success. He felt euphoric.

He would be the pride of his department, the cream that had risen to the top. He would be the best and some day, not too many years away, he'd be running this department and using his power to punish or reward his officers. He could feel the temporary power surge through him. He was hungry for that power to become permanent.

Jones's eyes sparkled with pride and, breathing deeply, he felt his chest expand as if inflating with power— his head expanded, also. He thought all he'd have to do is enter the school and capture Fang and Charlie before they had a chance to surrender, like Freddy did. He couldn't let that happen. He couldn't let them surrender and have them trip him during his first steps toward destiny.

He'd capture Fang first; Fang was the most dangerous. "Who cares about his size and meanness?" thought Jones. "Size and meanness can't stand up to 9 mm bullets." Jones had the equalizer in his holster. He would do what he had to do, what he was destined to do. When looking down the black hole of the barrel of a gun, the toughest men cringe and sweat. So would Fang and Charlie.

Accordingly, Jones left his guard position, where he screened anyone who tried to enter the parking lot. He walked to the side entrance, located by the school cafeteria. It was an entrance used mostly by cafeteria personnel to bring supplies into or out of the cafeteria. The entrance was concealed by a large dumpster.

The door was guarded by another rookie trooper named Jon Tuttle. Trooper Jones walked to Trooper Tuttle, with a friendly smile etched on his face, and his hand out for a handshake, like the two of them were *brothers in law*.

"Hey, Jon," Jones said. "How's it goin', man? Nice and quiet over here, huh?" Jones was doing his best to sound friendly as he shook hands with Trooper Tuttle.

Tuttle seemed startled and stared at Jones. They hadn't been friends during the past ten months as rookies. They graduated together, but weren't really friends at the State Police Academy, either. "Yeah, Hi Casey. Not much happening here," Tuttle said, smiling to cover up his embarrassment.

"Look, the captain said we should change places so we don't get bored. The change in positions'll help keep us alert. I was guarding the entrance to the parking lot. All you do is screen anyone who wants to come in. You keep all the reporters out. If you got any questions about who can come in, you just ask Captain Lewis or Lieutenant Hawkey. An easy job, really."

Tuttle picked up on the word *easy.* He liked the way it sounded. Easy was good. "Oh, sure," he said. "Hell, if that's the way the Captain wants it, I got no problems with it. This little cubby hole's all yours, Casey. Hope the smell of that dumpster doesn't get to yuh If the garbage smells anything like the food they serve here, then we'll be back here next week to guard the kids." Tuttle laughed, but Jones only grinned, with effort.

"No problem, Jon. You take it easy now, buddy," Jones offered.

"Yeah, sure. You too," responded Tuttle, smiling. He didn't realize that he and Jones were *buddies.* Jones had never been overly friendly as he was being now. As a matter of fact, thought Tuttle, Jones always had seemed to avoid him. "Wonder what that *buddy-buddy* stuff is all about?" he thought.

Trooper Jones thought, That was easy.

Trooper Jones watched Trooper Tuttle disappear around the corner, heading for the entrance to the parking lot. Then Jones walked to the cafeteria door and entered the school building without being noticed or authorized. Easy, he thought.

He had seen a schematic drawing of the school. It was a pretty simple layout. There would be no problem getting to the classroom. The problem would be avoiding Lieutenant Hawkey's SWAT team sentries. He wasn't sure where they were posted, but he assumed they were at the ends of the second floor hallway, near any stairway, in order to block the normal exit routes. He would have checked but was afraid of bringing suspicion upon himself and his intentions.

He was confident that he could avoid the sentries and get around them undetected. He wasn't sure how, yet, but he knew he'd think of something when the time came. After all, he was smart and it was his destiny.

/-/....../.-/-/-.--/---/../.-/....../.-/-/....-/./--/../../..../-/./-./

22

★★★★

"The belief in a supernatural source of evil is not necessary;
men alone are quite capable of every wickedness."

Robert Conrad

THE SCENE WAS FRANTIC. Roman stared in disbelief, for no sooner had
Fang left the classroom, dragging Alyson and Sam by their hair, when
Miller, like some long chained-up beast finally breaking free, erupted in
a maniacal rage and the first thing he did was yank the classroom phone
from the wall, rendering it useless. He threw it hard against Roman's
closet door and pieces fell to the floor.

Miller's bulging eyes showed the pressure of his rage, his lips
stretched into a snarl. He stood in front of the class looking back and
forth between Roman and the kids, deciding where to start first; his
borderline civility now stripped away by Freddy's and Fang's absence.
Blood rose to the surface of his flushed face. His tongue seemed wild
inside his mouth, and saliva squirted out occasionally as if his tongue
hand become a spitting serpent.

He turned toward Roman and shrieked, "Yur all mine now and
so're all the little bastards! All of yuh are mine." His finger swept across

the room pointing at all its occupants as he snarled like a rabid dog, exposing saliva froth and gnashing teeth.

Roman envisioned the rabid coyote that had attacked him and Grace in the Adirondack Mountains. He wished he had his trusty Ka-Bar. His attention was immediately refocused when Miller aimed his AK-47 at him and gloated.

The classroom boomed twice from the noise of the shots, almost deafening its occupants and assaulting their noses with the overpowering, pungent smell of cordite.

The children covered their ears and screamed in pain as the shock waves battered their ear drums. They started crying in unison as Miller laughed. And the louder the children's cries, the louder Miller's laugh became. It was a diabolical sound, a piercing cacophony like one might expect to hear coming from a torture chamber in Hell. But it was not a laugh born of fear, but rather from pleasure, the pleasure that comes from achieving ecstasy from someone else's pain. It was the sound of satanic sadism.

The two holes in Roman's desk were closely spaced due to the minimal recoil of the AK-47. The bullets had ripped through the thin metal at the side of the desk leaving nearly identical holes with curled and twisted shards of blossoming metal protruding where the bullets exited. Meeting little resistance from the thin metal, the bullets continued their unimpeded path through the other side of the desk, then penetrated the bottom of the metal filing cabinet which stood beside the desk. If Roman had had his knees under his desk, one or both would have been shattered by the bullets.

The bark of the AK-47, the crazed look on Miller's face, and the smell of gun powder terrorized the children.

Roman's hands and feet tingled from overly stimulated nerve-endings. It was an edgy readiness, not controlled by the emotional eruptions of rage. It was steadily taking control of every cell, fiber, sinew, bone, and muscle in Roman's body. The pressure of it was increasing geometrically, like the pressure inside an active volcano. It was time to act, Roman demanded of himself. Can't wait any longer. It was time to save his students, Sam and Alyson. Roman remained seated, glaring at Miller, feeling as if every brain cell had erupted into flames.

Miller walked to the opposite end of the room, near the wall of windows, where the kids were. He set the rifle down, then grabbed Steven by his shoulder length red hair. Miller unsheathed his knife. Roman leaped up, like a Jack-in-the-Box, ready to confront Miller. Roman paused when he saw Miller's intentions. Miller's knife sliced cleanly and without effort through a thick lock of Steven's carrot-colored hair.

Steven screamed. The children near him screamed as they attempted to squirm away. Miller threatened them. "Stay put," Miller shrieked at them, "or I'll cut yur throats!"

Miller kept cutting more and more of Steven's hair and each cut brought a grimace to Steven's lips as he looked at Roman with watery, terrified eyes.

Miller glared at Roman, balefully, each time he threw another lock of Steven's hair to the floor.

The room grew cold, which seemed quite strange to Miller. The kids didn't appear to be cold, but all of a sudden Miller felt a chill. He ceased cutting Steven's hair.

Roman walked— in spite of Miller's protests— to the closet, near his desk and removed the broom and dust pan. Then he walked toward the windows, toward the students, toward Miller, toward Miller's blade. He was steady, though disturbed— the kids were now in immediate danger, their lives depended on him.

Half-way to Miller, Roman said, adding a tone of meekness and fear to his voice, "Gotta sweep the hair off the floor. Cleanliness is next to Godliness, you know."

Miller thought Roman was having a nervous breakdown, or that Roman was simply not playing with a full deck. He laughed at Roman and figured him for a wimp, a fag or both, who got away with too much bluffing. That's why Miller hadn't reached for his rifle. He had the .357 magnum tucked into his belt and the knife in his hand. He felt safe. He concluded that the wise-ass teacher was faltering under the stress of the situation.

Roman saw the tears streaming down Steven's cheeks. Steven's whole body was trembling as Roman said, "It's just hair, Steven. You'll be OK. Do you trust me?"

Steven gave a slight, affirmative nod.

But the other children panicked, cried and hugged each other when they saw that Mr. Wolfe didn't do anything to Charlie. All the confidence and reassurance that he had tried to instill in them now looked fake. Seeing Mr. Wolfe's inaction, most students concluded that their teacher couldn't save them, so they were, once again, paralyzed by their fear of Charlie and their disappointment with Mr. Wolfe, their useless guardian. Mr. Wolfe had been their hope, but now he looked hopeless.

Roman glanced at Steven, winked, then placed the broom bristles on the floor as if to sweep up the hair that was a couple of feet away from Miller's legs.

Miller watched him, with a hint of silent laughter, his knife held at waist level, pointing at Roman. Now I'll humiliate this mouthy teacher, he thought.

Miller's knife was ready to slash at Roman, but reading Miller's intentions, Roman stepped on the end of the broom snapping off the bristled bottom, leaving the five feet long, green, wooden handle. Now it was a karate bo— a long, solid, wooden staff used as a combat weapon. Roman had used the bo over and over again during his years of karate training. He was as familiar with it as he was with his own arms.

The bo suddenly became a blurred shaft of lightening as it slashed through the air, crashing into Miller's right wrist. Miller's blade immediately popped free of his fingers and dropped to the floor with a dull thud. Roman kicked it away as Miller retreated a few steps, grabbing his painfully injured wrist.

Miller, trying to use his numb wrist, reached for the handgun that was tucked under his belt. Roman rammed the jagged end of the bo deeply into Miller's solar plexus. Air exploded from Miller's lungs; he gasped for air, still tugging at the handgun.

Miller's fear enshrouded him in a cold sweat when he felt the bo slam onto his thigh, with the sound of a wooden spoon slapping raw hamburger. Miller's fear increased exponentially when he could no longer get his right leg to move. He tried, but it was as if his leg was dead— the bo had struck a confluence of nerves, temporarily paralyzing the leg. Then the searing pain gradually seeped through the numbness, making Miller's leg burn as if it was in boiling oil.

Miller pulled the pistol free from his belt when another green blur of lightening passed before his eyes, filling them with shock from the anticipation of further pain. The bo, once again, slammed onto his right wrist, this time breaking bones. Then that terrible green blur broke his nose as blood and tears inundated his face. Miller fingers could no longer grip the gun and the gun fell to the floor as he screamed in agony. He staggered backwards, leaning on the blackboard for support— leaving a greasy slick on the board where his hair had touched it— his face contorted into a twisted grimace, blood and tears painting his face into a gruesome mask with grunts of intense pain ejaculating through his clenched teeth.

Roman had quickly and easily disarmed Charlie. Roman immediately took the rifle, the pistol and the knife, then set them on a student's desk. He unbuckled Charlie's belt, pulled it free, then picked up the knife sheath and placed Charlie's knife in it. He attached the knife to his own belt, then ordered the kids not to touch the rifle and pistol.

With Miller disarmed, Roman saw no further need for the bo. He winked at his students, who looked on in stunned amazement. Then Roman went to Steven, whose fear and tears had suddenly abated. Roman leaned the bo against the counter where Steven and the other children were sitting.

Roman kept an eye on Miller, who remained leaning against the blackboard, moaning and holding his wrist. Roman placed an arm around Steven's shoulder and gently hugged him while rubbing Steven's sliced hair in a fatherly gesture.

The other children peered at their teacher's compassionate smile and ceased crying.

"It'll all grow back, you know," Roman said to Steven. "You give it a couple of months and you'll have another head of long hair again." Then Roman glanced toward Miller and added, "And that creep will be back in prison."

Miller, unable to stand the pain, begged, "Help me. Help me . . . please."

Roman ignored Miller's plea, then spoke to his students. "Hang in there kids," he whispered, sympathetically. "Don't be afraid any more. It's almost all over now." He approached them, held their hands briefly, rubbed a few shoulders, tousled some hair, wiped away some tears and gave hugs to the needy. Roman returned to Steven.

While reaching into his pocket for a tissue to give to Steven, Roman saw movement from Miller who was off to his left side. Steven started to warn Roman just as Roman's left leg snapped out sideways, burying the ridge of his foot— from the outer side of the heel to the little toe— deeply into Miller's solar plexus. The resulting "whoosh" sound came, as all the air in Miller's lungs explosively exited in one sudden gush, like air escaping from a kid's party balloon. Miller was automatically doubled over at the waist by the powerful kick.

Then Roman was startled by another movement to his right, a high movement, coming quickly towards his head. He reacted instinctively, his nervous system sending chemical-electric impulses to his synapses, then on to his muscles within milliseconds of their origin. He turned immediately to face the yet unknown danger while raising both arms over his head, crossing them at the forearms to form an "X" block.

But the bo swished passed his arms and came crashing down on the back of Miller's head while he was doubled over from Roman's previous sidekick. Miller toppled to the floor, unconscious and lying at Roman's feet.

Roman brought his arms down, then looked from Miller to Steven with both laughter and amazement. Steven, too, was smiling as were the rest of the children. Roman noticed that Steven had held the bo as if it were a baseball bat; he grinned at Steven. The tears and crying had completely vanished as everyone stared at Miller's prone and unconscious body.

"Guess that'll teach him not to mess with us," Steven said with bravado and a sly smile, as he looked at Miller's inert body. Some of the other children added enthusiastic "yeahs" in support of Steven; their smiles growing larger with each "yeah," and with each further "yeah," their tear-stained cheeks dried as quickly as desert rain.

"You sure taught him," agreed Roman. "You handled that bo like a real pro. That was a heck of a hit, Steven. Couldn't have done a better job myself. He'll be out cold for quite a while and he'll have a nice goose egg, or we hope so, right?"

A chorus, the kids answered, "Yeah!"

Roman felt the tissue in his hands, looked at Steven's proud, smiling face and put the tissue back into his pocket. He took the bo from Steven and set it in the corner.

Then, collecting his thoughts, he suddenly spun around and ran to his desk, grabbed his sturdy, high-backed chair, went quickly to the door and wedged the chair up under the doorknob tightly and securely. Roman used the wooden door wedge, normally used to keep the door open, and wedged it under the door, thus, effectively locking the door so that Fang wouldn't be able to enter if he came back too quickly. Then, quickly, Roman took tape and construction paper and blocked the narrow door window.

Roman fought off a feeling of panic. His thoughts returned to Alyson and Sam who were on the roof with Fang. What if Fang went berserk like Miller did? What would he do to Alyson and Sam? Roman had to get on the roof, but not until he got his students to safety. This conflict of interest was agony for him. His frustration rose dramatically.

Then, suddenly, a noise came from the door. He snapped his head in that direction. Has Fang returned? he asked himself. If so, he knew Fang would be heavily armed.

Quickly Roman placed his right index finger to his lips in the universal sign for quiet. Roman whispered, "Get down. Hide." The children fell to their hands and knees, hiding behind the desks.

The room became as still and quiet as a buried coffin. Roman slipped off his shoes to prevent noises. He picked up the .357 magnum handgun, stuck it down the back of his pants so that his belt held it there, at the small of his back. He grabbed the AK-47. He stood next to the door, perfectly still, aiming the AK-47, from his hip, at the door. He checked the rifle's safety. It was already in the "off" position. He said to himself, "Charlie, you dumb-assed, shit-head."

But now the door was still. No movement of the knob, no rattle, no sound of a key. Had he imagined the noise? Perhaps he had been mistaken. Maybe, Roman thought, his nerves were getting a little frayed and his ears were picking up nonexistent sounds.

Roman reset the safety latch to "on," then lowered the AK-47 and leaned it against the wall, near the door. Roman then gagged Miller, while he was still unconscious, with one of the tennis balls that the kids used at play, then put loops of duct tape over the ball and behind Miller's head. When he had retrieved the tape from the bottom desk drawer of his desk, he also had grabbed a roll of copper wire that he used for electrical experiments for the students. He tied Miller's hands behind his back with the copper wire. He used the wire to tie Charlie's feet, also

He checked the handgun to see if it was fully loaded. It was. He tucked it back into the back of his pants— he knew better than to stick it into his pocket where the hammer would catch on cloth as he pulled it out, or to stick it down the front of his pants where it could blow-off his dick. He reached for the AK-47, but decided it was too cumbersome and unnecessary. Also, he didn't want Fang to have a chance to get at it. He decided to throw it out the window. He told the children to come to the front of the room, near Miller. He gave the bo back to Steven and said, pointing downward, toward Miller, "If he comes to, don't let him get up." Roman looked at the other students. "And if Steven needs help, then you people help him. Don't let him up off the floor. You can kick him."

Steven gladly took the bo and stood guard over Miller. Steven's helpers seemed to have itchy feet, wanting to treat Miller like a soccer ball.

Roman took the AK-47 to the window, then suddenly changed his mind, thinking that if he threw it out the window, it may discharge when it hit the ground. A split-second after he had turned away from the window, he saw and felt the window shatter, heard the report of a high powered rifle, then felt himself crash to the floor. The classroom looked blurry to him. In the background he thought he heard screaming. When it was quiet, Roman, still dazed, told the kids to crawl away from the windows. The windows were four feet higher than the floor, good concealment for little bodies or a prone adult body.

Roman stared at the white, rectangular ceiling tiles, each with myriad holes. He suddenly became aware of the pain in his back and then the feel of the warm flow of blood streaming down his back, to his waist, getting dammed-up by his belt and spreading horizontally along the contour of his waistline.

A voice kept repeating, "Mr. Wolfe? Can you hear me?"

Roman's dazed thoughts flashed to his previous action. So stupid, he thought. The sniper thought I was one of the bad guys. My fault.

Steven and three other boys tried to help him up, once he had moved away from the windows. As he rose off the floor, darkness and weakness began to claim him. He felt weak-kneed and momentarily lost his balance. He fell to his knees. The sounds of screaming children were distorted, as if coming from a tunnel. He felt the hard floor against his knees. Then he was on a fours supporting himself. He felt dizzy, then collapsed onto his chest, feeling his head bouncing off the floor, but he felt no pain. Just before his mind went completely black, he had a vision of his daughter, Grace. After that, the only thing he was aware of were tiny, flickering lights, as if he were looking up at the nighttime sky, seeing billions of twinkling stars. His mind, in a dream-like state, drifted to Arlington National Cemetery where so many of his Vietnam comrades and buddies were buried. He saw a freshly dug grave with a casket hanging over it, waiting to be lowered into the ground. His dream-self walked to the casket. The casket was open . . . he saw himself.

He thought, So this is what it had felt like just before his friends had died in Nam. He felt no pain. He saw dark clouds overhead then a squeaky sound, from the casket hinges, he supposed, as the casket was closed. He could feel the casket rocking as it was lowered into the hole. An obsidian blackness engulfed him, as if he were being lowered into a tar pit.

/--/./.../---/--/..-/-.-./..../..../.-/.--./.--/../-./././.../...../

23
★★★★

"The greatest fault is to be conscious of none."

Robert Carlyle

TROOPER JONES CAREFULLY PEERED around the corner and saw one of Lieutenant Hawkey's men guarding the hallway. Jones knew he couldn't get by the guard without being seen. He also knew he could lie and tell the guard something that would sound very convincing, something that would get him down the hallway and up the stairs to the second floor where the classroom was. But the guard had a walkie-talkie and could easily check his story. Of course, by then he could be all the way down the hallway. And what's the guard going to do? Shoot me? He asked himself. Yeah, he could do it that way, but it would be better if, somehow, he could sneak past this TWAT snob— jealously of the elite SWAT team caused him to denigrate that team.

Jones nervously waited, wondering what option to take. Then he got lucky. He heard the familiar crackle of the SWAT guard's walkie-talkie. The guard walked a few paces around the corner, swung the strap from his Heckler and Kock assault gun over his shoulder then removed the walkie-talkie from his belt hook.

Jones smiled. His continued good fortune was holding firmly. Then he realized that it wasn't luck at all. This was fate helping his destiny. Luck was just a random collection of positive circumstances, while destiny was preordained. These events were meant to happen like solid links in the chain of his life. His destiny was coming to him and he had to wait and let it happen. Things would fall into place for him, with an occasional push or prod to speed things up.

Quickly he used this opportunity to slip out from his hiding place and hurriedly made his way down the hallway. His silent strides enabled him to overhear the message on the walkie-talkie.

Hawkey said he was going to make his rounds with all the SWAT members who were guarding the school escape routes. But as Jones progressed farther down the hallway he could not make out any more of the message's details.

Lt. Hawkey was being thorough and careful. Jones arrogantly thought that he was doing his job just as well. This was meant to be. He was meant to be here, to be a hero, to walk undetected down this hallway, to rescue the innocent children and capture the gunmen. It was his destiny to gain early promotions and to enjoy the rewards of his heroism. His chest puffed up with pride.

When he reached the middle of the hallway, he found the stairs that led to the second floor. Before starting up the stairs, he looked back down the hallway, toward the guard. He heard the faint sounds of the walkie-talkie, but didn't see the guard.

He wasn't surprised that he had succeeded. He felt as if he were being guided. It was like he was doing God's work, just as his domineering mom had always told him. "Do God's work to help others," she would say, "and rewards will be plentiful for you."

Trooper Jones's confidence was like a pathological parasite spewing poison into his brain or, perhaps, a virulent virus eating away at the logical part of his brain. His vision of his destiny overpowered any reasonable thoughts and actions. He wasn't capable of seeing the remarkable similarity between the effects of that parasite and virus— overpowering logic, reasonable thoughts and actions— to religious beliefs.

He withdrew his handgun— Glock-21, .45 cal. (Psalm 21:45?)— from its holster and bounded up the stairs. Immediately he felt beads of sweat rolling down his forehead. His handgun felt slippery in his sweaty palm. He removed his hat and wiped his forehead with his sleeve. He placed the handgun into his left hand and dried his right palm by wiping it on his pants. He wondered why he was sweating so much as he placed the gun back into his right hand, then cautiously proceeded up the stairs. His holy arrogance dissolved slowly, as if his own salty sweat was washing it away.

His head tilted upward, looking upstairs for any warning of danger. He saw none, heard none. He grabbed the railing to steady himself. His legs felt weak, rubbery. He began sweating more heavily. Again he wiped the sweat off his brow, not being aware, yet, that he was in the tight grip of stress and fear which were slowly overwhelming him. His high level of arrogance could not match his low level of logic.

He reached the landing between the two floors, turned right and proceeded up the second flight. At the top, he placed his sweaty back against the wall to make himself less of a target. He wiped sweat from his eyes and silently cursed the salty sting.

He peeked around the corner and saw that the hallway was deserted. Each end of the hallway had large windows, so, in all probability, Captain Lewis had spotters, with binoculars, keeping track of the hallway. Big deal, he thought. They couldn't do anything about him now, especially since he had already turned off his communication radio. He knew he had good instincts, but he had to be cautious. He swiped more sweat off his brow and held his handgun close to his chest, gripping it as if it were a crucifix that offered supernatural protection. He heard faint noises coming from the first room on the left, then it was quiet again.

He noticed that there was a high barrier of desks precariously piled on top of one another. Some desks tipped down so that the writing surfaces filled-up most of the space between the legs of the front row of desks which formed a somewhat haphazard and unstable barrier.

Jones guessed that the two gunmen must have anticipated the SWAT snipers and built the barrier across the hallway in order to obstruct the snipers' view, plus give a warning noise if the desks were tampered with and fell.

As Jones stood at the top step he could hear the faint sounds of another walkie-talkie at the end of this second floor hallway. Lieutenant Hawkey must still be talking to his team.

Jones felt pain in both hands; it seemed like they were in a vice. He gazed down at them. He had been gripping the Glock so tightly that his knuckles and fingers had turned white, not just pale, but white, as if spray painted. His left hand, in a tightly knotted fist, was the same. He holstered the Glock, then clinched and loosened both hands repeatedly to gain flexibility and easy the cramping. Then he asked himself, "Why am I getting so fuckin' nervous? It's my fate. It's God's plan for me. I'm protected."

Jones closed his eyes, breathed deeply through his nose, then exhaled through his mouth to relax himself. His mind drifted to his mom's favorite psalm. He could hear his mom reciting Psalm 23:4. He mumbled, "Yea, though I walk through the valley of the shadow of death, I will fear no evil for thou art with me; thy rod and thy staff, they comfort me . . . ." No time for that now, he concluded.

He squatted, then crawled on all fours to the barrier of desks. Quietly and carefully he pushed one tipped-over desk out from between the leg of an upright barrier desk, nothing fell. He crawled under the desk then replaced the desk where it had been. Not much of a protective, warning barrier, he thought.

He saw the name Mr. Wolfe on the first door to his left. He turned the doorknob. It was locked. He peeked into the door's window; it was covered. "Fuck," he mumbled.

He put his ear close to the door, but heard no noise. How could that be? Did they leave? No. There must be another explanation. He looked around and found what he thought was the answer. He saw the open, hallway door leading to the roof. The door was ripped off its hinges, bits and pieces of scattered, shattered wood lying on the floor. So, the gunmen took everyone up to the roof, he surmised. Not a bad plan. Having the high ground gives an automatic advantage. "But it won't help them," Jones mumbled. God was on his side. His mom had pounded that into his head since he was a kid.

His head jerked toward the door. He heard yelling noises coming from the roof doorway. He ignored the classroom door, stood up, crossed the hallway and proceeded up the stairs to the roof. He could see another open doorway at the top of the stairs. He could feel the cool, refreshing air wafting down the stairway and he could see the clear sky as if, it too, had a doorway to heaven. This stairway was steep, but he would be on the roof quickly. He began thinking of the stairway as symbolic of his quick rise to fame, rewards, promotions and power. He thought these steps would bring him closer to his destiny. He was still cautious enough to move up them slowly. He felt joyously giddy at the thought of being a hero.

*   *   *   *   *   *   *

Fang pulled Alyson and Sam by their hair and dragged them along the roof top. The roof was weak in certain places. It shook and rumbled under Fang's massive weight, as if it were the last days of Pompeii. Fang pulled Sam and Alyson toward the edge of the school roof. Alyson screamed from pain and the terror.

Alyson grabbed at Fang's right wrist trying to loosen his fingers as she screamed, "Let go, you ugly jerk! You're hurting me! Let me go!"

Sam was digging into Fang's left forearm and kicking Fang's legs with no effect.

Fang wished he had had some of his stash of ketamine hydocloride—a veterinary sedative, sometimes used as a date-rape drug. That would calm them down, loosen them up and their legs would spread like warm butter across toast, Fang thought.

Fang marched to the edge of the roof so everyone below could see him and Alyson. Then, suddenly, he picked Alyson up by the hair and held her over the edge of the roof, effortlessly, even though Alyson was kicking and screaming in mid-air. Alyson was smart enough to grab Fang's forearm with both of hers, allowing her to relieve the pressure and pain of hanging by her own hair.

As soon as Sam saw this, she stopped scratching and kicking, not wanting an accident to happen to Alyson. She did try to pull Fang away from the edge of the roof with no success. Fang left fist suddenly let go of Sam's hair, then backhanded her in the face, the force causing her to stagger-step away from Fang and crash to the roof in a daze.

"Now yuh pigs ," Fang growled, "take a shot at me. Come on yuh brave assholes. I dare yuh!" he shouted through twisted lips and with a crazed look in his eyes.

The state policemen on the ground stared up at the rooftop, not believing what they were seeing: a muscular madman holding a fourth grade girl over the edge of the roof with one outstretched, massive, right arm. Some troopers aimed handguns at him.

Lt. Hawkey was not present. He was still making the rounds with his team members, checking their situations, making sure all the exits were covered.

Captain Lewis ran, carrying a bullhorn, to a spot that was closest to, in front of and under Fang's position on the roof. As she ran, she thought, sarcastically, Yep. That pervert is just a big, sweet, cuddly Pooka.

"Otto, this is Captain Lewis," she shouted into the bullhorn, "pull the girl back onto the roof. We can talk."

"Yuh took my brother, Bitch!" he screamed. "As worthless as he is, he still my brother, an' yuh took 'im. Now I got this liddle girlie, here." He moved his right arm slightly, making Alyson swing in the air like a pendulum, then said, "We don't negotiate nothing, liddle lady. Yuh do what I say or I drop this liddle brat an' then we all watch 'er go splat on the blacktop." Fang shouted the word *splat*. "Sounds like it be fun, right? Used ta do it with watermelons, when I's a kid. Has ta be much better when using a real head, donecha think so, Cappy-tan?"

Alyson was holding tightly onto Fang's forearm, as if she were attempting to perform a chin-up exercise. She realized that struggling only made matters worse for her. She looked down and could see how far up she was. She was scared of heights so she closed her eyes, squeezing out teardrops and trembling with fear.

"Pull her back in, Otto. I'll get you whatever you want."

"Yuh take me fer a fool, Missy? I pull 'er in an' one of yer boys'll shoot me right through this big ol' head o' mine,"

Captain Lewis turned the bullhorn to her men and shouted, "Men, lower all the rifles and holster all handguns. I don't want any weapons aimed at Otto. No one is to shoot without my order."

All her men complied, so she turned around to face Fang.

She said, "OK, Otto. There're no weapons aimed at you any longer, so pull the girl back onto the roof."

"Did I hear a *please*, Cappy-tan?

"Please, Otto," Captain Lewis added, with controlled impatience.

Fang's right arm pulled Alyson into his chest, then his left arm grabbed her around the waist. He positioned her against himself like a bullet-proof vest, just to be cautious. He yelled, "This is as good as I can do fer yuh, Sweetheart. I don't trust yuh. I know yuh got snipers 'round here, so if I get shot, she dies, too. Remember that, Bitch."

"Otto, the helicopter's already on its way," responded Captain Lewis.

"First thing yuh do, Bitch, is yuh stop callin' me Otto. I'm Fang, an' second, yuh send my brother back up 'ere!"

"We didn't capture him, Fang. He gave himself up. I can't send him back in there. He has asked for our protection."

"Why, that cowardly, fuckin' runt. Really did give himself up, huh? Shee-it! He always a goddamn, snivelin' baby!" Fang yelled. "He a hopeless retard. Yuh tell 'im that. Got no brains, no balls an' no guts. Fuck 'im. Yuh keep 'im. I want somethin' else."

"What is it, Fang?" Captain Lewis said into the bullhorn.

"I want that helicopter 'ere before dark. Yuh been stallin', liddle lady. Actually, I want it 'ere ten minutes ago. Yuh unnerstand?" Fang's face was livid.

"One of my people has already called for the helicopter, Fang. There can't be any more delays because they're already on the way. OK?"

"Better be or yuh know what 'appens," Fang said as he held Alyson out over the edge of the roof, again, for cruel emphasis. Then he pulled her back to his chest and stepped back from the edge of the roof so he couldn't be seen from the ground.

*   *   *   *   *   *   *

Trooper Jones proceeded up the stairs, to the roof, having trouble breathing. He raised his right index finger to his right nostril, plunged it inside and pulled out the obstruction, a pale-green nugget which he wiped onto the wall. It made him think about his mother. She was manipulative, but loving— too loving. She had always taken exception with his crude manners. That's when he would get angry with her and think of awful things to say to her, hurting her feeling deliberately and harshly. Sometimes he even fantasized of tying her up and doing things to make her scream. His mother was unaware of her incredible luck. Jones struggled with self control, but knew that he wouldn't get into the State Police Academy with a criminal record. His meanness was like an ugly birthmark. It came into the world with him and grew larger as he aged. He shook those thoughts off and refocused. He took another deep breath through his nose, felt satisfied, then let the breath out through his mouth.

Trooper Jones took one confident step out the doorway and onto the rooftop where he immediately saw Sam. Sam looked at him. Jones placed his index finger to his lips.

Sam pointed to the doorway and mouthed the words, "Get out of here. Go."

Jones smirked at Sam, showing his disgust with her words. He whispered, "You get out. Now."

Sam shook her head and mouthed the words, "Can't leave her."

Jones shrugged his shoulder and pursed his lips to indicate that now he didn't give a shit what she did as long as she was quiet. Then Jones looked toward Fang.

Jones saw Fang holding Alyson over the edge of the roof and heard him say, "or yuh know what 'appens."

Jones walked cautiously toward Fang, whose back was towards him. Jones knew he had the big guy dead to rights. He could see the glory of his destiny rushing toward him, like being in a fast car and seeing the trees appear to rush toward you. He was elated. The sight of this rooftop scene and the knowledge that he had Fang nearly captured caused his imagined destiny to sprout and bloom, like a daisy in June.

Jones saw Fang pull Alyson into his chest, then step backwards, away from the edge of the roof where he could no longer be seen by the police on the ground.

Jones was only ten feet from Fang when he gave the command, "Police. Freeze and put the girl down."

Fang, caught off guard, but thinking quickly, spun around, still holding Alyson to his chest as a shield. He reached between him and Alyson and pulled the .357 handgun out of his belt and aimed it at Jones. Seeing that he now had the advantage over this brash cop, he said, "Now whatcha gonna do, asshole?" Fang's laughter skipped across the rooftop, like a thrown, flat stone skipping across calm water.

Jones suddenly realized how big and powerful Fang looked. Fang's massive body was intimidating and Jones was suddenly cognizant of the fear and sweat pouring out of his flesh, like a squeezed sponge. He noticed, with repugnance, the stink of his own sweat. He had thought that the reports of Fang's strength and size had been greatly exaggerated, but seeing first-hand that he was wrong only made his fear grow. But he took control of himself because he was convinced that he was headed for glory. He forced himself onward, through the barrier of his growing fear and the unexpected fissure in his courage.

"Just put the girl down and no one will get hurt. The charges ain't serious, yet. You just go back to prison. That'll be a piece of cake for you. And there's no death-row waiting for you . . . yet . . . so let the girl go and drop the gun," said Jones as he looked into the barrel of Fang's gun. He had told Fang to freeze, but he was the one who was frozen. Surprisingly, he found it hard to move.

Alyson squirmed from discomfort as Fang's arm was crushing her to his chest.

"Nah. Don't think so, asshole. Yuh think they'll ferget 'bout that cop I shot in the parkin' lot? Nope. No 'lectric chair, gas chamber, or needle fer me. I die 'ere or I go free. Live free or die. That's me. So yuh drop yer gun or I just fuckin' shoot yuh where yuh stand. Yuh shoot at me an' hit the girl an' yer ass gets burned in some pretty hot fire, liddle man. Can't yuh see? Yuh simply didn't think this through, did yuh? Didn't know they kept stupid troopers. Guess yuh should only open yur mouth ta change feet, huh?" Fang laughed, then grunted, "Now put yer gun down."

Just then Jones saw his destiny descend like the flow of brown sewage into a putrid sewer of utter confusion and hopelessness.

What the hell's happening? he thought. If I try to shoot Fang and hit the girl, my career is over and if I put my gun down and I'm captured, without having the captain's authority to even be on the roof, my career is still over. If I put my gun down and get killed, my life is over. If I get wounded, my pride and self-respect ends, just like my career. I'll be laughed at and humiliated for the rest of my life.

Ultimately and quickly, however, his decision was made on the basis of self-preservation. Screw the girl! Better to have a career that's over than to have a life that's over, he thought in desperation.

Thoroughly humiliated, Jones lowered his gun to his right thigh, then released it with a scraping clank on the gravel and tar rooftop. He raised his hands head high, palms open, in surrender.

Fang grinned satanically at Jones while releasing Alyson to the rooftop. She immediately ran into the arms of Sam and cried hysterically.

Fang diverted his attention from Jones to Sam and Alyson who were sitting. To Sam he said, curtly, "Make a move fer the door an' yuh both die."

Then Fang turned his attention back to Jones. Fang smiled at Jones, humiliating him with his crazed eyes and twisted smile that soon turned into taunting, soul-piercing laughter, causing Trooper Jones to tremble as his head became dazed and dizzy from panic. Jones felt his legs becoming rubbery.

Fang, still a few feet away, continued grinning at Trooper Jones who stood helpless and looked pathetic.

Jones's eyes began to water and when Fang saw this it triggered his rage.

"Yuh sure be stupid. Yuh never, ever give up yur gun. Didn't they teach yuh that? Now what yuh goin' ta do? Ask me fer mercy? Beg fer yur life? Maybe I should kill yuh ta stop yuh from havin' dumb babies."

Fang walked to Jones while glancing at Sam and Alyson, who sat on the warm, sticky tar and pebbles, not daring to move. Fang placed his handgun into his belt and stood two feet from the trooper, daring him to make a move, wanting him to make a move, wishing, begging Jones with his eyes to make that mistake.

And Jones did. Jones thought he saw an opportunity to reclaim his destiny, as well as his dignity. He swung at Fang's face. Fang, not being agile or particularly quick, felt the fist slam into his jaw. Jones's fist bounced off Fang's jaw.

Fang said, with a laugh, "Yuh throws a punch like a girl. They let sissies like yuh be a cop?" Fang grabbed Jones by the front of his shirt with his left hand, raised his right arm, cocked his fist back towards his shoulder, then punched Jones in the chest with a cannon-ball sized fist that shot at him as if it were operated via hydraulic pressure. Fang heard Trooper Jones say one word before he collapsed.

As Fang's punch landed, there was a cracking, splintering noise. The bones in Jones's sternum shattered, cracked and were driven inward, the bone shards puncturing, then bursting Jones's heart and deflating one lung. Trooper Jones was dead before his body hit the ground. The look of shock and utter surprise was frozen to his dead face. His shocked eyes, dead man's eyes, staring at the sky as if seeking help from some heavenly source. His lips were parted as if to say something else. The last word he said before he died was *destiny.*

Alyson's head was buried into Sam's shoulder and Sam kept it there so Alyson couldn't see Fang's savage brutality. Sam knew that Fang was now out of control.

Fang bent over and grabbed Trooper Jones by the neck and crotch, lifted him over his head, as if he was a pillow. He walked to the edge of the roof and stood there. All eyes from the troopers in the parking lot were, again, on Fang. Fang stood on the edge of the roof like King Kong on the Empire State Building. He was breathing heavily and screaming unintelligibly. He was in a full-blown, crazed rage.

Fang knew that now he was a murderer, definitely an intentional cop killer and there was no way out except for the helicopter. He desperately needed that helicopter.

Fang glanced over his shoulder at Sam and Alyson, then stood on the edge of the roof for a few seconds with Jones held over his head— the other cops didn't yet know that Jones was dead— before he yelled, "Cappy-tan Lew! Yuh better git that helicopter 'ere soon or I got two girls that gonna git the same watermelon treatment." Quickly, Fang tossed Jones's body off the roof, then rapidly stepped away from the edge. He looked to see if Sam and Alyson had moved. They hadn't, remaining frozen by fear and shock. Fang corrected his mistake by jogging to the rooftop door and locking it.

Captain Lewis and her men watched the limp body falling to the blacktopped parking lot. To Captain Lewis, it seemed as if time slowed down and the body fell in slow-motion. The body hit with a thud and a crunch, then bounced a foot into the air. Captain Lewis and a few other troopers ran to Jones. She felt for a pulse, but there was none. She wasn't even aware, yet, that Jones's crushed chest and punctured heart, and not the crushed skull, were what had actually killed him. All she could see was his crushed skull. But when she saw very little blood, she was fairly sure that Jones was dead— a dead heart can't pump blood out of the wounds. Jones's hair was quickly becoming matted with brain fluid, his nose and jaw were both shattered. It looked as if at least one arm was broken. Bone shards, a little blood from Jones's mouth, hair and spongy lumps of brain matter were scattered at Captain Lewis's feet.

A trooper turned, ran away from Jones's body, then vomited. Most of the others walked away, in shock, some with hands over their mouths, but all with fear and anger glowing in their eyes. Hatred began to fester in these men. Their intellect was being washed away by a surging tide of primordial *hunt and kill* instincts.

Captain Lewis stayed with the body, temporarily immobilized by the shock of one of her men being killed, and a rookie, too. But, she thought, what the hell was he doing on the roof?

Captain Lewis looked up to the rooftop and said, "Oh my God. Now you've done it, Fang! You'll regret it." No one heard those words and her vengeful tone of voice.

/../---/--./.-/-/-/../-./--./---/.-../-../

24

★★★★

"Throughout history, it has been the inaction of those who could have acted; the indifference of those who should have known better; and the silence of the voice of justice when it mattered most, that has made it possible for evil to triumph."

Haile Selassie

LIEUTENANT HAWKEY WALKED TO the tower that over-looked the school track and football field. It rose into the air, about thirty feet, easily clearing the roof of the long, red-brick, triple door garage which was used to store the custodians' grounds-keeping equipment. The observation deck looked like a child's large tree-house built on top of four large poles that were spaced out into a fifteen by twenty feet rectangle. A wooden ladder was attached.

A green, three feet tall, solid-walled railing extended around the perimeter of the platform's floor and from the top of this railing to the rooftop was all open space.

From here, unobstructed photographs or videos could be taken.

It was also a sniper's paradise. Trooper Gus Kovalik, the best shot on the SWAT team, the guy that Hawkey once had bragged could shoot a cigarette out of a man's teeth at seven hundred yards, was on the platform.

Lt. Hawkey had, moments before, called on the walkie-talkie to say he was coming to the tower. A few minutes later K-O— the first two letters of Kovalik's last name were "K-O," and since he could be counted on to "**K**nock-**O**ut" any target that he was assigned, he was given the stunted moniker, "K-O"— peeked over the railing. He could see Lieutenant Hawkey approaching from a long way off, though Hawkey could barely detect the trooper's presence in the tower.

When Hawkey reached the bottom of the tower, he looked up and yelled, "I'm coming up, K-O." One didn't take a chance accidentally sneaking up on a man with a gun, especially one who used it as well as Gus did.

Gus used his special Marine sniper rifle rather than the official state trooper version. It was the Marine's best sniper rifle in Vietnam, classified as the M-40A1 in .308 caliber. The barrel was free-floating— meaning that it was secured to the chamber, but did not touch the stock. The gap between the stock and rifle barrel was about the same thickness as a piece of school writing paper, but this slight mini-gap served to prevent the stock from distorting the barrel from one shot to the next.

Gus, like Lieutenant Hawkey, was an older member of the team. And like Hawkey, he was a Vietnam veteran, a marine sniper with over fifty confirmed kills (ninety per-cent of them were head shots) from extremely long ranges.

Hawkey personally recruited Gus for the team. He spotted Gus on the State Police Marksman team during the National Rifle and Pistol Championships held each year at Camp Perry in Ohio (considered to be the World Series of shooting sports in America). Gus had easily won the competition the last two years. Lieutenant Hawkey used his influential connections and the borrowed power of his superiors to get Gus transferred, with Gus's approval, to Hawkey's SWAT team. They quickly became close friends, especially having both survived the hell of Nam. They became like brothers, not of genes and chromosomes, but of courage, honor and friendship— a brotherhood based not on blood, but on Semper Fi.

"Come on up, Joe," K-O responded. He could hear Lieutenant Hawkey coming up the ladder, his boots thumping and scraping on the wooden rungs.

Lt. Hawkey stepped onto the platform and asked, "See anything going on, K-O?"

"No. Nothing, yet."

Hawkey saw the sniper rifle leaning on the railing with its bi-pod extended for added support and accuracy. K-O took care of his rifle like a woman takes care of her diamonds.

Hawkey certainly couldn't argue with that.

K-O was a guy you could trust and really depend on; a cool head; a calm personality, with remarkable vision and an unusually steady hand. K-O had reminded him a little of Wolfe. But where Wolfe had his blade, garrote and martial arts skills to use at close range, K-O had a rifle, the element of surprise and camouflage that placed him in the elite of the elite status of snipers, enabling him to accomplish nearly impossible shots at extreme ranges.

Lt. Hawkey picked up the binoculars and looked toward the classroom windows. He said, "K-O, I want you to double check all your scope settings, check the rifle and ammo, too. If we only get one shot, I don't want some grain of dirt or dirty lens or unstable bi-pod to thwart your effort. Check everything, K-O."

Though the rifle and scope were already set and double checked, K-O checked everything again to ease Hawkey's mind. K-O reached out and gently picked up the rifle like one would pick up his own newborn child. He opened the bolt to make sure in was unloaded. He reached into his vest pocket and pulled out a velvet wrapping about a foot long. Each bullet had its own pocket to eliminate any chance of nicks, scratches or dirt getting on any bullet. K-O wanted pristine bullets so that nothing on the bullet could affect accuracy. K-O pulled out one bullet from its velvet pocket, checked it by rolling it on his fingers, making sure the business end of the bullet was tight in its casing, then he checked the primer. No problem there. The bullets were all match-quality and hand-loaded by Gus. Each bullet was a hollow-point, high grain, high power, micro-missile of death. Gus pulled the bolt back, carefully checked the rifle chamber for obstructions and to see if more oil was needed. No oil was necessary, so he slid the bolt forward, then downward to lock it into the loading chamber. The bolt closed easily, like silk across flesh. He checked the safety. It was in the "on" position.

"No problems with anything," Gus said.

Hawkey said nothing while K-O was checking all aspects of the rifle. He didn't want to upset any preparations, patterns or rituals that Gus might have. Hearing Gus's good news, Hawkey nodded, patted Gus on the shoulder and smiled at him. It was a strained smile.

Gus noticed the strained smile, then thought, Very unusual for Hawkey. Usually as cool and stable as a glacier.

They had both been squatting, but now K-O sat down and lifted both knees up so that each of them looked like an inverted "V" shape. He relaxed, took a couple of deep breaths and eased the rifle barrel onto the railing, saying, "The bi-pod won't be useful. The railing's slightly too high. That's fine, though. No problem."

Over the railing and under the rifle barrel Gus placed a piece of half-inch thick, non-skid rubber to prevent the barrel from accidentally sliding. Gus leaned forward slightly and pushed the stock securely into his shoulder.

Joe watched silently as K-O took a deep breath through his nose, then let half the air out through his mouth. K-O peered through the high-power scope, finding the cross-hairs and sighting on the second floor classroom windows. He could see, like before, that all the school windows were mostly uncovered, except for the teacher's classroom which, appeared to have all the shades pulled down. All Gus could see were faint, distorted shadows, small shadows. Kids. But the roof was a simple, clear shot, no harder than bitch-slapping a Viet Cong.

Through binoculars, Hawkey saw the same shadows. Neither man spoke.

K-O slightly readjusted a knob on the scope to give a perfectly sharp image of the windows. Then another knob was readjusted to match the two-hundred seventy-five yards from the tower to the classroom windows and to the school roof.

Now K-O rechecked the wind direction by looking at the football field's goal posts. Each of the four posts had a purple and gold banner—

school colors— used to indicate wind direction, mostly used by the field-goal kicker and the quarterback.

Hawkey saw K-O look at the wind direction banners and smiled at Gus's luck. There was only a very slight breeze from their right to left. The breeze was so minimal that it would not effect the trajectory of a high-powered rifle bullet.

Finally, having checked the rifle itself, one of the bullets, the scope's stable attachment and wind velocity settings, K-O pulled out the five-shot clip. Everything looked good, so he removed four bullets from his velvet pouch, plus the one he had already pulled out and loaded them carefully into the clip.

The oiled clip slid into the rifle easily, with a reassuring, secure "click."

Lt. Hawkey started to compliment his friend. "That's great—"

But Lieutenant Hawkey was interrupted by the sound of his walkie-talkie. Captain Lewis's voice sounded urgent. "Joe, come in. Over. Joe. Come in. Over," she repeated.

Hawkey heard the stress in her voice and responded immediately. "Hawkey here. Over."

"Joe, Fang's on the roof. He's holding one of the classroom girls off the edge of the roof by her hair so I had to speed up the helicopter arrival to get him to pull the girl back onto the roof. But that isn't the worst of it, Joe. A couple of minutes after pulling the girl back in, Fang appeared on the edge of the roof again, with one of my rookie troopers held over his head. Fang threw the trooper off the roof.

"It was trooper Jones, the one that brought the psychiatrist to us. I don't have any idea what he was doing on that roof. It was a totally unauthorized action. Never mind that for now. We'll figure that out later. Fang looked frantic, Joe. I think he's lost control. I want you to have your man take the shot if he can get one. Over."

"A termination . . . a kill shot, Bev?"

"Affirmative, Joe. He's too damn dangerous to fool around with any longer."

"Bev, I'm on the other side of the building with my best marksman, Gus Kovalik. We can't see Fang at all from our position. There're AC units and a chimney blocking our view. But if Fang's on the roof, then

Miller must be alone in the classroom. We've got no really clear, clean shot into the classroom either.

Whaddaya mean, Joe? You saying you can't see inside the classroom? Over."

"We've got a good view of the outside of the classroom windows, Bev, but we can't see inside the classroom. All the shades are pulled down and all we see with my binoculars and Gus's scope are distorted shadows, small shadows, kids. I suspect that there are kids still lined up on the counter next to the windows. Over"

"Shit!" Captain Lewis mumbled in frustration. "OK, Joe. If Fang or Charlie come into view and Gus can get a kill-shot at them, I want him to take the kill-shot at Fang, but a disabling shot at Miller. Once the helicopter gets here we'll be in serious trouble. Fang'll want to take hostages with him and we can't let that maniac and Miller leave, except in cuffs . . . or, if they force our hand, in body-bags. Over."

Hawkey smiled at Gus, then gave him the thumb-up sign— K-O opened the bolt-action of his rifle, then closed it; that action shoved one bullet into the chamber, ready to fire as soon as the safety lever was pushed to the "off" position.

Hawkey had originally believed that Bev wouldn't give permission for any of his snipers to take a kill-shot, especially when kids were present.

Trooper Kovalik heard the conversation, but still had a frown on his face as he silently mouthed the word "disabling?" with question marks flashing in each eye as if there were spotlights inside his eyeballs.

Hawkey saw the frown and knew what it meant immediately. "Bev, a disabling shot is real tricky and actually dangerous. If Gus shoots Miller and the shot doesn't put him down and out immediately, the guy will go into a rage and will shoot with any or all of his weapons at the students. Also, these cartridges that snipers use go through-and-through. If someone's next to one of those psychos, the penetrating bullet may hit an innocent directly or with a ricochet. However, the chances of that happening are much less with a kill-shot to the head. Over."

"Sorry, Joe, I understand, but I can't authorize a kill shot on Charlie, not yet, anyway. But if you or any of your snipers get a kill-shot on Fang, while he's on the roof, take it; however, taking a kill-shot into the classroom, at Charlie, is not authorized. That's a negative, Joe. Miller hasn't killed anyone like Fang has. Hell, he hasn't even hurt anybody, that we know of. He doesn't have a record of lethal violence; just violence as a pederast. I'm worried about the kids in there and not just the possibility that Charlie will use one of the boys as a catamite. Plus, a head shot would be terribly traumatic for those kids to witness. Blood, bone shards and chunks of brain will splatter all over the room. A sight like that will traumatize those kids for life, if it hasn't happened already. So I repeat. No kill shot is authorized on Miller, just a high percentage disabling shot is authorized on Miller. Fang's another story. He's already killed and he'll do it again without hesitation. Tell all your snipers that they're authorized to take a kill-shot if Fang is clearly visible on the roof, but it has to be a very high percentage shot." Bev emphasized the words, *it has to be a very high percentage shot.* "Joe, I gotta go. You understand what I want? Over."

"Roger that. I understand and I'll pass the message on. Out."

K-O looked up at Hawkey.

On a different, but secure channel, Hawkey ordered, "You heard the Captain, men. Obey protocol. You have authorization for a very high percentage kill-shot at Fang, on the rooftop, with no kids around, but only a high percentage disabling shot at Miller, inside the classroom. And, for the sake of safety I don't want any shooting without a status report for me and permission to fire from me, in case orders are changed at the last second. Please acknowledge immediately."

"Sniper one. I acknowledge."

"Sniper two. I acknowledge."

"Sniper three. I acknowledge."

Gus nodded his head at Hawkey, then said, "I acknowledge, Joe."

Hawkey placed a friendly, trusting hand on K-O's shoulder.

Each sniper would follow his orders, exactly, despite the fact that each man realized that a *disabling* shot was a pure misnomer— like saying that two planes that almost crashed in mid-air had a *near miss.* Bullshit! It was a *near hit.* Very few shots can completely disable a gunman, except a kill-shot, which, of course, if successful, disables him immediately and permanently. A disabling shot to the shoulder, arms, abdomen, waist or legs did not usually stop a determined gunman in the sense that he couldn't function. More often than not, he was still able to kill or maim his hostages because he was still conscious and still able to partially function, especially if he goes into an adrenaline saturated, vengeful rage. Even if the gunman was bleeding to death, he could still often function enough to do serious or fatal damage to some of his hostages before he grew too weak from the loss of blood.

The scenery brightened as the sun moved out from behind a cumulous cloud.

"Jesus Christ!" Gus said as he resumed looking through his rifle scope. "Joe. Look. The end window, on the left, just opened and the shade is up. Miller's standing with his rifle aimed out the window. Should I take the shot, Joe?"

Joe quickly looked through his binoculars, then at K-O. "Affirmative. A disabling shot," Hawkey reminded K-O, as he thrust the binoculars back to his eyes.

K-O quickly assumed his firing routine and had Miller in the scope's cross-hairs.

Hawkey stared through the binoculars. Now there was a sunshine window-glare on Miller. The bright sun was reflecting off the whole row of windows, but it looked like Miller. "High percentage shot," bolted through Hawkey's brain like lightening. Hawkey stared through the binoculars, but still wasn't sure what he was seeing. He concentrated, blinked to focus, squinted, then suddenly yelled, "I can't see his face clearly. Can you, K-O?" Then to himself, Hawkey spoke, "Shit! Miller isn't that tall." Joe turned, inhaled sharply and screamed. "No!" at K-O

But K-O was already pulling the trigger. Hawkey's shout made K-O flinch.

The shot rang out and Hawkey's heart felt as though it had ripped away from the arteries and tumbled into his stomach. Visions of disaster inundated his thoughts.

"Goddamn it, Gus! I don't think that was Miller. I think it was the teacher!"

"It was Miller with the AK-47 in his hands. Why would the teacher have the AK and aim it out the window?" K-O confidently responded.

"No, Gus. I don't think it was! There's sun glare on the windows. All you saw was an adult, male shape. Then you saw the AK-47 and were partially blinded by the glare. Both of us assumed that the AK-47 was held by the bad guy, Miller, but the teacher could have had the rifle, K-O. He could have disarmed Miller."

"Disarmed Miller, then aim the AK out the window?" K-O stated, incredulously.

"We don't really know if he was aiming it. Maybe Roman disarmed Charlie and wanted to throw the AK out the window and it just looked like he was aiming it."

K-O acknowledged the possibility with his eyes. "Oh, shit!" he exclaimed.

"Oh, shit, is right, K-O. I think you may have just shot the teacher. Both our fault, but Goddamnit! I think you shot my friend, Roman!" Joe held the binoculars to his eyes and looked at the bullet shattered window. He saw no movement.

K-O set the rifle down realizing that he may have shot the wrong person. If so, it would be the very first time. He was so sure of the shot. He dragged his hand across his sweaty brow, then rubbed his cheeks and mouth. He squinted through dazed eyes. He looked at Hawkey, open mouthed, but said nothing . . . just thinking, Who the hell's Roman?

/-.../..-/-/-/....//-.../---/-/..../---/..-./-.--/---/..-/

25

★★★★

"The problem with the world is that fools and fanatics are always so certain of themselves, while wiser people are full of doubts."

Bertrand Russell

ROMAN HEARD HIS NAME being called, as if by multiple voices traveling through a long, echoing tunnel. He couldn't rise from the floor. Numerous hands seemed to be pressing on him, holding him down. He thought he saw elves poking and prodding him. His vision was blurred; his hearing was being distorted by sounds of bees or insects. He thought about Gulliver's Travels, where Gulliver, on his back, is tied to the ground by civilian Lilliputians while Lilliput soldiers stand on him and hold him down with spears.

Roman was being pushed and poked. The myriad voices overlapped, giving Roman incongruent sensations of reality, cloaked in fantasy, seen through blurred vision, hazy thoughts, vague noises and dulled feelings. He grinned stupidly, as if drunk. He tried lifting his head and almost passed out from the sudden pain. His mind filled with blackness as tiny dots of silver light sparkled before his eyes, like diamonds floating in a sea of tar. He felt cold sweat running down his face and chest. His vision cleared slightly, as if half a layer from a gauze blindfold had been removed. Then he became aware of warm sweat slowly flowing down his spine, bringing to mind a lethargic snake. His senses struggled to peer through the mental and visual fog. "Warm?" his mind asked. He groaned, saw and heard chattering elves surrounding him, but not hurting him. He wiped the cold sweat off his brow, then reached to his back and touched the warm wetness, then grimacing from the pain. When he held his fingers to his eyes and saw red. Ah, he thought, it's blood, not sweat. Am I shot or stabbed in the back? Finally his mind cleared, eyes focused, the illusions departed, leaving him to face stark reality.

A small, but familiar animal crawled to him. He blinked, squinted, then refocused his eyes. Not an animal. He recognized Steven. He was crawling back from the sink dragging a small tub of water and paper towels. Roman thought, Damn! No insects, no buzzing, no elves, my chattering students.

A few children held Roman's hands and arms as they tried to help him get up.

"No. Not yet," Roman said through a frown of pain.

Steven and the other students sat on the floor and watched Mr. Wolfe. Whimpering children sat all around him, outlining his body as he lay on the floor. The whimpering, moaning and crying sounds, like buzzing bees all around him, made him feel like a queen bee in his classroom hive.

Roman thought, I couldn't have been stabbed; nobody here to stab me. Shit! Must've been shot.

Roman sat up, pulled off his tie, then awkwardly unbuttoned his shirt and removed it. As he did that, he realized that being shot didn't feel as bad as he'd thought it would. But then he'd often been told that you don't feel much just before you die and that just before death you felt a blissful numbness. But he had an optimistic and comforting feeling that this wasn't his time to meet death. He didn't feel any numbness yet. He did feel sharp pain in his back which proved to have a seriously debilitating affect on his right arm. He could only move that arm with great pain. But at least now his mind was clear.

Roman struggled to sit up. When he did sit up, he leaned his back against a cabinet for support, suddenly moaning and nearly fainting from the pain. The pain was excruciating, as if a double-edged dagger were being pushed, very slowly, into his back. He was forced to lean forward, away from the cabinet. He tried to remove his undershirt. He grimaced. The undershirt was too tight; it created too much discomfort to remove it. He tried to survey his other body parts to see if he was wounded anywhere else. He detected nothing else. It was just his back. "Steven. Some scissors, please," Roman painfully stated through clenched teeth.

Steven came back with a pair of scissors and started cutting Roman's undershirt off. Shirley and Judi wiped the blood from their teacher's back, often gagging, especially when seeing where it was pooling around his belt line. It was extremely difficult for them, but they both finished without actually vomiting.

As the girls were cleaning the blood, Roman noticed that he was having no trouble breathing, despite the pain in the upper right back area. He wiggled his toes, could move his legs, arms, fingers and hips. He could now see and think clearly. He felt the warm rivulets of blood trickling down his back. The blood flow had decreased considerably when he sat upright. He pulled all this information together, concentrated on it.

His conclusion was that he wasn't shot critically, didn't even seem as if the bullet penetrated very far. Maybe it was just a piece of bullet shrapnel or a glancing shot, he thought. He gently asked the children to move a little away from him. He needed room to maneuver. They obeyed. Then Roman saw the bloody paper towels. Plenty of blood on the initial paper towels, but not as much on the later ones, he thought. There wasn't nearly as much blood as he'd expected or imagined. His mind, stunned with the thought of being shot— and shocked with the irony of not having been shot in Nam— may have exaggerated the sensations and the quantity of blood, but not the pain. Something was wrong, but he couldn't put a handle on it yet. He focused his eyes and mind, trying to think of the next move to escape and free the students.

"People," he said to the students, "now is the time for bravery and all you have to do to be brave is not to cry, whimper or moan. That way I can think better and get all of you out of here. Be brave. Be quiet and listen."

Steven glanced bug-eyed at Shirley and Judi.

"What?" Roman asked, but all he saw was more kids pointing at his back. It certainly wasn't surprising news that he'd been wounded.

He tried to move his upper torso and was startled, then immobilized by the searing pain. He looked at Steven questioningly.

"Mr. Wolfe," Steven said. "It's a long piece of glass sticking out of your right shoulder blade area. It's slanted. Looks like it went in sideways and kinda deep.

Roman couldn't move his upper right arm normally; it felt numb.

"It doesn't feel like it's bleeding badly any more. How's it look, Steven."

"It's not bleeding much now."

"It doesn't hurt as much either," Roman added, mostly for the kid's comfort.

Roman smiled broadly at the children, reassuring them with, "Looks like Mr. Wolfe's going to live to be a hundred year old grandpa." Then he thought, A sliver of glass? I wonder how big it is? It may be a glass sliver, but it feels like an ice pick scrapping at my shoulder blade.

He fought to keep smiling at the kids. They smiled warily back at him, but were non-responsive when he winked at them. They're too smart, Roman thought. Can't fool them about the seriousness of the situation. Suddenly he thought of Blizzard. In his mind he said, "Blizzard. Come." Before Blizzard appeared, Roman said to the children, "My friend, a white wolf, is coming. You'll all be able to see him. Don't be afraid of him. He won't hurt you. I promise."

Blizzard appeared, ghost-like. He lay down next to Roman.

A few kids still screamed and scrambled away.

"He won't hurt any of you," Roman repeated. "His name's Blizzard,"

Blizzard panted; his pink tongue hanging out and his ribs expanding and contracting quickly with each breath. He licked his own mouth, then yawned and placed his head on Roman's thigh. The kids fell in love with him immediately, even the initially scared kids. They all looked as if they wanted to pet him.

"Pet him one at a time," Roman said to the kids and they did just that.

Roman shifted his position carefully, not wanting to break-off the glass sliver inside the skin. He couldn't pull it out himself because of its location. Nor did he want to have a student pull it out and expose the other kids to the sight of more blood, but, really, what choice did he have?

Shirley and Judi stood next to Mr. Wolfe.

"Girls," Roman asked, with a whisper, "is the glass broken off at skin level?"

"No," they answered in unison.

Shirley spoke, "Mr. Wolfe, it looks like one piece."

"Can you carefully pull it straight out so it won't break? Now listen carefully. Can you pull it out the way it's slanted? I don't want to have it broken off under my skin. Shirley, just grab it carefully with a piece of dry paper towel so your fingers don't slip off it, slowly pull it out, then Judi will hand you another paper towel and you press that paper towel against the wound."

Shirley cringed. "Oh, no, Mr. Wolfe. I can't do that. I'm afraid," she whispered.

Roman looked at Judi, who shook her head, indicating that she couldn't do it either.

Roman asked Steven if he would help. "Gee. I don't know, Mr. Wolfe."

Blizzard looked up at Roman and sent a thought to him. "I can do it."

Roman asked all the kids to sit in front of him so they wouldn't see what was happening. Then he asked Steven to get a bunch of paper towels from over the sink and the roll of duct tape from his desk. Roman reminded him to crawl so he couldn't be seen from the windows. Upon retrieving those items, Roman asked Steven to sit close to him. Then Blizzard moved behind Roman.

Roman said to Steven, "When I tell you, I want you to go behind me, press the paper towels hard against the cut, then attach them there with the duct tape, OK?

Steven looked a little hesitant, but said, "OK."

Roman, still in a sitting position, prepared himself for the pain.

Blizzard delicately grabbed the glass sliver between his lips and drew it out slowly. Three seconds later it was out. Blizzard dropped it, then licked the wound; the taste of blood was appealing to Blizzard, but was not the reason that he'd licked the wound. Something medicinal in the saliva would assist the wound to heal quickly.

Blizzard moved away while licking the bright red blood from around his mouth.

Roman, surprised at the lack of pain, said, "Now, Steven."

Steven quickly crawled behind Roman, wiped off one meandering rivulet of blood, then pressed a thick, folded wad of paper towels hard against the wound.

Roman still felt no pain, only pressure. He ripped off three long strips of duct tape for Steven. Roman then told Steven to tape the paper towels to his back. Steven placed three pieces of duct tape so they crisscrossed the paper towels in the shape of an asterisk. When Steven was done, he carefully picked up the piece of glass, showed it to Roman, then wrapped it into a paper towel and lobbed it into the nearby garbage can.

At the same time Roman grabbed his bloody undershirt. He tied the under shirt securely to the tip of the broom handle and waved it out of the shattered window. He and the children waited anxiously.

A couple minutes later, Roman heard a familiar voice coming from outside and below his window.

"Wolfe, if you hear me, wave the flag up and down, then say, "My name is Wolfe." said Lieutenant Hawkey.

Roman moved the broomstick up and down, then repeated the sentence.

"OK, now. I think I recognize your voice, but I have to make sure you're not Miller. Answer this question: 'What was the Spanish-sounding name that some of our Hispanic friends called you?'"

"Solo-lobo," answered Roman without delay.

"Good, Roman. Is Miller dead?"

"No, he's tied up and gagged," Roman said as he knelt on the floor below the shattered classroom window. "You the SOB that nearly killed me?"

"Roman. Listen. It's Joe. Remember Nam. Remember Khe Sanh? Remember the siege and your Mohawk Indian friend? It's me, Hawk Eye."

"Hawk Eye? . . . Damn you. You tryin' to kill me, old friend?"

Joe apologized, saying, "Sorry about that, Wolf Man. My sniper and I thought you were Miller and he was trying to get a shot at him. When I saw it was you I yelled at him. He flinched, but pulled the trigger. Luckily the flinch knocked his aim off. We thought he'd shot you anyway. You okay?"

"Yeah, I'm fine. Your man put a large glass sliver into my back with that shot, but nothing bad. I got it out and now it's bandaged. Not much pain now. Miller's lying here on the floor, unconscious. Steven, one of my students, his classmates and I put him down for a long count. And if he doesn't stay down, quiet and behave, they have my permission to put him down again. Kind of like in the book, *Lord of the Flies*."

Steven's face, and the faces of his classmates, burst with pride, then lit-up like a string of Christmas lights.

"Tell you about all that later. Holy crap!" Roman yelled out. "Hawk Eye, huh?. Never thought I'd see you again. You're a trooper? Didn't think they'd take Injuns. You scalp anyone yet? I gotta guy up here who needs scalping."

Besides Hawkey's relatives, Roman was the only one allowed to call Lieutenant Hawkey by his Mohawk Indian name of "Hawk Eye."

"This old Mohawk Injun renegade is at your service, Wolf Man." Then, to return the friendly insult, Lieutenant Hawkey said, "They let you be a teacher of young children, huh? Must have really lowered the standards to let you into that profession?"

"Yeah. Yeah, I guess so. They took pity on me."

"Is the coast all clear up there?" Joe stated.

"Yeah, Hawk Eye. It's all clear up here. Fang's on the roof with one of my girl students and Sam. The girl's name is Alyson. Does that damn sniper of yours know enough not to shoot at me again?" yelled Roman.

"He does, now, but I was spotting for him, so it's my fault too. There was too much glare on the window," shouted Lieutenant Hawkey. "OK, Buddy. Now I need your help. You have a better knowledge of the situation up there. So, how do we handle this?"

"This is your show, Joe," Roman said, puzzled.

"No, Wolf Man. When you were around, it was always your show. We all trusted you implicitly. How do you see this situation?"

"OK. Let me think."

While Roman thought for a minute. Lieutenant Hawkey called Captain Lewis on his walkie-talkie, wanting to update her about the current situation concerning this side of the building. Captain Lewis acknowledged him and said that she had a bad situation with Fang holding the girl hostage over the edge of the roof. She also said that she thought Sam was up there, but had not seen her yet. Captain Lewis said that she needed Lieutenant Hawkey to come back as soon as possible. She ended the transmission abruptly.

Hawkey called K-O, who was still in the tower and told him to stay there. And if Fang came to his side of the roof and K-O had a clear shot, he was still authorized to take a kill-shoot, but only if he could do so without harming the hostage and *if he was 100% sure that he was shooting at Fang.* Hawkey informed Gus that Sam may be on the roof, also. Gus acknowledged the message, then filled his lungs full of air and exhaled in a sign of relief for not having shot the teacher, though in his youth he would have like to shoot some of his teachers.

"All's clear, Wolf Man. You can look out the window now and talk to me," said Lieutenant Hawkey.

Roman pulled the broomstick into the classroom and gave it to Steven. Roman stood and hesitantly moved toward the window. "Give me an update, Buddy."

"My captain tells me that Fang's up to something that doesn't sound or look good for that little girl or for Sam. Got any good ideas? We need to work fast, man. The helicopter is coming. Can't let Fang off that roof into a helicopter."

"Yeah, Hawk Eye. I understand. I was going to lower Miller and the kids out the window and down to you with a long orange, heavy-duty electrical cord, but if you say that your captain has Fang in sight, on the roof and something bad is happening, then I have to get up on the roof ASAP. Get your ass up here, Hawk Eye and help me get these kids outta here. Meet you in the hallway."

"Be there in a few seconds," Hawk Eye yelled as he ran around the corner of the building, grabbed two of his men, then raced to the side entrance of the school while radioing Captain Lewis with the information.

Lt. Hawkey and his two men sprang, two steps at a time, up the stairs, passing another guard who was told to stay put. When they got to the second floor, Lieutenant Hawkey peeked through the doorway, then down the hallway. He saw Roman standing in the hallway with a handgun in his right hand and Miller draped, like a limp rug, over his left shoulder. A mass of children stood behind him, poking their heads out of the doorway, desperately wanting to get away.

Roman left hand pointed to the door that led to the roof. Hawk Eye, his men, then Roman and the children started walking toward each other.

When Hawk Eye reached Wolfe, Wolfe said, "Hawk Eye. Can you guard the roof door? Fang can't be allowed to come back down here. We need to keep him up there."

Hawkey's two men looked at each other with puzzled expressions when they heard the Lieutenant being called "Hawk Eye."

"Sure," Hawk Eye said. "I've got two good men to help." Hawk Eye stood guard by the open door frame pointing his H&K, MP-5, 9mm assault gun up the stairs.

Lt. Hawkey ordered the two other SWAT team members to assist Roman.

Roman pointed to his students and ordered, "You guys bring these kids and this asshole, Miller, out of here, immediately."

The two officers looked at Roman, strangely, taking offense at being ordered to do something by a civilian; a teacher who was giving them orders as if it were natural for him, as if he were their boss. They looked at Lieutenant Hawkey for confirmation, their expressions saying, "Do we take orders from this guy?"

"He knows what he's doing," Lieutenant Hawkey said, in a loud, authoritative whisper, "Do what he said and get out of here, now. But cuff Miller first."

One trooper placed handcuffs on Miller's wrists, which were still tied behind his back, then allowed Roman to transfer Miller's limp body onto his shoulder. Then the officer departed down the stairs.

The other trooper collected the scared kids into a small, tight group and immediately took them downstairs to safety, while his Lieutenant stayed with the teacher he mysteriously called, "Wolf Man," among other names, who, in turn, called his Lieutenant, "Hawk Eye" instead of Lieutenant Hawkey.

Roman looked anxiously at the roof door entrance. "I have to go up alone," he said to Hawk Eye. "Too dangerous with the both of us up there. He'll start shooting when he sees your uniform. Me? I can bait him into a fight. He sees me as a weakling teacher, so he won't shoot me. He'll want to play with me, like a cat with a mouse."

"Shit! Buddy, Captain Lewis will chew me a new asshole if I let you do that alone. I can stay outta sight, be your backup."

"I don't have time to argue with you, Hawk Eye. You know I'm right about this. Can you handle Captain Lewis's criticism?" There was a pause. "Hawk Eye, you always trusted me before. So trust me now. I know how to do this, OK? That's my student and my wife up there. Fang's an extremely dangerous bully and I've handled bullies every since middle school."

"The Captain won't agree with that, but, yeah, I know you're right. I'd trust you with my life. Did it nearly every day we were together in Nam. Go ahead, but be real careful with this guy. He's ultra-ruthless. I mean . . . stone . . . cold . . . ruthless. Not some skinny, half-pint Viet Cong or a midget-like NVA soldier.

"Oh, shit! I almost forgot to tell you. A custodian came to Bev and I when he saw someone on the roof. He said that the key to the roof door is on a hook near the door handle. I told him that that doesn't help us any because the ape on the roof would take the key, unlock the door, pass through it, then lock the door behind him. I had interrupted the custodian with my impatience and didn't allow him to finish. The guy said that there's a spare key, a hidden key to that door. You just reach up to the rafter that's above the door and feel around until you find it. So that'll help tremendously, giving you a quiet approach. I'll be waiting down here. Go," Hawk Eye said.

Roman quietly started up the stairs, mumbling something.

Joe thought, What the hell? Did he just say Blizzard? He's still the Wolf Man.

After calling Blizzard as he climbed the stairs, Roman said, "Consider yourself called to duty." When he reached the top of the stairs, Roman paused, felt above the door frame and, sure enough, found the key. He unlocked the door as quietly as he could.

He felt for the blade on his right hip and pulled it out with his left hand as he gripped the magnum handgun in his right hand— he wished that he had his throwing knife, but he never brought weapons to school. His thoughts meandered, thinking, The way public school are heading, teachers will soon need to be armed. He refocused, unlocked the door and opened it very slowly. Luckily, the door was facing away from where Fang was standing. Peeking around the corner, Roman could see Alyson and Sam. He could see fear in Sam's tense body, even looking at her from behind. Poor Alyson looked like she was in shock, as Sam held her tightly. As they sat, Sam rocked Alyson.

Fang stepped away from the edge of the roof, then glared at Sam as she held Alyson. Alyson was trembling, her face buried in Sam's shoulder while being held within Sam's embrace. Fang laughed at them, knowing that the door was locked, so they had nowhere to go. He had complete control over their minds and bodies, but it was their bodies that he was thinking about. Maybe, he thought, he should bring the girls on the helicopter with him. Once he was safe, he could have so much fun with the both of them, though it was Alyson that he desired the most.

* * * * * * *

Holy shit! Bev thought to herself as she looked upward from the parking lot. Did I just hear a coyote howling? Sounded like it came from the rooftop. No. Can't be. Must have been a dog, she said to herself, with a confused tilt to her head and a frowning brow. She thought, That's strange. It didn't really sound like a dog. And what would a dog be doing on the roof? Christ, this mess is getting crazier and crazier.

* * * * * * *

Joe smiled at the ghostly vision as he stood guard by the door. He'd seen the *ghost wolf* before, in Nam, but had never said anything to anybody about it. He had thought, Why waste my breath saying something that no one will believe.

/--/.-/-.-/./--/.!..-./././.-../

26

★★★★

"It is easy to go down into Hell. Night and day the gates of Dark Death stand wide, but to climb back again, to trace one's steps to the upper air — There's the rub, the task."

Virgil

ROMAN HID BEHIND THE upper roof doorway which projected upward from the rooftop like an ice-fishing shack.

He peeked, again, from his concealed position. He glimpsed Sam and Alyson. Roman noticed that Alyson had something tied around her waist. Something orange? "Shit!" Roman mouthed the word. Fang had securely tied a thick orange, extension cord around Alyson's waist. Must have gotten it from the room across the hallway, Roman thought. The cord, being used as a rope, stretched about twenty-five feet to where Fang was standing at the edge of the roof. The other end of the orange cord was tied around Fang's waist.

Fang stared downward and screamed, "Yuh see this orange 'stention cord? The other end is tied ta a little girlie! If I fall off the roof then she gets pulled off with me! How yuh like that? So, go ahead. Shoot me. Come on, shoot me, yuh sons-a-bitches! Hey, Cap'an Lew. Give the

309

order ta shoot me! I ain't goin' back ta prison. I don' mind dyin' right here! Better than life in prison."

Captain Lewis immediately yelled into her bull-horn, "Stand down. No one fires their weapon. That's an order." Then, gazing upward at Fang, she spoke. "No one's going to shoot you, Fang."

"Sure, I know. Yur all goddamn chicken-shits when it comes right down to it. All cowards. Yuh'd never face me man-to-man. None of yuh would. Yuh see, I know . . ."

While Fang continued his taunting conversation with Captain Lewis, Roman picked up a pebble and threw it near Sam. The loud talking covered up the sound so Fang couldn't hear the pebble land, then roll. The pebble had landed near Sam and attracted her attention. Her horrified face turned toward Roman, then, like magic, she grinned.

Quickly, Roman placed his right index finger perpendicular to his lips, indicating that Sam and Alyson shouldn't say anything. Roman then pointed at his eyes, then Sam's eyes, then pointed at Fang, who was still engulfed in his invective taunting. Sam knew that Roman wanted her to look at Fang so she wouldn't give away Roman's presence. Sam turned and gazed at Fang's gesticulating arms.

Sam waited, then suddenly, she felt the extension cord, around Alyson, drop loosely to the roof. Sam stared at the severed ends, then thanked God for her wonderful, atheist husband.

Meanwhile, Fang was openly daring someone to shoot him, using a maniacal tone of voice and sudden, jerky hand-motions, while spittle ejaculated from his mouth.

Roman, hiding behind the A/C equipment, whispered to Sam, "Door's unlocked. Run. Lock the door behind you. Don't show anyone the key. Go now."

"Lock the door?" Alyson whispered.

"Don't have time to explain. There's a cop waiting for you down the stairs. Do what I told you. Take this key. Now move."

Sam scrambled to her feet and ran for the door. Fang was oblivious to her.

Now that it was just the two of them on the roof, Roman went through a transformation. No longer was he a calm, patient teacher, but a skillful, violent protector; a wolf protecting its lair. His bare chest and back stood out in a strange contrast against his navy blue, dress pants and black belt. His back was smeared with old blood and rivulets of new blood, but no pain. Roman leaped away from the A/C equipment.

Fang stood still and erect, finally sensing that something was wrong. Then he felt the answer— the slackened extension cord. He spun around to see that Sam and Alyson were gone; his face was distorted by his fury. His jaw became a granite cliff jutting away from his thickly muscled neck. He immediately turned around and stepped away from the edge of the roof, then untied the extension cord, allowing it to fall off.

Fang paused to glare at a strange-looking sight— the skinny, gangling teacher. He looked into Roman's ominous eyes and felt a disturbing surprise. Fang had been expecting to see immobilizing fear in those brown eyes. But what he saw and felt was an intense, feral heat, radiating toward him like a flame from a flame-thrower. And, yet, in contradiction to the heat, Roman's eyes seemed covered with a film of ice, the fire blazing somewhere inside. Staring into Roman's icy eyes was like seeing a lit welding torch through a block of clear ice.

Fang thought, Damn Teach is clever ta get those bitches away silent. Somethin' very odd 'bout that puny man.

The flames of anger leaped from Roman's eyes like molten lava spewing from a volcano. The absence of expected fear in those eyes worried Fang. The grim slash of the teacher's mouth had a determined edge to it, but Fang had seen that before and had also seen it crumble under the impact of his fists. Yet Fang's primal urge was to retreat in the face of this skinny, bare-chested man with the fiery eyes and ominous grin. Roman's eyes reminded Fang of something . . . some animal. Yes, Fang finally realized. Those were a rabid dog's eyes. The repeated urge to retreat brought immediate shame to Fang, filling him with a rage that was aimed, like a rapier, at Roman's heart— *retreat* was a repulsive word in Fang's limited vocabulary.

Retreat was an abominable term and action for Roman, too.

So Fang used an old, but often successful ploy, to spook Roman into forfeiting his psychological advantage. Fang took a sudden, menacing step forward and raised his open hands chest high, palms facing each other, fingers spread out and slightly curved, as if to grab or choke Roman.

Normally, when Fang made this motion and stepped forward, his opponent would turn and run or freeze from panic or at least retreat a few steps. When the opponent showed any of those signs of fear, Fang knew he would overpower him easily.

However, this scrawny teacher didn't run or retreat.

Then, to Fang's surprise, the teacher took a step forward, did not cower and did not appear intimidated. Fang felt the fangs of confusion and doubt as he stared at the teacher.

Roman's eyes appeared to glow, then flicker like a candle flame. He glared at Fang with the chilling hardness of a block of granite.

Roman knew that in order to beat Fang, he'd have to stay as cold and slippery as ice and as hot and intense as fire. He knew that he needed to keep out of Fang's grasp, where those massive arms could squeeze the life out of him. Speed and technique would be his shield. No chance to overpower someone of Fang's stature. Maybe, Roman thought, I should just shoot him. But that implied that Roman couldn't handle Fang in a hand-to-hand confrontation. That disturbed Roman's sense of pride and honor.

Fang thought, How could this teacher think a standin' up ta me, physically? Can't he see how strong I am? Must be a damn fool ta face me man-ta-man . . . unless he knows somethin' I don't know. But what? Fang's mind raced in a frenzy before the unexpected and the unthinkable happened.

Fang experienced the cowardly doubt and hesitance of the classic bully whose bluff has been called. His thick muscles were pulling at him to retreat, but his mind, his pride and anger were pushing him to a confrontation. His own masculinity was in doubt and his mind was screaming in pain and shame for his reluctant muscles to prove his manhood.

Fang's pride and rage dominated his reluctant muscles. He pushed himself psychologically, determined to squash the skinny fucker who was standing defiantly in front of him. Fang's muscles pumped up with blood as the adrenaline flowed. His heartbeat raced and his blood pressure climbed. He felt his muscles twitch with newly found energy, waiting to explode into action.

Fang spotted Roman's handgun and knife. Roman's handgun was held by his right thigh, barrel pointing at the roof. Fang quickly reached for his own handgun, pulling it out of his belt, then aimed it at Roman.

Fang noticed that Roman didn't raise his handgun. The only movement from Roman was a strange twist to his lips, a sort of mocking smirk that further enraged Fang. Fang aimed his gun at Roman's face, but Roman's mocking smirk grew.

Roman's eyes were a chilling sight to Fang. Those eyes burned into the growing confusion and instability of Fang's psyche with such mental torment that Fang felt forced to release his fury orally.

Fang thought, Challenge me? The bastard dares ta challenge me? I'll crush 'im, break 'im in two. The son-of-a-bitch thinks he can challenge me? He must be fuckin' crazy. But Fang felt humiliated by the challenge. He was used to everyone backing down from his bullying ways. The challenge shocked him, disturbed him, but worse, it disoriented him.

"Yur a goddamn fool, Teach. Yuh act too damn confident fer a skinny whelp. I could pull this trigger an' blow yur head off right now!" Fang exclaimed.

Roman smiled calmly, further agitating and irritating Fang. Roman thought, agitation and irritation will upset Fang, but his agitation and irritation could produce a pearl of an advantage for him.

Roman responded, "You could, but you won't."

"Wha' the fuck's tha' mean, Asshole?"

"It means that I know that you won't shoot me."

"Yeah? An' how do yuh know tha', Asshole?"

Roman smiled. "Well, because you're supremely arrogant and way too cocky, but there's also a tiny shred of doubt growing in you, and it's because you're scared of me," Roman said, continuing to smile. Then Roman added, "Yeah, I'm certain of it. You're scared of me and I'm just a tall, skinny teacher. Now isn't that ironic? Mr. Muscles is scared and over-confident all at once. You a girlie man, perhaps? Whaddaya think I'll do? Beat you to death with all my frail bones?" Roman laughed.

Fang said, "Yur bluff's pathetic. I'll throw yuh off the roof like I did that cop. It take 'bout as much effort as throwing a pebble off a cliff."

"No. I don't think so. You won't shoot me and you won't throw me off the roof because you won't end it that way, that's all. You need to prove yourself to be stronger, tougher and meaner than the other guy. You need to use your body, your muscles, to defeat someone and still expect to gain pleasure from it. Using a bullet would only cheat yourself of the need for all that ego-stroking, hands-on pleasure. Hell, anybody can pull a trigger. Even little kids can do that. But you're not a little kid are you? Are you? No. Of course not. You're not just anybody. You're the mighty Fang, the big bad Hercules standing on the peak of Mount Muscle preaching to your followers, right? You won't let a cowardly bullet strip you of your pride and deprive your muscles of the macho pleasure of crushing me. No, you're not going to shoot me, Fang and we both know it. You want, and you need, to get your hands on me, don't you? Your such a big, fuzzy, cuddly bear. Oops! Sorry. I meant, you're a mighty, mean, vicious . . . um . . . fool.

"Hell, we both know you don't want to fight me because behind that mad-dog body, you're really a scared puppy. If you had a tail, it would be between your legs right now. But I'll let you save face. That's why I came bearing a gift, a gift in the form of a deal that I'm certain you'll like."

Just then a distant noise captured their attention and distracted both of them, but only for a second. Like a metallic eagle, the State Police helicopter soared overhead searching for prey.

The rotor wash grabbed and pulled at loose clothing and sent hair in constantly changing directions. Bits and pieces of debris swirled around, stinging bare skin. It reminded Roman of Nam. Disturbing glimpses of Nam flashed across his mental projection screen. The memories gave him a sudden chill. His hair, skin and clothes rippled from the effects of the rotor wash. He felt as if he were covered in fur and that his fur was being blown around— Blizzard? His vision turned blood-red, as images of punctured flesh and the contorted faces of soldiers, in agony, screamed silently in his mind. Flashing images of comrades in unendurable pain seared his brain, followed by visions of wounded comrades who were waiting for a chopper to get them to where they would get medical attention. Roman snapped back to the grit-blown reality.

As the helicopter flew low over the roof, on its way to the parking lot, the rotor wash blew cooling air onto the two deadlocked opponents. But nothing could cool the heat than was emanating from each opponent's eyes.

* * * * * * *

Lt. Hawkey had already brought Sam and Alyson to the parking lot. They were in the ambulance now, getting medical attention.

Hawkey and the Captain were standing close by. Hawkey knew that a mighty confrontation was about to take place and once he knew that Sam and Alyson were safe, he grabbed his walkie-talkie and ordered all his men to hold their fire until further notice. He made all of his men acknowledge the order so that there were no errors or misunderstandings. When that was done he pulled his new Glock-21 handgun from its holster, then told Captain Lewis that Roman was going to fight Fang.

"You know that's not following regulations. Did you OK that approach?"

"Yes, Bev, I did. You want the best man for the job up there on the roof? Well, he's there right now, Bev."

"What? Are you crazy?" responded Captain Lewis.

"You don't know the Wolf Man, Bev. So far everything's been foreplay. Now Fang's going to get fucked."

Then, without giving Bev a chance to reply, he ran for the side entrance to the school. Once inside he ordered the nearest guard to follow him upstairs where they both guarded the doorway to the roof. They heard muted talk coming from the rooftop.

* * * * * * *

"Well," said Roman, "you know the cops have Freddy and I handed Miller to them. It's just you and me now. There're cops all over the hallways downstairs," he lied, "and it's all just a matter of time before the snipers are repositioned to get them in locations where you'll be exposed from one angle or another. There's no hiding any longer, Snaggletooth— Fang reached up and pulled his lip off his tooth. You've got, perhaps, fifteen minutes, at most, before you're a dead man or a convict, again. So I—"

"Yeah! Yeah!" Fang interrupted. "Snaggletooth, huh. Tryin' ta piss me off? Fuck yuh, wimp. Yeah, I can see the writin' on the wall, so quit usin' up my fifteen minutes with all yur bullshit. Git ta yur fuckin' point, Teach."

"OK. Well, then, here's the deal, Fang. We unload our handguns, together, of course, and throw them, as well as the bullets, over there." Roman pointed to the area. "Then you and I fight each other. If I win, I take you to the cops. If you win, you have me as a hostage to help you get to that helicopter and, let's face it, you'd never make it to the chopper without a hostage. And that helicopter's the only way you'll ever be able to get out of this mess. Whaddaya say? You got cojones big enough for that? You know, mano-a-mano . . . or were you just blowing hot air out your ass?"

"Fuck yuh! What's the trick, man?" blurted Fang. "Yuh looked in a mirror lately? Hell, I seen toothpicks bigger than you. Why would yuh want ta make such a deal, 'less there be some trick ta it? I'm not stupid. I know the door's unlocked. Yuh opened it. Must be another key. So now the cops rush up here an' use me for target practice? Is that it?"

"Yeah, you're right, Fang. There's a trick, but first you should know that the door is locked. I told Sam to lock it when she escaped. I gave her the spare key when she left. So the cops won't be rushing up here without breaking the door and giving you plenty of warning. I also told Sam to hide the key and not tell anyone. You have the original key and Sam has the spare key. The door's locked.

Now Roman did some acting, down-playing his skill. "So . . . now here's the trick. The trick is that I'm going to kick your ass all over this roof. Hell, you don't have a chance, really, because I mess around with martial arts once in a while. You know, like, in my cellar? I can break one-inch boards, so I think I can take you down. Now, if I was a coward like you, I would guess that a better alternative than getting my ass kicked would be to give myself up to the cops. You could save yourself a shameful beating that way. Hey, you don't really want to go back behind bars with a bunch of cuts and bruises, maybe a black eye or broken nose. What'll the guys think? That'll only show that you got you're ass kicked. The guys'll laugh at you. So what're you going to do, chicken shit? Give up or get beat up?" Roman laughed tauntingly, humiliating Fang to the brink of desperation and uncontrollable rage.

Fang pointed to Roman's knife. "The knives get put down, too?"

"Up to you," Roman responded laconically, but still grinning tauntingly at Fang. "Actually, I kind of like blades. Good things for whittling large chunks into small objects. You know what I mean?"

Fang thought Roman was bluffing about the knife. What he did know, however, was that he wasn't real good with one or he'd slice this fucking teacher's heart out. But he also hated the thought of his skin or muscles getting cut; it wasn't in his own self-image to see his muscular body sliced up and scarred.

Roman saw that his planned sarcasm and humiliation had gotten to Fang, whose face took on the color of a beet and whose facial expressions were contorted.

Roman was not nearly as self-confident as he pretended to be. Roman's own doubts set in, but he shook them off like a dog shaking water off its body. Roman knew that self-doubt had to be pushed aside in any confrontation, if the expected outcome was to win. Even in a losing battle, not acknowledging self-doubt enabled one to put in a "good showing." He didn't fear losing as much as he feared giving up, quitting, not doing his best, acting cowardly. Roman hoped he was skilled enough to meet this challenge successfully. It was time for action, not words, he reprimanded himself.

Fang and Roman cautiously watched each other unload the handguns; they each drew out their knives. Roman walked a few steps away and placed his empty gun, bullets and knife on the roof. Then Roman walked back to his spot. He stared at Fang.

Fang hesitated. He looked at his knife, then looked at the smiling teacher. He walked a few steps away and put down his gun and bullets, but kept the knife. His cruel eyes and twisted lips smiled at Roman.

"My goodness, Snaggletooth. With all those muscles and your size, you don't think you can take me without that knife? See? I told you before that you were afraid of me. Man, look at you. You're proving what I said about you. You're afraid of me. You're a chicken. You stand there with your legs apart, as if you have bowling balls between your thighs. With balls that big, you really think you need to have a blade to have an edge on me? Pardon the pun, but it'll be fun, to see you run, without your gun, like a girlie nun, in the hot sun, until I've won, and you are done." Roman laughed heartily, then made clucking noises like a chicken and flapped his arms as if they were wings. Roman continued taunting, "You're simply a muscle-bound coward after all, aren't you?" Roman howled. He howled so loudly that all the people in the parking lot and in the hallways were startled by the wailing, animal-like blast and haunting, wolf-like howling.

Then the howling changed to a deep throated growl, the growl of a hunter confronting its prey, exactly like the howl that exited from the gnashing teeth of a wolf.

Fang, out of red-faced embarrassment, tossed the knife aside, saying, "I don't need this ta kill yuh, Teach. All I need's me bare hands."

Fang rushed brutishly, but not cautiously toward Roman, wanting to completely destroy him— to break him in half and toss him over the roof like garbage.

/-.--/---/..-/-./--./.-/-./-../.-../---/...-/./-../

27

★★★★

"I have read many obituaries with great pleasure."
Clarence Darrow

"I didn't attend the funeral, but I sent a nice letter saying that I approve of it."

Mark Twain

CAPTAIN LEWIS SAW LIEUTENANT Hawkey vanish into the school. She knew that he and his men would have the school completely sealed off. She didn't question his actions. Lieutenant Hawkey was here because she trusted him. She didn't agree with his complicity concerning the rooftop situation, but she knew that it's during times of disagreements when trust is forged into an unbending bond.

She knew that Lt. Joe Hawkey was the kind of guy that thought it best to hurt you with the truth, rather than please you with a lie. She also knew that Hawkey thought, that when seconds counted, sometimes the chain of command had to be broken. She also knew that, on occasion, Joe could be as nasty as a threatened badger.

Fang and Mr. Wolfe were reported to be on the rooftop. But Bev couldn't see this for herself. She became frustrated, but it was a controlled frustration. Then her eyes lit-up as if a jolt of electricity shot through her when she realized that she did have the means of seeing what was happening on the roof. The helicopter.

She ran to the helicopter, grabbing one of her men by the sleeve, almost jerking him off his feet and nearly forcing him to drop his rifle in order to keep his balance. They both reached the helicopter as the trooper pilot was exiting the aircraft. The rotor blades hadn't yet come to a complete stop.

"Take us up!" she shouted to the pilot.

Seeing her severe expression, knowing her imperious stature and reputation, and hearing the determination in her voice, the pilot obediently responded, "Yes Captain." The pilot jumped back into the chopper, followed by Captain Lewis and trooper Decker. Captain Lewis sat in the front seat, adjacent to the pilot, with trooper Decker sitting in the back seat. In seconds the chopper was in the air again, where Captain Lewis had a clear view of Fang and the mysteriously, foolish teacher that Lieutenant Hawkey had so much faith in. She wished that she could share that faith.

Her first impression was that she was startled by the obvious mismatch in size between the two opponents. That first impression was followed immediately by something more mysterious, something unsettling. Something else was on that roof. She thought she saw white flashes streaking in circles around the two men, like the contrail of a jet. She stared at the whitish blur, disbelieving what she saw. Swirling dust? An illusion? Suddenly the blur stopped and stared directly at the helicopter, canine's gleaming.

Holy shit! Is that a white dog? she thought. Then, "Oh-my-god. It's a wolf." Her eyes bugged out as Blizzard bared his teeth. Then Captain Lewis saw the flashing sparks in the wolf's eyes, sparks that burst into flames, giving a reddish glow to its eyes. She rarely felt fear, but now was one of those times. She looked at the teacher and saw exactly the same thing in his eyes— a burning, glowing, red-eyed fury.

Then something else occurred that she couldn't explain. The wolf, in a streak of blazing speed, jumped at Roman with a howl that made her automatically flinch. Her jaw dropped when Blizzard disappeared into Roman's chest cavity. It was only then that she realized that Roman would have a chance against Fang. Startled, she thought, What the fuck is going on here?

She looked at the pilot and asked, "Did you see that white wolf?"

Looking at her, curiously, he said, "What white wolf, Captain?"

Looking over her shoulder, she asked trooper Decker, "You saw it, didn't you?"

"No, Captain. I didn't see anything, but those two men. Kind of a mismatch isn't it? Good thing the ambulance is here. That teacher will need to be treated immediately, that is, if he survives the confrontation."

As Bev stared out the window, the pilot and trooper Decker looked at each other and shrugged their shoulders, not knowing what the hell Captain Lewis was talking about.

"Don't be so sure," Captain Lewis remarked in a stunned voice.

*　*　*　*　*　*　*

Roman was a couple of inches shorter than Fang and that fact was hardly noticeable from the helicopter. What was readily noticeable was the mass of each person. Fang clearly out-weighed the teacher by about fifty pounds of muscle. Fang looked massive. Christ, Captain Lewis thought, they look like a barrel and a pencil.

She noticed that the teacher was bare-chested and she wondered why.

As the helicopter circled, Captain Lewis saw a patch on Roman's back. A wound, maybe? The tape holding it on was crisscrossed three times. But what crossed her mind the most, as she stared at him, was how vulnerable he looked compared to Fang, and yet, there was something dynamic and athletic about him. He possessed an aura and vitality that seemed to radiate a shimmering wave around him, like a full-body halo. He's a *Berg*, she thought. He's one of those extremely rare people who doesn't look like much on the surface because the best of him is concealed below the surface like an iceberg. Jesus Christ, she thought, Snap out of it, as the helicopter circled the roof again.

Captain Lewis remembered that Hawkey had said he'd bet his own life on this guy, and that, for the time being, anyway, was good enough for her because she felt the same way about Hawkey. Hawkey trusted this Wolfe guy implicitly and that's how she trusted Hawkey. So she would allow Hawkey to do things his way, within reason— her reason.

"I may be able to get a shot at Fang," trooper Decker yelled over the rotor noise.

Captain Lewis looked back over her left shoulder and responded in a loud voice that couldn't be mistaken; a voice she seldom had to use, but didn't hesitate to use now.

She yelled, "Trooper! You keep that rifle away from the window until I or Lieutenant Hawkey tells you otherwise. Hawkey gave the order for no shooting and no one breaks that order, but me. And just what kind of goddamn shot are you going to get, anyway, from a jerking, vibrating machine that's swaying as it hovers in the air? You've been watching too many of them damn James Bond movies, Trooper."

She continued to stare at him for a couple more seconds. Her glare was like twin laser beams boring into him. The force behind her reprimand seemed to actually push him back into his seat. Embarrassed, he said, "Sorry, Captain."

"It's OK, Decker. Just keep calm, but ready."

Her gaze then returned to the men on the roof.

Roman and Fang continued to glare at each other. What Roman saw, was body parts; the vulnerable parts of Fang's body to strike: eyes, nose, neck, solar plexus, ribs, testicles and knees.

What Fang saw was a long piece of string cheese that he wanted to tear apart, chew and spit out.

As the helicopter hovered high over the roof, the three occupants saw Fang take a step toward the teacher. These two mismatched opponents were about to enter into the struggle of, and perhaps for, their lives. The helicopter's occupants watched as if mesmerized by a video that they could not turn away from.

"Yuh stupid pile a shit!" Fang growled angrily. "Yuh could *never* match my strength. Yur jus' a skinny, shriveled-up faggot."

Fang laughed tauntingly, his upper lip snagging on his tooth. He moved his lip around to free it from the tooth, then paused. He stared at Roman. He looked into Roman's obsidian eyes. They looked cold, but then bright lights of unknown origin burst into flames that reflected inward, illuminating the caged wraiths that hid within the shadowy depths and crevasses of Roman's mind.

Fang sneered and, again, caught his upper lip on the tooth. He removed it. Embarrassment engulfed him?"

"That's OK, Fang. You go ahead and fix that snaggletooth of yours before we get down to business."

Fang rushed toward Roman, his outstretched hands preparing to grab Roman's throat. Roman darted sideways and delivered a blocking knife hand (shuto) strike to Fang's right elbow joint. The shuto strike served to not only block Fang's arms out of the way, but it also inflicted pain into the elbow joint. Roman then followed up with an immediate and powerful right-foot round-house kick (ma-washi-geri) which slipped in under Fang's arms and rammed into his solar plexus.

Fang grunted from the sudden impact and was thoroughly surprised by the technique. He turned slowly to face Roman, who was surprised that Fang didn't.

Fang rubbed his solar plexus, then his elbow, trying to relieve the pain. He inhaled deeply and shrugged his shoulders. "So that's the trick yuh had up yur sleeve? Yuh knows a little chop-chop karate crap, huh?"

Fang used this break in the action to catch his breath, to prepare for the kill. "I knew a guy in prison who knew a little of that chop-chop crap. He tried to use it on me." Fang smiled broadly, flashing his yellowish front teeth. "I bashed his fuckin' head inta a brick wall a few times. Poor little fellow has hisself some brain damage now. Doctors say he be a vegetable for the rest a his life. So I wished 'im well an' hoped that he'd have a long life." Laughter from Fang. "Goin' ta do the same thing ta yuh, boy. Yur gonna be a mashed potata. I'm gonna shove that Jap crap up yur ass so far yuh'll choke on it."

"Well, then, I sure hope you had a good night's sleep. You'll need all the energy you can get. By the way, how's a big, muscular guy like you sleep? I'll bet someone as big as you sleeps in the *fecal* position, right?" To Fang, the slanderous pun went totally unnoticed, like a stealth plane over his head.

Roman thought he was being witty and that went unnoticed, too.

"Naw, Asswipe. I sleeps on my back. What's it ta yuh?"

"Just curious if a bed was ever made to hold a lump of crap as big as you, that's all. Your karate man must have been a novice. Novice? It means a beginner. I've known plenty of karate masters who would have killed or maimed you already. And they're only half your size."

"Bull shit!" Fang responded.

Both men stared at each other. Fang was squeezing his fingers into a fist, then relaxing them as if he were squeezing a tennis ball. Roman was in a modified horse stance, knees slightly bent to spring into action.

"Don't need no word lessons, sonny boy. Jus' want yuh ta know that I'm gonna change the look a some a yur body parts. " Big grin, then laughter from Fang.

"Let me ask you a few questions," Roman said, 'Why is it that the biggest bullies have the biggest mouths? Does that take a lot of practice or does it simply come naturally? Are you an orator or a fighter? Don't get me wrong. Hell, I'm OK with talking and delaying things, if being a verbose coward is your style, but why be a big-mouthed idiot and bully if you're afraid to fight me?" Roman's sarcastic smile out-shone Fang's like the sun outshines the moon.

Roman continued, "You want to quit now, or do you want me to continue with my karate lesson? Or maybe you can simply talk me to death. Hell, I'm dying of boredom. I'm already slightly brain damaged just listening to your bullshit."

"There be no quittin', boy. Don't care about no Jap crap neither."

"That's OK. I only know enough to teach a beginner like you a good lesson. Now, are we going to chat all day? Should I order tea and Danish pastries?" Roman grinned, but his eyes blazed. "Do you want cream and sugar in your tea?"

Fang's smile slackened. The skin around his eyes pulled tight. His teeth clenched.

Both men had been concentrating so thoroughly on each other that they hadn't noticed the noise of the helicopter. Now, as it circled around them, they became aware of it and felt the cooling breeze from its whirling blades and the sting of flying debris.

Roman was suddenly distracted. To Roman, the chopper was a symbol of all the tragic, human horror that he had witnessed and participated in while in Nam.

To Fang, the helicopter represented a savior— a hovering angel coming to scoop him up and carry him away to safety. And this wise-ass teacher was his free ticket to accompany that angel on a trip that would take him far away from his pursuers. Then he'd push the teacher out the door of the helicopter and watch him plummet to his death.

During Roman's karate training the sensei (teacher) almost always stressed that karate was for defense, not offense. But Roman knew that one cannot always live by strict codes, rules, laws, standards or philosophies. For Roman, this was one of those times. Like a wolf, he leaped toward Fang's, burying a tremendous sidekick (yoko-geri) into Fang's unsuspecting abdomen, then planting that same foot back down on the roof and spinning his body around backwards, he smashed a left-footed back kick (ushiro-geri) into Fang's ribs and heard the sound of a pencil breaking— one of Fang's ribs.

Fang staggered backwards, grabbing his side, his eyes bewildered, his face red with rage and pain; his fists knotted into white-knuckled marble. Just as he caught his balance, Roman quickly approached with what should've been a devastating front kick (mae-geri) to Fang's groin. However, Fang had been fooled enough by this frustratingly deceptive teacher, so Fang swung his left hip forward, so both hips were in line with Roman's front kick. Then Fang widened his stance and bent his knees slightly for a stronger stance, while at the same time raising his left arm and fist to head level.

The heel (kakato-geri) of Roman's right foot came crashing into Fang's bony hip a split second later. This time it was Roman who grimaced in pain as the smaller bone of his heel collided with Fang's larger, stronger hip bone. Then, before he could withdraw the foot completely, Roman's pain doubled as Fang's left arm and fist came crashing down onto Roman's shin bone, slamming that leg to the ground, causing Roman to lean forward. Fang took this opportunity to punch with his piston-like right fist, toward Roman's face.

Roman anticipated Fang's strike and when he saw the fist coming at him, he snapped his head backwards like a boxer slipping a punch. This action, though it avoided the full impact of the punch, didn't prevent Roman from getting hit with a glancing blow. It did cause Fang's fist to strike slightly lower than the bridge of the nose, with less force, on the rubbery, cartilage tip of the nose that could more adequately absorb a punch than could the brittle bone at the bridge of the nose. The injured nose bled immediately and profusely, but instead of feeling warm, it felt cold as it was fanned by the rotor wash of the helicopter. Neither man could hear the rotor blade noise, their concentration on each other being so intense. Besides each other, all they seemed to sense was their own pain, their own rapid heartbeats, their own heavy breathing and the rush of blood through their arteries causing a sound like ocean waves in their ears.

Roman staggered backward, the result of jerking his head backwards so quickly, while trying to avoid the impact of Fang's punch. He lost his balance, tripping over an uneven spot in the roof, then fell onto his back. The jagged gravel that was imbedded into the roofing tar slashed and punctured his upper back area, leaving droplets of blood to stain the grayish tips of gravel. The paper towel bandage ripped and Roman could feel the wound bleeding again. Roman couldn't feel any pain, yet.

Fang rushed in as quickly as his huge body would allow. He was like a bull in heat, anxious for an orgasm. He lifted his right knee chest high, leg bent downward, then sent the heel of that leg thundering down toward Roman's face.

Roman recovered in time to roll over and spin his body around at the same time, avoiding Fang's lethal heel stomp, the force of which jammed several stones deeply into the thick, hardened tar, leaving a large and deep crescent-shaped heel print in the rooftop. Roman tried to get up, but couldn't move fast enough. Then, seeing Fang bending over and reaching for his left ankle, probably wanting to twist and break it like a chicken wing, Roman immediately withdrew both legs toward his buttocks, while at the same time turning his body onto his right hip leaving his left leg in perfect position to kick. And kick it did. Like a bazooka thrust, Roman slammed his left heel out so it was foremost and struck a violent, crunching blow to the bridge of Fang's nose. The blow must have felt like being hit with a baseball bat. Blood spurted where the broken, white shard of nose bone protruded through Fang's skin, the sound like shale cracking during an earthquake.

Fang saw red, literally, as the blood gushed onto his lips, teeth, cheeks and chin. His knees began to buckle. He staggered toward the still prone Roman, covering his nose protectively with both hands, forming a gruesomely bloody, finger-painted mask, blood oozing between his fingers. His eyes blinked rapidly, desperately trying to clear away the flood of tears that had inundated them and blurred his vision.

During this momentary pause, Roman rolled onto his left hip leaving the right leg already cocked and released a straining grunt from his lips, then sent the blade of his right foot— the ridge that extends from the little toe to the heel— into Fang's crotch, as Fang was standing over him, legs apart, trying to regain his balance and clear his vision.

Fang let out a agonizing grunt as his testicles compressed from the sudden force of being rammed up into his crotch. His hands dropped to his crotch as he fell to his knees, helpless, the blood and tears streaming down his cheeks, around his mouth and dripping from his chin. Tortured sounds and a spray of blood ejaculated from between his red-strained, tightly clenched teeth as he kept both hands covering his groin.

Roman immediately performed a gymnastic backward somersault from his prone position and landed on his feet, assuming a deep, knees-bent, horse stance (shiko-dachi).

Roman saw the opening immediately. Fang, still on his knees, swayed back and forth, his eyes closed, head bent down with the anchor of pain. Fang's neck was exposed. Roman leaped to the side of Fang and with an open-handed, edge of palm strike. He slammed his hand viciously into the back of Fang's neck, hoping to hit the occipital bone at the very base of the skull. If hit properly, with enough force, it would render Fang unconscious. But the continuous movement of Fang's neck made the blow miss its mark.

Fang pushed himself up from the roof. The big man wasn't through. The chop to the back of the neck wasn't accurate, though it was painful.

Fang stood as his pain assuaged, though blood frothed from the corners of his mouth as he strained to keep his bodily bulk in action. His lips turned upward into a feigned smile, his snaggletooth hooking onto his upper lip. Fang brushed his lip off the troublesome tooth, then glared at Roman saying, "Shit! Yuh be a surprise. Thought yuh was a bluffin' bastard."

Roman remained in his horse stance as he watched to see what Fang would do. He knew that by facing Fang sideways, in the horse stance, he was offering very few vulnerable targets to Fang. Roman's eyes tracked Fang like radar; his mind screaming at him to attack Fang and, yet, he didn't. He was trained for this, but he did not attack.

When Fang took a threatening step toward him, Roman modified his horse stance to a leaning-back stance (kokutsu-dachi) which is strictly a defensive position where, from a horse stance, Roman simply leaned his previously straight torso backward with about seventy percent of his weight on the back leg and the remaining thirty percent on his front leg. His upper body remained sideways, with his upper torso leaned back, out of Fang's reach. The line extending from his front leg to his head would made a forty-five degree angle. His front fist was held at thigh level with the forearm and upper arm protecting his ribs. His back arm was cocked and held at shoulder level, ready to counter-attack.

As Fang circled him, Roman pivoted his stance to remain facing Fang. Fang moved more slowly, more cautiously. He wished he hadn't been suckered into this fight with the cunning teacher. He'd seriously misjudged the guy. The teacher's every move, offensive and defensive was an obvious indicator of his superior, martial arts, combat abilities; his competence and confidence showed on his stoic face. Teach was dangerous and Fang didn't like having to admit that to himself, but he did because recognizing the danger is always the first step in any plan to successfully overcome that danger. He desperately wanted to land a fight-ending, solid punch.

Fang was disappointed in himself for not seeing the danger in this teacher earlier. The had been hints of danger, but nothing concrete. He wished, now, that he'd shot the bastard. He had let the tall, skinny appearance dominate his perceptions. When he saw the teacher's six feet, two inch, one-hundred eighty-five pound frame, he simply disregarded the teacher as being any kind of a real threat to him. He was sure that the teacher was bluffing with the karate talk or, at least, that he was only a novice karate student. Now he knew that he'd been played for a fool.

But, Fang thought, that didn't mean that he couldn't still turn the table on this teacher, and still beat the crap out of him, leaving him lying on the roof like a lump of bloody pulp. Fang's only regret now was that he had to keep the teacher alive because he needed him as a hostage in order to get a helicopter ride. Fang thought of some ways that he could make death very painful and long for the teacher. He found hope and a cruel satisfaction in these pathological thoughts. He even gained energy from them, but when his thoughts cleared, he knew there would be no time for torture. He'd teach the teacher how to fly . . . from cloud level.

Fang eyed Roman's extended lead leg and quickly tried to kick it, hoping to knock Roman off balance. But Roman's reflexes were simply too fast for him. Roman had plenty of time to lift the leg, then replace it.

Realizing that Fang had too much at stake, so he would probably never give up and that he couldn't remain in a defensive posture indefinitely against someone as massive as Fang, Roman decided he'd have to be the aggressor to keep Fang on the defensive.

Roman immediately and smoothly switched his stance, again, to the American Free Fighting Stance. In this stance, keeping his feet closer together, and by standing more erect, Roman was able to achieve greater mobility, speed and power. This higher stance also allowed him to perform punches and kicks with less chance of telegraphing his intentions, as often occurs when a lower stance is taken. Best of all, the American Free Fighting Stance was a surprisingly versatile stance offering many opportunities to perform offensive techniques, while at the same time allowing Roman to immediately switch, if needed and with minimal effort, to an excellent defensive posture.

But as Roman realized that he'd have to go on the offensive to defeat Fang, he found himself the target of a sudden flurry of Fang's arms, like being attacked by a windmill. Roman took a punch to the chin that jarred him back to reality.

Roman knew it was a chance he'd have to take, so, instead of retreating, he stood toe-to-toe with Fang, blocking punches with lightening speed, power and accuracy. Then just as suddenly, he stepped toward Fang, jamming him and releasing an upward, close-quarters palm-heel strike (teisho) under Fang's chin— when striking into bony areas, Roman preferred not to punch with his knuckles because the force of the strike travels into the small, delicate bones in the fingers and wrist. So Roman used the palm-heel strike which, when delivered correctly (with the fingers curled inward to protect them, the wrist bent back so the strike is delivered from the bottom of the palm, the area at the base of the thumb) the pressure is no longer on the smallest bones of the hand, but on the radius, the ulna and the humerus bones, larger bones that can better absorb the force of the strike.

Ducking his body under Fang's arms, he viciously slashed his right elbow (empi) into Fang's ribcage. Quickly pulling his right arm downward and standing more erect, he arched a looping ridge-hand (haito) strike over Fang's flailing arms. It struck like a hammer into Fang's sensitive temple. He immediately followed that with a back round-house kick to Fang's left, outside thigh, striking the peroneal nerve causing an immediate numbness in the leg that nearly buckled Fang's left knee.

Roman cursed when Fang's knee didn't collapse.

Fang gained his balance with his good right leg, but felt the numbness of Roman's tremendous blow. But Fang would not retreat. Roman started thinking, Why me? Why do I get these big, muscle-bound fuckers to fight? Shit! Some day I'm going to meet one of these apes that has tremendous martial arts skills and I'll get crushed.

Fang took the blows and, although they were painful, he kept coming at Roman. Roman knew that neither of them could keep up this furious pace for very long, but he was determined that he would outlast Fang's tenacity, no matter how long the fight continued. He felt himself breathing hard, but saw that Fang was not only breathing hard, but weakening considerably.

Fang staggered toward Roman, like an exhausted boxer, flailing wildly as exhaustion and weakness took a tight grip on his heart, muscles and lungs. He couldn't get enough air and was gasping for breath. His muscles burned from lack oxygen. His breathing was rapid and raspy. He continued throwing punches, weak, slow punches, but they still had the force to punish, especially the more delicate facial bones.

Roman was cautious, looking for an opening to Fang's face. When the opening occurred, he attacked suddenly with a thrusting spear-hand (nukite) to Fang's eyes, then withdrawing the hand and switching to a knife-hand (shuto), he slashed a blow to the side of Fang's neck, followed by a heel-stomp (ushiro fumikomi) to Fang's instep, all while weaving and bobbing in and out of Fang's range. The flurry of punches and kicks were all successful to varying degrees, but only knocked Fang off balance, backing him up and turning him slightly.

Roman, now fighting off his own exhaustion, seized this opportunity for another heel stomp to the back of Fang's knee, finally collapsing the knee, sending Fang down to the roof on all fours. This move put Roman behind Fang. Roman bent and lifted his right leg, pulling it backward as high as it would go, then thrust the knee violently forward into Fang's spine, at the base of the neck. Fang's neck muscles tightened in agony and he grimaced. Roman then grabbed Fang's hair, yanking his head upward and backwards so that Fang was now back up on his knees, his throat exposed. Roman smashed a vicious left handed knife-hand strike (the open hand strikes with the area from the base of the little finger to the wrist) toward Fang's Adam's Apple. Fang lowered his chin protectively, making Roman's strike glance off his chin, then into his Adam's Apple with much less force than Roman had intended. Roman groaned in pain, but shrugged it off. Roman still held Fang's hair so he violently shoved Fang's head forward. Fang's body snapped forward as if from a spasm, his chest and face crashing onto the graveled tar rooftop. He lay there motionless, except for the rapid expansion and contraction of his stomach as he gasped for breath.

Roman stood erect, over Fang's body, staggering slightly from his own exhaustion and breathing heavily, spittle dripping from his mouth. His chest was heaving; his heart was trying to escape from his chest cavity. It had never taken Roman so long to best an opponent and it had never taken such a toll on his body. Roman thought, That bastard was tough, but I outlasted him. Roman wiped the sweat out of his eyes and looked down at Fang's nearly motionless body.

Roman relaxed, put his hands on his thighs and breathed deeply through his nose several times, each time slowly releasing the air out of his mouth— a karate training technique— through pursed lips, in an attempt to control his rapid heart beat.

Roman was surprised that he hadn't killed Fang, though society-at-large would probably think that they were better off with Fang dead. But if he'd killed Fang, then part of society would label him a reckless killer. Roman, though, had had enough killing in Nam— and another country which had a TOP SECRET classification by the Department of Defense— then in the Adirondack Mountains just two years ago. He hoped that the killing could finally stop. All he really wanted was to be a normal, average teacher, enjoy his job, genuinely care for his students, then, each evening, go home to his wife and daughter. He simply wanted a quiet, relaxed life.

Roman walked away from Fang's prone body, toward the edge of the roof so he could let the people in the parking lot know it was all over.

He heard the roar of the helicopter for the first time. He looked up at it and wondered if Hawk Eye was the pilot. He'd heard that Hawk Eye had learned how to fly those things in Nam, after he, Roman, was gone. He'd heard that somehow Hawk Eye had manipulated the pilots into giving him free lessons, then had been certified and received his pilot's license as well as Warrant Officer status. Roman thought that it must have come in handy, especially since he had heard that Hawk Eye had gotten so good at piloting the helicopter that he could fly it at top speed through tight, forest and bushy places where only a tampon could fit. Roman chuckled as he started breathing easier.

Roman sluggishly waved at the helicopter. He couldn't see its occupants clearly, though he thought he saw a woman's windblown, long hair swirling out the window, her mouth contorted as if screaming at him. But he could only hear the whipping, whirring sound of the helicopter blades, the same noise that had once meant death and dying to him. He didn't know that that woman was screaming a warning to him.

He was a few feet from the edge of the roof when Fang's massive arms encircled him in a vice-like, bear hug. Now he realized why the woman was screaming. Roman's upper arms were pinned to his sides, but years of karate practice made him act instinctively. He immediately bent his lower arms— below the elbow— upward and grabbed Fang's little fingers as Fang dragged him near the precipice. Fang instantly stopped when Roman mercilessly yanked Fang's little fingers backward, toward his wrists, breaking both of them as if they were dry twigs. As each finger broke with a pop, Fang's grip slackened. That's what Roman was waiting for. He sent the heel of his left foot slamming onto Fang's instep, breaking the long, thin tarsal bones. Roman heard the agonizing squeal of pain and immediately slammed a fist backward toward his right hip, but into Fang's groin. Then, as Fang screamed and bent forward from the blow, Roman snapped his head violently backward so it crashed into Fang's nose and mouth. Finally, Roman's waist was unrestricted. He raised his right elbow in front of him, then spun around so the elbow went crashing into Fang's cheek and jaw. Roman heard a crack, but didn't know if he'd broken the cheek bone, the jaw, or both. He did see something white fall out of Fang's mouth. One look at Fang erased all doubt. The snaggletooth was gone. Now that he was facing Fang, Roman made a tight fist that tipped forward so only the two biggest knuckles would hit. He took quick steps toward Fang, then slammed his fist into Fang's solar plexus with such force that he thought he'd hit Fang's spine. Then slipped behind Fang.

Fang was stumbling backward from the punch, but he was looking at his broken little fingers, then placed one hand on his jaw and the other on his groin, not knowing which area was hurt the most. He turned to face Roman— now Fang was the one closes to the roof's edge. Fang's eyes watered profusely, temporarily blinding him and mingling with the nose blood. Not being able to see well, he moved his injured foot outward, widening his stance so that Roman couldn't repeat the painful, numbing leg kick. He staggered backward. He took a wider stance to stop staggering and maintain his balance. Roman sprang forward bringing his right leg swiftly upward, executing a powerful front snap-kick into Fang's broken rib, with a startlingly loud kiai— a loud, ferocious scream that scares, startles or stuns the enemy, while at the same time calling up all of one's reserve strength.

The air escaped Fang's lungs in a gush, like flood-water out of a drain pipe, forcing him back even closer toward the edge of the roof.

Fang rubbed the tears away and cleared his eyes enough to see Roman facing him.

But before Fang could recover, Roman sprinted toward Fang, jumped and threw up both legs— the right leg extended and the left leg curled back toward his buttocks; his whole body parallel to the roof top— and performed a flying side kick to Fang's solar plexus. The kick knocked Fang backward even farther toward the roof's edge.

Roman landed on the hard pebbles, cutting his hands and forearms, but stood immediately.

Fang grabbed his chest in agony, then screamed with a howling, frustrated roar. He walked, like an angry grizzly bear, right into Roman's range, not caring, just wanting to get his hands on Roman.

Roman brought both his hands together, palms touching, parallel to the roof, and when they entered between Fang's outstretched arms, Roman snapped his arms upward and outward making Fang's arms snap outward so he looked as if he'd been crucified. Then Roman summoned up reserve energy and brutally used a hammer-fist to strike to the side of Fang's neck. The sound was like a loud slap, but deeper and the consequences much more telling as the collapsed vagus nerve shut off blood to Fang's brain. Fang lost control of his body and staggered, attempting to regain his balance and coordination.

Roman took advantage of this moment and heel-kicked Fang's chest. It didn't appear to affect Fang, other than to knock him back a step, now precariously close to the precipice.

"I'll kill yuh, mother-fucker! I'll rip yur heart out an' crush yur skull! I'll tear out yur eyeballs an' eat 'em," Fang screamed. "Come on! Come ta me, yuh goddamned asshole. Yuh son-of-a-bitch!"

Roman sensed that Fang's obelisk of solid, muscled power was beginning to crumble like a sand pillar, so Roman obliged, rushing straight at Fang, leaping into the air at Fang— diving at Fang— and just when it looked like their two heads would collide, Roman snapped his right elbow into Fang's face, hearing and feeling and the crunching contact. Fang was thrown backward by the sledge-hammer force of the elbow strike.

Roman fell to the roof top. When he lifted his head to look for Fang, all he saw was Fang's feet disappearing over the roof's edge. Then, even over the helicopter's loud rotor noise, he heard Fang's elongated and terrified scream. Roman didn't hear Fang's body crash into the ground, but his imagination was vivid— a watermelon thrown off a two story building onto a hard surface.

Roman pushed himself up from the roof and walked to the edge. He looked beyond the precipice, then below as a plethora of faces stared upward at him.

Roman peered at Fang's shattered head. Roman's expression was sullen; he showed no shock, no pity, no guilt. He focused on Fang's head, crushed and bloody. Roman could see a growing pool of blackish blood, in the center of which was a dislodged eyeball. The eyeball was still attached to the string-like, optic nerve that resides inside the orbital bone structure.

As if the crushed skull, blood pool and dislodged eyeball wasn't bad enough, Roman noticed that Fang's head lay at a odd angle— a broken neck. Roman thought that it didn't matter how he died, just as long as he did die. Roman covered his face at that sudden, surprising and undesired thought. Suddenly remorse and guilt speared him from all directions. "I am a killer," he mumbled to himself, "but if I can use it for an anti-evil purpose, maybe I can still live with myself and have some semblance of happiness, family life and career."

Roman looked out over the parking lot, searching for Sam. Roman simply muttered, "Sam. Grace. I love you," to himself.

Roman turned away from the applauding law officers, thinking, I killed again and I thought I was done with that life. I'm damn tired of feeling the burden of guilt. If someone uses deadly force against me, I shouldn't feel guilty about using deadly force against them, whether they be the enemy on the battlefield or criminals at home. And I'm especially goddamn tired of being reminded that I'm good at killing, as if I should feel additional shame about my skill. I was forced to fight and kill for my country, and then I'm forced to kill to save lives in the Adirondack Mountains, as well as right here at school. But there was a lingering, shred of doubt that burned within him, like a red-hot coal, as he subconsciously wondered if he really had needed to kill Fang. Roman mused, Why should I continue to feel guilty about being good at killing? I only do it in life and death situations. I don't get pleasure from it. Dammit, I shouldn't have to feel guilty any more than a person who's forced to play tennis, then becomes good at it, then very good, then excellent and eventually an expert at it and becomes a professional who wins contests and gets rich from his/her skill. Should that person feel guilty about becoming an expert and becoming rich due to their skill? Hell, no.

Roman walked unsteadily across the roof, down the stairs and into the parking lot. He found Sam in the crowd. She was holding Alyson close to her, protectively, like she'd done for Grace so many times. It made Roman think of his precious daughter and how badly he wanted to see her, to kiss her forehead, to hug her tightly, to love her forever.

But as he stared at Sam and she at him, tears came to his eyes, tears of joy as well as tears of pain. He was happy to see Sam and Alyson safe and to know that all his students were safe, but he was also in controlled, emotional pain knowing that he'd killed again, and that he was much too good at it. Suddenly his sub-conscious thoughts surfaced and an epiphany jolted him. He realized that he had started out wanting to capture Fang, but ended up killing him, not by accident, but by intent. He not only wanted revenge, he also wanted to rid the world of one more ruthless, sub-human criminal. This revelation did not sit well with him, yet it didn't bother him enough to make him sorry for what he'd done. After all, he thought, the truth is, I *am* a killer. I do it well and with the law as a shield and a conscience to guide and reprimand me. The trouble is, Roman surmised, that a killer with a conscience must live a troubled life. But, he thought, I've saved lives, made some lives better and prevented torture and death to other people whom Fang would have abused. I'll have to slip guilt and shame into my mental Pandora Box, lock it and conceal it in a remote area of my brain's subconscious, he thought. Then immediately changed his mind because it was his sense of shame and guilt that often guided his decisions and without them he might lose control of his positive thoughts and beneficial actions.

When in the parking lot, Roman again gazed at Fang's shattered, lifeless and bloody body. He thought, How many lifeless or severely wounded bodies have I seen on the sacrificial battlefields of Nam and elsewhere? When a person witnesses death enough times, the sight of it becomes less and less distressing, even while viewing a shattered corpse. Seen enough times, death loses its shock value; it may even become mundane.

Roman concluded, Isn't Death the price we pay for our life?

Roman felt as if in a daze. He felt a hand on his shoulder and almost lashed out at it. It was Hawk Eye. Hawk Eye put his arm around Roman's shoulder and led him away from Fang's battered body. Hawk Eye noticed that Roman was staring at his palms-up hands, but had no idea what Roman was thinking.

Roman felt as if he was in a dream, dazed and sluggish, as Hawk Eye led him to Sam. Sam put Alyson down and clutched Roman in a tight, emotional hug. Roman gingerly enclosed her waist with his arms, closed his eyes, then buried his face in her neck, feeling the tenderness of her flesh, the fragrance of her perfume and shampoo and the tickle of her hair on his cheek, all the delights of being held, loved and alive.

Captain Lewis walked to Roman and introduced herself.

Roman forced his mind to clear, shook Captain Lewis's small, delicate hand and immediately wanted to lie by saying, "I didn't intend to kill him. Really."

Captain Lewis saw exhaustion in Roman's eyes and body movements as well as a resigned sadness in his eyes. Was it a sign of remorse or of satisfaction? she wondered. Captain Lewis said, "Fang's death was self-defense, an accident during a life or death struggle. That's what my report will say. Would you like to add anything, Mr. Wolfe?" Captain Lewis stared into Roman's eyes for his reaction, wondering what he'd say or do.

Roman knew better than to talk before thinking. He wondered if he should tell the truth. He glanced at Hawk Eye who now stood behind Captain Lewis.

Hawk Eye read in his eyes what Roman was thinking and subtly rotated his head side to side, indicating, "No. Don't say anything."

Captain Lewis knew that men who have to kill, especially soldiers and police, usually become hardened towards death. But this man, Roman, seemed confused, even regretful. Maybe, just maybe, he intended to kick Fang off the rooftop. That would be breaking the law, a technicality of sorts. And if it was true, she hoped that Roman would be quiet about his intent and simply let her write the report as a case of self defense that led to the death of a hardened, brutal criminal.

There would be no threatening or embarrassing investigation of Mr. Wolfe for this killing, she thought. She and Joe would see to that.

Captain Lewis noticed that Roman was about to respond to her last question and quickly interrupted him. "That's fine, Mr. Wolfe. It's a question that I have to ask for my report. I'll just write that you had no further details or comments to offer."

Captain Lewis turned to Hawkey and said, "You were right about him. There is a dark shadow that follows him. He seems to be in a constant struggle with it. As long as he struggles with it, he'll be a good man. If he stops struggling and lets the darkness consume him, he won't be any better than Fang."

Lt. Hawkey took offense at that statement, then regretfully admitted to himself that it was probably true. He replied, "Yeah, I know, but that dark shadow saves more lives than it takes and it does not, so far anyway, kill unnecessarily."

"Do you think it was necessary to kill Fang?"

"Taking the long view and realizing that if he lived he'd kill, maim and sexually abuse both children and adults, then, yes, I'd say Fang needed to be killed to prevent him from ruining and/or ending future lives."

"That's not the way the law works, Joe, but, in this case, perhaps you're right."

Suddenly Bev and Joe heard a howling noise. They looked around. It appeared that no one else had heard it. Bev and Joe looked up at the school roof top. A pure white wolf prowled along the narrow ledge, following Roman with its eyes, then it leaped off the roof and glided toward Roman, then slowly disappeared, with the echo of its howl continuing, but fading until no sound remained.

"What the hell!" Bev shouted as she stared at Lieutenant Hawkey.

"Yeah, I know," Hawkey responded. "I've seen it before. Tell you about it sometime. It's not an explanation that I can give in just a couple of minutes."

"Bullshit! I'm too curious to put it off, so be in my office tomorrow morning, Joe. Make it at 8:00 A.M. That time OK with you?"

"Fine with me, Bev. See you in the morning."

/-./././-../././-../.-/-./.-/-../.-/.-/.--./.--./.-././/.-./-../././-../.-/-/././-../

28

★★★★

"Changing the world is good for those who want their names in books. But being happy, that is for those who write their names in the lives of others, and hold the hearts of others as the treasure most dear."

Orson Scott Card

GRACE SAT OUTSIDE ON the back lawn of Dave's and Linda's dairy-farm house. She sat on a swing facing south. The setting sun glared at her profile, reaching over her right shoulder as its waning rays caressed her cheek. She swung lazily, but rhythmically, soothing her worried mind. She looked at a cumulus cloud in the fading daylight and thought she saw her dad's smiling face in the contours of the cottony texture. She smiled at the thought because, when she stared at things, they often took definite shapes and, mostly, those shapes were people's faces. She wondered if that was a strange thing, a unique characteristic of hers, or was it just a normal, human thing.

She continued to stare at the cloud as she swung lazily, drifting back and forth in a short arch. Then she was overcome and consumed by a feeling of complete euphoria, like she has on Christmas morning. She'd had rare feelings like that before and —

"Grace! Grace!" Linda called from the back door. "It's time for dinner, Honey. Time to come in and get washed up."

Grace turned, acknowledged Linda, then, again, looked to the south, in the direction of her dad's school. She heard the door click shut before she spotted the dragonfly, which, for a yet unknown reason, created a joyful purring inside of her.

She dragged her feet to stop the swing.

She was about to stand up when the dragonfly snatched her attention, again, and held more tightly. The dragonfly, at first, seemed like an insignificant, buzzing, speck in the sky, but she was entranced by it now. Her eyes were pulled to it as if by some unknown force. She spoke. "It's not a dragonfly. Too far away. Not a bird either. An airplane? Helicopter, maybe? Well, I guess I better go in and wash for dinner."

*　*　*　*　*　*　*

Captain Lewis had asked Lieutenant Hawkey to fly Roman and Sam to Strong Memorial Hospital, in Rochester, so Roman's injuries could be checked and, if needed, stitched up. Originally, Alyson was to go too, but Alyson's parents showed up and whisked her off, saying that they'd take care of whatever she needed.

Captain Lewis informed Lieutenant Hawkey that she'd take care of all the details at the school and at headquarters, and that she and the principal would make sure that all the students were returned to their parents. That set Hawkey free to fly the helicopter, after he contacted his SWAT team, informing them that he transferred command to Captain Lewis.

The regular pilot was asked to accompany them so that he could return to the school after departing from the hospital. Hawkey took the controls, while Roman sat next to him. Sam and the regular pilot sat in the back seat.

Hawkey looked at Roman as the helicopter climbed towards the clouds. "Been a long time, Wolf Man," he said with a beaming smile.

"It's good to see you, Hawk Eye. I've thought about you a lot and actually missed you a little bit," Roman said with a teasing smile. "How long you been with the troopers?"

"Oh, about a decade after Nam, I guess. It took awhile for me to get my head straightened out. I've been working in the New York City area for about ten years and just got back to the Rochester area a year ago. Didn't hear anything about your Adirondack experience until this school hostage thing happened. So I didn't figure out who you were until today. Shit, man, I never even knew your last name. Last names were unimportant in Nam, remember? And even if you knew a guy's last name, at one time, it was forgotten quickly. It was the faces, the macho nicknames and the action that was remembered, right? It was the brotherhood, the closeness and the shared fear that was remembered mostly. But I did seem to remember that you lived somewhere in New York State. Just didn't know where or even if you still lived here. You used to talk seriously about moving out west. Montana I think. Then I wasn't sure if you'd want me to contact you because it would dredge up some terrible memories and emotions. I felt confused, indecisive. We'd lost touch so fast and I didn't know how to get back in touch, so I let it slide and didn't try to look you up. I thought I should let sleeping dogs lie undisturbed."

Roman looked at the terrain below him; cars looked like beetles, trees looked like bushes, the cornfields looked like plush grass. Looking off into the distance was like looking through the wrong end of a telescope. He took a deep breath and turned away from the window to smile at Hawk Eye. He explained, "I departed Nam faster than I'd expected. I assistance was requested for one last mission before my DEROS— Date Eligible for Return From Overseas. It involved top secret, black-ops, *head-hunting* missions into North Vietnam, Cambodia and Laos. We were supposed to—"

"Head-hunting missions?" Joe interrupted.

Shit. You asshole, Roman said to himself when he realized that he'd slipped-up. Roman glanced back at Sam, disappointed in himself for letting a monster out of the bag. He hadn't told Sam about this part of his Vietnam experience. Looking back at Hawk Eye, he said, "Yeah. It was called head-hunting. It was top-secret missions to assassinate high ranking enemy officers who controlled sections of the North Vietnamese army. Some of those officers were in North Vietnam and some set up their base of operations across the borders of Cambodia and Laos. As you know, China and Russia were aiding North Vietnam, and Cambodia and Laos were giving the enemy a safe haven within their borders. So about four weeks before I was to leave our squad to return states-side, I departed abruptly for a top secret mission. I couldn't tell the squad about it. Sorry.

"Our group wasn't elite special forces, or special operations, or anything like that. Originally, we were supposed to go with Navy SEALs, Green Berets or Army Rangers, but that changed when the top brass wanted to be able to cover their asses and be able to claim that we were a rogue outfit, especially if any of us got killed, captured, or left behind. Basically, what we really got were tough volunteers from line infantry companies, men who compensated for their lack of elite training with a lot of experience in the boonies and on the battlefield. They used quickly learned, survival skills, and sheer nerve and muscle, instead of elite, special-forces training, to get the job done. No American officer could go, for fear of being captured. I was appointed the leader of the group.

Joe, I requested you for second in command, with your permission, of course, but that request was denied. Guess they didn't want any renegade Injuns, but like I said, the mission was a top secret, so I had to leave suddenly and didn't tell anyone about it."

"Renegade Injun? That's blasphemy, you lily-white heretic."

They both laughed at each other.

Hawkey pulled and pushed on some manual equipment as well as stepping on some other gadgets to operate the helicopter. He asked, "That group have a name?"

"Yeah." Roman laughed. "They were called *lerps*."

"Lerps? What the hell are lerps?"

"The acronym is the letters: L... R... R... P, meaning Long Range Reconnaissance Patrols."

"Never heard of the LRRPs," Joe said.

"Well, that's no surprise. They were another secretive outfit, almost anonymous compared to the well-known American, elite special forces. Kind of like the minor leagues in baseball. If a guy got good enough in the LRRPs, he might get called up to the big leagues, the Rangers, Green Berets or SEALs.

"The lerp teams went out on five or six men, long range patrols that sometimes lasted a few days, or a week or two, and occasionally longer. Their job was to pinpoint enemy positions, set up ambushes, carry out high-level enemy officer assassinations. Black Ops is the term used to refer to it now. Usually they went deep into enemy dominated territory, places where no one else wanted to go or dared to go or, more importantly, couldn't go, like crossing over another countries border. Anyway, I DEROSed for the states immediately after those missions. I didn't have a chance to say good-bye. Sorry I didn't try to find you, Joe, but I was really messed up mentally, and physically exhausted. After I got home, I didn't want to be reminded of Nam, any part of it, not even you. I tried to forget everything. Besides, all I had was the name 'Hawk Eye.' I didn't know your surname and didn't know what state you lived in. I decided not to look up old friends and take the chance of having to deal with more old, horrible memories. Plus, I figured that once I found old friends, what condition would they be in? Worse than me? Amputees? Mental patients? Maybe they didn't need me as a reminder either. So I isolated myself, slipped into a self-made cocoon and stayed there for a long while. It was no picnic for Sam and my daughter, Grace. But, luckily, after about six months, I came out of my cocoon and was able to face the world again."

Joe understood exactly how Roman had felt. Joe had been messed up, too. They all had except, perhaps, the guys that enjoyed the killings.

Joe increased altitude and sped northward.

Sam remained quiet. Roman didn't look back at her again. Feelings of guilt caused his neck and face to turn red. Someone once said that, "The more guilt and shame you feel, the better man you are." Maybe. Maybe not, he mused, but if it's true, then I'm one hell-of-an awesome guy. Might even be able to walk on water.

Joe grinned at the quotation, then said, "Well, if that's true, then we are saints."

Their conspiratorial laughter filled the cockpit like fog.

Sam thought, Why hadn't Roman told me about the head-hunting missions? Probably just trying to protect me from gruesome stories..

Joe asked, "Why'd you go on that patrol when you were so close to getting back to the world?"

"They wanted me to train the LRRPs in practical self-defense, especially stealth killing with a knife and/or garrote, and basic jungle survival skills. There was no boxing or street fighting with rules and all that crap. To teach them as much as I could in two weeks prior to the long range patrols, we worked twelve to sixteen hours a day. I taught them the various choke holds, garrote usage, how to break a neck quickly and quietly, where to stab and where to slash with their knife; you know, stuff like that. The brass never told me why they couldn't use special forces instructors. They just said that they'd heard about me and that I they wanted me. Actually, I think they wanted me for their own deniability. Then having elite training from the regular special forces could be denied.

"Those LRRPs were good, though. They were highly motivated and a lot better than they were given credit for, especially with only two weeks of training. The other special forces guys looked down on them, but the LRRPs learned the hard way, not at some safe training camp, but out in the lethal fields and jungles where an error meant instant death, and not some higher ranking asshole chewing you out for making a mistake."

"Sounds like you didn't like it, but you OKed the request?"

"Yeah, my ego got the best of me. It was a stupid decision. But at the time, I thought I could save more lives by training men to take lives. After LRRP experience I knew that I'd had enough, Hawk Eye. I had seen and participated in too much pain, agony and death. Didn't want it any more, so when my time was up I left and didn't look back. All I wanted was Sam and Grace, and a place to hide."

"I understand that," Joe said as he looked at Sam, then at Roman and teasingly stated, "Yeah, man, I can see why you'd want to come home to Sam. She's a looker. And you sent her down the stairs and into my open arms, remember? You shouldn't tempt a guy like that, Buddy. You don't just go around dumping a lovely lady like this," Joe motioned to Sam, "into a friend's arms, especially if the guy is as handsome as me. Know what I mean?" Hawk Eye said with a laugh and a wink.

Sam blushed deeply and took an immediate liking to Lieutenant Hawkey. Now she knew another person who knew Roman just as well as she did. Actually, he knew a side of Roman that she knew very little about. She was intrigued by that thought, especially since Roman was often like the moon to her— she knew a lot about the light, bright side, but almost nothing about the dark side. Hawkey knew a lot about

Roman's dark side. She wanted to know some things that Hawkey knew about her husband, things that Roman would never tell her, things that she decided not to ask him about, such as those head-hunting missions.

* * * * * * *

On the way to the back door, Grace looked over her shoulder at the distant object. As it drew closer, it grew in size and noise. It slipped through the air smoothly and gracefully. Grace rubbed her eyes. Now she could see that it was really a helicopter. Maybe a weather helicopter, she thought.

She began to have another pleasant feeling about her dad. She could see his face in that cloud again. She could hear his voice whispering words of love. Then her heart raced with excitement. She rushed back to the swing to get a better look at the helicopter.

* * * * * * *

Sam peered through the helicopter's side window and saw farm fields. "Grace is at Linda's and Dave's house," she said to Roman.

Roman gazed through the front window to see where they were, then smiled at Sam, understanding the implication of her message.

Looking at Hawkey, Roman requested, "Can you land this shit-bird in a pasture without a problem?"

"Sure, but why would I?" Hawkey questioned.

"I'd like to pick up my daughter, Grace, and bring her to the hospital with us. She's at a friend's farm house. Roman pointed, then said, "You can see it there. You see the barn?" Roman pointed to the faded, red barn, then at the white, ranch house.

"Well, if your daughter's as nice as, and as pretty as Sam, then I'd better meet her. That pasture behind the house OK to land in?" Hawkey said and pointed.

"Don't see any cows that you can scare the milk out of, so I'd say it's OK, unless Dave comes out of the house with his gun. But don't worry. He's a really bad shot."

"Shotgun or rifle?" Hawkey asked, knowing he was being teased.

"Considering what we're arriving in, I'd say a shotgun loaded with *bird*-shot."

"Jesus! Your jokes haven't changed. Birdshot, huh?" Hawkey smiled and moved the control stick a little to the right so the chopper leaned in that direction and veered toward the farmhouse and adjacent pasture.

"I don't get the joke," Sam said.

Roman waited for Hawk Eye to respond to Sam.

"Well, in Nam, a helicopter was often called a 'bird,' so if your friend came out with a shotgun with 'birdshot' in it, it would be a shotgun for shooting at helicopters."

"Oh, dear. That stinks like the cow droppings in the pastures," Sam responded.

*   *   *   *   *   *   *

Grace stared at the helicopter and was mesmerized as it grew larger and larger. A giant dragonfly, an eagle, a pterodactyl, she thought, with a silly grin. Then she heard the familiar "whop-whop-whop" helicopter sound. At the same time she, again, sensed the growing closeness of her dad. He's in that helicopter, she thought. She could feel her dad's presence getting closer. It was one of her rare premonitions, premonitions mostly concerning her dad and almost always true.

Dave and Linda ran out of the house, to see what the noise was, just as the helicopter landed in their empty field— Dave didn't have his shotgun.

Grace looked at them, then at the helicopter. She started running and screaming joyously, "Papa! . . . Papa!" before anyone could be seen getting out of the helicopter. Then she stopped at the pasture fence, struggling to climb over the horizontal, white boards as she saw a man exit the helicopter. The man was running with his back bent forward due to the still spinning helicopter blades. Then the man stood fully erect and Grace paused on the first board of the fence to look at him. The tall man wasn't wearing a shirt, but he was running toward her, his arms outstretched, yelling, "Grace! . . . Grace!"

Grace climbed up and over the top board, jumped to the ground and ran to her father as he ran toward her. Within seconds she jumped into her dad's arms and he spun her around so swiftly that the centrifugal force made her legs swing out away from him. Then he stopped and they hugged each other closely, neither of them saying anything, just appreciating the warmth and mutual love they had for each other. Roman kneeled and kissed Grace on the lips, forehead and cheeks. He pulled her close, again, then saw the tears running down her cheeks.

Roman turned toward Dave and Linda, waved vigorously, then yelled, "Thanks! I'm taking Grace with me in the helicopter. We're going to Strong Memorial Hospital. I may need a couple of stitches. Sam and I will explain things later."

Dave shouted, "OK!" He and Linda both waved goodbye as Roman carried Grace to the helicopter, where she sat on her mom's lap during the short trip to the hospital.

Grace got to meet Lieutenant Hawkey and sensed something different, but nice about him. He looked different, too. When he shook hands with her, he was very gentle, warm, sincere, yet she sensed that, like her Papa, Mr. Hawkey was really tough, too. But any friend of her Papa's was a friend of hers and, besides that, she liked the way Mr. Hawkey smiled at her. It made her feel extra special.

Then, on the spur of the moment, Grace asked Hawkey, "What's a helicopter called when a skunk is the pilot?"

"Don't know, cutie. What's it called?"

"A smellicopter, of course," Grace said, followed by a giggle.

"Oh, Grace. You've been hanging around your dad too much," Sam said.

Then Lieutenant Hawkey reached toward the console and turned on the FM radio. It was tuned to Rochester's WKLX, a classic oldies station. A song was just ending. When a new one began, it happened to be one of Roman's favorite oldies singers, Roy Orbison. The song was "Pretty Woman."

Roman turned and looked at his pretty woman, Sam, then reached back and held hands with her, one arm around Grace and one arm going between the seats to Sam. He closed his eyes and got lost in the melody and the lyrics. He finally relaxed.

When they arrived at Strong Memorial Hospital's helicopter landing pad, Lieutenant Hawkey asked the regular pilot to take the bird back. The regular pilot was also to call Captain Lewis to see if she needed the helicopter. Then the pilot was to call headquarters and have someone meet them at the hospital with a car so he could drive Roman and his family to their home in Calford.

When Hawkey finished giving orders to the pilot, he turned around and walked toward Roman. Hawkey saw Roman hugging both Sam and Grace. Then Roman placed his left arm around Sam's shoulders and his right hand on Grace's shoulder. They were all pulled close to Roman's hips, like the three-fingers in a Boy Scout salute.

Sam saw Hawk Eye smile as he approached her with something in his hand. She said to him, "You'll be coming for dinner sometime soon, right?"

"I'd love to, ma'am. You tell me when." Then shifting his gaze to Roman, Hawk Eye handed him a Native American dream-catcher. "This'll trap those bad dreams Buddy."

Roman remembered the dream-catcher that Hawk Eye gave him in Nam. It was lost during a chaotic firefight. Roman knew that the purpose of the circular dream-catcher was to catch bad dreams in the spider-like webbing, while the allowing the good dreams to easily slipped through.

Hawk Eye turned back to face Sam as she asked, "You back to calling me 'ma'am,' again?" Sam asked teasingly.

"Sorry. It'll be 'Sam' from now on. I promise," Hawkey responded.

"Good," Sam replied, "I'm one-fourth Seneca Indian. We'll have plenty to talk about."

"And I'm one-hundred percent, renegade Mohawk, Sam, so if you get me started on Native American heritage, you'll never get me to shut up."

"So who's trying to shut you up?" replied Sam, with an over the shoulder smile.

Hawk Eye responded, "You have lovely hair, Sam. It would be a most honored scalp to wear on my belt."

"And yours on my belt would be a great honor, too," Roman interjected, humorously, then listened to further repartee between Sam and Hawk Eye.

Grace was puzzled, especially when Sam's hands covered her ears so she could no longer hear.

"You wouldn't want to do that Hawk Eye, because then I'd be forced to cut off your balls and pecker, then make them into cuff links and a very short tie for you to wear." Sam winked and demonstrated a comically, evil smile.

Hawk Eye, stared bug-eyed and cherry-faced at Sam after that blunt comment, then realized that he wasn't going to best her at this contest. Hawk Eye glanced at Roman and said, "Whoa! Man. Where'd you find this wonderful squaw?"

Roman replied straight faced, holding his laughter inward. "At Geneseo State College. But I didn't find her, she found me and, like Robert Frost said at the end of one of his poems, ' . . . that has made all the difference.' And even though she's five years older than I am, I kind of fell in love with the old lady."

Sam let go of Grace's ears and smiled at her, saying, "Part of our conversation wasn't for your ears to hear, Bugs." Sam's nickname for Grace was Bugs. Then Sam smiled at Grace whose confusion was only partially relieved.

"Ouch! Damn!" Roman exclaimed, as he tried to rub the pain out of his shoulder where Sam had slugged him. She was actually five years younger than he was.

As Roman, Sam, Grace and Hawkey approached the hospital's rooftop door, Roman rubbed his stomach and said, as he licked his lips, "I'm hungry."

Grace saw a chance to jump into the conversation and quickly said, "What are you hungry for, Papa?"

Roman gazed at Grace, with just a trace of a smile, winked at her and said, "Oh, I do think I could go for an apricot and some black licorice." Roman laughed heartily.

Hawkey didn't understand and thought, Roman's up to mischief.

Sam joined the laughter.

Hawkey was still confused until he heard Grace's reply.

"Oh, Papa, you're so crazy. You can't eat my cats. Don't be so silly."

Pets? Hawkey wondered, as his curiosity peaked. He thought, I'll have to ask the Wolf Man when I getta chance.

They took the elevator to the first floor emergency room entrance as if nothing serious had happened.

Roman temporarily lapsed into a daydream, thinking how wonderful that two old survivors and close friends had found each other after many years and that he, Roman, and his family were safely reunited.

* * * * * * *

They were all moaning in pain as they approached him shortly before dawn. His dread increased with each of their shuffling, staggering steps, like drunks, with their hands extended outward as if wanting to choke an invisible neck. Their faces were pale with bloodshot eyes that didn't need to blink. They stiff-stepped closer and closer, some drooling and some sneering ominously with bloody teeth. They were dressed alike in tattered black robes with hoods, as if they were sinister monks. As they came closer he saw that they were bleeding, but not profusely, from their noses, eyes and ears, which made their necks look as if they were encompassed in large red collars. The moaning changed to shrill wailing as their teeth began gnashing at the air. Then, over the wailing and gnashing sounds, a louder sound stabbed his ears like double ice picks. The rumbling sound grew louder and louder, dominating and overpowering the wailing, as if a monster was roaring from a dark cave. A sinister gust of wind blew all their hoods open, exposing the face of each black-robed wraith, their mouths locked open in screams of torment and agony. He felt paralyzed and panicked, as if confined in a straight-jacket and leg shackles in a small room. When their heads started falling off and their hoods began collapsing upon the bleeding stumps of their necks, he had difficulty breathing. The wraiths kicked their heads toward him, as if they were in a ghoulish soccer game. Blood from the rolling heads sprayed the ground, coating the wraiths' boots like thick paint. The battered heads sailed off in all directions around him, but their eyes kept looking at him, unblinking, as they soared past him. He was surrounded, the bull's-eye in a menacing circle of headless souls, their hands outstretched, reaching for him, but not yet grasping him. The lengthy sleeves of their oversized robes covered their outstretched hands, until they all raised both arms into the air, which allowed their sleeves to slide down their scab-crusted arms. They each held a knife in one hand and a garrote in the other hand, waving them like flags, in Roman's face. They started closing their threatening circle. The wraiths began stabbing him. The man was terrified and in pain from his confinement. He screamed as he felt blood pouring down, then dripping off his body as—.

Roman jerked himself up to a sitting position in bed, his sheet and pillow damp with sweat. He got out of bed smoothly and quietly so Sam wouldn't be awakened. He glanced at the dream-catcher, disappointed, then went to the living room. It was too early to get ready for school.

He sat in his reclining chair and stared at the opposite wall. Something was bothering him, but he couldn't quite grasp it. He closed his eyes. Something about the nightmare, the hooded wraiths. All Asian. All, but the leader. Then it came to him and so did the tears. The hooded Asian wraiths were all the Vietnamese and North Koreans that he had killed, but, incredibly, their leader was Billy. Roman buried his sweaty face into both hands, feeling the slick wetness and tasting the salt from his tears. He mumbled, "Sorry Billy. I'm so very sorry that I killed you. It was a miserable and unforgettable accident. I'll live with the misery of it because I won't forget it, Billy. Keeping you alive in my thoughts is the least I can do for you, even though you'll haunt my dreams."

Ten minutes later and much calmer he said, "Another dream-catcher that doesn't work. I guess that's another nightmare for my Pandora Box."

Roman turned on his reading light, then picked up the book *TESTAMENT* by David Morrell. Roman relaxed and started reading, not knowing that the story would be an emotional read for him.

/./.-../---/...-/./-.--/---/..-/-.--/---/..-/./-../.-../.-/